RUMBLE AND THE GLORY

JA HUSS

Copyright ©2024 by JA Huss
ISBN: 978-1-957277-19-6

Edited by RJ Locksley
Cover Design by JA Huss

THE
RUMBLE
AND THE
GLORY

JA HUSS

Collin Creed is a killer. But he's Lowyn's killer. And after a twelve-year separation, she wants him back.

Deep in the hills of West Virginia, three small towns have found a way to flourish in the face of extreme poverty. Disciple runs a side-show tent revival that brings in millions of dollars a year. Bishop flaunts traditional ways in the vein of Colonial Williamsburg, luring weary city people to the slow-living lifestyle. And Revenant offers them an experience of sin filled with tattooed bikers and live-music dive bars.

It's a sacred trinity that worships the almighty dollar and everyone plays their role like a well-trained Broadway actor.

But these hills have secrets, and so do the people.

Twelve years ago, when he was just eighteen and dreaming of a future with his high school sweetheart, Collin Creed learned something about himself. Something so disturbing he left Disciple to join the Marines and didn't once look back. But all that came to a screeching halt with the congressional hearings, forcing Collin to return home and rebuild his black-ops empire brick by brick.

Lowyn McBride's heart broke when Collin shut her out and left town without an explanation just as they were getting ready to start their adult lives together. The death of her mother the following year was a make-or-break moment and Lowyn rose to the occasion, giving up her university education to parent her younger sister while building an empire of her own as a specialty antiques dealer.

Anger and desire, guilt and shame—the return of the enigmatic Collin Creed ignites the town and sparks an explosion of emotions inside Lowyn. But he's not the only one with a secret in his past. Lowyn has always played the good girl to Collin's bad-boy reputation. But it turns out—she's just like everyone else up in these hills—not as wholesome and pure as she looks.

The Rumble and the Glory is a cinematic and spicy small-town secret, second-chance romance wrapped up in a cloak of mystery and suspense. It honors the themes of found family, redemptive anti-hero, and is filled with bigger-than-life, morally-grey characters against a backdrop of deceit and deception.

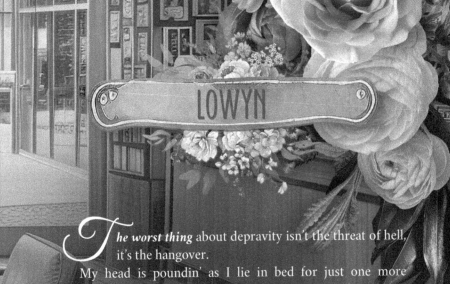

LOWYN

*T*he **worst thing** about depravity isn't the threat of hell, it's the hangover.

My head is poundin' as I lie in bed for just one more second. My eyes are crusted over and opening them up is gonna be a process. So I just stay still, letting my mind remain blank for a few more seconds. Maybe I'll even fall back asleep.

It's not like I have to work today. For me, this day right here is a holiday. A sacred day.

Well, maybe sacred is a tick too far, but at the very least the Day After is always a quiet day for me. A time to reflect on my mama and how much I miss her.

That's what last night was about.

I don't make a habit of getting drunk. In fact, I do it exactly once a year. So this headache of mine, though annoying, isn't familiar enough to be distressing.

Besides, this bed is warm, and the covers feel good, so I let out a small sigh, enjoying the little bit of time I have left here in the in-between, before life starts back up again.

In the same moment that my sigh is leaving my body, there's another sigh behind me.

My eyelids fly open and all the little crusties that should've been massaged slowly with gentle fingertips just split apart without a bit of fanfare.

The first thing I see is the sexy face of young Jim Morrison in black and white staring out at me with a rock-god expression like he's about to take over the world. And while I study that sexy face a very heavy, very strong arm glides over my waist and pulls me close.

Oh, no.

Oh, no, sir, this is not happening. I did not bring the one-night stand *home* with me last night. I did not! Immediately my mind is racing, trying to put all the pieces of what happened back into some kind of coherent order.

Woke up, went to work, blah, blah, blah. Bryn and I had lunch and, of course, she tried to talk me out of what came next—which was my annual 'get drunk day,' in honor of our mama, of course.

See, our mama died when I was nineteen and Bryn was seventeen and yesterday was Mama's birthday. Some people remember lost loved ones on 'the day,' as in the death day. But not me. That day can go to hell. That day sucked.

But Mama's birthday was always a happy time for us. It was a day when Bryn and I would take care of her instead of her taking care of us. And she would let us do that. She would let us make her meals that day, and do her laundry, and pick out her clothes, and bake her a cake.

If it was a school day, we got the day off because we would go into work for Mama. She ran the flea market right on the edge of town, just this side of Disciple. She would go in with us, of course, but Bryn and I took over that day and we greeted and cared for the customers who wandered in from outside places.

I was always someone else on those birthdays. Louder than my normal self. Carefree like a butterfly on a summer day. And spontaneous, like anticipation was my motor and I was just lookin' for a reason to press my foot on the gas.

And it was all that much more special because in my

everyday life I am nothing like that at all. I'm quiet, and careful, and deliberate.

Now that she's gone, this is how I honor her. Not the one-night-stand thing, though that is part of my be-more-spontaneous plan. It's not the purpose of the letting go, just the end result. And if I'm being honest, if I didn't give myself permission to let go once a year, I might be in a dry spell something terrible as far as sex goes.

No, I honor her by being the girl I was on her birthdays. Because Mama noticed how different I was this one day a year. How much I laughed and smiled on those birthdays of hers. How I let go of the burden I felt to be *good*.

On this one day every year I am Lowyn the Laughing. Lowyn the Lighthearted. Lowyn the Lover. In other words, I'm not Lowyn the Lonely, or Lowyn the Laborious, or Lowyn the Leftover.

Which is a harsh way to characterize myself, I do realize this, but why fight it? It's sorta true. Because the other three - hundred and sixty-four days of the year I am a responsible business owner. I am goal- oriented. I am diligent, and hard-working, and nonconfrontational. I am in control one - hundred percent of the time.

Control works for me. Schedules work for me. Ten-year plans, exceeding expectations, and organized growth all work for me. I thrive in this environment.

And I don't always throw so much caution to the wind on Mama's birthday. Some years, if I have a steady boyfriend, I don't have a one-night stand at all.

But if I'm being honest with myself—and what's the point of having a rolling internal monologue if you're not gonna be honest?—I have noticed over the years that I tend to break things off about a month prior to the Day.

Not that I *want* a one-night stand. Not particularly. It's just... what is the point of pointless dating? I mean, a girl knows if he's 'the one.' You just know. And I would not want to skip my one day of giving Mama the version of me she liked best for some random nobody who barely passed the Valentine's Day test and is never gonna make it to Christmas.

My mama loved me for the studious, serious overachiever I was. She did. I know she did. But when I would let go, let my hair down and just flow, I saw the way she looked at me. Like this was the girl she knew I was.

I try to be that all the time, but I'm just not her.

Even on the Day I'm mostly pretending to be this girl. If Mama's up in some spiritual realm looking down on me, then I want her to see me as the Lowyn she knew, and not still-single, too-picky Lowyn who will never fall in love again.

However... it is not like me to bring the one-night stand *home*.

Granted, this is the ten-year anniversary birthday of Mama being gone, so... perhaps I got a little overzealous?

I reach up and push some hair out of my eyes, gently rubbing the crusties so I can see better. I let out a long breath. Who was it? Who is in bed next to me?

Please, I silently beg. *Please, if there is a God above, and if you care about me at all—please, please, please do not let the man in bed with me be Grimm.*

Please.

This is a small town. In fact, the entire Trinity area is small-town 101. I grew up with everyone in my dating pool and there are only so many single men to go around, one of them being Jameson Grimm.

But I don't get drunk in Disciple. No. No, no, no. That's a big fat no. I go over to Bishop. Which is the unlikely choice given my nearby options include the small town of Revenant, but I'm not ready for that kind of letting loose.

So Bishop it is.

I get a room there at the Bishop Inn where my sister, Bryn, works as a chef, and then I walk into the center of town and get drunk at the Pineapple Pub. I drink, I dance, I might even karaoke. And then I take a man—most years, it's a tourist—back to my room at the inn, have a lovely romp in the sack, then wake up and go home. Alone.

Grimm doesn't care for Bishop. His first choice for a night out is typically Disciple, but he would go drinkin' in Revenant long before he'd go to Bishop. So after giving myself this common-sense pep talk, I let out a breath of relief because I have a better than reasonable chance that the man in bed with me is not Grimm.

My once-a-year celebration is as safe as a plan as one can make when letting loose to drown sorrows that are not sorrows, but only because you refuse to give in to the idea that you are the kind of person who drowns her sorrows.

Or... *has* them.

In addition to being goal-oriented and fastidiously organized, I'm also perpetually optimistic. Bryn calls it my worst fault. Says I hide behind rose-colored glasses. Literally. She tells me this all the time. And my response, every time—and with a perpetually optimistic smile—is that I can live with it. Rose-colored glasses are right up my alley. Also literally. Because my go-to sunglasses are those round John Lennon ones, tinted rose.

It makes sense in the world of me.

However... it is curious that I didn't stay in the room at the inn. Surely Bryn was babysitting me. That's kind of her job. So... how did I get home?

Must've been the guy.

OK, Lowyn. It's time to turn and see who he is. This is the Day After now and while you might be hungover, and Mama's birthday is a holiday so you won't be going into work, reality is something you face, not hide from.

I grab the covers and pull them up to my chest so I don't flash him accidentally when I turn, but this is when I realize I'm not naked.

Hmm. In fact—I wiggle my toes—I've still got my boots on.
And my pants.

What the hell happened last night?

I mean, I didn't even get laid?

I turn over and study the man in bed next to me.

He's massive. Like broad massive. And fit. He, unlike me, is
not fully dressed and I can see all the hills and valleys of his
muscular back, shoulders and biceps. But he's got his head
tucked under the pillow so I can't see his face.

One good thing—this is not Jameson Grimm. Grimm has
dark hair and the hair peeking out from under the pillow is
something between blond and brown.

Plus, this man has tattoos. Kind of a big one that covers the
shoulder I can see. Something military, I think—an eagle, and
one of those shield things they put on badges or patches. Inside
the shield, in neat thin-line lettering, is the word 'Silence.'

Weird.

But not important. I need to get this guy out of here. I can't
start my day with last night's… whatever. He's still got one arm
around my waist, but it's not tight. So I just slip it off me, sneak
out of bed, and tiptoe out of the bedroom.

I close the bedroom door behind me, sighing with relief
that he didn't wake up, then hit the bathroom. When I come
out, I've got my boots in my hand and I take them over to the
front door and put them in their cubby.

My foyer is a testament to order. Every pair of boots, sneak-
ers, and flip-flops has their place in a cubby. Every coat has a
hook to hang on. Every pair of gloves, every scarf, every hat
has a basket to live in on the long maple bench and there are
two cupboards on either side that hold anything that is too
ugly to display.

I'm a freak about organization and presentation. It's everything. Having an ordered home with pretty things on display
just makes me feel good even when my head is pounding with a
Day After hangover.

I hit the kitchen for vitamin C and coffee. Orange juice first, then a steaming cup of Sexy Cinnamon with a splash of cinnamon-vanilla creamer.

I take that first sip leaning against the counter and sigh as I stare up at my disgustingly cheerful kitchen.

My cabinets are old—like pretty much everything in this house—but they have been brought back to life with lots of sanding, and paint, and love. My favorite color is sea-foam green, so that's the color I painted the cabinets. There is a splash of tangerine orange here and there—curtains, dishtowels, bowls—to make it all pop and all of this looks pretty fun contrasted with the dark walnut butcher block counters. The floor is also walnut, wide planks that were harvested a hundred years ago. I salvaged them from a house three hours away in Kentucky and since my house is modest in size, I was able to do the entire first floor with that wood.

I love this place. It's not the biggest house in Disciple, but it's definitely the most loved, at least in my opinion. Our town is cute. The homes in Disciple were all built right around the same time about a hundred years ago. They all started out pretty much the same—Craftsman-style—but over the years people have customized them. Most have two floors, but some have three now. The paint colors change every once in a while. My house is not sea-foam green on the outside, but it's as close as you can get without being obnoxious. More of a sage, I guess. The porch is the best thing about this house. It's all cobblestone with cedar trusses and beams. In fact, all the trim and accents on the outside of the house are cedar and cobblestone. It looks like something out of a woodland fairy-tale and it's all just so lovely, I sigh every night when I get home.

To say that I am a vintage girl would be an understatement. It's literally my life because I own McBooms, a retro antique shop that was made world famous when Jet Shadows, host of *Jet's Junk* on that one cable channel we all love, came to my store and did a whole episode. Then he came back! Three times over the next two years.

One of those years—mmm. I take a sip of coffee and chuckle—he was my one-night stand for the Day. That was fun.

I look over at my bedroom door and wonder if that's Jet in there. But no. Jet doesn't have tattoos. Plus, we haven't talked in a couple years now. He got engaged, then broke it off, then married the woman in Vegas. He called me that night to tell me goodbye and his life was over and that he secretly loved me. He's kind of a dramatic guy.

I haven't heard from him since.

It's not Jet and it's not Grimm. So who cares? I'll wake him up in a few minutes and kick him out and then get on with my life.

I look out my window as I sip the coffee. It's a nice spring day. The leaves started coming back on the trees a couple weeks ago and even though there are still a few gaps on the hills, they will be an almost impenetrable cover of green in just another week or two. April in West Virginia is extraordinary.

When evaluating one's life, and looking down at a diagram where chaos lives on one side of the line and perfection lives on the other, I'm solidly in perfection territory. Business owner, homeowner, same friends since childhood. It's all pretty nice, and organized, and in order. But becoming an adult started off kinda rough in my case.

Losing our mama was an unexpected blow and it completely derailed my college career and dreams of being a veterinarian. I came home from West Virginia University to take care of Bryn—who isn't the kind of girl who normally needs taking care of—and, well, I never left Disciple again. Not in the literal sense, of course. I leave town all the time for my picking adventures. I do that one week a month. This week, in fact.

But I don't have plans to move out of Trinity County. I

don't have plans to go back to school. I'm here. And I'm gonna stay here.

Much to the chagrin of my best friend, Clover. She's always bugging me to go on adventures with her. Her life didn't get derailed in college. She was at WVU too and she went on to graduate with a degree in business. Now she works for a super-fancy-fancy hotel in Virginia as an event planner. She's two hours away, so we don't get together all the time, but we have a regular once-a-month date where I check in to her super-fancy-fancy hotel and we spa together. Sometimes she comes down this way and we will drink a little bit of wine, play old vinyl records, and dance in my living room.

Clover was born rich. Well, rich for these parts, which is to say her family *looks* rich, but cash flow around here is almost always a problem. Her parents own a huge Civil War-era mansion on the very western edge of town just as you go down the hill towards Revenant and Clover has been paying the reno bills for a few years now since her parents retired to Florida.

It's a lovely estate. And every time she comes, we go over there and walk the grounds, and reminisce about how we spent our childhoods riding her horses through the surrounding woods. She's been working hard on that place for nearly five years now and the reno's still going. I really hope—

A noise from the bedroom pulls me out of my thoughts and back to reality.

I cringe a little. I don't like the awkwardness of the morning after. I don't want to see this guy, let alone serve him a cup of coffee. My one night of reckless behavior is over and he needs to go.

I'm just about to go in there and give him a hint when the bedroom door opens with a creak.

I hold my breath, preparing for the inevitable. But he doesn't appear from around the hallway. Instead, he goes to the bathroom.

The breath comes out. It's a short reprieve, but I'll take it.

I'm just about to start rehearsing my you-need-to-go speech when a noise from outside distracts me. A tune. No. A ringtone. Specifically, *my* ringtone. The chorus to *Son of a Preacher Man*.

What the hell? Did I drop my phone outside last night when I came home?

I go to the front door, pull it open and swivel to my right. The sound is coming from the hedge. I have a big porch. It's wide and long and there is a railing between me and this hedge, which is formidable. I've been carefully shaping the shrubs surrounding it for the better part of three years now, so the only way to really get to the phone—which is somewhere inside the one on my right, hidden from view—is to lean over and shove my hand into the soft green leaves.

I smile when my fingers find the phone and then straighten back up so I can look at the screen.

Bryn. Calling to check up on me. I accept on speaker. "Hey, sis. I'm fine—"

"Oh, my *Gawwwdd*!" She says this loud, her voice scaring some birds away in the nearby elm tree. "I've been calling you for six hours, Lowyn! What the actual fuck!"

My sister is as loud and obnoxious as I am quiet and contemplative.

"Sorry. I was sleeping and just found my phone in the hedge."

"You're not in your room!"

"Oh. Yeah. I went home."

"Went. *Home?*" She says these two words in a weird way. Like I'm speaking a foreign language or something. "With *him?*"

I huff out a small laugh. "Yeah. He's still here. In the bathroom. I'm just about to kick him out. And I didn't even have sex with him, Bryn. Was I like super drunk or what?"

Silence.

"Bryn?"

More silence.

I shake the phone. I do this sometimes. I don't know why, but it's a habit I have because of all the vintage phones I've owned over the years. Sometimes the speaker wires get loose and if you shake it a little, it pops it all back into place. Of course, this is irrelevant for a cell phone. It's just a habit. "Bryn? Did I lose you?"

She lets out a long breath. "OK. Let me get this straight."

"Oooo-kayyy."

"You took him *home*?"

"Yeah. I don't remember how we got here. I don't actually remember anything."

"Wait. You don't know *who* you took home?"

"Nope. I woke up, looked over at the guy next to me—who is fucking hot from the back, Bryn. But I didn't see his face. He had it buried under the pillow, but—" Then I pause. Because this head-pillow behavior reminds me of a guy...

Now *I* go silent.

"Lowyn?"

No. No, it can't be.

"Loooowww-wyn."

And just as she says this, the floorboards—those perfect, hand-scraped, carefully salvaged and repurposed walnut floorboards—creak behind me.

"I'll call you back." I press end.

"Mornin', peaches." His voice is a low, husky growl. "How ya feelin'?"

No. *No!* This is not happening.

"Lowyn?"

My head slowly turns to the left and this is when I see the Jeep. It's not the same Jeep, obviously. That thing was already forty years old when he left here for the Marines twelve years ago. But there *is* a Jeep in my driveway.

Correction. *His* driveway.

And this Jeep is sleek, and black, and lifted, and... ya know, like... sexy. As all fuck.

"No." I say it out loud this time. Just a small whisper. But he's barely a breath away.

"Oh, this really is happening, Lowyn. It really is."

I turn and there he is. Collin Creed. The man who broke my heart. The guy who joined the Marines without even discussing it with me, left town, and never came back.

Until now, apparently.

He's smiling at me, his eyes dancin', laughing at me. "You don't remember anything from last night, do you?" He points over his shoulder. "Can we talk about this house of yours?"

"Get out."

"In fact, let's start with that bedroom."

"Get. Out." I point at the Jeep, my finger shaking.

"Lowyn." He laughs out my name like it's a joke. "You didn't even take down the Jim Morrison poster."

"Get. The fuck. Out of my house!"

"*Your* house?" His smile falters. His voice lowers. His eyes narrow. "*Your* house, Lowyn? This is *my* house. What the actual fuck have you done to it?"

"It's not *your* house. I bought it from your parents eight years ago, you asshole. It's mine now."

He points to himself. "I grew up in this house. There are still marks on the fucking bathroom door that say 'Collin, age eight.' You bought my childhood home, turned it into a retro freak show, are sleeping in my teenage bedroom, and didn't even take down my *fucking posters*?"

He guffaws now. And I go fire-hot with anger and embarrassment.

Collin taps my head and I step back to avoid contact, but not fast enough. "That's mental, Lowyn. Completely fuckin' mental."

I push past him, trying to get back inside. In this same moment my phone rings again and he blocks me with an arm.

I look up and meet his eyes. Oh, God. Those fucking eyes. With those mesmerizing swirls of golden brown mixed with sea-foam green. They are so familiar, but at the same time distant and strange.

Twelve. Years.

I yank my arm from his grip, go inside, and slam the door right in his face.

COLLIN

*A*mon is *kicking back* on his bed—feet stretched out, PlayStation controller in hand, machine-gun sound effects blaring—when I get back to the motel on Route 60.

He is blond, he is blue-eyed, he is broad, and as dangerous a man as they come. But he's smilin' right now like a kid on Christmas Eve.

That's funny. Kinda. True—the Christmas Eve part. People say that all the time because kids are happy on Christmas Eve. They have presents coming. But here, in these parts, where he and I both come from, Christmas Eve comes with a whole other kind of happy.

I kick Amon's duffle out of my way and slam the door behind me with a foot while pushing my sunglasses up my face.

Amon glances over at me. "What's your problem?"

"Nothin'."

He smirks. "Nothin', my ass. I bumped into Rosie Harlow at the Rise & Shine when I was getting coffee this morning. She said you drove Lowyn home from that pub in Bishop last night. What the hell were you doing in Bishop? I mean…"—he laughs —"you could've gone over to Revenant. That's where I was last night. And Lowyn? That was unexpected. Especially after all the protesting you've been doing since we came up with this plan."

"I'm failing to see a point here." I walk past the beds, heading for the shower.

"We're not here so you can reconnect with your high-school sweetheart, Collin."

I pause my retreat to look at him. "Says the guy who's having breakfast with his parents this morning. I'm not reconnecting anything. I drove her home because she was wasted. And do you wanna know where she lives, Amon? Take a guess."

He doesn't answer right away, too busy with his virtual battle on screen. But he's grinning so I'm gonna guess that he does.

"My *house*, Amon. She sleeps in my fucking bedroom. She's still got my posters on the wall."

Amon almost spits out his laugh. "Shut the fuck up."

"I swear to God. The Doors, Led Zeppelin. Ozzy. Everything's still there. There's even a few old shirts of mine in the closet."

"Shut. Up."

"She's mental, right? She's crazy."

"Wow." He pauses again so he can kill someone in the game, then chuckles and puts the controller down. "That's really weird. She lives in a shrine to you?"

"Yeah. It's... disturbing. There's something really wrong with that girl."

Amon laughs. "Come on. It's just Lowyn. She's cute and harmless."

"And crazy."

Amon has always liked Lowyn. Maybe he even had a crush on her back in the day. But she was so out of his league back in high school. Smart Lowyn. Goal-oriented Lowyn. They would've never worked.

Amon's never going to date Lowyn, but still. I'm not gonna stand around and listen to him compliment her. I slam the bathroom door and turn the shower on. I hate motel rooms. I'm already in a bad mood from the whole wake-up confrontation and the thought of spending another day in this room is turning my sour mood into something more like pissed off.

We're here for a reason and I want to get on with it.

Just as I take off my shirt Amon knocks on the door. "What?"

"Bryn's outside. She wants to talk to you."

I open the bathroom door and peek my head out. "How did she even know where to find us?"

Amon smirks. "Guess we know Rosie Harlow hasn't changed."

"Tell her I'm in the shower. I don't need a lecture from Bryn." I close the door on Amon, strip off the rest of my clothes, and walk under the hot water, trying to put Lowyn McBride's face out of my mind.

What is she doing? And how come no one told me that she bought our old house? I haven't seen my parents in over a decade. I haven't even talked to them in eight years. I knew they sold the house because that's what we fought about the last time I called them up. But we fight about everything.

Yes, I was pissed when they said they were moving to Florida and if I wanted any of my old shit, I needed to come home and pack it up. Which wasn't even possible because I was guarding a sheik in Saudi Arabia at the time. We had just made a twelve-day trip through the fucking desert—by camel—to get to this throwback fucking oasis that didn't even come with a road.

It was Christmas and I had my satellite phone, so I figured, *Meh, yeah. I'll call the parents. Wish them happy holidays and all that shit. Be a good son.*

What a joke. Less than five minutes into the convo my daddy was screaming at me, my mama was crying, and I was just way too tired to deal with the news that my entire childhood was about to be packed up and donated to Goodwill.

I actually scoff. Because obviously they didn't pack it up. They sold it to my ex-fucking-girlfriend.

I'm the bad son. The black seed. The offspring they probably wish they never had. Especially when you compare me to my little sister, Olive. She's everything I'm not—honest, dependable, friendly, and obedient. The perfect daughter.

I like Olive. Hell, she is my sister so I love her, of course. But she's nine years younger than me so we never did get to that 'friend' stage before I left to join the Marines. I haven't seen her since she was kid and even now, at twenty-two, she's still too young for me to have anything in common with. The last time we spoke she was in the middle of her freshman year of university and all she wanted to talk about was frat parties and spring break.

Having never gone to university myself, I couldn't relate. And since Olive doesn't know the first thing about elite private security, she can't relate to me either.

Of course, this isn't anything new. There aren't many people anymore who can relate to me.

Just the guys I'm here with, really.

They're all I have left.

WHEN I COME **out** of the shower wrapped in a towel, Amon is gone, and my bad mood is blossoming into anger.

Lowyn. I almost growl her name in my head.

I grab a pair of jeans and a t-shirt from my duffle on the floor and throw them on my bed. Then I light up a smoke and take a seat at the small table and chairs next to the window, kicking back and stretching my legs out as I pull the stiff blackout curtain aside to check the parking lot.

My eyes wander to the clock next.

I've got another twenty minutes to waste.

I'm waiting on Grimm to call me about a deal we're making. He and I used to be good friends all growing up. Boy Scouts, Midget Football, Little League and finally Eagle Scouts and varsity for both sports. We did all the things. Aside from my eclectic taste in Seventies rock and vintage Jeeps, I was the most disgustingly perfect kid you'd ever meet.

And then... well, New Year's Eve happened. That one night changed me forever.

Amon and I weren't actually friends until we joined the Marines together that same year. By the time we were both dishonorably discharged two years later I already knew my old family didn't exist anymore.

When I'd call home that first year in the service my daddy had a hard time finding things to say, my mama would always start crying before we hung up, and my little sister didn't even want to talk to me. Though I don't think that last bit was personal. I think Olive was just too busy being a bratty nine-year-old and pushing all the boundaries.

By the time Amon and I were on our first post-military job, I had already accepted reality. The only family I had anymore were the guys from Silence, our security company.

Me, Amon, Nash, and Ryan will probably always be tight. I mean... when you've done the things we've done, who else can you count on? Who else is gonna have your back but the boys who did that shit with you?

Nash and Ryan are driving in from DC this morning. They're not involved in the real estate deal. I'm the only one putting my name on that deed. Amon is just here to see his parents—who apparently still love him, despite the fact that he never calls home, never sends presents, and, for all intents and purposes, is a giant fuck-up.

I'm kinda jealous. Actually, looking back, I've always been jealous of Amon. He was the wild kid in school. He was always in detention, always in fights, the first in our year to get drunk and arrested, and talk about a man whore. There were no fewer than three pregnancy scares before he was eighteen and each time the town went wild with gossip. Thankfully, no teenage girls were actually pregnant and if ever there was a guy who gave no fucks about town gossip, it's Amon, so each and every incident just slid off his back like water.

He was the town asshole. And still, his parents couldn't wait for him to get home. They've been calling him constantly for the last few days. Wanting to pick him up from the airport, wanting him to stay at the house, wanting him to come to dinner, blah, blah, blah.

Anyway. After the whole congressional hearing thing, Silence was liquidated. I guess that's the best word for what happened. Everything was sold off and the whole endeavor was dissolved.

Everything but us, of course. The four of us aren't going anywhere. And we've got a new company starting up as soon as I put my signature on those real estate papers.

We're buying a compound on the edge of Disciple. The place started out as housing for coal miners back in in the late 1800's, then it was a Baptist church, a summer camp in the late Sixties, and then, once that ran its course, forgotten about. It's been abandoned for almost twenty years now, so we're getting a killer deal on it.

Apparently, Grimm is the local real estate mogul around here these days, so that's who's doing the paperwork.

A sharp knock at the motel room door makes my head jerk.

"Collin! I know you're in there. Open. The door."

Shit. Fucking Bryn is back.

"Collin!"

I sigh, get up, and crack the door open. "What."

Her eyes flash down to my towel, but recover quickly. "What the hell is wrong with you?"

I take a long drag on my smoke, then blow it in her face. I

quit smoking ten days ago, but quitting things is a process for me. I like to take it slow so I don't beat myself up when I fail.

Bryn coughs and waves the smoke away. As a kid, I never even looked twice at her. But as a teenager, I never liked her much. She's loud, and aggressive, and always sticking her fucking nose into shit that's none of her concern.

May I present Exhibit fucking A.

She points her finger at me. "My sister is in a good place—"

I laugh so loud she has to stop talking. "Good place?" I laugh again. "She bought my fucking childhood home and made my teenage bedroom a shrine, Bryn!"

Now it's Bryn's turn to laugh. It's a good one too. Just as loud and aggressive as her personality. "You think..." She stops, almost doubles over, then giggles as she continues. "You think that room is a *shrine* to you?"

I take another drag, really annoyed. "Sure looks like one to me. Sure looks like she's stuck in the past from where I'm standing."

"Stuck in the past?" Bryn guffaws. "She owns a world-famous retro shop, Collin. That room is filled with shit for *sale*. Everything in her house is *for sale*! It's all on the fuckin' website, you idiot."

"What?"

"God, you're really full of yourself. Do you really think she's been pining over you for twelve years? She's rich, Collin. And happy. And you"—Bryn points that finger at me again—"will leave her alone. Do you understand me?"

"Fuck off, Bryn. And you're full of shit. That was *my* Jim Morrison poster!"

"Are you kidding me right now? Do you really think you're the only teenager in the history of rock and roll who ever had a Jim Morrison poster on his fucking bedroom wall? She sells. Retro. Items!"

"This is such bullshit. She had my shirts in the closet."

"Oh, my God." She's not laughing now. She's looking at me

like I'm the crazy one, not Lowyn. "You're..." She blinks and shakes her head. "You're *insane*. She has not kept your smelly, gross t-shirts from high school in the closet for twelve years. You saw t-shirts. Vintage fucking t-shirts, Collin. From Trinity High."

Is she right? Did I get this whole thing wrong?

"Stay away from my sister, do you hear me, Collin Creed? I don't know why you're here, or what's going on with Amon and Grimm or whatever, but you stay the fuck away from my sister."

Then she turns on her heel, walks over to her car—where Lowyn is waiting in the passenger seat—gets in, and drives away.

Lowyn watched that entire encounter. I slam the door and pace the small room. What the hell? Lowyn has never been confrontational like Bryn, so I guess the proxy ambush makes sense, but what the hell? Lowyn just sat there and watched as Bryn tried to make me look like a crazy asshole.

I get dressed, grab my keys, and drive the Jeep down to Grimm's office. Thirty minutes later, papers all signed, money all wired, I am the new proud owner of an ex-mining town.

When I get back to the motel Amon is there waiting for me, breakfast with parents over, already packed.

"Everything good?" He's got his eyebrows raised, like maybe Rosie Harlow has already filled him on the way I got everything wrong about Lowyn and Bryn pointed her finger in my face.

I don't answer. Just grab my duffle and put the town of Disciple behind me.

OUR NEW COMPOUND is not in Disciple, it's about eight miles outside city limits. That's why it's perfect—not subject to any of the town regulations as far as what we do with the land, but still close enough to be convenient.

Though I won't be going into Disciple for my fucking groceries. I'm so done with it. It's not even like I have family there. Amon is my family. Nash is my family. Ryan is my family.

Everyone else can just fuck off. I will buy gas, milk, and bread in Bishop from now on.

We found this property online, so this is actually the first time we've seen it in person. Nash was skeptical about spending so much money on something sight-unseen, but realistically speaking, we didn't have a lot of choices. We were looking for a very specific type of property in a very limited geographical location and this is the only one that ticked all the boxes.

When I pull the Jeep into the long, gravel driveway, the first thing I see is the used armored truck, recently acquired. It's parked inside the carport attached to the first house, so obviously Ryan and Nash are here.

The compound has fourteen houses in various sizes and states of repair. Plus a barn, the church, a huge metal building —not original—that looks like a community center, and several smaller outbuildings. Chicken coops, run-in sheds for livestock, and tool sheds—stuff like that. Most of the eighty-nine acres is wooded—really thick West Virginia forest—and hilly too. But at least twenty acres, where the houses all are, is flat and grassy. There's also a big pond with a dock, two small streams, and a valley with no fewer than three excellent spots for the shooting range.

I cut the engine of the Jeep and just kind of sit there, taking it all in.

"It's great, right?"

I look over at Amon and nod. "It really is."

Amon grins. "All right, let's do this." A moment later he's out, already crossing the expansive lawn and heading towards the church.

But I allow myself another moment. Because this is kind of a big deal. Actually, it's the biggest of deals. We didn't all make it, and we lost more than we ever gained since this whole thing started, but those of us who got out alive will at least have this.

More than just a job.

More than just a base of operations.

This place will be our sanctuary.

NASH SKINNER IS A CALIFORNIA BOY. Monterey born and bred, so he's a rich fuck too. We've known each other for ten years now and I still don't quite understand how he went from silver-spoon trust fund to one of the most dangerous men on the planet.

With dark hair and eyes, a body built like the Hulk, and the reflexes of an MMA fighter, he comes off as formidable and scary. Which he is. How else would we have ever met?

Nash has a huge family out west and they all own a part of some famous beachside inn. His brothers and sisters bought him out last year and he got a windfall of nearly one million that he chipped in for the new business we're starting.

Amon and I don't come from money like that, so we've been living frugally and saved nearly every penny from the last four years to chip in our share.

The last guy in the group is Ryan Desoto. Italian as they come. Probably a Mob background, since he's from Newark and all his cousins have colorful names like Tony 'Two Toes' Russo and Ivano 'Ice Pick' Bianchi.

I've never been a hundred percent sure if the stories he tells are true or not. They're so far-fetched. But then again, he's Ryan 'One Shot, One Kill' Desoto, so why wouldn't the rest of his family be as crazy as he is?

He didn't save up for his share of the business, either. He called his uncle—Bosco 'Bang Bang' Bianchi—and the money was delivered in person, in cash, one week later. It was a pain in the ass, that cash. I had to launder that shit just in case it got traced back to us down the line.

When I get to the church and check the semi-truck—also recently acquired—I see that it's already been mostly unloaded.

To be honest, the church is what sealed the deal for this place. It's pretty nice as far as churches go—really great wood-work, dark-gray slate floors, and stained glass to die for—but the reason we all fell in love with the church was the bunker underneath it.

The Cold War was still a thing when this church was built. People took that whole threat seriously. With three-foot concrete walls, steel doors fit for a bank vault, and a mostly outdated air filtration system, the basement of this church could probably withstand a nuclear bomb.

We're just gonna use it as a munitions depot, so to us, it was better than perfect.

Nash greets me first. His grin is wide and his eyes lit up like he's about to get into a firefight. "Did you see that first house? I called it."

I saw the pics online, and yeah, the first house—the one closest to the road—really is the nicest of the bunch. I don't really care which one I live in. In fact, I'm kinda hoping I can room with Amon for a while. And anyway, Nash is a rich fuck, so whatever. If he needs all the creature comforts to feel whole, he can have them.

I know Amon doesn't care either. And I'm sure Nash and

Ryan have already sorted it out, because Ryan walks up behind him and doesn't object. So I say, "It's yours, dude. You've earned it."

Nash lets out a breath, then nods at me, getting my meaning. "Anyway." He points to a door that leads to some stairs. "The bunker's through there. Wanna take a look?"

Again, I've seen the pics online, but this actually does interest me. So I wave a hand for him to lead the way and follow him down.

"*ood morning, peaches!*" I look up from my computer at the front counter of McBooms to find Rosie Harlow breezing in. She stops in front of me and scowls. "What are you doing here? It's the Day After."

I sigh, then spin the vintage barstool I'm sitting on so that I'm looking out the front window—past the brightly painted letters that say 'McBooms' in a huge varsity font, orange and yellow with a thick shadow of brown—it's such a great vintage combination—and then let out a long exhale.

Rosie drops her giant leather purse onto the counter. "Don't bother, I already know."

I spin back to face her. "You already know what?"

"About Collin, peaches." I roll my eyes and she grins, because that's what Collin called me all through high school while we dated. "Yep. Collin. And you." She grins bigger. "And Amon."

I knew this. Bryn told me she saw him.

Rosie rests her elbow on the counter, cupping her chin as she continues to grin. With a perfectly heart-shaped face, she's the definition of cute. Kinda short, a little bit skinny, long, straight, dark brown hair, and the grayest eyes you've ever seen. It's really hard to look at anything else when she's staring you in the face. She's Valerie Bertinelli circa 1976, complete with bell bottoms and red-checked flannel over a tight black tank top. She's a walking billboard for McBooms because everything she's wearing right now came from my store. Even the chunky platform sandals, which are totally impractical since it's really not sandal weather, but practical has never been Rosie's middle name.

She got pregnant in tenth grade and is the proud mama to a twelve-year-old boy called Cross. Not an uncommon pathway for girls who grow up in West Virginia, but Disciple isn't just any old Appalachian town. It's got a special relationship with God, and if you want to call it culty, that works just fine. No one minds because all of us, every single one of us, is descended from the sanctimonious town founders.

The main one being a preacher man called Justin. He named the town Disciple because that's what he called his followers and the town was built for them.

Here's the most ironic thing about current-day Disciple, West Virginia—there's not a single church in this place. That preacher did everything out of a tent. A real fire-and-brimstone show every frickin' Sunday complete with holy water, miracles, and promises of Hell.

I've got reels of him somewhere around here.

The Revival. That's what the show was called back in the day and that's what it's still called now because the Revival show still happens in the field just south of Jerry's Hardware store. Simon West is the preacher these days and everyone in the town—including me, including Rosie, including Bryn—plays a part in the show that gets put on.

Because that's what the Revival is—a show.

We might all have a special relationship with God here in Disciple, but that doesn't mean we can't make a dollar off it at the same time. Or... ten, as it is. Inflation and all that.

Anyway, church or no church, believers, or not, living in Disciple comes with expectations because we gotta live up to the hype. The Revival is what keeps us going. And, if I'm being honest, the Revival is how McBooms first got noticed. The whole reason Jet Shadows was in Disciple in the first place was to attend a revival. The fact that he wandered down the street and into McBooms was... well, the hand of God, I suppose.

Rosie is the only single mother within a five-mile radius. And I'm not saying that teenage girls from Disciple are any better than teenage girls from anywhere else—it's just the rest of them had the good sense to leave town limits once the baby bump started showing.

Rosie rode it out though. Hung in there. She said, to anyone who scowled at her that year, "I was born in Disciple and I'll die in Disciple. So you people had best just get over it."

And... they did, I guess. She's been working three jobs to support Cross for as long as I can remember and no one really much cares where the kid came from. He's a town treasure. Everyone loves Cross, even if they do think his mama is goin' to some kind of hell for it.

Rosie fills in for me at McBooms when I go out picking. And she's in charge of the books. Not the accounts, I like to do those myself, but the catalog books. Everything in this store is meticulously photographed, listed, and filed in the appropriate reference binder. I have binders going back to the day this place opened.

I get a lot of online sales. I mean, who the hell has time to make a trip to the hills of West Virginia to hunt down retro décor? They come for the Revival, yes, and I do get a fair amount of foot traffic on the weekends, but nothing like I do online.

Everything I sell is on the website. And I buy a lot of things online too. But that's not sustainable. Not if I want to make a profit. So every second week of the month I pack up my truck and my trailer and I go picking around Appalachia and the surrounding states, usually returning on Thursday night. Sometime I drive a whole day to get somewhere, then stay the night, pick around the towns, and spend the last day driving home. One week a month I have a wandering sort of lifestyle and I like it.

Love it, actually. My life is filled with cherished heirlooms, undiscovered treasures, and fun. I really don't do drama. I hate it, in fact. So I'm all kinds of out of sorts today.

"I ran into him at the Rise & Shine this morning."

Shit, my mind wandered. "Who are we talking about again?"

"Amon!" Rosie giggles, her back to me now because she's flipping through the pile of mail that I stack on the far side of the counter. I never read mail.

"Oh, right. What did he say?"

"You know." She's still got her back to me. "How Collin found you at the Pineapple Pub and drove you home." She turns to face me now, her lips all pouty. "Did he see... the room?"

"We woke up in the *bed*, Rosie."

"Together!"

"Together."

She covers her mouth with one hand and presses the other against her heart. "What did you say? I mean, how did you explain that?"

"Well..." I sigh and look out the window again. "I didn't. Bryn lied for me. She told him it was... some kind of show-room and everything was for sale on the website."

Rosie practically snorts. Then she points to my computer. "Is that what you're doing? Putting it all online?"

"Yep."

"Oh, my God. Did he believe her?"

"I don't know. She just yelled at him and got back in the car and we drove away."

"You were watching?"

"From the car."

"You wimp."

"You know how I hate confrontation. I just... I don't want him to know why I really have that stuff."

36

Rosie makes a serious face. "I get it. I'll push the story to Amon tonight."

"Tonight? Are they staying in town or something?"

"Apparently they bought the old coal-mine compound."

"What? You mean the church camp? Does that mean he's back for good?"

"For good. Amon says they're opening up some kind of private security company and West Virginia is home base."

"Security. Is that what they've been doing since they got kicked out of the Marines?"

Rosie shrugs. "Dunno. So… you goin' pickin' today?"

"Nah." I point at the computer. "I'm gonna finish adding all this stuff to the website and then meet Bryn for lunch in Bishop. I'm starting the trip tomorrow."

Rosie grabs a bunch of binders and a stack of photographs and takes them over to a Fifties dinette set in the middle of the store, plopping them down with a thump. "Well, let me know if you need anything. I'll be here all mornin'." She pops a cassette tape into the nearest boombox sharing the table, presses play, and begins to gyrate to the beat of 'We Got The Beat.'

My head hurts and I can't do the Go-Go's this early in the morning, so I save my work and go into my office to finish.

Adding all this stuff to the website is so stupid. I mean, why do I care? It's Collin Creed. I've hated him for more than a decade now. Why should I rearrange my day over his stuff in my house?

It just burns me. I mean, I know it looks bad and I'm sure he's picturing me yearning for him all these years, so I just can't have that. I can't let that be the final impression of me in his head.

Not after what he did to me back in high school.

He broke my heart.

And then he left town.

I didn't mean anything to him and so… he sure as hell doesn't mean anything to me, either.

MY SISTER BRYN is the head chef at the Bishop Inn. Which is where I was supposed to stay last night. I still don't understand how I got home and how Collin and I ended up in bed together.

Obviously, we didn't do anything. I still had my boots on when I woke up.

But I need the whole story and Bryn barely had time to drive over to the motel on Route 60, chew Collin out, and then chew me out as she raced us into Bishop so I could pick up my truck at the bar and she could still get to work on time. She said she had receipts—text messages and screenshots, and, unfortunately, a vid one of her co-workers sent to her around one a.m.—but she wasn't in the mood to go over it then, so that's why I'm driving back to Bishop to have lunch with her.

It would be better to not fill in the blanks. To just move on and chalk it up as just another wild night on the Day. But it's Collin Creed and he's not leaving town, he's staying.

I need to know the details. Even if I will hate myself when it's over.

The Bishop Inn is everything you imagine a B&B to be. A large eleven-bedroom Victorian home that has been lovingly restored and cared for over the years, boasting dark hardwood floors and trim, fancy embellishments, and way too much wallpaper.

People love it though. It doesn't attract superstars or anything, but it is a favorite place for local couples to get away from the rat race on the weekends. Bryn has been working at the inn since she was in high school. She was a maid at first. Then Bryn helped Mrs. Maroo in the kitchen—back when she did all her own cooking—and she even helped

Mr. Maroo in the gardens for a summer. After Bryn finished chef school, Mr. Maroo decided he and Mrs. Maroo needed to see the world, so their thirty-something son, Michael, became the concierge, their daughter-in-law, Jessica, took over bookings, and my sister, Bryn McBride, became the new head chef.

That was one of the best days of my life. Watching Bryn grow up and make her dream come true like that—it was amazing. She's wanted to be a chef since she was nine. When I was nine, I wanted to be a veterinarian. And I know that almost no one grows up to be what they thought they would be when they were nine, but my sister did it.

It's special, I think. I'm not bitter about my non-existent veterinary career. The hours are horrible and the pay isn't great. I'm just really impressed with my sister's fortitude and focus. She's always been a take-charge kind of girl and that's why I enlisted her to go lie to Collin and tell him that bullshit story about why I still have his stuff.

She doesn't even blink when a confrontation presents itself. She's a fighter.

I'm more of a nurturer. And while I would never call myself doubtful or pessimistic, I am very cautious. Pulling our lives back together after Mama died wasn't easy and one misstep— one frickin' misstep—and everything turns out different.

That's what I learned from that experience. That successful people are careful. That's not to say they don't take risks—I know risk is a huge part of success—but successful people calculate their risk and can steer around the rapids.

Bryn just plows her boat straight through the whitewater. And it works—for her.

But not for me. I am slow and steady. (Says the girl who picked her truck up from a bar this morning.)

I snicker a little as I pull up in front of the inn.

Inside, the place is filled with people lugging boxes of pastel-colored spring décor and Jessica is too busy giving out directions to do more than wave at me and point to the kitchen when I pass by, as if Bryn would be anywhere else.

Indeed, my sister is in the kitchen. She's flitting around a stove manning a skillet and the grill at the same time.

"Wow. Do you need help?"

She shoots me a look over her shoulder. "You? Cook?" We both laugh. I'm a terrible cook. Why should I practice a skill that my sister can do better? She cooked for us, even back when Mama was alive.

"Seriously, though. I can flip that burger."

"I'll have to cancel lunch."

"What? No! You have to fill me in on last night!"

"There's some wedding thing going on over in Revenant and for some reason the entire wedding party wanted to come *here* for breakfast."

"*Some* reason?"

Bryn and I both look at the swinging door where the comment came from. Michael is standing there smirking. "The reason they came is for you, Bryn." He directs his attention at me. "Apparently, some bigshot from Williamsburg with a cooking channel on YouTube was here a couple weeks ago and spent twenty minutes of his last vlog raving about Bryn's French toast brioche and her avocado burger."

I make a face. "That's... an odd combination."

Bryn sighs. "They do it on purpose."

"Do what on purpose?"

"Arrive just in time to order both breakfast and lunch."

"Apparently, it's to see how well the chef handles the two meals." Now Michael is beaming. "And our girl here did spectacularly. The inn is booked through July, Lowyn. Can you believe it?"

I smile at him. "That's great, Michael."

"I'm giving her a raise."

Bryn snickers. "You can't afford to give me a raise."

"I can now." Michael chuckles, then leaves the kitchen to resume his duties.

Bryn sighs, wiping her sweaty brow with the back of her sleeve. "What I need are a few more cooks in my kitchen."

"And that's not in the budget?"

"Nope." Bryn plates the burger and the French toast, then pauses to look at me. "It's great that we got all that attention, but we're always booked through July at this time of year. Our problem is winter months. People just don't want to make this trip in the winter. So he really can't afford to give me a raise, let alone hire me some help."

"Oh. Well, that sucks."

"Yeah." Bryn pouts a little. "But it's fine. I mean, the inn has been here for fifty years. Surely it will be here for fifty more."

"Surely."

"Take my phone." She points to her chef's coat pocket. "All the evidence you think you want is in the message streams between you, and me, and Taylor."

"Taylor Hill was the one who saw me last night?"

"Oh, boy, did she ever."

"Great." Taylor is the waitress here at the inn. But she's actually from Disciple and runs the kiddie tent during Revival. So this means it's gonna be all over town.

"Go sit outside, Lowyn. It's nice. I can't concentrate with people in my kitchen."

I just shake my head, but go outside so she can boss herself around in private.

THE BISHOP INN gardens are pretty spectacular. Even though this property is only about two acres, Mr. Maroo used every single square inch judiciously. Spring bulbs are blooming, the trees are budding, and the evergreen hedges have been trimmed to crisp, clean lines. He made a maze of sorts—not tall enough to get lost in like that kid from *The Shining*, the hedges are only about four feet high, but it's kinda cool that you can go for a half-mile walk in the diameter of two hundred and fifty feet.

I enter the hedge maze flipping through Bryn's phone to find my name.

Oh, my God. That's my first reaction to the last text, which reads, *He's s0 h0t, Br4n, I'm g0nna take him h0me with me.*

Only all my O's are zeros and the Y in Bryn's name is a 4.

I was wasted.

I scroll up, cringe as I read the entire conversation, then go looking for Taylor's stream and find the vid of me cackling like a fucking high schooler as Collin just sits there and grins at me.

No. *Laughs* at me.

And my God, look at him! I didn't pay much attention to him this morning, I was too flustered. But he's hotter than ever. How is that fair?

I stop looking. It's over. I don't need to know this stuff. Obviously, I threw myself at him and I wish I hadn't.

I *wish* I hadn't.

Here's something most people don't know about me—which is kind of meta, because it's about people knowing stuff about me.

I don't want people to know me. I can't even explain this properly, but I don't want people to know anything about me. I just feel that… people don't have the *right* to know me. Not without my permission. Which is so stupid, I understand this. But it's how I feel. And now Taylor and Collin both know something about me that I didn't give them permission to know.

I hate this feeling. It's vulnerability mixed in with a violation of privacy.

And the worst part is—Collin is the whole reason I'm this way to begin with.

It was him. And what he did to me when he left that year.

He broke my heart and he didn't even care enough to say goodbye.

COLLIN

When it comes time to choose a house for myself—Amon is not interested in a roommate unless they have four legs—I choose the house in the back, right up against the woods. When you turn in the driveway it's the one straight ahead at the end of the gravel cul-de-sac. It's a two-bedroom, one-bath that looks like it was last updated circa nineteen sixty-nine.

This particular house didn't have pics online, so once I get inside, I discover that someone has pulled up the carpet to reveal the original hardwood—which is cool, but they are a mess. Every room has a grid of carpet tack strips running across it, and prying those up will be a necessary, time-consuming job, but other than that, it's not bad. And while there is some leftover shit from previous occupants, it's not garbage. It's just thrift-store kind of stuff.

The kitchen is… I dunno. I can't make up my mind. It's either amazing or gross.

All the appliances are avocado green, the flooring is dark brown linoleum—matching the dark-brown cabinets—and the countertops are orange. The backsplash is actually brightly colored daisy wallpaper and even the sink and cooktop were made in matching enamel avocado.

What the hell were people thinking? How could anyone want a green and orange kitchen?

It's not amazing, I decide. It's gross.

But the truly ironic thing about this house is that I bet Lowyn McBride would love it.

I didn't get a good look at what she did to my childhood home, but I saw enough that this is totally her style. Maybe the green in her house isn't avocado and maybe the orange in her place is a little softer than this, but it's all very reminiscent.

I do like the porches though. It has a nice-sized one in the front, but a really huge screened-in one in the back. And the screens are not even ripped. Like maybe this work was done recently.

It needs a total reno. Work I don't really have time to mess with, but I am not unhappy with the purchase or the place I will now call home.

Maybe I'll never love it, but it *is* my first house. And it's on a compound that will soon be overflowing with men so dangerous and so fucked up in the head, they can't survive in the real world anymore.

And I love the fact that this will be their home too so much more than I ever will the house.

I grin all the way over to Amon's place, which is actually about a hundred feet to the right. I find him in his kitchen, sweeping the floor.

"Where the hell did you get a broom?"

He points to a skinny closet next to the fridge. "There's a built-in ironing board, dude. And look!" He picks up a handset of an old-fashioned rotary phone hanging on the wall. His kitchen has dark cabinets too, but his countertops and appliances are turquoise. And so is the phone. The wallpaper is actually patterned black velvet.

The phone has a dial tone. This delights Amon because he's grinning like a stupid kid. "Can you believe it works?"

"How does it work, though? I mean, whose number is that?"

"Fuck if I know. Fuck if I care. It's mine now."

"You don't even know what the number is."

He taps the center of the rotary dial. "Look."

I lean in and I make out a set of faded, barely-there numbers—four, one, one, two. "What the hell does that mean? Where are the rest of the numbers?"

"This is how they did things back in the day."

"Yeah, but this is the present. So how does it work if it's only got four numbers?"

"Collin. You're killin' my buzz, dude. What do you want?"

"I'm just... bored, I guess. Aren't you bored?"

By the time Amon and I got to the compound Ryan and Nash had already unloaded all the weapons and were in the process of arranging them neatly onto pegboards and shelves in the bunker.

We don't have any furniture, just our duffels. And the only other thing we brought with us was the armored truck. So there's no unpacking to be done. I mean, I guess I could hang up my t-shirts, but they're just as usable folded neatly away inside my bag.

"How can you be bored? Isn't your place a mess?"

I shrug. "It's... whatever. I got a sleeping bag."

"Well, I'm not a heathen. I like a clean house."

"Since when?"

"Since now. I'm a homeowner, Collin. I'm responsible for this place."

He says this with the most serious face, so I can't tell if he's joking or not. "Are you gonna start cooking too? Are you taking on new clients? How much do you charge an hour? I'm looking for a maid."

"Fuck off." He goes back to sweeping.

I'm kinda jealous of his kitchen. Turquoise and black is a little bit badass.

He stops his sweeping to side-eye me. "Why don't you go shopping?"

"Shopping for what?"

He pauses his sweeping to stare at me. "Dude. Are you gonna eat MRE's too?"

"Oh, *food.*"

"What did you think I meant?" He's laughing at me now.

"Couches?"

Now he's guffawing. "You're hilarious. Go grab some lunch then. Not fast food. I've eaten enough fucking crap these past few years to last me a lifetime. I'll call in an order at the inn in Bishop. You go pick it up. What do you want?"

"What do they have these days?"

"Same shit they've always had, Collin. This is Trinity County. Nothin' ever changes. Burgers, spaghetti, pizza, meat-loaf. Just pick something."

"Steak, then. Medium rare. And baked potato."

"Salad?"

"Sure." I point at him. "With ranch. No onions."

"No one puts onions in a house salad, Collin."

"I just like to make sure."

He's shaking his head as he takes out his phone. "Go. I'll order and it'll be ready by the time you get there."

I let out a long breath, then throw up my hands. What the hell. If I'm driving at least I won't be bored all by myself in an empty house.

BISHOP IS *a curious place* if you're not from around these parts. It's got a historic district right smack in the middle of town that's cordoned off and no modern modes of transportation are permitted, just the ol' horse and buggy.

Authentically restored to 1700's specifications, it's a lot like

Colonial Williamsburg—in fact, that's what it's modeled after—but on a much smaller scale.

It's about four blocks wide on all sides and the whole downtown is nothing but people in old-timey costumes, peasants tending to pigs and chickens, and time-period-appropriate businesses like a blacksmith's, the general store, and the Pineapple Pub.

The Bishop Inn in Bishop has been in business longer than I've been alive. It's not technically inside the historical zone, but it is right on the edge. So if you're coming to do the whole Trinity County thing, it's a nice place to stay and it's close to everything.

The Bishop Inn was a once-a-week thing for my family when I was a kid. Every Sunday we'd go for brunch. And after I was done eating, I'd take Olive out back to the gardens so my mama could sip her mimosas and my daddy could read the paper. I started doing that as soon as she could walk. We were close when she was really small like that. But that's because I was still basically a kid and playing hide-and-seek wasn't a distant memory yet.

That was every Sunday morning until I was almost sixteen. And by that time Olive was in school and too big to play hide-and-seek because the hedges were only four feet tall.

I smile thinking about those days. I had no idea that in just two short years my whole life would be flipped upside down and it would stay that way forever.

I am going to be this guy *forever*.

Even after all these **years** the Bishop Inn mostly looks the same when I enter the foyer and wait for my turn to talk to Jessica. It's bustlin', and busy, and packed with people. Jessica looks a little flustered.

It kinda surprises me that she's still here. It also surprises me that I remember her name.

She finishes with the people in front of me and she's still looking down at her book when they move along and I step up, so I catch her full reaction when we finally lock eyes. She starts to say, "Hi, how can I help—"

But that's as far as she gets.

There are about five seconds of awkward silence and then she lets out a breath. "Collin. I didn't expect to see you here."

"Yup. I'm back." I shrug, not sure I owe her an explanation, but also not sure I don't. "I'm picking up food. Amon called it in."

"He did?" She looks over her shoulder to her husband Michael. He's on the phone—taking orders, probably—so she just looks back at me. "Is it under Amon's name?"

"I dunno. His or mine, I guess."

Jessica smiles. "OK. I'll go check and…"

"I'll hang out in the gardens. There's no rush."

"I didn't… I didn't mean you had to leave, Collin. That's not what I was saying."

"It's fine. I'll be outside."

When you kill someone when you're eighteen, people look at you different afterward.

Jessica watched me grow up. Saw me once a week, every Sunday at brunch. She probably thought she knew me. My parents used to be invited to the New Year's Eve party here every year. One time, when I was fourteen, they even brought me along.

So Jessica might actually have thought of me as family once upon a time.

And then, one night when I was home alone with my nine-year-old sister and my parents were right here at the afore-mentioned New Year's Eve party, a man broke into our house and tried to steal my sister right out of her fuckin' bed.

Like all boys growing up in the hills of West Virginia, I had been hunting since I was small. Turkeys, mostly. But I had gotten my share of deer too.

Lowyn was over at my house. Her house now, but still my house then. We were making out on the couch when she heard a noise coming from the back mudroom.

"What is that?"

"The wind." That's what I told her. And we just kept kissing.

I would think about these moments every fucking day for years.

What if I had gotten up and looked? Would I have scared the guy away? Would he have walked off, found another house with kids in it, and tried for them instead?

There's no way to know, of course.

It happened the way it happened.

That guy broke into our house, crept into my sister's bedroom, gagged her with his hand, dragged her out of bed and was already in the hallway outside the back mudroom when Olive was able to scream.

I don't know if that's exactly how it played out because obviously the guy is dead and Olive never gave a statement. She said she couldn't remember anything but a hand over her mouth, and then she screamed, and then... then she was covered in blood.

Lowyn said she didn't see anything. That I told her, "Stay here and don't move," after Olive screamed, and that's exactly what she did.

But she didn't stay there. She got up with me. She was right next to me when I pulled the rifle out of the front closet—I meant to get the shotgun. That part gets me every time. Because I wasn't thinking clearly and if I had the shotgun instead of the rifle, I'd have killed Olive too. I checked the magazine, snapped it back in, and walked into the hallway with my eye looking through the sight like I was on patrol in fucking Iraq or something.

That guy took one look at me, let my sister go, put his hands up, asked me not to shoot, and I shot anyway. I hit him right between the eyes.

Lowyn saw the whole thing.

Olive saw the whole thing.

And neither of them contradicted me when I lied to the police ten minutes later.

I became another person that night. Maybe I was always that guy, maybe not. But no one gets to walk into my fuckin' house, manhandle my fuckin' sister, and then live to tell about it.

No one.

This is the part that gets me though… why would Lowyn want to buy that house? Why? After what I did in that hallway, why would she buy that place?

The whole reason my parents moved was to get the fuck out of there. There were bloodstains all over the wall. The carpets had to be pulled up. We couldn't even live there for a week because of the investigation.

My parents couldn't wait to put that place behind them. And Lowyn McBride *bought it*?

What the actual fuck, ya know?

And my stuff in the room? I don't get it. But she really does have it up on her website. I checked a couple hours ago and sure enough, there's a page titled 'Get the Look—Retro Rock Teen Boy Bedroom' and pretty much everything that was in my room is for sale on that page.

I go out onto the back porch of the inn and skip down the stairs, automatically heading for the hedge maze. It never occurred to me that it wouldn't be here, but as I enter, it does occur to me and I'm suddenly grateful it is.

That's when I see Lowyn. She's walking the maze too, but

she's got her head bowed looking down at her phone. She stops, puts a hand over her mouth, and even from thirty feet away, I can hear her gasp.

"Somethin' wrong?"

Her head jerks up, her eyes meet mine, then they narrow down. "What are you doing here?"

"Picking up food."

She scoffs.

"What? I'm not allowed to eat here or somethin'?"

"Well…" She pauses, maybe wondering if she should have this argument with me. She decides in the affirmative. "Bryn is the head chef here, so—"

"So what? Are you really telling me that I'm not allowed to eat here?"

"It would just be a common courtesy if you found somewhere else to frequent." She starts walking forward in the maze, which is actually walking to my left. I start walking forward too, which is also to my left.

"Are you following me?"

There is no way to stop my laugh. "We're in a hedge maze, Lowyn. I'm not following you."

But I… sort of am following her, because for some reason my part of the maze lines up perfectly with her part of the maze and the next thing I know, we're walking side by side.

"Oh. My. God." She whispers this under her breath.

"Look." I sigh and run my fingers through my hair. "I'm sorry I was such a dick this morning. What Bryn said makes sense. It was just weird, ya know? I've been gone all this time, and I come home, meet up with my ex-girlfriend in a random bar, and when I drop her off at home, I discover she's living in my house. I mean, you can see my point, right?"

"Why are you here?"

"That's your answer? Why am I here? I told you, I'm picking up food."

She stops walking and faces me, jaw set, eyes narrowed,

anger coming off of her like heat. "Not here at the inn, Collin. Why are you *back?*"

"I... we... we started a business."

"You don't sound too sure of yourself."

She's right, I don't. "Private security. Amon, me, and a couple other guys from work—"

"Work? What is 'work' these days, Collin?"

For a moment I'm at a loss. I didn't prepare for this. Of course, I know what to say, but that's to strangers and clients. This is Lowyn. Still, the practiced monologue is all I've got. "Private security, I just said. We offer bodyguard service, cyber-security, home and business security, firearms training, and protection dogs."

She doesn't say anything. Just stands there, staring at me.

"What?" I'm still a little hostile and it comes out in my tone, even though I don't mean it to. Everything about Lowyn feels provocative. And not in the sexy way. The confrontational way. Which is ironic, since she's never been a confrontational kind of person. "*What?*" I demand again.

"That's what you've been doing this whole time? Since you were kicked out of the Marines?"

"I wasn't kicked out. Who told you that?"

"Your... daddy."

My jaw is clenched now too, and I look up, trying to control my anger. "I didn't get kicked out. And neither did Amon. We... just... got pushed in a different direction."

"I thought it was a dishonorable discharge?"

"It was, but—"

"So you got kicked out."

"That's not how it works, Low. You've got no idea how it works."

She folds her arms across her chest. "OK. So how does it work?"

I open my mouth to tell her it's all private. There are NDA's involved and worse. Were, at least. The congressional hearings kinda made all those things moot.

But there have been some threats since then. Thickly veiled ones, but threats nonetheless. It's not the kind of thing the military-industrial complex wants the general population hearing about. Or, God forbid, talking about.

But I'm saved by Jessica, of all people, calling my name from the back porch. "Collin! Food's ready!"

I look back at Lowyn and shrug. "I gotta go."

And that's exactly what I do. I don't even say goodbye.

WHEN I GET BACK to the compound all the guys are hanging on my front porch waiting for the food. Sitting on various pieces of outdoor furniture that weren't there when I left.

I pull the Jeep right up to the porch, parking a little sideways and balancing one tire on a rock the way I used to back in high school. I look up at the guys, find Amon's face, and see him smile as he remembers this miniscule act of rebellion.

I was such a good guy back then. Before that asshole broke into my house, I had the whole world at my fingertips. I was playing the game and I was playing it honestly too. I didn't drink, or smoke, or cheat on my girlfriend. I worked out five days a week, was the star receiver on the Trinity football team, and got good grades. I went to the Revival and played my part every fucking weekend—and I know it's not church and it's got almost nothing to do with God, it's just a fucking sideshow, but I would play my part. I would sit up there, watching my daddy preach his message, and I would close my eyes, and think on the words coming out of his mouth—time-honored things like respect, and honesty, and working hard.

I know it's easy to assume that the whole thing from top to bottom was a fiction. His showmanship, fainting women in the crowd, the whole 'amen' thing.

But there are people who come regular. People not from Disciple. Like it's an ordinary church or something. And it's meaningful to them.

It meant something to me too. It meant a lot to me, actually.

I *was* the Revival. An honest-to-God son of it. And yeah, everyone in Disciple is part of the Revival. We're all descendants of the original organizers, but I come from a long line of tent preachers and even though that was never gonna be my future, the tent had always been my sanctuary.

It grounded me. Helped me be good.

That was then, though. This is now. And these two whens have almost nothing in common.

Three scouts had come to see me play ball junior year. Two full scholarships were offered in the fall of senior year. I was gonna play for Ohio State. I was gonna major in business—not so I could climb some corporate ladder, but so that, once the football career was over, I could start my own business. Make my own way.

I guess that part's still true. I do have my own business and I certainly have made my own way through this shitty world.

But so many things are different. My family used to love me. They used to be proud of me. My sister and girlfriend didn't look at me like I was a murderer.

But I am a murderer.

I murdered that guy who thought he could touch my sister. Scare her, and my girlfriend, and me. And the moment that bullet hit him, everything I ever was just... stopped.

And the moment after, I was this guy right here.

BEFORE WE EAT, we drink. Four little stainless-steel canisters with twist-off caps are lined up on the porch railing. The smoothies are not quite cold, but it doesn't matter. We drink them anyway. We don't really have a choice.

I'm quiet as we eat, but the guys are so busy talking shop, they don't even notice this about me. Nash is in charge of renovations. We need every one of these houses fit for livin' in before the rest of the guys get here in June. We're about six weeks out, so it's gonna be tight. Nash is ticking off all the people he's gonna need as Amon holds his burger in one hand while jotting down notes in the other. He's in charge of the hiring since he's local and, unlike me, charismatic. Which is kind of ironic considering who my daddy is.

Ryan is in charge of heavy machinery. We have a good place picked out for the shooting range in one of the valleys, but it needs some dirt work done to make it safe, not to mention a proper road leading out there.

I'm the business end. I take meetings, make calls, and do the interviewing for the new hires. And I'm not talking about the locals, obviously.

It took us forever to agree on a name for the company since we're all equal partners, but finally Amon suggested Disciple's Edge. I didn't want Disciple in the name, so I said no. And then we tossed around about a dozen other contenders, but in the end, we met halfway and stuck with Edge.

Edge Security.

I don't know what Lowyn is thinking about our choice of location, but there's a very good reason behind it. Lots of them, actually. Number one is the close proximity to DC. Number two is the gun regulations. West Virginia is firearm-friendly.

Not that we don't have all the fuckin' permits, but it's just easier to work here than it would be in Virginia, Maryland, or, fuck's sake, DC.

I personally find it hilarious that all the politicians up there on Capitol Hill hate the guns but want people like us around them twenty-four seven for protection. The hypocrisy is jaw-dropping.

But hey, their personal philosophy is none of my business as long as they pay the bill every month.

And actually, it's only one asshole that we need to deal with. Charlie Beaufort is what's called a 'staffer' for the government. He's never been elected, never made any campaign promises, and gives absolutely zero fucks about anyone not on his payroll. He's not my boss, but he's the closest thing I have to one because all the security contracts for the government go through him.

Maybe one day, once we're all settled in, we won't need the government contracts. But that day is not today, so whatever. Charlie says bark, I'll give him a growl if it keeps the money flowing.

*I'M JUST ABOUT **to turn in***—the guys having gone back to their own houses long ago—when my phone starts buzzing across the floor next to my sleeping bag.

It's only about nine, but still. I hate when people call me. Especially this guy. "What's up, Charlie?"

"Just checkin' in on ya." Charlie Beaufort is a Southern boy. People think West Virginia has an accent? Fuck, Georgia is the mother of all accents. And down there, if you know how to finesse it in just the right way, no one thinks you're ignorant and uneducated—if you drawl those vowels out just right, you're not a hick hillbilly like us guys up here, you're just a good ol' boy. And if you're from the South, being a good ol' boy is a goal one aspires to. Sometimes.

It's a confusing title, to be sure, because these days it's almost lost all meaning. You see, if you are a traditional man in the South you are one of two things and both of those things are good ol' boys. It's how you present yourself that matters and Charlie here is the height of good ol' boy aspiration, polished and rich. He doesn't drive a pickup or a Jeep. He hunts, but only because we all hunt. But he's not hunting for dinner, he's hunting for sport. And not the way a man from Ohio might hunt for sport, either.

It's all very nuanced. And maybe you just gotta be from here to get it.

Or care about it, for that matter.

I tried really hard to give up my accent. And I can turn it on and off—mostly. But it's hard to do that when I can't even hear it.

"Yeah, I'm good. We all made it OK."

"So..." Charlie stops there and I already know what he's gonna say before he can manage to spit it out. "Did you think about my offer?"

"I did. I did, Charlie. But the answer is still no. I'm runnin' the business here. Someone's gotta run it and that someone's me. I need to be here, ya know what I mean? I need to keep tabs on shit because the guys we're gonna be dealing with—the kind of guys you *insisted* we deal with—are gonna require a lot of supervision in various forms."

"Well, you make it sound like I prefer murderers over good, honest men. And that's just not true! I'm all about second chances, Collin. You know that, right?"

Do I? Uh. No. Let's refresh our memories, shall we? Charlie Beaufort is a good ol' boy of the highest caliber. He's interested in power and money, order interchangeable. But do I say that? Fuck no, I don't. I just agree with his delusions of grandeur because he signs the checks.

And anyway, I don't mind the guys. I want them here. They deserve to be here.

"I know that, Charlie. And these men really do need a second chance. You're a fuckin' angel, you know that? A goddamn saint, as we say around these parts."

"Oh, come on now. Don't be blowin' no smoke up my ass, Collin Creed. Son of a tent preacher. Goddammit, you're so fuckin' Southern. Have I told you how much I love that about you, Collin?"

He has. About a million times.

Charlie had never heard of Disciple, West Virginia, but when I told him how I grew up and what this town is about, he looked at me like I was some kind of mythological creature that just stepped out from between the pages of the New King James.

He's the one blowing smoke up my ass, not the other way around.

Well, maybe it's reciprocal.

"I just want to make sure you know how much I respect you, OK? Is that so bad? And I would like you to keep in mind that I would take you over any of those boys of yours in a fuckin' heartbeat. And I would pay you the money you deserve."

"Well, I certainly appreciate that, Charlie. But you know I'm not much of a money man."

"I do, I do!" He's chuckling now. "OK. Well, I'll let you go. I just wanted to make sure you boys are settling in OK and that we're on track for delivery by August one."

"We are. It's gonna go down smoother than a shot of Whistlepig."

This makes him guffaw. The more hillbilly I act, the more he likes me.

So be it.

"You take care now, Collin."

I end the call.

I set the phone back down in the floor, crawl into my bag, and turn off my little pop-up solar lantern before deciding to reach for the phone again. I don't have her number, but I have my number. And that's the number I call.

Lowyn answers on the thirteenth ring, all out of breath. "Hello?"

"Hey."

There is almost ten seconds of silence. I don't say anything, I let her work it out. Who else is gonna call her on the landline?

"Collin?"

"It's me."

"What... what are you doing? Are you drunk?"

I laugh out loud. "No, I'm not drunk. I just thought of something and I wanted to tell you about it."

"It's nine-fifteen at night."

"Is it past your bedtime, Lowyn?"

"What do you want?" She's irritated now.

"I'm not sure if you heard, but we bought that old mining town down the highway between Bishop and Disciple."

"Yeah, I heard. Amon told Rosie and—"

"Rosie told everyone." She and I both laugh. "Some things never change."

"So... why are you calling again? And how did you get this number? It's the landline."

"It's *my* number, Lowyn."

"Oh." She huffs a little. "Right. I guess I never turned the phone off." There's a pause here as she works out the details. "Wow. I'm a really bad bookkeeper. How have I been paying this bill all these years and never knew it?"

I bypass her rhetorical question and skip straight to my own explanation. "I don't have your cell number. And I wanted to tell you that there's all kinds of fuckin' retro shit up in these houses."

"Really?"

"Is that excitement I detect?"

"Obviously, I am in love with the retro shit."

"Obviously. Well, I was just wonderin' if you'd like to come up and take what you want."

"Take what I want?"

"Help yourself to whatever's here."

"Don't you want it?"

"It's crap, Lowyn."

"It's treasure, Collin."

I really like it when she says my name. I don't know why, but I always have and that has not changed. "Our opinions diverge here. It's yours, if you want any of it. And I really am sorry for jumpin' down your throat this morning. Being home is... weird."

"Especially with your family gone. It's got to be a shock."

There's a silence after she says this. It wasn't a shock. She has no idea what kind of conversations I had with my daddy since I left. It wasn't a shock.

"It was, I guess." I don't like liars and I don't like to lie, but I will do it on occasion to spare a sadness. Mine, in this case. Not hers.

She lets out a breath. "Well, thank you. And to repay you for this kindness... you can eat at the inn."

I laugh again. And this time, it feels good too. "You are the most generous woman I have ever met."

"And you're the most..." I wait for it, dying for it. "The most... talented... wordsmith."

I just shake my head.

"Seriously. I had forgotten how you speak."

"How do I speak?"

"You choose your words so carefully. And you say things in the most interesting way."

"Do I now?"

"'Our opinions diverge here.'" She says this in a low tone, imitating me, but not mocking me. "That's just so… *good*."

"Good?"

"Yeah. I've missed it."

She doesn't say, 'I've missed *you*.' But I know that's what she means. 'Cept she's not talking about this me. She's talking about the old me. The good one.

"I've missed you too." And that's not really what I mean, either. What I'm saying is that I've missed us.

"The rumble and the glory."

"What?"

"The sermon that plays on the speakers? It always reminded me of you. Maybe you don't remember it."

I do. How could I forget that? They were my daddy's words. And his daddy's before him. And his daddy's before him. *When you look upon the hills, the sun shining on the peaks, and you hear the rumble in the distance, don't you ever forget that behind it comes the glory.*

Lowyn huffs a little. "I guess I know where you get it from."

"Get what from?"

"That wordsmithing you do."

I smile. "You come up any time you want, Lowyn McBride. I'll be here." And then I end the call and this time, I really do go to sleep.

LOWYN

I *didn't really have time* to assess the hotness factor when I kicked Collin out of my house this morning, but I swear, when I saw him in that hedge maze, I about lost my breath. And I had already been looking at him on the video on Bryn's phone for several minutes before he caught me.

Not that anything I was doing was illegal. Of course I'm gonna look at the video. I cannot remember what I did.

Well, let's just say that thanks to that video, my memory has been jogged. I was sitting at the bar alone, just doing my thing. Getting drunk. And yes, I was looking for a man to take home.

This part isn't on the video because probably no one was paying attention to me until much later. But I do recall the moment I first saw Collin Creed walk through the bar door. Except I didn't know it was Collin. I didn't even have an inkling. Why would I? I haven't seen him in nearly twelve years. Haven't even thought about him really.

And I know, I know, I know that the bedroom doesn't look good on my part. Might make me appear dejected. Or jaded. Or possibly even unhinged. But I really haven't been pining over Collin Creed since high school. That's just not how it went.

And my proof, should anyone confront me on this point, is that I didn't even recognize him. All I saw was a very handsome man with a chiseled—yet slightly scruffy—face, mesmerizing hazel eyes, and that hair that has never been able to decide if it was blond or brown. He was wearing a leather jacket, jeans that hugged those thighs of his, and a t-shirt that said... well... something. I don't recall the t-shirt slogan.

He and I locked eyes. I remember that part too. That's how I remember what color they were. And then he headed in my direction and took the empty seat right next to me.

It was the only empty seat at the bar, to be fair. So it didn't immediately mean anything. Still, my heart was racing like crazy and when he turned on the stool to get his wallet out of his pocket, and his knee accidentally bumped into mine, I felt like I was back in junior high.

He said, "I'm sorry, I didn't mean to—"

And that's as far as he got. His eyes went wide. Then he squinted them down into slits. "Lowyn?"

I was confused at first. I was still not thinking this man was Collin Creed. So I said, "I'm sorry, do we know each other?"

He pointed to himself. "Collin Creed. Dated you for three years in high school."

My mouth. Dropped. Open. I think I even gasped. In fact, I was taking a swig of my beer in that moment and I actually choked on it. Which made Collin start pattin' me on the back like a fuckin' baby.

When I finally calmed down, he squinted at me again. "You really don't remember me?"

Remember him? That was not my problem. The problem was the boy who killed a man right in front of my eyes when I was sixteen—the very one who walked out on me after we made all those plans—was back. And I was just supposed to... what? Take it all in stride?

Typically, as Bryn pointed out when I was telling her this story, this is my style. I take everything in stride. Except Collin Creed walking back into my life after almost a dozen years and sitting down at the bar stool next to me on the very night when I was out looking for a good time and had plans to get drunk.

I have never been much of a numbers girl—exhibit A, I had no idea I was paying for a landline phone all these years, maybe it's time to hire an accountant?—but what are the odds that he would show up in that bar, on that night?

So then I just started ranting and raving about fate. And the longer I talked, the more I drank.

I am pleased to report that I was a happy drunk until I woke up this morning and became a thoroughly humiliated, nearly-sober, respectable member of society once again.

Normally I do not do uptight. But there I was, caught in that maze, being a total bitch.

You can't eat here? God, what a childish remark.

And what did he do? What did Collin Creed do? Call me up on a phone that has been hanging on my kitchen wall for almost eight years and never once rang so he could invite me over to pick through his treasures.

What is a girl to make of that?

Is he coming on to me?

Do I *want* him to come on to me?

I mean... the guy was the love of my life. Until that night stole everything from us. In a matter of moments my perfect future with this man was shattered into bits and pieces. He was never the same after that.

I get why he shot the guy. He was scary. He looked home-less, or maybe he was on drugs. There was a lot about that intruder that was off even before you added in the fact that he was in the middle of kidnapping a little girl right from her bed.

And I get that Collin Creed, even back then, was kind of imposing and big. An athlete, tall and muscular. But he had just turned eighteen. He was still a kid, really. I looked at him after it was over. There was blood splattered everywhere. All over Olive—she was a horror show. Some of it even got as far as Collin. Little dots on his face. But when I looked at him, I saw someone else. Someone I had never met.

His eyes were raging wild, his breath coming out hard and

fast. Olive was screaming. Just screaming her head off. And then someone was knocking on the door. Pounding, really.

It was the next-door neighbor asking if everything was OK. Jim Rush. That's who lived there back then.

We didn't plan anything. There wasn't time. Collin looked at me, panicked, then he looked at Olive and let out a breath. "Are you OK?" That's what he asked her. She had stopped screaming when the door pounding started.

We didn't plan the story. We didn't. Jim Rush broke through the locked door. Just kicked it open and came barreling through. He stopped and just stared at the body. Then each of us. We were all standing exactly where it happened. The dead man was crumpled around Olive's feet. Collin still had the rifle pointed where the man used to be. I was still hiding behind him with my hand to my mouth in shock.

Jim found us all in the hallway like that and he was screaming, "Oh, my God! Oh, my God! What the fuck? What the fuck?" Asking everything twice. "Are you OK? *Are you OK?*"

We were OK, I guess. Bloody and traumatized, but we were not hurt.

I kinda lost time, but the next thing I remember is that me, Olive, and Collin were all outside, standing in the driveway. And the police—Jerry Cane and Matthew Reed—were telling us to calm down, take our time, and tell our story.

Olive and I didn't say anything and Collin lied. Said the guy came at us.

When they asked Olive and me for our story, I repeated what Collin had said. I don't know why. To protect him, I guess. I mean, I think he was justified. I know the guy was surrendering, but later—days later, actually—when the final report came out, it said that the man had a gun in the waist-band of his pants.

So I think Collin was justified.

Olive didn't say anything that night and no one made her

give a statement. Some days later, I think she did corroborate the story. And in two weeks the whole matter was put to bed.

But Collin, the one I knew, anyway, was gone.

He didn't hardly talk anymore. He skipped classes in school or just didn't go. And by March we all knew he had joined the Marines. He and Amon both.

I don't think they planned it that way. Amon ran with a different crowd. Most of his friends were from Revenant. Since the towns are all so small around here, Disciple, Revenant, and Bishop all share schools. The three towns make up a crude triangle on the map, so back in the Seventies or Eighties the county built a school compound smack in the middle of that triangle so we'd all have a 'better school experience.' They were just being cheap. They wanted three schools for everyone in the area instead of nine. But it was kinda nice going to school with kids who didn't live down the street.

Amon lived in Disciple, but his crew was from Revenant, so I can't even imagine that Collin joined up because of Amon.

But they are friends now, I guess.

Weird how one night—literally the span of seconds—can change the course of an entire life.

I was so mad at Collin. I screamed at him when I found out he had joined up. And I never scream. Not about anything. I don't even think I screamed when the gun went off. But when Collin joined the Marines, I lost it. I lost my mind. It was a terrible night. I was crying so hard. And it was for so many things. The shooting, the lies, the way Collin just withdrew. And the fact that I was not important enough to stick around for.

He didn't yell back. Just looked at me as I screamed and cried.

That was Easter night. I remember that. It came early that year, so that whole week prior the town was scrambling to get the tent up and everything ready for the first Revival of the year. They always start on Easter morning and end on Christmas Eve.

And of course, Collin's daddy, Mr. Creed, was the preacher. So he was busy. So busy. We were all busy, I guess. My family, the McBrides, we ran the souvenir booth, plus my mama had the flea market. And the thing is, when Easter comes early like that it's cold outside. Some years it snows. And that particular year, I remember, it was snowing.

There were brightly-colored tulips everywhere, their pale yellow and pink blooms peeking up from the blanket of snow that had formed overnight. The tent is an aged cream color, stained brown in some spots, which made it look vintage and charming surrounded by the snow and the bits of green grass as the day warmed up. This was before we had the scaffolding built around it so we could put up an even bigger tent over the Revival one, should the weather call for it.

But it was still nice. There were rabbits scurrying around and a few deer in the field. And the sun was peeking out, shining scattered rays of light down on us like God was pleased. The whole scene was beautiful. It looked like an Easter card you'd get in the mail from your nana.

I was walking to the tent that morning to get ready for work and I had stopped in the street to just look at it. That's when Amon came up to me. Pinched me on the arm in a playful way. We weren't friends, but we were friendly. "Never thought I'd see the day that Collin Creed would join the Marines."

My head whipped to the side to look at him. "What?"

And then he spilled the whole secret.

That's how I learned that my boyfriend broke up with me.

From Amon fuckin' Parrish.

*THEY LEFT **at the end** of May after graduation. And even though they came back together one time that first year, Collin didn't even call me.

Easter night, twelve years ago, was the last time we spoke. He listened to me rant and rave and then he said, "I'm sorry, Lowyn. I gotta go."

I thought he meant he had to go home or something. That we'd pick this conversation up at some point. But on Easter Monday, he didn't show up for school. And when I went to his house that afternoon, his mama said he moved out.

Moved. Out.

"Where did he go?"

"He didn't say."

"Well, he can't just move out! He's in high school!"

But that wasn't true. He was eighteen.

I never did find out where he was staying. He had a Jeep, but he wasn't living in it. And knowing what I do now, I imagine he was staying with Amon, maybe.

I was so hurt. And back then, kids didn't have cell phones. Not kids where I grew up, anyway. So I could call that landline all I wanted, he wasn't gonna be there.

He came back to school, and I did try and corner him once, but he wouldn't even look at me. He turned his head as I yelled in the hallway in front of his locker. And when I was done, he just walked away.

Not another word.

I gotta go. That was the last thing he ever said to me until last night at the bar.

So how am I supposed to feel about this?

On the one hand, I'm giddy at the thought of him being around again.

But sad, too. Because of how we ended. And because I don't know him anymore. It didn't really hit me until he said those words, "Our opinions diverge here," that I felt all the missing pieces inside me.

Because he always had the heart of a poet. He used to say the most beautiful things to me. Not telling me I'm beautiful, though he did do that. Just the way he always had a new word to take the place of an old one, even in the most ordinary of situations.

Our opinions diverge here.

It's art.

In the morning, I'm packing for this week's pickin' trip and Rosie's mouth is runnin' like a motorboat as I gather up everything I need from the back of the shop. She's been talking about some guy named Scar who lives in Fayetteville, which is a big town down the river from Disciple.

I don't even bother mentioning that a guy called Scar is probably not the best choice because she already knows this. Rosie picks the bad ones every single time. She doesn't ever pick anyone from the Trinity area. But she doesn't ever bring them home to meet Cross, either, so everyone in Disciple gives her a pass on her dubious taste in men.

Whatever happens between her and these men is her business, I guess.

But just as I'm putting my little travel bag into the back of

72

the truck, she changes the subject. "So... what's up with you and Collin?"

"What do you mean?" I close the back passenger door of the truck, walk around, and open the driver's.

She huffs at me. "He's back. Obviously single."

"How do you know that?"

"Amon told me. Said they're both single. In fact, all the men up there in that compound are single. Every girl in Disciple just let out a sigh, Lowyn."

"Good for them. We're not together, Rosie. We're not going to get together, either."

"Why not?"

"Why not?" I scoff. And I don't feel like talking about this. So I just change the subject. "I'll be back on Thursday night, as usual. My itinerary is on the board in the break room. Call me if you need anything."

Then I get in the truck and close my door before she can say anything else.

She's still smirking at me as she waves goodbye from the parking lot.

I'm heading southwest for this trip. I've got appointments set up near Knoxville, Chattanooga, and Memphis. That's probably as far as I'll get. Then I'll just turn around and drive home on Thursday morning. I love pickin' Tennessee, and I haven't done it in a while. Almost two years, maybe. I've spent the better part of the last year up in the Great Lakes region, so this will be a nice change.

About three and a half hours into my trip I make my first stop at a beautiful farm just outside Johnson City. There's a wrought-iron gate with a stone wall on either side, so I just let out a long sigh as I make my way up the driveway.

This woman is a dealer. Her specialty is mid-century toys. Which is a hot item, all the time. Everyone loves toys and they just don't make them the way they used to. Haven't for decades.

I warned this woman on the phone that I would not be

paying top dollar. She said, "Just come out and look. You just come out and look."

And I thought, *OK. She was warned.* But this... dear God. The house at the end of the long, smooth blacktop driveway is made of stone too. River stone. It's *gorgeous.* A sprawling rambler that fits neatly into the curves of the hillside.

I'm instantly irritated because I know she's gonna have good stuff in that house. And I also know that I'm not gonna get much, if anything, because I've got a flea-market budget and this is boutique-class all the way.

But I'm here, so I might as well take a look. I get out and she's already coming down the front walk saying my name. "Welcome, Miss McBride. Welcome! I'm Sassy. So good to finally meet you."

Sassy's middle-aged. Maybe forty, maybe a little older. Well-kept, with make-up and blonde hair in an old-fashioned updo that is just the right amount of messy. She's wearing a long cotton dress with a muted floral pattern that drops just below her knees so she can show off her designer cowboy boots.

She's a country fuckin' music star, I just know it.

"It's just Lowyn."

"Lowyn, come in! Let's talk." Then she grabs my hand and takes me inside.

There is no way I can stop my gawking once I go through that door. The stone fireplace, the wide-planked salvaged floors, the gray and black tones, and the view of the forest outside just about takes my breath away. Her home is so beautiful. It's something out of a magazine. "Do you sing country music?"

She laughs. "I did, I did. You got me. What gave it away?"

"Well, everything. But listen—"

She puts up a hand. "Ah, ah, ah. I already know what you're gonna say."

"Ya do?"

"I'm too fancy for your blood."

"Well, you are. I'm sorry."

"No, no, no. You're jumpin' the gun. I'm not interested in making top dollar."

"Why not?"

"Because I don't need the money, sugar. I'm not selling this stuff for money. I'm selling this stuff for revenge."

I smile, then giggle. "Divorce?"

She points at me. "Nailed it. That bastard. He was a lying, cheatin' fool. But I got the house, and the horses, and the guitars, and the toys."

"What he'd get?"

"The yacht. The mansion in the Bahamas. And the dog." She makes a face, a sad face that turns into an angry face. "I'm pissed off about the dog."

"I see."

"I loved that dog. She's my baby. And he's taken her prisoner. Don't worry!" Sassy puts her hand up again. "She's gonna be fine. I'm gonna steal her back as soon as I can find someone to do that for me. But first, I'm gonna sell his toy collection and"—she pauses to wink at me—"make a little country-music comeback." Then she takes my hand and starts leading me through the house. "Now listen, I've got a proposition for you, Lowyn McBride…"

COLLIN

hen I come outside the next morning, I stop short on my porch. The whole place is crawling with people. Hundreds of them. Even from here I can see the front part of the property is filled with cars. Amon and Nash are talking to a group of men in the road that leads down the middle of all the houses, and there has got to be about a million dogs barking.

I forgot about the fuckin' dogs.

That was Amon's thing in the Marines—for the short time we were legit with them. Right out of basic they hooked him up as a Marine Corps dog handler. He was not qualified for this, of course. Same way I wasn't qualified to be a counterintelligence specialist. But nonetheless, this is where we ended up.

How they found us, I never did figure out. Or why. I still don't know. But the moment Amon and I got off the fuckin' bus and stepped onto the base in San Diego, they were there. Two MP's came up to us. Called us privates and everything. "Private Creed, Private Parrish, please come with us." As if we had a choice.

And that's how this shit started.

We didn't do anything but show up. The rest of it was the US fuckin' government.

Of course, we didn't stay in the Marines. That's why we had

to agree to the dishonorable discharge as soon as our second year was up.

All that is beside the point. The point is, Amon is dog-crazy. Never had a dog growing up, his daddy's allergic, so he didn't even know he was dog-crazy until he got his first partner, Angel, a beautiful black German Shepherd who was probably smarter than most of the people in this town.

The only time I've ever seen Amon Parrish cry was when he walked away from that dog. And when he said he wanted our private security business to offer up K-9 protection for sale, I didn't even blink. I just said yes. We got four breeding pairs, seventeen juveniles, and eleven puppies. They'll be staying in an outbuilding just past Amon's house, in the woods.

He sees me coming down the porch steps and waves me over. And he's grinnin' like a fuckin' fool. "My dogs are here."

I smile too. "I hear 'em. They're fuckin' loud."

Amon claps me on the shoulder. "Don't worry. They'll be inside soon. The kennel people are already setting up."

I look over in that direction, then take in the rest of the camp. "We're... very busy right now."

"Shit yeah. Ryan's got bulldozers ripping up trees back there"—Amon points behind us where a bunch of hard-hat guys are yelling things—"and Nash and me are pickin' out the men we need for reno."

"There's like a hundred people here, Amon. We didn't agree on a hundred people."

"I know. I maybe put the word out that we were hiring a little bit too good. But don't worry. I got your place covered. They're gonna rip it up and put it back together and you don't have to do a thing."

"Wait. What about the stuff inside?"

"What stuff?"

"You know, all the shit lying around."

"I feel like there's a reason you're asking me this question, so maybe let's just skip ahead to that."

"There is. I told Lowyn she could come pick through it."

"Did you?" He slips his arm around my shoulders. I didn't think he could grin any bigger, but he is. "That was so sweet. Saving all that crap for your dumpster-diving girlfriend."

I push his arm off. "She's not my girlfriend. And it's not crap, Amon. It's treasure."

"She told you to say that, didn't she?"

I chuckle. "Nah. But that's what she calls it. Isn't it better to repurpose than throw it in the dump?"

"It is. I will put together a box team and all Lowyn's crap will be packed up and put in the church. How about that?"

"Maybe she'll come over today and look through it."

"Well, that would be spectacular, friend. And since you've got nothin' better to do, why don't you go make that happen." He turns, whistles loudly, and starts yelling at some guys over near the dogs.

Then he just walks off.

But he's right. I should go make that happen.

I DON'T HAVE **her cell number** and when I call the house phone, she doesn't pick up, even though I let it ring twenty-five times. I need to get that woman an answering machine. Do they even sell those anymore?

So I take a ride into town. Having already deduced that she is not at my house, I go looking for her store. Disciple is like four blocks square, so I just take a little drive through town until I find it. Then I park out front.

I get out and look at the front window for a moment, taking it all in. McBooms, it's called. Like McBride married a boom box, I figure. It's clever, and I always did like clever. Plus, the lettering is stand-out good. Varsity font. Like the letters on that jacket I used to so proudly wear. And her colors are bright. Yellow and orange. Well, let's call them... pineapple and tangerine.

Yep. This is so her. I pull the door open and go inside. A little bell jingles above my head and someone calls, "Be right there!" in a sing-songy voice.

Which gives me time to take in the interior of her shop. From the outside, McBooms looks like any other building built at the turn of the twentieth century. Red brick, three stories tall, huge picture window running down the front side, and lots of many-paned windows trimmed in white on the second and third floors.

But from the inside, it's somethin' else altogether.

Same three stories tall, but most of the upstairs has been removed and turned into an open ceiling bedecked with large wooden beams and curved trusses that might remind a person of a railroad bridge or the inside of a church, depending on which way one leans.

There is shit everywhere. But it's not disorderly. In the center of the massive, almost warehouse-sized room sits a living room, something right out of the Sixties with a modular, tapered-leg couch the color of dark champagne taking up a significant portion of the space. Opposite the couch sit two wood, tapered-leg chairs with cushions the color of a Caribbean sea. And in between is a minimalist coffee table in the shape of a circle and the color of walnut. There is a credenza in the kitty-corner, top open to reveal a record player inside. And across that diagonal is an old-time black and white TV on a wheeled stand showin' off its rabbit-ear antennas.

Pulling the look together is a massive orange rug, but underneath, and running throughout the store, the floor is made up of wide-plank boards of wood so old, they look like they have stories to tell.

There is a jukebox over in the corner and another seating

arrangement—this time a dinette set with a Formica top, chrome legs and accents, and in Fifties diner checkered red.

And when I spin in place, I spy several more 'get the look' rooms, including a rope hammock hanging from a beam, a wave lounge chair in black velvet that can fit two people, and a whole wall of posters with the faces of dead rock-and-roll gods lookin' back at me.

On the far side of the room is a set of wooden stairs that lead up to the second- and third-floor lofts where I presume the details are kept. Throw pillows, and bedding, and accent pieces.

Stepping in here really does feel like stepping into the past and I love it. Everything about it says 'Lowyn.'

A woman appears, dusting her hands off, directing my attention back to the task at hand. This is not Lowyn. I'm not exactly sure who she is—people change over time, after all. But she sure as hell knows me.

"Collin Creed. As I live and breathe." I must not have my best poker face on because she points to herself. "Rosie Harlow! Come on now! Amon picked me out of a crowd yesterday morning at the coffee shop."

I raise an eyebrow. "A crowd?"

"There were half a dozen people in there at the time!" I grin at her and she makes a little swoony motion with her body, pretending to faint. "That dimple, my God. I had forgotten how fuckin' handsome you are, Collin Creed."

"Nothing gets past you, Rosie."

She snickers. "Lemme guess. You're here for… a mix tape."

"A mix tape?"

"We make those, ya know. You can order them online."

"Really?"

"Really. You can pick out songs and everything."

"How is that legal?"

"We don't charge for them. It's free when you buy a hundred bucks' worth of shit. And we record them the old-fashioned way." She points to the jukebox, which, I notice now that it has been pointed out, is positioned next to a table with a stereo system and a wooden crate filled with cassette tapes. "We play 'em and press record, just like the good old days. It was my idea."

I point at her. "I had forgotten how brilliant and funny you are, Rosie Harlow. Thank you for reminding me."

She blushes, then fans herself. "My God." Then blows out a breath. "You're lookin' for Lowyn, right?"

"Is she around?"

"She's not, actually. She's gone for the whole week."

"Shut up. She told you to say that, didn't she?"

Rosie laughs. "No. She really is out of town. It's a pickin' week."

"What the fuck is a pickin' week?"

"That's when Lowyn goes out of town to pick through people's junk so she can buy it up and bring it back." Rosie waves her hand at the store.

"Oh." Well, now what do I do? Lowyn was my whole plan for the day.

"She's not far, though."

"No?"

"Not yet. She had an appointment down near... Oh, I don't remember. Somewhere in Tennessee. You could show up and surprise her."

"I don't think she'd like that."

"Are you kidding me? She would *love* that." Then Rosie winks at me. "Hold on. I'll go get her itinerary." Then she whirls around and goes back the way she came.

Rosie comes back out with a piece of notebook paper. Like, the actual shit we used back in school. She notices me noticin' it. "Isn't Lowyn so damn cute? She uses notebook paper for everything. And look!" She holds the note up so I can see it. "Cursive!" Then she bursts out laughing.

I take the paper and stare at Lowyn's handwriting, memories flooding back like crazy. God, I would know that handwriting anywhere. It's not long and slanted, like a John Hancock, but upright and loopy, like a teenage girl's. The fact that it is written in baby blue ink with pink accents makes me happy in a way I haven't been in a very long time. I can see her clicking that two-color pen right now, her tongue gliding over her lip as she carefully writes her note.

I look up at Rosie and she looks unsure. "What?"

"You OK, Collin?"

"I'm fine. Thanks."

"Good." She's more serious now, not smiling anymore. "Ya know, we're all glad you're back. It sucks the way it turned out, but they're gone now, so…"

"What?" I'm confused.

"Nothin'." She points to the letter. "Show up. Her number's on the top, so you can call if you want. But by the time you get down there, she'll probably be heading to that motel. She drives a black truck. Got a trailer hitched to the back. You should surprise her. She needs a good surprise. And you are the best surprise she could ever dream of, Collin Creed."

I don't know if that's true, but I would like to think that it is. "Thank you. And… nice to see you again, Rosie. It's been a pleasure."

"Oh, stop now. You're gonna make me faint." And then she does faint. Dramatically. All the way down to the floor with the back of her hand pressed to her forehead.

I leave shaking my head, but smiling too.

It's… maybe… good to be back.

Four hours later I pull in to the parking lot of Motel Pool and there she is. Lowyn McBride, her ass sticking out of the back seat of her truck as she gathers shit up. I don't park next to her, I park down the lot a little so I can watch her for a moment. And just as I think that, my phone rings.

Unknown number. And just as I see that, she backs out of the backseat with a phone to her ear.

No.

I accept the call. "How did you get this number?"

"What?" She sounds scared. "Sorry, I—"

"I'm kiddin', Lowyn. I know it's you."

"How'd you know? Did Amon call and warn you or something?"

"No, should he have?"

"No. But that's who I got your number from."

It's kinda fun to simultaneously watch her kick her hip to the side and toss her hair as she says these words to me. She's flirting. Over the phone. I'm *dead*.

"Anyway. Don't you wanna know why I called?"

"You miss me?"

On the phone, she chuckles. But in real life, across the parking lot, she puts her hand over her mouth and bends over —my effing God, Lowyn. She's showing that ass off right and left. But the reason she bent over was to hide her expression, which I catch just a bit of when she almost turns around. She puts the phone against her chest, gulps a breath, then brings it back up to her mouth. "This is business."

"Yeah? What kind of business?" It takes every bit of willpower I have not to laugh at her.

"OK. But you're gonna—" She turns as she's saying this, pauses mid-sentence, and squints her eyes at me. "Is that your Jeep?"

I laugh. "That is my Jeep."

"You're here?"

"Surprise."

"Oh, my God." She hangs up the phone and comes stalking towards me, mouth going a mile a minute, cursing me out, I'm sure. But I can't hear a single thing she's saying.

God damn, she is so cute.

How did I ever walk away from her?

When she gets to me, I buzz the window down.

"What are you doing here in my motel parkin' lot?"

"I have come to invite you over to my new culty compound" —I pause to appreciate her giggle—"so you can pick your treasure out of my fuckin' junk."

"Oh… that was dirty, Collin Creed."

"Dirty how?" I can't stop the laugh.

"'Pick your treasure out of my fuckin' junk?' How is that not sexual innuendo?"

I guffaw. "Woman, what is your business with me?"

"Well." She blows up some air, which make her bangs poof up. "You're gonna think I'm crazy." I want to say a million things back to that, but she doesn't give me time. "You're running some kind of security operation, right?"

"Yeah."

"Well, does your operation take on any… questionably legal operations?"

"Have you been spying on me?"

She gets the joke, because she laughs, and I love this. "Seriously, Collin. I'm being serious."

"What kind of questionable operations?"

"How do you feel about canine kidnappings?"

"I… have… zero feelings about those. And they are not on the menu."

"But if, by chance, some rich, ex-country-singer star—sorta —wants her dog kidnapped from her filthy, no-good ex-husband, would said security operation be able to, perhaps, make that happen?" Lowyn ends this sentence with a lilt in her voice, like she's asking me for jelly beans.

"Lowyn."

"Collin." She smiles and rests her chin on the part of the door where the window glass disappears.

"If you want me to kidnap a fuckin' dog, then... I will tell Amon to do that."

She giggles. "Amon, huh?"

"He's gonna love this job."

"So I can tell her yes?"

"Tell her maybe. We gotta get details."

"Should I be wary of the fact that you agreed to this so quickly?"

"Oh, yeah. You should."

"That's what I thought." She's serious now. The way Rosie got all serious back at the shop at the end there.

I let out a long breath. "I drove a long way. I would like to have dinner with you. Would you like to have dinner with me?"

She smiles again and nods. "Just let me lock up my trailer and I'll be right back."

I watch her ass the whole way across the parking lot. The other night I was thinking there was no way we'd get back together. I didn't even let myself daydream about it. Because a dozen years are a long time and Lowyn McBride is a fuckin' treasure. I thought for sure she'd be married. Have kids. A nice house. She does have a nice house, but I mean a bigger house. With all the things she deserves.

But she's not married, she's a business owner, and as far as I can tell, she's not gonna hold my exit from her life against me now.

More importantly, she knows I'm a murderer, and now she knows I'm a kidnapper too.

Well, an accomplice, at the very least.

As she makes her way back across the parking lot to me, I have to take a moment. Because a week ago Lowyn McBride was a... well, I won't say a distant memory. I have always regretted how things ended between us. But I had given up on the delusion that one day we might reconnect. I mean, really.

How is it possible that she's not married? And I know she doesn't have a boyfriend because she let me come home with her the other night and the Lowyn I know would not have done that if she had a boyfriend.

I feel like I just fell into an opportunity.

She gets in the truck, smiling, jostling a little as she pulls her seatbelt across her chest. "OK. I'm hungry. I didn't eat all day. Were you driving all day, Collin? Did you eat anything?"

Just like that. Just like… just like we are still the same people we were. Like no time passed at all. "I didn't eat, no."

"Good, then I won't embarrass myself when I scarf my food down."

I smile as I slide the Jeep into first, then pull out of the motel parking lot.

"Where we going? Is it barbecue? I'm maybe a little bit hungry for barbecue."

"Lowyn, I can't remember a time when you would ever pass up barbecue."

"Some things never change." She kinda sighs these words out. But she's not looking at me. She's looking out the window.

"We are going to barbecue. I know a place."

She turns to look at me and giggles. "You know a place in Johnson City, Tennessee, do ya?"

"Just you wait."

She giggles again. An easy laugh. One that takes me all the way back to junior high when I used to watch her before school when she was hanging with her friends. Rosie was around back then too, and Clover. "Hey, whatever happened to Clover?"

"Oh, she's a fancy-fancy events coordinator up in that super-fancy-fancy hotel in Virginia. The Dixie Yonder. You ever heard of that place?"

You know what I like about people in these hills? The way they keep a conversation goin' with a question at the end. I've been all over the world and in most places, people just want you to shut up. And maybe it's just because we're reconnecting, that could be it. But I think it's just something we do in these parts. Keep the conversation going, I mean.

"I have not. But if you say it's super-super-fancy, then it must be impressive."

"Super-fancy-fancy."

"I stand corrected."

She laughs and so do I. Why the hell did I ever walk out on this one?

She turns her head and looks at me. I can just barely see this from the corner of my eye. "Collin."

"What?" I glance over at her, then look back to the road because this little section of highway is kinda curvy.

"Where have you been?"

My breath comes out unexpectedly. "Shit, Lowyn. Where haven't I been? All over."

"Start from the beginning. I want to hear about all of it."

"You really don't."

"No, I really do. I have been picturing you in my head all these years."

I look over at her again. "What?"

"Sure. Of course. I mean… the way you left, and—"

"I'm sorry about that."

"No. I mean, OK. That's fine, apology accepted. But that's not what I'm talking about. Not in a pining way. Just a casual, every-once-in-a-while way. Where is he right now? Thoughts like that on a Christmas Eve. And maybe a year later I'd say, what is he doing? And then, months after that, for no good reason whatsoever, I'd think, what does he look like? Almost the same, by the way. But older. And…" She pauses and when I look over again, she's nodding her head. She smiles at me. "Nice."

"I look nice, huh?"

"You do. So maybe it did drive me a little nuts after you left because I had lost something, ya know? Initially, I was a teeny bit desperate for news, so I would try to corner your daddy every once in a while, in those early years, to ask him about you. But he was less than forthcoming, if I'm being honest. You don't have to tell me everything, of course, just paint me a tiny picture."

I tap my fingers on the steering wheel, thinking about this. "A tiny picture... well, I went to basic. That was San Diego."

"Oh, that sounds nice."

I shrug that comment off. "Then..." I sigh. How much can I tell her?

"Then you got discharged."

"Right." I can tell her this part, because none of that's classified anymore. There was a fucking congressional commission about the whole thing, so it doesn't even matter. "Well, about that. First thing is, I *did* get dishonorably discharged—and so did Amon. But it was planned."

"What's that mean?"

"They kinda... picked us, I guess. Me and Amon. Reasons unknown. And put us in this special program. Not the SEALs or Rangers, but something kinda like it."

"Ohhhhhh. Wait." When I look over at her, that beautiful face of hers is all crinkled up. "I think I heard something about this."

"I think everyone heard something about this. It was a big fuckin' deal in Congress the last two years."

"Yes. They had a commission about it."

"They certainly did. All the people running it—all my superiors—well, most of them went to prison over the whole thing. And not the super-fancy-fancy kind, either." She giggles. "They all got ten years in the fuckin' brig."

"Yeah, I do remember that. Did you get in trouble?"

"Well, not officially. It was a military operation, but we weren't military. That's the part Congress took offense to. See, these generals, they made a... a private army, if you will.

According to Congress, we were mercenaries. But according to our contracts, we were security."

"Well, this sounds sticky, Collin."

"Oh, you have no idea how fuckin' sticky that whole thing got."

"But you're out now? I mean, you are, right? You're here, startin' a business. It's not some front for the US government, is it?"

"Fuck. No."

She relaxes a little. "Good."

"That's all you got to say about that? Good? I'm not government, so that's good?"

Her smile is real, but not big. "It's very good."

I decide to leave it at that because we're coming up to the little place I'm taking her for dinner. She leans forward when I pull into the parking lot of a log-cabin restaurant on the Watauga River. There's an old painted sign over the huge front porch that says 'Watauga Waffle House.'

Lowyn huffs out a little laugh. "The Waffle House?"

"Not *the* Waffle House. The Watauga Waffle House. But don't worry, the online menu says they serve spaghetti and meatballs."

She slaps my shoulder in a playful manner that makes me so homesick for high school, my stomach aches. "I still do like a good meatball."

I laugh too. Turn the Jeep off. Then I look over at her and take her all in. She's got on a white tank top and a white over-shirt that makes her look girly and feminine. There are no buttons or anything on this overshirt, it's a cotton jacket with eyelet lace on the collar and the bell sleeves, with two pieces of white satin tied in a bow at the dip of her waist. She's wearing jeans too. Tight jeans that really show off her curves. And boots. Lowyn McBride always did like a good pair of vintage cowgirl boots.

"So... listen, Lowyn—"

"You don't have to."

"You don't even know what I'm gonna say."

"I kinda do. Whatever happened, happened. That's how I see it. I understand why things went the way they did. It was a really fucked-up night, ya know?"

She's talking about the night I killed that man. "Yeah. It certainly was."

"And... well, we were too young to process it. I'm really glad you're back though."

"You sure? Because you were pretty mad at me when you realized it was me you took home that night."

"That reaction was a combination of things. And I'm not gonna pretend that I wasn't hurt when you left, but it's not about that. Not exactly."

"What's it about then?"

She unsnaps her seat belt and turns in the seat so we're more facing each other. Then she starts wringing her hands in her lap. "I lied about something. That was part of it. It was embarrassment, maybe. And... yeah, I was mad at you for leaving me. But that was a long time ago. And then you made that nice offer to let me come pick your place and... and I realized we don't have to be mad at each other. Ya know? That... I dunno. Maybe we just needed time apart and it wasn't meant to be back then."

"And now?"

She shrugs. "I don't know. But before this goes any further" —she points at me, then herself—"I have to tell you something about that room of yours in my house."

"My room?"

"Yeah. You see, it's not for sale."

"But I saw it on the website. It's all on there."

"Yeah. It is. Because that same morning that we woke up in your bed, I put a bunch of pictures up on the website to make you think that."

"So... you're telling me... you've kept my childhood

bedroom like a shrine for… for why?" Her face goes sad, which confuses me. "Lowyn, what is going on?"

She lets out a long breath and then reaches for my hand.

This startles me, so I pull back. And I don't mean to do that, but before my mind can catch up with my reaction, it's already done. "I didn't… I don't… just tell me what's going on."

"OK. But I'm sorry ahead of time, OK?"

I shrug. I don't even know what to do with that statement. "OK."

"OK. Well, after you left, the preacher, your daddy, well he got weird, Collin. The sermons got dark. People stopped comin' to the Revival. The towns started losing money. People just… glossed over it the first year. He's upset, he's… whatever. They thought it would pass. But the second year, he was worse."

"Worse how? What was he sayin'?"

"Oh, Collin. It was…" She blows out a breath. "Fire and brimstone, ya know? Like… Sinners in the Hands of an Angry God kinda shit. Really angry. Real dark. Still, people didn't know how to approach it, ya know? He's the fuckin' preacher, right? What can one do?"

"Yeah, OK."

"But then Bishop and Revenant started to complain about it and… well, things got ugly."

The three towns of Disciple, Bishop, and Revenant are all tied together through the Revival. Disciple has the tent and we play the part of God, or whatever, because this whole thing is kind of a living carnival. A sideshow of epic proportions.

And if you have a God, of course you have to have a Devil. That's Revenant. Revenant plays the part of debauchery. A real Babylon kind of place. Bars, and neon signs, and bikers. Really rowdy kind of stuff. Plus some pagan stores and stuff like that. Nothin' illegal, of course. It's all a show.

Bishop is the path of redemption through traditional ways. It's a Colonial town and it has a historical district in the old downtown where people live like they did back in the day. Horse and buggy, butter churns, spinning wheels, and raising livestock. All that kind of shit.

We got a thing going up here in the hills of West Virginia. Like a theme park, except the people of Disciple, Revenant, and Bishop all live inside of it. We all play a part. And we're all tied together. The tent revival really brings them in. It's legend. And without it, Revenant would just be... well, a place you really didn't want to be. Same with Bishop. People would come and see the buggies going down the road and all that, but really, the three towns need each other to make it all work.

All our lives are tied together through this carnival we produce like a three-legged stool. And if one leg goes wonky, it takes the whole thing down.

"All right." I nod at Lowyn. "I guess that's reasonable."

"Right. So. Well, they fired him. That's why your family moved."

"*Really.*"

"Yep."

"Huh. All this time I thought they just wanted to get rid of that house."

"Well..." She's cringing.

"There's more?"

"Yep, there's more."

"OK, Lowyn, just spit it out. Tell me. What the hell is going on?"

She looks out the window for a moment, then takes a breath and looks back at me. "So... they needed to sell the house, right?"

"As one does when they move."

"And I offered to buy it because... well, maybe this is stupid, but I spent a lot of time in that house, ya know? It felt like... like it was part mine already."

"Makes sense."

"So I make the offer, your daddy accepts, and they're packin' up to move."

"Keep going."

"So on the day before we close on the house I'm over there helping out. And I say to your mama, 'Would you like me to pack up Collin's room?'" Lowyn's shoulders shrug up and she blushes. "I did like your things, Collin. I did want to explore it all, OK? I admit that. But then your daddy says, 'Just put it all in the trash, Lowyn. That's where it belongs.'"

I look away. Get lost lookin' out the window. Trying to process this. Not sure how to feel. I mean, I haven't talked to them in eight years. I have no idea what Olive even looks like these days. My mama hasn't called me on my birthday, or sent me so much as a card at Christmas. And those last few conversations I had with my daddy on the phone—well, he made it perfectly clear that I was trash to him, so I'm not even surprised that he wanted to throw me out altogether.

"I'm sorry, Collin. It hit me that way too. So I told them to leave it and I'd take care of it."

"And you just left it." I look over at her and she nods. "The exact way it was when I took off."

She nods again. "There are memories in that room. Memories they had no right to throw away." Now she straightens her back and lifts her chin up in a defiant posture. "And to be honest, some of those memories were mine. They didn't have any right to do that. And then... well, I didn't know what to do with that room. So I just closed the door and went along with my business. Then time passed. I redecorated everything and remodeled around it. I didn't need the space. I don't sleep in your bed, Collin. I'm not staring at your posters on the wall, pining away about something that never happened, OK? I sleep upstairs. I turned the bonus room into a master suite. It's real nice. You should come see it."

There is no way to stop my laugh and just like that, all the melancholy that was filling up this Jeep dissipates. "Did you just invite me into your bedroom, Lowyn McBride?"

She blushes as she smiles, then shrugs. "It's just... a really nice room."

I chuckle and look out the window again. Only this time, I'm not thinking about those asshole parents of mine. I'm not thinking about the past at all.

I get out, walk around to Lowyn's door, open it up, and offer her my hand. "Come on. Let's get some fuckin' meatballs."

*M*y *God*. I cannot believe this is even happening. I mean, Collin showing up at my motel while I'm on a trip? That's... that's the daydream. That's how you picture a reunion in your mind.

It wasn't a lie when I told Collin that I haven't been sitting around pining for him. I am nothing if not a multitasker. I pined for him while I was busy doing other things. And no, I don't go in his room and sigh over his things. Not often, anyway. On the every-once-in-a-while occasion though... yeah. I have.

And now we're sitting a picturesque little restaurant that's all decorated like a vintage cabin. And when the waitress took our order, he looked at me with one squinty eye, like he was making a determination, and then ordered me the spaghetti and meatballs. With wine. Red. And how does he even know I like red? We didn't drink when we were kids. We didn't even want to. That's not what our lives were about. We were Disciple kids.

Not that we don't have an errant teenager every now and then. Amon Parrish, exhibit A. Rosie Harlow, exhibit B. But, for the most part, Disciple kids did Disciple things. We ran the Revival nine months out of the year. Of course, it was most busy in the summer and we only did once-a-month revivals from September through Christmas Eve.

The Revival was our life.

The McBrides were in charge of souvenirs. My daddy died when Bryn and I were small. He was not from Disciple, he was from 'over the hills'—that's where all strangers come from as far as we're concerned. Before my daddy's death, the McBrides were in charge of tent construction and maintenance. After, of course, we weren't able to do that anymore, so we got the souvenir booth and the Harlow family—Rosie had four brothers and a daddy—took over the tent stuff.

Most of the things for our little tent my mama bought, of course. Custom-made crap with the logo on it. But each family was expected to contribute a certain amount of high-dollar handmade items for the booth. Some people made quilts. Some people made soap. My sister and I made folk art. Little collages of images we'd cut out of magazines and stick on flower pots and such. It was a lot of découpage, and it was nothing fancy, really. But we had a good eye for things and people liked our stuff.

Still do. We still make it. I collect all kinds of vintage magazines in McBooms and the ones that really aren't worth much Bryn and I use for our crafts.

Now that Amon and Collin are back, I wonder if they will have to take part again?

"My Lord, Lowyn. The look on your face right now, is that bliss?"

I take a sip of my wine so I can chuckle into my glass. "You wanna know what I was picturing in my head?"

"I'm positively dying here."

"You, in the Revival tent, standing up at the lectern, preachin'." Which is a little bit of a lie. I didn't get that far in the daydream, but it was coming.

He guffaws. People turn and look at us from a nearby table. "That's not gonna happen."

"But you're gonna do something though, right?"

"No. That's the whole reason we bought outside city limits.

Well, not that the city limits had any compounds for sale. But no. We're not gonna play a part in the Revival."

"You're in the triangle."

"Trust me. It's not gonna happen."

"But you talked to Jim Bob, though, right? Told him that? Because if not, they're gonna expect you to contribute."

I wait for an explosion. His vehement denial that he will not participate. But he sits back in his chair across the table from me and smiles. "What do you do to contribute?"

"Same thing."

"Your little crafty projects?"

"Yep. They're a bit more complicated these days, but I am nearly thirty now, so that's to be expected."

He presses his elbows onto the table, clasps his hands together, and leans forward. "Lowyn, can I ask you something?"

"You may."

"Where is your husband?"

I am just about to take another sip of wine, but thankfully it hasn't hit my lips yet or I might've spit it out. "What?"

"You must be hiding him somewhere. It's the only logical conclusion. Else, what the hell is wrong with the men out here? Why are you still single?"

I take a deep breath and smile. "Well, I have had my share of men. And I do have that once-a-year one-night stand in Bishop on Mama's birthday."

"Ohhhh." He laughs again and it's a hearty one. All deep and rumbly like thunder. "Is that what that was?"

"Yeah. One night a year I get to be a trollop."

"Ya know, we didn't—"

"I know. I woke up with my boots on, Collin Creed. To say that I was disappointed would be an understatement."

For the third time, I delight him. He leans back in his chair, making it creak. "I would like to go on record—"

"You do that."

"—and I would like to say that the men of the Revival have officially missed their chance."

"Is that right."

He nods. Slowly. Eyes stuck on mine. "That is a fact."

"What about you?"

"What about me?"

"No ex-wife anywhere?" I ask. He chuckles and looks away. "Holy shit, Collin Creed, you were *married*."

He lets out a breath between his teeth. "Almost. Like..." He holds his thumb and forefinger together with the teensiest bit of space between them. "This close."

"What happened? Runaway bride?"

"Nah. Nothing so dramatic. Well, that's not true, I guess. When you call off a wedding, it's always dramatic."

He and I lock eyes as I slowly nod my head. "Yep."

"So. I guess I got cold feet." He's still looking at me when he says this. Then he turns his head. "That's not true, either." He looks back at me. "You might be the only person I've ever admitted this to, but I just didn't love her. Not enough to marry her. Ya know, maybe I'm old-fashioned about this shit, or, I dunno, maybe I've been to one too many Revivals. But I don't wanna get divorced, ya know? I want it to be the way it was meant to be. Forever. And I knew that she and I were never gonna make it to forever."

"Well, you must've felt somethin' for her. Or why were you engaged?"

Collin just shrugs. "Well... I thought we were friends." His eyes narrow a little. "And I thought friends would be enough. And maybe it would've been. But then I realized she and I weren't friends. She was, pardon my language, a fuck buddy." He shrugs again. "I dunno, Lowyn. I just made a mistake. I think that's all there is to it. I thought I wanted something, but it turned out I didn't."

"Was she crushed?"

"Maybe? A little? And that's part of the problem too. She married one of my friends about three years later."

"Ouch."

"Whatever. Good for them. I sent them a subscription to the Beer of the Month Club so every thirty days or so they could toast their future, or, alternatively, wallow in their mistakes."

I smile. Then giggle. Then take a sip of wine.

"You do look good, Lowyn. I know I told you that the other night, but I'm not sure you remember the other night."

"I saw some video. Taylor Hill sent it to Bryn."

"Busybodies."

"Shit, Collin. You know how this place is." I make a yapping bird-beak with my fingers. "Gossip, gossip, gossip. I mean, the way you left... and the rumors that came after... I think people are surprised that you came home. And maybe you don't believe it, but I think they are relieved too."

"Why the hell would they be relieved?"

"Well, no town likes to lose people. Not towns like ours. There's no rule that everyone has to stay, of course. There's not even an expectation, really. Look at Clover and her family. But you were different. You know that, right?"

He lets out a breath and looks over my shoulder, eyes watching things distant to me. When his attention shifts back, he's gone very serious. "I..." And that's all he can get out.

I put up a hand after a few awkward seconds. "I was there, Collin. I know."

"But... what do you know, Lowyn?"

"That you were scared. That all three of us were scared. And then, when he—when that guy—when he surrendered and let Olive go, you were *pissed*. And you took that shot because that's what happens to assholes who come into your house and fuck with your people."

He blinks. Purses his lips a little. "I would like to deny that. I would like to say my finger slipped. But you're right. And you have *no* idea"—he pauses to look deep into my eyes—"no idea at all, how much that night changed me."

I'm shaking my head. "It didn't change you, Collin. It just... *revealed* you."

He guffaws and leans back in his chair. "Is that an insult or a compliment?"

"Neither. Both. It doesn't matter. You wanna hear my confession now?"

He nods without saying anything.

"I'm single because you ruined me that night." He looks shocked. But I put up a hand. "You see..." I have to pause here to think about how to say this. How to explain it. "You didn't even hesitate, Collin. If you had seen it from my perspective— you didn't waste a single second. You got the rifle, told me to stay put, went into the hallway, and two seconds later, it was handled. Two seconds. That's how long I was afraid. Two. Seconds. That man, he had a gun on him. If you had hesitated things could've turned out very different. You could've been the dead one. Olive could've been the dead one. I could've been the dead one. Everyone knew that, Collin. And if you think the sheriff didn't know that maybe you acted *too* quickly, *too* efficiently, well, he did. He asked me. He came over every couple of months, even after you left, to ask me questions."

"Why? Was he gunnin' for me?"

"No. He wasn't. I think maybe he thought I was trauma-tized. And he was trying to make me understand that when a stranger comes into your home and tries to kidnap your baby sister, this is what one does. Because any man who would even think about doing that, well, he just isn't a good man."

Collin allows himself a grin. It's small, but it's there. "I thought you were telling me the story of how I ruined you."

"I am. You ruined me because every guy I dated after you I would ask myself—how quickly would this one act? How long would I be afraid if some bad man forced his way into my life again? And the answer was never two seconds, Collin. So the answer was always too long."

We stare at each other for a good long moment. He picks up his glass and I, in return, pick up mine. "I've missed you."

I huff a little. "That's not a toast."

"To being back."

"Welcome home."

WE EAT A NICE DINNER. The restaurant's low lighting makes it intimate. And it's not loud and obnoxious, but quiet and... calm, I guess. We talk about other things after that. The night of the shooting was something we needed to discuss so we could clear the air. And now that it's over, it feels... easier. Like no time has passed. Like we're still in high school. Still dating. Still planning a life together.

I know what Collin was talking about when he said that woman he was gonna marry wasn't even his friend. That's how I've felt about the men I've been with. The fact is, I didn't just size up all my dates and boyfriends against Collin's action-readiness. I sized them up against him for everything.

And I was so used to doing it, Collin wasn't even part of the equation anymore. It's not like I went on that date six months back and said to myself, *So how does this one measure up in the looks department? How good is his aim? Does he even own a gun? Is he the right height? Does he have ambition? Can he catch a football?*

It wasn't like that. I just had this internal checklist. Like I already knew what I wanted. Like I was looking for a blouse on the rack and I already had a vision of it in my mind so I could just skip past all the things that weren't that.

Skip past all the men who weren't Collin Creed.

Collin and I walk outside the restaurant. It's a really nice evening. Still warm, like maybe summer's right around the corner. We head down a little path that leads to the parking lot. It's all very picturesque. It's dark, but there are fairy lights everywhere. Add in the sound of rushing water from the river and the little cabins tucked into the trees on either side of the path, and it's actually pretty romantic.

There's a little dock on the edge of the river. Decorated with more fairy lights. And no one's on it, so Collin takes my hand and leads me over there.

While we're walking, I'm freakin' out a little bit. What is this? A date? I mean, like a real date? Is he going to kiss me? Why is my heart beating so fast? I think my palms are sweating.

We stop at the edge of the railing and he lets go of my hand, then leans his elbows on the railing. I push up against it. Being shorter than him, this evens us out. He looks over at me with those teal and brown swirly eyes of his—now dotted with fairy-light reflections—and smiles. "How disappointed?"

"What?"

"When you woke up and realized you still had your boots on."

My laugh is immediate. "I didn't know it was you when I woke up. I just opened my eyes and saw that fuckin' Jim Morrison poster. It confused me for a moment, then I remembered what day it was. And my head was spinning, so I knew I got kinda drunk—"

"Lowyn." He turns his body so he's facing me. Straightens up so I have to tip my chin up to keep eye contact.

"What?"

"How. Disappointed?"

I let out a breath. "That I missed an opportunity with you? Or that I just missed an opportunity?"

"Ya know, the correct answer here is *very*." I giggle. "'I was *very* disappointed, Collin.' That's the right answer. And then I say, 'Well, perhaps there is a way I can ease your disappointment, Lowyn McBride? Perhaps there is a way I can redress this issue.'"

"Are you coming on to me?"

"Yes."

"Are you gonna invite me to stay the night?"

He lets out a breath now too. "No. But I want to. It's just…"

His pause is too long. "It's just what?"

Collin Creed's eyes are so pretty, I could stare at them for years. They search me now. Like I'm hiding some secret and he desperately needs it. "I was a dick, ya know?"

I smile. Can't help it. "It was a pretty dick move."

"And even though I may have premeditated this night—the cabin, the dinner, hell, the fuckin' fairy lights—they had pictures of all this on the website…"

I giggle. God, I've missed him.

"I don't think I've earned a second chance yet."

He hasn't. I love him. Will always love him. But I haven't been a teenager for a very long time. And even though he and I reconnected on the one night a year when I allow myself to be irresponsible, it's only ever been one night a year and I'm not about to change that now.

"Wow. What is going through your mind right now?"

I shrug. "Just… I agree."

"That I'm a dick?"

"No. Well, yeah. A little. But mostly I agree that you really haven't earned it yet, Collin. This is all very nice—the river, and the dinner, and the cabins, and the lights—and I would love nothing more than to give us another chance. But I'm not gonna jump into anything just for a night under the sheets."

"That's not all it would be, ya know."

"Maybe. I mean, I do know that. We're more than that, even now. After all these years, we're more than that. But I've got a life, Collin. A damn good one. And here's an addendum to my answer earlier about why I don't have a husband. I don't want one." I shrug one shoulder. "It's really as simple as that. I don't want one. Because I don't need a man to protect me now. I'm all grown up and I can do it myself."

He presses his lips together, nodding. "Would you like to go bowling with me?"

"What?" And then I'm laughing again.

"You know how I feel about bowling."

"Bowling *shirts*, you mean?"

"See how well you know me, Lowyn McBride?" He pauses to grin here. And damn, it is a charming one. "We got in just in time to join the summer bowling league. So our regular nights are gonna be Tuesdays."

"Are you asking me to join your team? Or do you just wanna use me for practice?"

"Join, for sure."

"Hmm. Well, I go out of town a lot on Tuesdays so I would not be able to commit to that."

"Our regular nights are gonna be… Mondays."

"Mondays? Sometimes I'm packing my bags on Monday nights."

"For Tuesday's trips?"

"You're catching on."

"Our regular nights are gonna be Fridays."

I laugh. God, this man. "I might be able to swing Fridays."

"Then it's a standing date, I guess. I should warn you that there is quite a battle going on in the background about our shirts and the name of our team. I think you should join in on these conversations."

"Do you?"

"Mmm-hmm. I do. What time do you get home on Thursday?"

"Usually late."

"Well, then I will drop by your store on Friday morning so I can prep you for the discussion that will be coming."

"So you can tell me how to vote?"

Now he makes a face at me. "You're joking about this stuff though, right? I'm not gonna use you, Lowyn. And I'm not gonna tell you what to do, either. But I would like to comment on something here. Something I remember about you. You did want to get married. We had plans. I've been gone—"

"You weren't just *gone*, Collin. You walked away."

"Right. I did. I've been gone, and I can see how your explanation makes sense. The part about taking care of yourself and measuring other men up to that one night. But I didn't ruin you, Lowyn. I mean, look at you. You're better than ever. You've got your own business and this interesting life. And if we keep going, then this is a complete fresh start."

I look away and sigh a little. I don't want to have this discussion with him. There's so much more to the twelve years since we last spoke. It's a long time. He's changed, and I've changed, and yeah, I could fall into a pattern with him very easily.

It would feel so good.

It would feel so familiar.

But would it be the right thing to do?

I'm not sure yet.

I look up at him. "I think I should turn in now."

He nods, then waves his hand to the path that will take us back to the parking lot.

We walk side by side, but he doesn't take my hand this time. I hate that I had to knock him down a peg, but I'm not the woman he met the other night.

I'm the woman he met the other *morning*.

WHEN WE GET BACK my hotel there's a moment of awkwardness as his Jeep idles in front of my room door. I decide to just end it bluntly without a promise of anything else. "Thank you. It was a nice dinner, Collin. And thank you for driving all this way just to see me."

His smile is still there, but it's sadder than it was. "It was my pleasure. Now, about that dognapping job…"

"Oh, right. I should tell Sassy that you will consider it?"

He nods. "I will not be able to commit until I get details, but it doesn't sound too complicated. And Amon will be enthusiastic about this prospect, so I really will just hand it over to him."

"This is the second time you've said that. What's the deal with Amon and dogs?"

Collin smiles for real now. "I'll show you when you come over to pick my junk. We can have our little bowling meeting."

"OK." There is a moment here when I waver in my determination to stop this before it starts. But it's the only way this can end, so I rip the Band-Aid off, flick him a little wave, get out of the Jeep, and go inside.

COLLIN

I don't stay the night at the cabin I rented, I just drive home.

I'm an idiot. Why the hell would I think that Lowyn McBride would just jump in bed with me? She was never that kind of girl, so of course she's not that kind of woman, either.

We did have sex as teenagers. Once. Just once. The presentation was five stars. We went camping up in the hills above Disciple. There's a little waterfall up there that empties into a small pool and in the early summer, when the temperature is rising and the air is getting thick with wet heat, the water is still very cool to swim in.

The Revival has lots of tents. Hundreds of them, maybe. They are not the modern pop-up kind, but the old-timey canvas that comes with wooden poles and requires rope, stakes, and patience.

But if there is one thing every kid in Disciple knows how to do it's put up a fuckin' old-timey tent. So we took it up there, and we brought lanterns and candles to put inside, and we took our sleeping bags and spent the night up on the hill.

And if Lowyn really did save all my stuff in that room, then the memories of this night are in there too because we took lots of pictures of this date.

It was the first time for both of us, so naturally I was way too excited and she never got past anticipation.

I smile at this. Kids, man. We don't know shit when we're kids.

But I did know one thing—she was special and she deserved that beautiful night, even if my performance and skill weren't quite up to par.

"So. Are ya feeling dejected?"

I look over at Amon, who is sitting in the passenger seat of my Jeep because we are now driving back to Johnson City, Tennessee, so we can meet with former one-time country-music star Sassy Lorraine. I'm not sure if Lorraine is her real name and Sassy is just a descriptor, but it doesn't matter. She told me to call her Sassy.

I told Amon the whole story when I approached him about her kidnapping job this morning. Then I got a call from Sassy asking if we would come meet her in person. So here we are.

"I'm not feeling dejected. I just should've known better. I treated Lowyn like she is just any other woman and she's not. She's different. She's always been different."

"Ya wanna know where I think you went wrong?"

"Why not. Tell me."

Amon points at me. "You should've offered to go pickin' with her."

"Why would I do that?"

"Because pickin' is something she loves. And she was already out on the road. All travelling alone and shit." He leans back in his seat. "Nope. I would not let my woman go out on the road alone like that."

"She's not my woman."

"When you're away, she's not your woman. But when you're back, Collin, she *is* your woman. Even if it just means she's your responsibility."

I stare at him for as long as I can before I have to turn my attention back to the road. "Who are you and what have you done with my man-whore best friend?"

He chuckles a little. "We're home now, Collin." Then he

sighs. "It's all so fuckin' different than every other place on earth. After what we've been through, I feel protective of these hills and these people. It hasn't even changed, ya know?"

"Yeah. I've noticed."

"It's all so fuckin'..." He puts his hands out in front of him like he's trying to capture the proper descriptor between his palms. "So fuckin'... *good.*"

All that drama for the word 'good.' But he's not wrong. I'm sure we've got our share of liars, and cheaters, and thieves around here, but I'm also fairly positive that we've got less than most.

"I even called up Jim Bob."

"What?" I almost slam on the brakes. "Why the hell would you do that?" Jim Bob Baptist has been the mayor of Disciple for more years than I've been alive. He runs everything to do with the Revival. We do have a city council, and they vote on shit, but it's pretty much a dictatorship around here with Jim Bob at the top.

Amon is still talkin'. "Because I love it here. I'm happy to be back. I'm glad we chose this place and I'm gonna settle down here and raise me some little asshole kids one day."

I just shake my head at him as I laugh.

"Anyway. Next time she goes out on the road, you need to go with her, Collin. We both know that the world is a dangerous fuckin' place. And while I would generally call the Trinity area safe, your woman is driving clear across Tennessee." When I look over, I find him shaking his head. "Nope. I've heard about Tennesseans."

"Shut up."

"I've heard the rumors of what goes on down there."

"You're stupid. She's been doing it for years, apparently. I'm sure she's fine." And just as I say that my map app tells me that the driveway I'm looking for is coming up on the right. We turn in and come face to face with a formidable wrought-iron gate.

Amon whistles out his first impression, which is one of appreciation. "We're gonna charge this one double, right?"

I don't answer him. Just buzz my window down and press the call button. No one asks questions, but they don't have to because I've already counted up three separate cameras, one of which is staring right at my face from the other side of a teeny-tiny hole on the keypad.

The gates open and we pull forward up a long blacktop driveway that leads to an impressive stone house. Sassy Lorraine greets us from under a nice portico, waving her hand, a smile on her face.

Two hours later we've secured the information for the recon, Amon is in love with Sassy's missing dog—which is one of those pocket chihuahuas that wears clothes—and we're also on our way home.

Amon brought his laptop, so he's already putting together a plan to bust the dog out of a mansion in the Bahamas.

"Hey."

Amon doesn't even look away from his computer. "What?" His fingers never stop tapping.

"You never said what you're gonna do for contribution."

"Oh." He pauses his typing and looks at me. "Security, of course."

I shoot him a look. "Please tell me—"

"Listen." He puts up a hand to full-stop me. "It's what we do. One or two guys making the rounds every weekend, it's not a big deal."

"He's gonna pay us? Because we don't live in town, Amon. We're not gettin' a share of nothin'."

"It's not exactly profit share, but you're wrong. You'll see. Just talk to him about it. And don't say no just to be a dick. Hear him out."

I let out a breath.

"Will you do that, Collin?" Amon studies me. "Just... hear him out?"

"Why should I? I don't want to be a part of it."

"You say that—"

"Because I mean it."

"You say that because this town left a bad taste in your mouth when you lit out. But now that you're back, can't you at least admit that there's parts of it ya missed?"

I sigh again. He's not wrong. I did miss Lowyn. And the memory of her as she played her part in the Revival. And I did leave here with a wad of money in the bank. More than most eighteen-year-olds have, thanks to profit share.

Some years the profit share is real good. Last time I checked there were a hundred and twenty-seven people playing their part in the Revival and every man, woman, and child inside Disciple town limits gets a percentage of the profits. Babies and children under eighteen get what you'd expect. It comes out to a couple thousand dollars a year after all is said and done. It goes straight to the bank, of course. Ya can't touch it until you're eighteen. But when you're collecting that profit-share money your entire childhood, it adds up. Amon and I both had over thirty-seven-thousand dollars when we left.

It's enough to get started in life. Take the money and run, if ya want. Plenty of us did that.

But some people stick around, buy a little house, start a little business.

I guess that's what Lowyn did with hers.

Married men all get one percent of net and everyone else over eighteen gets point two-five percent and it is not uncommon for the Revival to net several million dollars a year. Hell, there were some years back when I was a kid where we got up in the ten-mil range. That means the married men get between twenty and fifty grand a year. Which isn't making anyone rich, but it's paid lump sum on January first and that money sure starts the new year out right.

It's not just money though, it's hope. If you had a bad year—if you were struggling—you always knew that on January first you had a fresh start comin'.

Plus, every man in town, even Jim Bob, has a day job. And if you ever find yourself lacking, this town will take care of you. So being in the Revival does have perks. Being a married man in the Revival even more so.

Still... "Amon, there is no way that Nash and Ryan are gonna agree to work for profit share."

"Nope, they're not. They're not even invited."

"So it's us? Me and you? Every fuckin' weekend? Amon, how do you not remember what it's like to be *in* the Revival? It takes over your life. I don't wanna do it."

"It's not every weekend. Things slow down in the fall and we get all of winter off. It's not a bad deal."

"What if we're busy? We're just starting our company."

"Yeah, but you're not going on any jobs—you're running things. And I'm not going on any jobs—I've got the dogs. We'll be here. And besides, Lowyn will be there too."

"That's not making it better. Now we're gonna have to contribute something crafty to her fuckin' booth! I still have nightmares from those non-stop fucking craft projects in high school."

"You do not. And anyway, Lowyn made all yours for you after you turned thirteen. She'll make them for you again."

"You don't know that. And it's not the point. I specifically told you that I didn't want to be a part of the Revival. You should not have spoken for me."

"What do you think of this drone?" He simultaneously changes the subject and turns his laptop so I can see the screen.

I state the obvious. "You're changin' the subject."

"It's twenty-five thousand. But we'd use it again. It's got a payload of nearly fifty pounds." Amon's big plan is to do recon for a few weeks, then fly a drone in, pick up the dog, and fly away. He's convinced this is gonna be no big deal.

"The dog weighs five pounds. Why do we need a drone that can carry fifty?"

"Because we can expense some of it. And like I said, we'll use it again in the future. That's a guarantee. You know how they come in handy. We've got plenty of money, so I'm gonna get it."

He plops his laptop back down into his lap and starts typing again.

He's right about the drone, I just feel like arguing with him because I'm pissed off about the Revival. I'm not gonna be security. But now everyone in town is gonna hear about how I refuse to do my part. And they're all gonna have opinions about it.

I stew in this discontent the rest of the way home. Amon makes conversation about more drone plans, but I'm only half listening. My mind is spinnin' with imaginary Revival scenarios. How this place is gonna suck me in and never let me go.

I suppose it was naïve of me to think that we could move in so close to Disciple and keep our distance at the same time. I mean, maybe it could've worked that way. If Amon wasn't so enthusiastic about doing his part. I didn't see that coming, I guess. Never once, in all these years, has he ever mentioned anything about missing the Revival.

His parents, yes. He's close with his family. And he's got four sisters. All much younger than him, the same way Olive is much younger than me. They are a close family despite their lower status on the Revival ladder. They were in charge of set-up when I was little. I do remember that. They didn't do the stage—that was Clover's family, they were in charge of the stage—but the Parrish family took care of everything else inside the tent back when I was a kid.

Then Amon got his bad-boy reputation and the Parrish family was demoted because of it. They did clean-up, after that. But everyone gets the same share. Clean-up, set-up, who cares, I guess.

Security is a step up, though. Maybe that's why Amon wants to do it? Maybe he's gonna get his family in on it?

"Hey."

"Hmm?" He's still busy typing and we're nearly home.

"What does your family do to contribute these days?"

He looks up from his laptop. "My sisters have this marketing thing going. So they all run the social media. My mama and daddy just do the crafty shit for Lowyn's booth now."

"Wow. It never even occurred to me that the Revival might have a social presence."

"Speaking of, you wanna pay for ours? My sisters said they'd make room for us on the client list."

"Do we need that?"

"We do. It's the easiest way to get visibility these days."

I shrug. "What the hell. We're spending twenty-five grand on a fuckin' drone."

"You're gonna love this drone!" And then he proceeds to spend the last ten minutes of our drive telling me why we should consider getting an entire army of drones.

WHEN I PULL **into our driveway** I don't get far. And when I side-eye Amon, he says, "I can explain."

"Amon."

"I can *explain*."

"What the hell is this? There are a million people here."

"Stop exaggerating. It's not a million."

It might as well be. The reason I can't get down the driveway is because there are hundreds of cars and trucks parked haphazardly on the front part of the property and what feels like an equal number of men walking around doin' shit. When we left this morning, there were maybe a dozen cars and trucks here. It felt appropriate. This is a deluge of people and vehicles.

"Listen." Amon turns in his seat to face me as we wait for a group of guys who are blocking our way forward with loaded-up hand trucks and forklifts. "You know how starved for jobs the people are around here. They closed up all the fuckin' coal mines, Collin. People are desperate. I interviewed every single one and they are desperate for jobs."

"So you decided to hire *all of them*?"

"No! Of course not! If they had a felony on their record, I turned them away."

I stare out at the sea of activity in front of me. Every single house has people around it. A *team* of people. "I thought we were gonna prioritize shit?"

"I did. But"—he holds up a hand to shut me up so he can continue—"I figured, why not just get this renovation shit done as quick as possible?"

The path forward clears and some guy I have never seen before starts to direct me on where to go. I look over at Amon. He buzzes the window down, yells at the guy to get out of the way, and we continue down the driveway, towards our homes.

When I get to my new house the door is wide open and shit is flying out the second-story window into a dumpster. This is a familiar scene because every house we passed had this same scenario going on.

"It's demo day." Amon is laughing. But then he puts up a

hand again. "Don't worry, I had all the junk boxed up and taken into the church so Lowyn can pick through and find her treasure."

We get out, walk up my porch, peek inside, and I turn to him. "I have no windows. None. Every single one has been removed. How am I supposed to sleep in here?" Everything has been torn up and there are at least a dozen men in my house doing reno shit.

"Don't worry. It's all gonna be put back together real quick. I swear, Collin. Two weeks. It'll all be back to normal."

"Two. Weeks? I'm pretty sure that's a *meme*, Amon."

He grins, his eyes dancing with mischief. "Two weeks, I promise. Until then... well, last I heard you still had a room at Lowyn's." Then he claps me on the back, raises a hand to someone across the compound, and hops down the porch steps, leaving me there.

I go inside, find my stuff, pack it all up, and put it in my Jeep. Then I get in and drive into Bishop to get myself a room at the inn.

When I get there, Jessica tells me they're booked up. Which I think is a lie at first. But then, when I call the motel out on the highway, they're booked up too. And so is every other motel, and hotel, and B&B in a twenty-mile radius.

Because I had forgotten—the Revival starts this weekend.

*I am idling **outside*** my childhood home when Lowyn answers my call. "Hey."

"Hi."

"What's up?"

"Listen, this is gonna sound stupid, and forward, and like I cannot take no for an answer, but I need a place to stay." There is silence on the other end of the line. "Lowyn?"

"You need a place to stay? But you literally just bought like a dozen houses, Collin."

"Yes. That's accurate. But every single one is being torn up for renovation at the moment. Apparently, Amon took it upon himself to hire every jobless man in the state of West Virginia to do the work we had planned on doing in stages."

"Oh." Her tone softens. Amon Parrish has that effect on people. I have never really understood *why* he has this effect on people, because 'asshole' really is the correct descriptor for him.

"My place, and every house on the compound, is uninhabitable. Amon is staying with his dogs in the kennel building. Everyone else is staying at Nash's house. There's not really room for me unless I take the floor. But... I guess I can sleep on a church pew or somethin'." I'm guilting her now, but I don't care. I can sleep anywhere and I have laid my head down on many a rock in my time, but it doesn't hurt to ask. "It's only for two weeks." I cringe as the meme comes flying out of my mouth.

"Two weeks?" She's mulling it over, always a good sign. "You need to sleep there tonight? Because I won't be home until tomorrow."

"There's a key hidden in the shed out back. But please tell me you changed the locks, Lowyn."

She blows out a breath. "The locks are the same. I mean, who the hell is gonna break into my house, Collin?" It comes out before she can stop it, but she corrects herself quickly. "Wow. That was a really dumb thing to say."

"For what it's worth, I really don't think anyone is gonna break into your house." *Not after I blew the last guy's head off,* I don't add. "And I think this says something about your mental health that you're so totally not worried about it."

This makes her chuckle. "You and your words. Fine. You can stay. But only if you stay out of my stuff. Don't go peeking around."

"Why? You hiding something?"

"None of your business. But if you don't promise, you can't stay."

"My promise means that much? You'll just trust me if I say I won't?"

"Did you already forget about how you ruined me?"

I let out a breath. "I will not look through your stuff. But I'm allowed to check the fridge and make a cup of coffee?"

I can hear her smile on the other end of the line. I'm sure she's thinking this is a very bad idea, but we were much more than a couple in high school. We were best friends. And it's always nice to be around your best friend. Even if you are mad at him for ghosting you a dozen years back.

"You can help yourself to the kitchen, living room, and your old bedroom."

"That's very gracious of you. What time will you be home tomorrow?"

"Oh, probably around four. But I'll have to unload the trailer at McBooms."

"Call me when you're close to home. I'll meet you over there and unload that trailer for you."

"You don't have to. I've been unloading this trailer all by myself for long time now."

"Call me when you're close and I'll unload your trailer for you. Oh, and Amon had everything boxed up at the compound. It's all in the church waiting for you to pick through it."

She smiles again, I can hear it. "That was nice of him. What are you gonna do now? Just hang out at my place?"

"Well..." I sigh, already tired of thinking about what comes next. "I guess I have to go talk to Jim Bob because Amon signed us up for security and I had actually forgotten that the Revival starts this weekend. I did try to get a hotel, you know. They're all booked."

"Yep. This weekend. I think my booth tent is going up tonight, so I guess, if you're gonna be at McBooms to unload my trailer tomorrow, you can help me load it back up and take it over to the grounds."

"Yes, ma'am. I will do that."

"OK."

We're both silent for a moment.

"OK," I finally say back. "See ya tomorrow."

She says bye and I end the call, then find the key in the shed, sitting on the top of the same window trim where I left it when I was a kid, and put my stuff inside.

After that's done, I get back in my truck and make my way over to City Hall. I have to pass the Revival grounds and since it's really the first time I've gotten a good look at it since I got home, I stop the Jeep and stare at it for a minute.

It's the same, but different. Most notable is some kind of scaffolding that pops up from the telephone-looking poles that line all the makeshift 'streets' around the main tent. Teams of people are stringing lights from them. But there are more poles like that too. Not in the center of the streets—which are not streets, but really wide gravel walkways—but attached to the other tents that are all around the property in aisles. Like an outdoor flea market. This is where things are sold. Food, and souvenirs, and even clothes. Each corner tent is elevated on a platform about six steps high. And these same telephone-looking poles are shootin' out from the roofs.

It takes a me a moment to understand what it all is. A scaffolding. For what, I don't know. This wasn't here when I left. But it all looks really nice. Very nice, actually.

The tent grounds are a madhouse. I think everyone in town is over here, trying to get things straight for this weekend. When I start moving again people look my way. Lots of them wave—word travels fast around here—and I park down the street in front of the tiny stone building where Jim Bob Baptist does his government business.

Everything about this place is the same. Even Ester, the town clerk. She's typing on a keyboard when I enter, but she looks over the glasses perched on her nose to check me out without slowing her pace. "Collin Creed. What can I do for you?"

"Is Jim Bob around?"

"He is. Do you have an appointment?"

"Ester, you know I don't have an appointment."

She pauses her typing to sigh. "Is this Revival business? Because he's neck-deep in Revival business right now and you know how he hates to change the subject once he gets started on a task."

"I do, and it is."

She nods her head at the thick, maple double doors that Jim Bob Baptist has been working behind since before I was born. "Then go right in."

Even before I open the door, I can hear Jim Bob havin' a fit with someone on the phone. I look over my shoulder at Ester, wondering if I should wait, or knock, or something, but she is ignoring me on purpose.

I open the door and find Jim Bob pacing his office, phone to his ear, round face red with frustration. He looks at me, squints his eyes, then points to a chair in front of his massive antique desk.

"I don't care, Leonard. How many times do I have to state this out loud before you accept the fact that I have stopped giving out fucks about your personal business? Either you have those new programs printed and delivered to the Revival grounds by six a.m. Saturday or I'll make sure that Revenant gets docked five percent over this bullshit. Are we clear?"

I'm not sure if Leonard is clear or not, but Jim Bob assumes he is because he slams the phone into the cradle on his desk. He sits his considerable ass down in his executive chair, wipes his forehead with a handkerchief, and stares at me. "Are you offended by my profanity?"

"No, sir. I'm not."

"Good. Because if I have to hear one more asshole in this town chastise me about the f-word, I will lose my shit, Collin Creed. Lose. Mah. Shit."

I try my best not to smile, but it's not good enough.

He laughs too. "Should I assume you're here for your schedule?"

"Well—"

He points at me. "Don't you dare. Don't even say it."

"Jim Bob, here's the thing—"

"I just said don't say it!"

"Amon was speaking out of turn when he volunteered us for security."

Jim Bob leans back in his chair, making it creak from his considerable weight. He's a huge man. Not really fat, either. Just massive, like the desk in front of him. Easily six foot three, probably pushing two-fifty, he's a giant among mortals. And he is as sly as the summer day is long. He tries out some of his slyness on me now. "I know what you're thinking."

I squint my eyes at him a little. "Is that so?"

"That is so. You're thinking... *Well, I've been missing for a dozen years and even though I'm back, I'm not back because I bought a place outside city limits.*"

"Well, that would be accurate, Jim Bob."

"In outside-world terms, it would be. But we don't live like outside men, Collin Creed. We live like inside men. And I don't care if you're shufflin' through the sand in Saudi Arabia, or crawling through sewer muck in Prague, or standin' out front of the Nigerian Embassy for weeks at a time—"

"How the hell—"

"I just don't care where you've been or what you've been doing. Because you're home now and there is a place for you here. There is always a place for you here. Now. Where did I put that contract?" He shuffles through some papers on his desk as I continue to wonder how the hell he knew where I've been all these years.

It's very secret shit.

"Did Amon tell you all that?"

"Here it is." Jim Bob holds up a folder and looks up at me. "No, Collin. Amon did not tell me all that. I've been keepin' track of you since the day you left, son. You are part of the Revival, whether you like it or not."

"Well, that's not creepy."

"Call it whatever you want. Your daddy did a number on us."

I laugh and put up a hand. "If you're gonna say what I think you're gonna say, you can just forget it."

"There will be no forgettin', Collin." And he says these few words with weight, making them heavy. "It's too late for you to do anything but security this year, but you know where your place is, son. It's behind that pulpit." He flops the folder down on his desk before I can object, then opens it up and slides out a contract. "Amon already signed, but I'm gonna need your name right there on that line." He taps a blank line at the bottom of the contract.

I slide the piece of paper out from under his fingertip and pick it up, scanning the details. My eyebrows furrow together in confusion. Then I look at him. "What the hell is this?"

"It's a contract."

"It says you're gonna pay me a million dollars a year, Jim Bob."

"Indeed it does."

"Why would you do that?"

He smiles and once again leans back in his creaky chair. "Collin, nothin' is ever what it seems. Not around here, not around anywhere. The world doesn't run on percentages and contracts. It runs on negotiation. And the town of Disciple is negotiating a lifelong contract with you to stick around."

I just stare at him for a moment. "How many people have a contract like this?"

"All the ones we can't afford to lose."

"Which would be?"

"Myself—"

"Of course."

"—Ester—this place would fall apart without Ester—Joseph, Ruth, Tommy, Abel, and Grimm, of course."

The town clerk. A quarryman. A jewelry maker. A diesel mechanic. The Chief of Police. A real estate agent. "What the fuck is going on around here?"

"Read the contract, son. You have to be one year in to be vested. When that one year is up, we'll have ourselves another chat. Now sign your name on that line."

"What if I don't?"

"Then Collin, God help you. Because this town needs what you're offering and if you bow out, people will get hurt. You don't really think that man who broke into your house to steal your sister was just a random event, do you?"

"What? What's that mean?"

"Sign. The paper. And at the end of the year, you'll know."

"I don't like the sound of this. It sounds a little bit like extortion to me."

Jim Bob laughs. "Do you know what your daddy did after you left?"

"In regards to what?" He's about to answer, but I put up a hand. "Never mind. I don't care if he went crazy."

"Crazy." Jim Bob thinks about this word for a moment. "I guess that's one way to think about it. However, your daddy did some good things for this town. And some of the greatest happened after you left."

"Well, that's special. Thanks for letting me know."

"He had big ideas for this Revival. Came up with an engineering miracle. Four-season festivities, that's what he gave us before he left. Four-season festivities."

"I have no idea what you're talking about."

"Well, it's gonna rain on Sunday, so you'll find out soon enough."

TEN MINUTES *later* I'm rolling down Main Street towards the Revival, dollar signs and mysteries spinning through my head. I call Amon as I ease my truck to the side of the road near the main entrance of the park where the tent stands like a testament to my life here in Disciple.

He answers on the first ring. "Listen—"

"What do you know?"

"Jim Bob just texted me. I know what you're thinking, but you're wrong. I know exactly as much as you do."

"Which is what, specifically?"

"We're to do security for this season. We collect a million dollars each on January first. And then we learn the truth about the Trinity Towns and become vested members of the... whatever it is."

"Whatever it is? What if it's some death cult, Amon?"

"I don't think it's a death cult."

"But you don't know. He said the man who tried to snatch my sister that night wasn't a random event. What do you know about that?"

"Far less than you do. Since I wasn't there and we weren't even friends back then."

"What if we don't want in? I mean, after one year? What if we want to leave?"

"We might have a fight on our hands."

"And you're OK with that?"

"Why wouldn't I be? We're trained killers, Collin. We have enough weapons in our new bunker to start a war. I've got a kennel full of K-9's who speak four languages and we've got the entire population of able-bodied men outside of the Trinity on our payroll. Which, when one looks at it objectively, qualifies us as an army. It's a nice paycheck for a little bit of time. And how can you not be dying to know what the hell is going on? I mean, if we learned anything while we were gone, it was that this place is weird. Right?"

"So why would we join up, Amon?"

"Because it's in our blood, Collin. It's in our blood."

"Did you know about this before we bought the compound?" But even before these words are out, I know that he did. Amon was the one who pointed out that the compound was for sale. He was the one who got me interested in it.

He didn't push it on me. Just printed out the online listing and left it with my shit, a note attached. *What about this place?*

Amon has gone quiet.

"You set this up."

"It's not a set-up, Collin. It's destiny."

LOWYN

When I pull into the back alley behind McBooms on Thursday afternoon I am greeted with the sight of Collin Creed's Jeep, and the man himself, leaning against the driver's door with his arms crossed and his shades down. He's grinnin' at me.

I smile back at him. It's hard not to get excited about his return. I mean, we were fated to be together and we made all those plans back when we were young. Maybe this is just how it was supposed to be?

He goes one way, I go another, and we meet up later in the middle.

We are different people now. But not so different, either.

I spent all of today thinking about him. He's stayin' at my house. We're living together. In his childhood home, which I have redecorated to look like we're living back in a better time.

It's… kinda dreamlike, if I'm being perfectly honest. A little bit magical too.

Growing up in Disciple isn't like growing up anywhere else in the world. There's something special going on here in the Trinity Towns. I mean, I know it's all a show. I know the motorcycle club that runs Revenant isn't really full of murderers. It's an act.

And I know that the farmers who plow the massive gardens

with horses in Bishop go home every night to wives who work online and kids who own cell phones. It's an act.

I also know that no one in the Revival is as pious on the inside as they seem on the outside. Hell, almost no one in Disciple even believes in God.

It's *an act*.

But I also know that you don't want to cross those men in that motorcycle club, and those farmers really do grow food for the whole town, and the preacher standing behind that pulpit in our Revival tent really can bring out the magic.

It's much more than an act. It's something bigger. Something you do not find in other places.

Collin Creed is a man much like these towns.

One of a kind.

Before I even have my engine shut down, Collin is at my door, pulling it open for me. "Welcome home. Did you find anything good?"

I found you, Collin. That's what I want to say, but I don't. Instead I say, "It's really heavy. You might need to call a few friends."

"Woman, what did you buy?"

God, I love the way he talks. That mouth of his, it's always been what attracted me most. I have a sudden urge to kiss him. Just… place my hands on his face, and pull him close to me, and kiss him like we're still in high school.

Instead, I get out and walk to the back of my trailer, where I key in the code to unlock it and pull the doors open. "Ta da!"

"Holy hell, what is that?"

"A woodburning cook stove!"

He laughs. "Do people still use those?"

"Over in Bishop? Are you kidding me? Alice—she runs the bakery inside the Colonial perimeter, remember her?" Maybe he does, maybe he doesn't. "She's been lookin' for one of these for two years. It needs some tender loving care, for sure. But I'm about to make her scream in delight."

In the end, Collin Creed does not need to call friends to help him move my new stove. His mind comes up with a plan that involves four solid-top dollies and together we maneuver the stove up the ramp and into the backroom of my store.

When we finally get it in place, we're sweaty and huffing. Smiling and happy.

He tilts his head at me. "What?"

"Nothin'. It's just... I can't believe you're here."

"Yeah, me either. It's as weird as the bad acid trip I never had as a teenager."

I laugh. This man's mouth, my God. "For sure, Collin. For sure. Well, should we load the trailer back up and take my stuff over to the Revival?"

He sighs, like he'd rather do anything else but that. But he says the exact opposite. "Tell me what to do."

It takes *a little over an hour* to load the trailer back up, so by the time we get it over to the tent, it's full-on evening. And supper time during Revival set-up is a catered event because no one gets to go home to eat. We usually work well into the night, trying to get everything just right, or as near as to perfect as we can, because people show up early for opening weekend.

There will be no preaching on Friday, but all shopping booths will be open from nine a.m. to six p.m.

"I hope you have reserved your lane at the bowling alley, Collin. Otherwise, we will not have our standing date tomorrow night."

We're at the buffet table inside the main tent grabbing barbecue. He gets ribs and I get chicken. And then we take our plates over to one of the tables set up for just this occasion, and have a seat.

"Amon's in charge of the bowling alley arrangements. But I'm pretty sure he's on top of it. He seems to be on top of everything around here these days."

"Hmm. I detect a hidden meaning inside that statement. What's he up to?"

"Aside from signing us up for security?"

"Aside from that."

"I'm not sure." His face makes a look of concern. "I want to tell you something, but I'm not sure if I'm allowed."

"Interesting. Did you sign an NDA?"

His eyebrows go up. "Did you?"

I giggle a little. "I did not."

"But some people do?"

"I don't think so. It was just a question."

"Well." He looks around nervously. Then he lowers his voice. "Jim Bob offered us a... a kind of bonus contract."

"Oh, that."

"You know about those?"

"Yeah. Pretty much everyone gets one eventually. You have to prove yourself. But come on, Collin. You don't really think people work this hard just for twenty or thirty thousand dollars? If you own a business in town, you get a bonus offer."

"So you get one?"

"I was offered one, but I didn't take it."

"Why not?"

"Because I make more money than I need."

He tsks his tongue at me. "Oh, Lowyn. You're just..."

"Stupid?"

He laughs, shaking his head. "Good. I was gonna say good."

"Did you take your bonus?"

"I signed the fuckin' contract, but we have to work for a year to be vested. But now that I know that you didn't take yours, I would feel like a first-class asshole if I were to take mine."

"Well, don't let me stop you. I'm kinda rich, Collin. I really, truly don't need the money."

"Ya know..." But he stops.

"What?"

He opens his mouth to finish his thought, but at the same moment, a group of kids come up to me and interrupt the moment. Two girls giggling. Two boys pretending to be brave. Bonnie, Lydia, Matthew, and Mark. They've been assigned to me this season as helpers. I know it, and they know it, but this is the first time they've actually had to talk to me, so they're nervous and it takes about twenty minutes for us to sort out the details back in my tent. By that time, whatever Collin was going to say to me isn't forthcoming.

What did I miss? What was he gonna say? What kind of poetry was gonna spill past those lips?

I wonder about this as the evening turns into night and the night gets old. Collin helps me set up—I put him in charge of the two boys—but then he's called away by Jim Bob, so when I finally have the booth in order almost an hour later it's nearly ten o'clock at night and I need to go looking for him.

Not that I require a ride home. Every house in Disciple is just a few blocks away from the Revival grounds and mine is no different.

But he's staying with me now. Shouldn't we go home together?

I can't quite wrap my head around how we got into this position, but honestly, it feels very inevitable.

I find Collin leaning against a post inside the main tent. There's a little meeting going on between Jim Bob and Simon, the preacher. Collin has a severe scowl on his face and he's not even taking part in the conversation. So when he sees me, he pushes off the post and starts heading my way without a word to the other two men.

"Collin." Jim Bob calls after him.

Collin doesn't turn. Just growls over his shoulder. "I'm going home. I'll be in tomorrow at eight thirty." Then he pauses, just a few paces off from me, and turns to face Jim Bob and Simon. "For *security*."

"Fine, fine." Whatever they were talking about, Jim Bob gives up.

Collin puts his hand in the small of my back, leading me back the way I came in. When we're outside the tent he sighs. "Thank you."

"For what?"

"Rescuing me."

"What was going on in there?"

"Never mind. He's just pulling my strings. And if he keeps doing it, I won't honor that contract."

"He wants you to preach, doesn't he?"

"It's not gonna happen. That's not why I'm here. And it's not fair for this place to have expectations of me about this Revival stuff. I don't want to walk that path. I don't want to be my daddy."

"I know." When he was young, because his last name was Creed and his daddy was literally the star of the show, he was required to sit up there on the stage and play his part as... disciple, I guess.

I used to love watching him up there. It was the highlight of my weekend, if I'm being honest.

But I guess, now that I'm older, I see his point.

It's not fair that we're all connected to this thing and the part we play is determined by bloodlines.

Our family was never in the spotlight like that, so I never cared much. But it was different for Collin. Much different.

We've reached my truck and he opens my door for me. It makes me wonder if he's just remembering his manners, or if he took them with him when he left. Did he open every woman's door? Was he always a gentleman with them the way he is with me?

I'll never ask him that question, of course. But I still wonder.

We go back to McBooms so he can pick up the Jeep, and then he follows me back to his house.

My house.

His house.

It's a little bit crazy that it worked out this way.

When we walk through the door, I'm not sure what to do. So I just start asking questions. "Did you sleep in your room last night?"

He puts his keys on the counter. It's not the same counter that was here all during his childhood. It's all new. But it's in the same place, so this one act—of putting his keys in a familiar place like it's a habit—makes the whole thing even weirder.

"Nah. I slept on the couch." He nods his head to the living room.

I look over there, but don't see any evidence that he slept on the couch until I spy a duffle bag set neatly against the wall near the opening to the hallway. "Is that where you're gonna sleep tonight?"

His grin is immediate. "That's the second time you've invited me up to your bedroom, Lowyn McBride."

I didn't mean it as innuendo, but it definitely came out that way. I want to say something clever back. Maybe even something flirty. But I can't. So I don't. I just... stand there. Unsure what happens next.

Collin can read a room. So he does that thing he does, trying to smooth over rough edges. "Yeah. I'm gonna sleep on the couch."

He looks disappointed, but only for a moment. That's not his style. Not at all. Collin Creed isn't a beggar. And he's polite to a fault. Even if he wasn't all these years he's been gone, he's reverted back to that nice young man he was a teen. And he's not going to pressure me, or make me feel guilty, if I'm not sure where this is going.

Truthfully, I know damn well I will be sleeping with Collin Creed. And it's probably gonna happen sooner rather than later. But tonight it's late, and I'm tired, and I don't know how to have the conversation that we must have before anything can go any further.

So I just walk to the stairs on the far end of the living room, and start up them. But when I get to the top I stop and look down. He's not there at the bottom. "Good night, Collin."

"Good night, Lowyn."

He hasn't moved. But he *was* waiting.

COLLIN

After Lowyn goes up to bed, I just stand there on the edge of the living room that used to be mine. I didn't snoop last night, and I did sleep on the couch, but I did look around. At least down here. Only because she changed the layout a little. The hallway where I blew that man's brains out is gone and in its place is a pantry. She made the two other small bedrooms down here into one big office. And she moved the stairs, which used to be at the end of the death hallway, opposite the back door, to the other side of the living room.

The living room here in her house is a lot like the one in her shop. Same look and feel, at least, even if the pieces are not twins. The color scheme from the kitchen—tangerine and seafoam green—continues into this room too. A couch that looks aged—but I don't think it is—is the centerpiece. It's a sectional, like the one in the store. But this one is wide and is covered in a peachy-gold velvet. A very nice textile to fall asleep on, I know from experience.

The chairs are overstuffed here, a contrast from the sleek, minimalistic ones in the get-the-look set-up at McBooms. But they are nearly the same color of a Caribbean sea, except this pair's brightness has been toned down with a shadow, like a storm hanging out in the distance.

There is a large, overarching umbrella lamp and the familiar credenza. But this time I feel like there might be a hidden bar inside instead of a record player. I can't help myself, I go look.

Indeed. There is. All the fixings, at least. But no booze.

Lowyn's house—Lowyn's version of *my* house—it's got a family feeling to it. Like teenagers hang out here on Friday nights and play Monopoly and records. It's comfortable. And safe. A room filled with colors once bright, now even better slightly muted.

It's nice. I approve.

But it's all very weird.

I was gonna sleep in my room last night, but I went in there and found some old pictures and it was just too much.

It's too much tonight, too. Especially after dealing with Jim Bob and Simon, my dad's replacement. He was trying really hard to make me like him. He was telling all about his sermons, and his son, who is his disciple on stage for the show, and I just didn't wanna hear it.

That part of my life is over. And I'm not stupid, so I know that all the people in charge of the Revival—up to and including the new fuckin' preacher himself—are thinkin' that I might just slip back into my old role.

Which was never mine in the first place, so what the fuck, ya know?

I think signing that contract was a mistake. I think I should maybe try to get out of it.

But it's probably not possible. And it's just one year. Not even. It's one season. Which is only eight or nine months long, depending where Easter falls each year.

How much can go wrong in eight months?

I blow out a breath, pick up my duffle bag, and hit the bathroom for a shower.

When I'm done, and I come back out to the living room, I find a pillow and a blanket sitting on the couch for me. The pillow is down—pretty much the softest thing my head has rested on in over a decade—and the blanket is tan chenille with big old orange flowers woven into it.

And so, despite how this night went sideways, I put it to bed with a smile.

THE SMELL of coffee wakes me in the morning and the first thing I see is Lowyn McBride, standing in the kitchen wearing her Revival costume.

I recognize the style—straight, low-waisted dress, short, ruffled sleeves, and lace. Good lace. Handmade lace. Lowyn is wearing a springtime version with a muted floral pattern overlaid on an antique white base layer of rayon. There's a cloche hat on the countertop and a small, beaded change purse on a chain sitting next to it. Even through half-lidded eyes and all the way across the room, I can tell that she's wearing makeup because her lips are pink and smooth, like her powdered cheeks. She's got her hair up in her trademark faux bob, and good God, the sight of her both takes me back fifteen years and pulls me right into the present.

She is a twenty-first-century woman standing in a retro Eighties kitchen, wearing a dress that was reproduced by the best seamstresses in Disciple to resemble high fashion back in tent revival days.

There was a period of time, back when the Revival was still figuring out what it was, when the opinion of the day was that people should look demure, and poor, and downtrodden. Tent revivals were at their height during the Great Depression, after all. I guess these founders were thinking they should be authentic, the way Bishop is with their Colonial downtown.

They take great pains over in Bishop to make the wagons just right, and the cooking just right, and the clothes just right.

It's all very 'just right.'

But like Revenant, Disciple is its own thing. And so eventually the town came to a decision to not even try to be authentic.

I mean, what's the point? The tent is a theatre, and the preacher, and the children's choir, and the fainting women in the audience—they are all actors. So when the founders were deciding on costumes, they went for eye-pleasing.

No one wants to see a tired-looking housewife in a dirty apron.

No one wants to see a broken man with coal so far under his fingernails, it has stained the skin beneath.

No one wants to see crying babies and hungry children.

People don't come to Disciple to learn about things or be reminded of the past. They come here to be entertained by the contradiction. Same reason they go to Revenant. Same reason they go to Bishop.

They want an escape. They want the women to be pretty, the children to be sweet, and the men to be strong. They don't care about the message inside the tent—no one does. As long as it's filled with flappin' hand fans and dramatic shouts of 'amen.' As long as it's filled with bowed heads and closed eyes rejoicing halleluiah. As long as it's entertaining—well, that's all it needs to be.

The Revival was never meant to be relevant. It highlights the hypocrisy. It's meant to remind everyone that this whole thing, this whole world, all around us, is nothing but a well-planned, well-financed production.

Disciple's Revival is just a contrast set against the backdrop of Revenant.

And Revenant, with its motorcycle gangs, and pool halls, and rowdy bars, is just another contrast set against the back-drop of Bishop.

The Trinity Towns are a funhouse, or a circus, or a Broadway show.

And everyone in town has a leading role in the deception.

"Cross came by and dropped you off a package."

My lazy, drooping eyes are staring right at Lowyn as these words come out of her mouth. "What kind of package?"

She points to a parcel wrapped up in brown paper and tied with jute twine. "Open it up and find out."

I grumble as I swing myself up to a sitting position and sigh, bending over to cover my face with my hands and rub the stubble on my cheeks. Then I get to my feet and catch Lowyn looking at my chest because I didn't wear a shirt to bed. Just gray sweatpants.

Her eyes flit up and meet mine. Immediately, she is turning pink.

I just grin, walk over to the counter, and start pulling the twine on the package. I already know what it is, so I'm not surprised when I find my own costume on the other side of that paper. I hold up the shirt—black button-down, handmade in thick cotton—and look at Lowyn. "They're gonna make me into a gangster?"

She's trying not to grin. "You *are* security."

"Yeah, well. I figured I would just wear some tactical pants" —Lowyn is already laughing—"and a t-shirt. Maybe, if I wanted to dress it up a little, I'd put on some body armor."

"You're dreaming, Collin. You gotta play your part. There's no getting around it. Now give me that. I'll steam the wrinkles out." She comes around the counter and I catch the scent of her rosewater perfume. Every costume has accessories and when you're acting in the equivalent of dinner theatre, this kind of sensory detail matters.

Her fingertips brush against the back of my hand as she reaches for the package. She looks up and our eyes meet once again. "Hi," I say.

She smiles at me. "Good morning. Did you sleep well?"

"No. Well, yeah. Thanks for the blanket and pillow, by the way. I was ordered not to look around without permission, so I had to forgo those two luxuries that first night."

She's still smiling, but she doesn't say anything back. Just takes my clothes and disappears down the hallway. "Don't shave." She calls this out as I hear her opening up a cupboard in the laundry room.

I scrub my hands down my face again. "You don't think I should?"

"That's one perk of playin' the bad boy, Collin. You get to keep that sexy shadow on your face."

Oooooh. She called me sexy. My grin is wide and my whole body gets warm.

I help myself to a cup of black coffee and then wander down the hallway to watch her as she waves the steamer wand over my black trousers, making the wrinkles disappear like magic. She's smirking at me, giving me a side eye, but not in a bad way.

I tease her about this smirk. "Lowyn McBride, you look like you've got yourself a secret."

Her cheeks puff out with her laugh. Like she had every plan of holding that laugh in, but there was no way she'd manage it.

"What? What's so funny?"

She takes a deep breath and pauses her magic-wanding to look at me. "What were you talking about in your little meetin' last night?"

"Which one? I feel like the whole town had me cornered at one point or another."

"The one I interrupted. The one with Jim Bob and Simon."

"I told ya. Preachin' shit. Which is not gonna happen." She's still looking at me. Not smirking, but... "You *do* have a secret. Spill it. What's going on?"

She sets her magic steamer wand down on the laundry counter and takes my trousers off the hanger. Then she folds them at the new crease and offers them to me. I put out an arm and she drapes them over it. Then she picks up my shirt and puts it on a hanger. She resumes her steaming and her talking. "Well, Collin, ya see, things have changed a lot around here since you left."

"I'm followin'. So continue."

"And part of those changes is a… a…" She makes a face, like she's desperate to find the correct word to describe what comes next. "A *narrative*. Yeah." Now she smiles, proud of herself. "A narrative. A story that runs the whole season. It starts on opening day—today."

"OK."

"And it comes to a crisis on Fourth of July."

"All right."

"And it ends with a cliffhanger on Christmas Eve."

"They play this story out all the way up to Christmas Eve? Doesn't that kinda ruin the festivities?"

"We need to set the story up for the next season, right?"

I sigh. "OK. So what's the story?"

"Well, it *was* a story about a girl from Revenant who runs away with a boy from Disciple. We've done this one before. Twice, actually. First, the girl was from Disciple and the boy was from Revenant. Then we did a side story with Bishop once, too. Boy running away, et cetera, et cetera."

"Maybe I'm just being paranoid here, but I'm getting the feeling that this is somehow leading up to me."

She points at me with her wand. "You are correct. It does. I got a fat envelope with your costume delivery this morning."

I narrow my eyes. "What was in it?"

"A new story."

"About me?"

"Not you personally. But yeah. You're the story." She points to the shirt and waves a hand at my trousers. "You are a gangster. You left town for Revenant twelve years ago—walked out on your daddy and your family. And now you're back—"

"And I'm the bad guy? But I'm security!"

"You seem to think that being security involves walking around with the word 'security' printed on the back of your body armor, Collin. And that's just not how things work anymore. You'll have your gun, or whatever you're gonna carry, but you're gonna act out your part just like all the rest of us."

I sigh and rub my hands down my face for a third time. "I should've never signed that contract."

"Oh, it's not so bad. It's actually quite fun."

"What part do you play?"

"I'm not a real player. I've got too much going on with McBooms. So I'm mostly just a nameless face in the background."

"Where is this envelope?"

"On the kitchen counter. Right by my little purse."

I go out to the kitchen and find the thick envelope made of tan paper. It's got one of those string-tie fasteners over the flap, the kind where you tie the string around a little paper button to keep it closed.

I untie the string and take out a thin, spiral-bound booklet. On the front it says, "Season Nine: The Prodigal Son Returns."

I take the whole thing back down the hallway to Lowyn, who is still busy making my button-down shirt presentable. Then I start my complaining. "I'm not the prodigal son."

"It's not really about you, Collin. It's… it's just a story."

But she's wrong. It *is* about me. "How can you say that with a straight face? You just told me that the story, up until this very morning, was about a boy who falls for a girl in Revenant. And now the whole story is"—I hold up the little booklet—"this!"

"You should read it. It's got a good start."

I growl a little, which makes Lowyn laugh. "Calm down, Collin. You're a gangster looking for salvation. Just look at it that way for now."

"For *now*?"

"Well, that's hardly a prodigal son story, now is it? I don't know what the writers have planned, but I'm sure we'll find out soon." She turns her little magic wand off and pats my arm. "Don't worry. Whatever it is, it'll all come to a head by Fourth of July and then the story will turn."

"One season." I grit these words through my teeth. "And then never again."

She pats my bare chest, then presses her palm flat against it. Kinda takin' my breath away for a moment. Kinda wiping my mind of all complaints, too. "Go put the costume on. It's gonna be fine."

I PLAY those words over and over in my head as I get dressed in the bathroom. I think about how her hand felt against my bare chest too. I had a sudden urge to kiss her in that moment. But I can't. Because we've had that opportunity a couple times now, and both times she was sending me signals that it's not gonna happen.

Actually, she's sending signals that it *is* gonna happen, but not yet. I have a feeling there's something between us that must be dealt with before she will relent.

A feeling, Collin? Please. You walked out on her twelve years ago without an explanation. She wants a fuckin' explanation.

Yes. This is what's between us. She wants some truth from me. And she might steam the wrinkles out of my clothes and let me sleep in her house, but she's not gonna invite me into her bed—or even let me get a teeny-tiny taste of those lips—until I... *repent*, for lack of a better word.

Actually, it's an appropriate word. And while I by no means have been out in the world squandering my inheritance, I did go out there and leave this whole town behind, and then came back like it was no big deal.

And it was a big deal. A very big deal. If I want to live around here, I will have to repent. By playing my part in the story, by being security for the Revival, and by having an honest conversation with the woman I walked out on when she was just a girl.

Fine.

I come out of the bathroom and find Lowyn still in the laundry, steaming the wrinkles out of a silk tie. She smiles at me, then carefully lays the tie down on top of the washing machine and turns the steamer off.

I walk into the little room and she's immediately reaching for the pearly-gray buttons on my unbuttoned shirt. Her fingers quickly and smoothly slide them into the little slits and she works her way up.

This simple act of buttoning up my shirt pretty much blows my mind in the best way possible. It feels very intimate for some reason. When she gets to the top button, she smiles at me and flips my collar up so she can feed the silk tie around my neck to form a perfect Windsor knot. She flips my collar down, straightens it out a little, and grins. "You have to roll up your sleeves."

"Why?" This comes out without thinking. I'm still caught in the magic web she just wove all around me with her fingertips.

"Because that's what it says." She picks up a little pre-printed card that has been lying unnoticed by me on top of the washer. "This came in the package. 'Shirt half tucked in, sleeves rolled up, tie in a Windsor knot.'"

I just stare down at her. Right into those blue eyes of hers. I want to slip my hands behind her thighs, lift her up and set her down on top of the washer. Then I want to open her knees, slide between her legs, and kiss her like I might never get the chance again. I want to put my hands on her face, and press my lips against hers, and taste her.

"Collin?"

I let out a breath and the fantasy goes with it. "Yeah."

She's holding up suspenders. "You have to put these on too."

The braces are pinstripe gray with brown leather runner ends that button directly to the waistband of my trousers. I almost lose my breath when Lowyn slides the slim elastic over my shoulders and says, "Turn around."

Her voice is soft and low. Like an easy breeze blowing ever so slightly over a flower petal. I turn and she attaches the suspenders to the back of my trousers.

Then she says, "Turn again," in that same low and sexy tone.

I do as I'm told, facing her once again as her fingertips continue to wrap me up in a web of magic. She finishes the last four buttons and then takes a step back as she sucks in a breath.

"Wow." She lets that breath out. "You look..." She doesn't finish her thought. Just nods her head and bites her lip.

"You look that good too," I say back.

And this makes her smile.

THERE ARE **two ways** in and out of Disciple, West Virginia. Just one main road going east and west. Both directions are packed with cars when Lowyn and I leave her house and make our way over to the Revival tent at a walk.

I want to hold her hand, but I can't. Not until I give her that explanation. But it's still a very nice walk. The air is crisp, but not cold. Lowyn put on a little sweater—pale yellow with pearly white buttons that she did not button up. She's wearing that cute cloche hat and holding her tiny purse—just big enough to hold her cell phone—by the silver chain.

There are hundreds of people already lined up at the main gate that leads into the tent grounds, but we go down a side street where the side entrance is, and that's where I find Amon, Nash, and Ryan—all dressed up the same way I am—checking people through as they pass.

Lowyn grabs my hand. "I'll see you later, OK?"

"Yeah, OK." And I'm just getting used to that hand when it slips out of reach again.

She waves her fingers at Amon and the guys. "Have a good day, men."

I almost fall over with desire for that woman. And when I turn to Amon, he's smirking at me.

"What?"

"You're staying at her house, aren't ya?"

"Where else am I gonna stay? You've torn up my whole house. And what the hell are you two doing here?" I look Ryan and Nash up and down, noticing the slight differences in our costumes. "You're not even part of this."

"They're on the contract now. Jim Bob came by the compound last night. In fact, I've got forty-seven people on the contract with us."

"What? How's that work at the end of the year?"

Amon nearly guffaws, pulling me away from Nash and Ryan, telling them to check people in as they pass. We only go about a dozen feet away. "Don't worry. None of them are figured into the bonus structure. They're all hourly."

"What about Nash and Ryan? We can't pay them hourly. They're partners."

"In Edge, yeah. But they're not from here, Collin. Even if I wanted to give them bonus money—and I don't"—he gives me a stern look here—"there's no way."

"So why are they here?"

"They offered."

"Well, how the hell did they get a fuckin' costume?"

"They're wearing mine. We get three sets."

I look around, sighing. "I dunno, man. This is turning into a much bigger thing than I signed up for." I look back at Amon. "Did you know there's a fuckin' script?"

"Yeah." He laughs. "And for a couple of assholes who walked out on this place a dozen years ago, we get to play a pretty big part."

"See, this is what I mean. We're supposed to be security. Not... *gangsters.*"

"It's just a costume. Oh, I brought your Glock. It's in the security barracks." He nods his head to a tented building off to the left. "There's a safe in there where I've stashed the weapons. The dogs are in there too."

"Weapons? Dogs? It's the fuckin' Revival, Amon. What kind of heat are you expecting?"

"You never know. I like to be prepared. On a lighter note"— he nudges me with his shoulder—"how are you and Lowyn doing? Good, right?" He winks at me. "I mean, you're living at her house now. That was some quick work there, Creed. In town less than a week and already lining up the old lady."

"Shut up. Where do I go? What do I do?"

"Do you wanna dog?"

"Do I *need* a dog?"

"What's that got to do with anything? It's a dog, Collin. It'll keep you company."

This guy, I swear. "Sure. Why not."

Amon grins. "I knew you'd say that. Be right back." He goes inside the barracks and comes back out a couple minutes later with a dog. She is an all-black German Shepherd with light-brown eyes that almost look yellow. Her fur is rather long for a Shepherd, and fluffy, not sleek, so she doesn't look as menacing as some of the dogs that Amon keeps in the kennel. "This is Mercy. She's only just turned two, but she knows all the standard commands in German, English, Russian, and Hungarian."

"Dammit, Amon. How much did you pay for this dog? I

thought we had a budget? I said twenty grand apiece. This one sounds like a genius."

"Nah. I got her on special. She flunked out of cadaver school."

I don't wanna laugh at him, but it's kinda hard not to. Still, I don't give in. There's no point in denying that Amon is charming. He is. It's just... he fuckin' annoys me too. So I growl, "I don't know Hungarian."

"So talk to her in English." Amon rolls his eyes at me like I'm the dumbest motherfucker he's ever met. "You take the north gate. I'm taking east, Nash is taking west, and Ryan's taking south. All the other guys will do the interior."

"What are we looking for?"

"Assholes, Collin. We're lookin' for assholes." He pats my chest, hands me the lead attached to Mercy's harness, and walks off.

Mercy and I look at each other, then I shrug and we head north.

LOWYN

t takes me hours to stop thinking about Collin Creed and how he looked in his costume this morning. My God, why didn't I sleep with that man last night? Why?

He kind of explained himself, didn't he? I mean, I get it, don't I? Do I really need a formal explanation with a formal apology?

"Stop it."

I turn and look at Bryn, who has taken the day off at the inn so she can help out on opening day. There's no Revival on Fridays. It's just a look around. But all the booths are open, and the food venders are cooking up a storm, and the children's choir will be singing at least three times today.

There are also a few rides. Classic ones. A merry-go-round, a Ferris wheel, some bumper cars, and a helter-skelter slide. It's Good Friday and even though it's not a national holiday, here in these parts the kids don't have school. So most of the people are locals from the surrounding towns outside the Trinity.

Our booth is going crazy with customers, so Bryn is here for support. She's not required to be here every day we're open any more than I am, but you gotta be pretty much dying to get away with a no-show on opening day.

"Stop what?" I ask her.

"You're daydreaming. Did you sleep with him yet?"

"No. I'm still mad. He walked out on me twelve years ago. One does not just get over that in a week."

"He's living at your house, Lowyn."

"On the couch!"

"Please. Just sleep with him and get it over with. The two of you have been in love since he first saw you singing in the children choir and you first saw him holding the Good Book open for his daddy when you were back in kindergarten."

"How would you even know that? You weren't even there back in those days. You were in the play tent."

Bryn winks at me, then turns her back to help a customer.

She's right, though. Inside the Revival tent, the children's choir stands stage right and Collin was always seated stage left, so we were looking at each other all growing up. I used to imagine that he could pick my voice out of the chorus and I would sing extra loud to make sure that happened.

Did it work?

Maybe. Of course, he's almost two years older than me, and when you're five, that's a big deal. So maybe it didn't. Maybe he never saw me at all. Not until I was in high school, that is.

We started out as friends first. I was on the cheerleading squad at Trinity High my freshman year. I wasn't interested in cheering, I was there for Collin. That was it. And I did everything in my power to make him notice me. I'd do backflips across the field right in front of him. I'd decorate his locker on game days, even if I had been assigned some other player's locker. And I would leave him notes. Not signing my name, at first, but a little picture instead.

I wasn't an artist, but Clover was, and she and I were besties since first grade. She taught me how to doodle flowers when we were little. And this was what I drew for Collin. That was how I signed my name when I left him notes.

There was nothing scandalous in the notes. They said things like 'good job' and 'nice catch.' He was the receiver for the football team. But then, one night, after the game, I slipped a new note into his helmet that was lying on the bench. This was the last game of the season. They didn't go to state or anything. It was just a regular game. And in this note I asked him to meet me at the Revival tent at five a.m. And I signed it with my flower.

I didn't think he'd show up. I really didn't.

But he was there. Sitting on the top step of the stage.

There were a lot of people around. The Revival grounds never sleep when we're in season. And Collin's role in the whole affair was on that stage, so no one questioned why he was there, sittin' on that step.

When I came into the tent, he smiled at me and stood up, always the gentleman. "I knew it was you."

He said these words like they were no big deal.

But to me, they were the biggest deal ever.

And that was how we started.

I knew it was you.

THE FOOT TRAFFIC is busy well past lunch, so when Collin Creed enters our booth with a dog and a funnel cake and asks me if I have time for a break, I just sigh at him like he's my hero.

We walk towards the river on the far side of the tent grounds where it's quiet and no visitors are allowed. There are a few dozen picnic tables, a couple self-service drink carts, and a dock.

Collin unclips the leash from his dog—who is called Mercy and belongs to Amon—and then he and I take that funnel cake over to the dock and sit down on the creaky benches that line one side. There's an awning over the end of the dock, so we get to sit in the shade.

"Did everyone love your costume?"

Collin smiles at me. "My men gave me the wrinkle-free award." Which makes me laugh. "Nah. I don't know what the deal is with all this security. Jim Bob is paranoid or something. Do you always have this much?"

"I've never paid much attention, to be honest. We've never had dogs before, that's for sure. But if they were dressed up in costume, I probably wouldn't have noticed. I'm not here all day, every day. I'll work this weekend because it's opening day and all, and I'll be there for all the big tent shows, but I've got a business."

"Yeah, you do. I was wondering about that. I see some booths where they combine the two. MaisieLee is selling fittings for custom clothes in her costume booth, and April Laver sells her own cookie recipe from the bakery in her booth."

"Yeah, but they like to share profits, and I don't."

"Ah. I knew there had to be a catch."

"If I sold McBooms stuff here, I'd have to give the town some profit. And to be quite honest, I don't need the business. I'm pretty busy all on my own."

"That's smart. To keep it all separate, ya know?"

"Mmm. Do I detect some cynicism?"

"No. I'm just saying. Legally speaking, you did a smart thing."

"Who got your hackles up?"

"Why do you presume my hackles are up?"

"Was it Simon?" I point at him. "It was Simon."

"I'm not saying I don't trust him. I'm just saying I don't know him." He pauses. "Well? Do you have an opinion?"

I just shrug. "No one likes him. There. I said it. But the reason no one likes him is because they're still loyal to your family. And even though it's been almost a decade now, they're still holding out hope that the Creeds will come back."

"And now that I'm here?"

I laugh. "Oh, Collin. Now that you're back, they're gonna push that man and his whole family right out of town."

"I hope not. There is no way in hell I will preach in that tent. Like hell will be freezing over before that happens. My daddy will come back and take that job before I ever will. Please relay this message to whomever it may concern, every chance you get."

I just shake my head. "Anyway. Aside from your suspicions and hesitations, how is your day going?"

He nods, looks out over the river, maybe concentrating on the cliff on the other side. The river that runs through Disciple runs deep. And by deep, I mean over the course of the life of this planet, this water has carved out a place between hills. There used to be a working bridge that went from one side to the other, one of those old-timey train bridges with intricate trusses. But that thing started falling apart decades ago and no one had the desire to put it all back together.

They've been talking about tearing that bridge down for a long time now, but again, no one really cares enough about the damn thing to get rid of it, either.

"It's the same and different."

I look over at Collin and find him looking back at me. "Of course it is," I tell him. "You've been gone a long time." He just smiles at me. For quite a few moments. Too many moments to not be awkward, actually. "What?"

"We're still on for bowling, right?"

"You spent all those moments being silent and awkward, and that's what's on your mind?"

"You're on my mind, Lowyn. Just you. The bowling alley is just a way to get more time."

"You're living at my house. Bryn thinks I should just sleep with you and get it over with."

He huffs out a laugh. "She's always been a genius."

We go quiet after that. Not for long, but long enough for us both to know that we're thinking about sleeping together and why I've turned him down so far.

"So... listen, Lowyn. I know I don't have any right to ask this—and, in fact, it could ruin things between us—"

Oh, shit. Here we go.

"—but... I can't explain it."

"Can't explain what?" I know what he's talking about. I just have an urge to make him spell it out.

"Why I acted the way I did after... you know. After I killed that guy."

"You mean why you just... stopped talking to me? Then silently broke up with me? Then joined the Marines without telling me? Are those the things you can't explain?"

He sighs. "I'm a dick. I... don't deserve a second chance. And if you walk away, then..." He throws up his hands. "Then I guess that's how it was meant to be."

I scoff. We're gonna have a fight. He's been in town less than a week, he's staying at my house, and just a few minutes ago I was thinking about sleepin' with him and now we're gonna have a fight.

I take a deep breath. Collin Creed is the love of my life. I am twenty-nine years old and I've had plenty of chances to move on.

And I haven't.

I won't.

But I want him to know how I feel about this. So I turn a little and look him in the eye. "Collin, I love you, I have always loved you, and if you think I've been waiting around for you to come back, well"—I tip my chin up—"you'd be right. So I'm not even able to get up and walk out on you right now. I'm not capable of giving you an ultimatum the way you just handed one to me."

"Lowyn—"

"No." I put a hand up. "That's what that was. And fine. I agree. I won't ask any more questions about that night, or what happened in the weeks afterward, or why I wasn't important enough to you to even leave a note."

His face falls. That was the intention of my speech, so I'm pretty pleased with this reaction.

"But I want you to know that you did more than ruin me for other men, Collin. You crushed me. You ripped my soul into pieces. You... you... you made me *sad*."

He's still staring at me. And he swallows hard when this last word comes out of my mouth. I'm a quiet fighter. I do not scream, or throw things, or make threats.

When I fight, I just tell the truth.

It hurts Collin a lot more to hear these things I just said than it ever would if I had simply slapped him across the face.

"I'm sorry."

"I know. You've already said that."

He lets out a long breath. "I wish I could take it back."

"You can't. It's done."

"So what do we do now?"

"Well, I think you and I have a date tonight."

There is a glimmer of hope in his eyes. "We do."

"But I'm not in the mood for a date. Especially with your friends. I don't think I want to be on the bowling team. So I'm just gonna go home. In fact, I think I'm gonna work tonight."

"Work?"

"McBooms? I have to catalog a bunch of stuff, and..." I shrug and let it go. Stop trying. It's not a lie. At all. I do have to catalog that stuff. I don't have to do it on a Friday night, but I am.

"OK. Should I find another place to sleep?"

"Well..." I don't know what to say to this.

"I'll find another place to stay."

"I'm not..." I scoff. "I'm not even sure what to say here, because we're not even dating. But I want you to know that I'm not over you. I'm not done. I'm just..." I shake my head. "I don't know what I feel right now. Do I love you? Yes. That was my first point. I love you, Collin. I will never stop loving you. But you hurt me. And that scares me. I don't want to be a woman who hands out her unconditional love to a man who hurts her."

"Fuck, Lowyn." That cut him deep. It was meant to. He runs his fingers through his hair and then he scrubs his hands down his face.

I stand up. He stands up. "I'll see ya tomorrow. OK? We'll start over tomorrow."

He nods at me, his face long and somber. "OK. I'll see you tomorrow."

I turn my back and walk away. I don't want to. I want to ask him... where will he stay tonight? I want to ask him if he's OK. I want to take his hand, and take him home, and lock him up and never let him get away again.

But he's a grown man. It's none of my business where he sleeps. If he's not OK, that's not my fault. And locking him up and never letting him go is a felony.

So I keep walking.

I go back to my booth, and plaster on a smile, and chat happily with Bryn, and when six o'clock comes, I pack up my things, close down my booth, and walk over to McBooms.

It's dark in there.

And I don't turn on the light.

Because I want to have a good cry and I don't want anyone to see me do that.

*W*hen *my day is over* and Amon is handing out instructions to the night shift, I slip away and start walking back to Lowyn's house. I know I told her I'd find another place to stay—and I will—but I still have to pick up my Jeep in front of her house and get my things.

The whole place is dark when I get there and that's when I remember that she said she was gonna work tonight. I could go inside. I actually have the key.

But I don't want to. Because if I go inside, this sets a course of action. It sends a message. It means that I respect her wishes —which is fine. That part's fine. But it also means that I'm a quitter. And despite the fact that I quit on Lowyn McBride when I walked out on her twelve years ago—I'm not a quitter.

So I do not go inside her house and collect my things. I don't even drive my Jeep. I walk over to McBooms and leave everything the way it is.

But when I get there, it's dark.

Hmm. Did she lie to me?

I don't think so. Even though Lowyn started our reconnection with a lie about my teenage bedroom, she is not a liar. She was doing nothing but handing out truths this afternoon.

It's possible she got an offer and took it. Perhaps Bryn invited her to dinner? Maybe Rosie Harlow talked her into goin' dancing? Maybe.

But I can't go on that assumption until I thoroughly check out McBooms for any signs of life. I press my face against the window and get an immediate payoff. A little bit of music. Fleetwood Mac. But there are no lights on and I can't see any people inside.

So I knock.

Immediately, a head pops up from the couch in the middle of the store. I can just barely make out her face when Lowyn turns towards the window, wiping her eyes like maybe she was crying, and then, even from the other side of the glass, I can hear that sigh, even though I can't. It's long. Like she's tired.

I knock again. "Lowyn. It's me. Open up, please."

Lowyn McBride is a quiet fighter. She's never gonna show up at my motel room and rip me a new asshole the way Bryn did the other day. It's not her style. But I can say, with one hundred percent certainty, that Lowyn's calm anger, and the way she delivers her truth in the most soothing way, and that soft manner in which she shows her disappointment—her *sad*, as she put it—is enough to crush a man and make him feel ashamed.

It certainly did crush me this afternoon. And I can't let this day end like this.

She gets up off the couch, walks over to the door, unlocks it, and opens it up a crack. "What are you doing here?"

It's not an accusation, though she's entitled to that. She did tell me to fuck off, in her own way, of course. And here I am, inserting myself back into her life when she's just trying to have a quiet moment of sadness.

"I just wanna say something. And then you can close the door and I'll leave. But I wanna say... No."

"No? No what?"

"It wasn't an ultimatum. This is not how it's supposed to be. And even if it is, I'm not walking out again. Ever."

That sigh she gives me. It's a whole lotta disbelief.

"You don't have to believe me tonight. Or tomorrow. Or

next week or next year. But one day, Lowyn McBride, you *will* believe me. Because one day, when you're old, I'll still be here." I point to the ground. "I'll be right here. Because I made a mistake when I left you behind. I made a mistake when I broke your heart. I made a mistake and maybe I'm not the smartest guy around, but I'm a rather quick learner. And I don't tend to make the same mistakes twice. You were my best friend and I let you down. But I will not do that again. And like I said, you don't have to believe me. I'll just show you."

Then I tip an imaginary hat at her, turn, and I walk away.

"Collin?"

I stop. Force myself not to smile. And turn. "What?"

"Do you wanna come in and make Jell-O?"

"We're having a serious conversation here, Miss McBride."

"I realize that."

"I have no idea what Jell-O has to do with anything."

"It's a thing I do for the kiddie tent. They sell Jell-O squares for a nickel. But I had forgotten because you're such a fuckin' distraction. So I need to make some Jell-O before I go to bed tonight and I thought I'd invite you in to help me do that so you didn't have to look like a sad little puppy who just lost his mama."

"Is that what I look like?"

She doesn't answer. Just opens the door.

Of course I will not say no. And she knows this.

I smile at her as I pass through and enter McBooms. But then I remember something. "Were you crying?"

"Of course I was. I just lost my best friend. Again."

"You didn't lose me."

"I sent you packing."

"But I'm not leaving."

She walks past me to the couch and flops down. There's a boom box on the cushion next to her. I guess she had turned the music off when I knocked, but she turns it back on now and Fleetwood Mac resume their lament about dreams.

"I thought we were makin' Jell-O?"

"We are." But she doesn't get up. Just turns the music down a little so it's not interfering with our talk.

I take the hint and sit down. Not too close, but not too far, either.

"I thought you were goin' bowling, Collin?"

"I'll show up later, maybe."

"They're gonna pick shirts without you."

I smile. "Maybe it's for the best."

She turns to me and her mouth is poutin'. "I want to trust you. And love you like you never left. But... it's hard, Collin."

"What's gettin' in the way? My past actions? Or is it more the uncertainty of my future ones?"

"Future."

"You think I'll take off again."

"Why wouldn't you?"

"I literally just bought fourteen houses eight miles out of town."

"That's not enough."

My eyes widen in surprise. "It's not enough?"

"No. Not for me."

"Should I propose?"

I get a teeny, tiny smile from her. "No."

"You don't want a husband."

"Nope."

"Should I... give you a promise ring?"

"Hmm."

"Oooh. I'm gettin' warmer. Should I... write you a love poem?"

Her smile is big now.

"Damn, woman. You want me to write you a poem?"

"You do have such lovely words. A letter would suffice."

"Words, in written form, can fix this?"

She presses her lips together, smiling. Nodding. "But you can recite it. You don't have to write it."

"Right now? Do I have to do it right now?"

"A rough draft would go a long way."

Now it's my turn to smile. "OK. How about this?" I clear my throat. "Dear Lowyn. No. My *dearest* Lowyn." I pause to think, but the memory comes right up, like it's been waiting for this moment since the very day it happened. "I was in Bali one early morning. I had been up all night working—three days, actually —and I was so tired, I could barely make it back to the hotel from my post. So I took a shortcut through the fruit and flower market and the scent of it all, it struck me dumb. For about ten seconds, I just stood there, in the middle of the market, and slowly turned in a circle."

"Why?"

"Why?" I look right at Lowyn. "Because I smelled you, that's why." She smiles. "It was the flowers. Baskets filled with little flowers. They call them jepun there in Bali, but they're called plumeria here."

"Oh." She smiles bigger now. "I love plumeria."

"I know. You wore that scent every day in high school. But the story gets better. Because an old woman saw me, and came up to me, and asked me who I was missing."

"Did she speak English?"

"No."

"You speak Balinese?"

"No."

Lowyn laughs. "Then how did you know what she was saying?"

"I dunno. But I did. I didn't answer her, though. Because, obviously, I don't speak Balinese. So then she said, 'Come with me.' Then she took my hand and took me out of the market to a tree filled with pink and white flowers. The trunk was goin' this way and that and the top was shaped like an umbrella. A pink umbrella. The old woman said, while waving her finger at me, 'You don't pick them. You gather them.' And she pointed to the ground. There were children there too, picking up flowers that had fallen off the tree. But there were so many flowers, there was more than enough for all of us. So I picked up the flowers and..."

Lowyn tries to be patient, but I've caught her imagination now and she can't help herself. "And what? What happened?"

"I woke up." She smacks me. Playfully. "I woke up, Lowyn. In my hotel bathtub, surrounded by those same pink and white flowers."

"What? I don't understand. It was a dream? Or it was real?"

"I don't know. But I was thinking of you, and those flowers, and the next thing I know, magic happened. You're my magic, Lowyn. And that's my love letter."

"Rough draft."

"Right." I smile. "I will polish the fuck out of that story and turn it in."

She chuckles a little, mostly to herself. Then she draws her legs up to her chest and settles back against the couch cushions.

"So. I've been thinking about our conversation this afternoon."

Her eyes dart to mine. They are bloodshot because she's been crying. Her make-up, while not streaked down her face or anything, is smudged under her lower eyelashes. She's still wearing her costume, but no shoes, I notice. And she's taken the jewelry off.

"And I think I know where I went wrong."

"Oh?"

"Yeah. Ya see, Lowyn, I forgot to tell you how those two seconds affected me too."

Her sad look becomes even sadder. I don't want to have this conversation because it won't paint me in a nice light. It won't soften my edges, it will make me hard and sharp. And I hate that this is the man I turned into, but there's no way around it. I am this guy.

"Before I got up from the couch to go see what was happening, and before I picked up that rifle—thank the fuckin' God above, it wasn't the shotgun—and before I squeezed that trigger—even though the man in front of me specifically, and deliberately, asked me to spare his life—before all that I was..." I sigh. She's entranced by this story, even more so than the last one. "I was... *good*, Lowyn. Good enough, at least. I was a good enough ball player to get a scholarship to Ohio State. I was a good enough son to my daddy to still be worth his time. I was a good enough student, and a good enough boyfriend, and pretty much a good enough everything. And then, two seconds later, I was a murderer."

She exhales. "It was self-defense."

"Maybe." I shrug. "Maybe it was. Maybe he was gonna kill one of us. He did have a gun and he was kidnapping my baby sister right out of her bed. But he put his hands up, Lowyn. He asked me not to shoot. And I didn't even blink. I blew his fuckin' head off. And it's not because I was scared, either. It's not even so much about the anger, though I was angry. There was just this..." I let out a sigh. "This very strong voice inside my head, ya know? This voice that said, 'No, sir. *No. Sir.* You don't get a second chance after this. You. Are. Dead.'"

Lowyn presses her lips together. "I think that's what the sheriff was trying to tell me, Collin. Sometimes a person crosses your line and they don't get to come back from that."

"Right. I get it. I've even accepted it. That I'm one of those men, ya know? But the hard part for me was how I felt about myself afterward. You told me the other night that I made you feel safe. That what I did was something that ruined you by lifting me up."

"That's not what I said."

"Those aren't the words you used, but that is what you said, Lowyn. I don't make myself feel safe. I scare myself. That's what you don't know about me. You *see* me, this man with pretty words, or whatever, and think I'm him. And I'm not. I'm... that kid who blew that guy's head off. I'm that guy. I didn't feel safer after I murdered that man. I felt… powerful. But also dirty. Awful. Ugly. Evil. And you…" I stop here, because her eyes are watering now. "You, Lowyn, you're like the nicest, purest thing these fuckin' hills have ever seen. You're just… one of *them*, ya know?"

"One of who?"

"The good ones. You're one of the good ones. You're like… like the glory that comes after the rumble. And I used to be one of them too. At the very least, I had it in me to maybe be one of them too. And then I killed a man. And since that night, I've killed a lot more."

Her face falls. "Where? In the Marines?"

I nearly scoff. "No. No, Lowyn. I told you the military made a private army. I killed people as a hired gun."

"What kind of people?"

"Bad people. They were bad people. They were all trying to kill someone I was hired to protect. But you see, that night… it turned me from good enough to no good at all. And so, when we were having our conversation this afternoon, I was not trying to be flippant about our destiny, or lack of one. I was just trying to say all this, all these words, with the fewest number of letters as possible, and it came out wrong. It's not that I am content to let us be, or not be, based on fate. It's that I am content to let us be, or not be, based on whether or not I deserve you."

"What does that even mean, though? I mean, there's no Grand Poobah controlling the world handing out badges with the word 'Deserving' written on a banner. You just got to accept what people offer, Collin. Whether or not they choose to offer it isn't really any of your concern."

I just stare at her for a few seconds. Because she's right. It's not up to me what other people think. Or what they offer me, even if it's something I don't feel I deserve, like trust. She should not trust me. But it's not my place to tell her who to trust. And honestly, I know with one hundred percent certainty that she *can* trust me. Because if this really is a second chance then there is no way I will fuck it up again.

Without saying anything Lowyn hikes her dress up and slips into my lap, her legs straddling mine, her fingertips gently touching my cheek, and our eyes locked—the same way we used to do it in high school.

And automatically, and without a single thought or hesitation at all, my hands slip to her smooth, cool thighs and reach around her ass to tug her closer.

She sighs. And smiles. "Thank you."

"What for?"

"For all those letters you didn't want to string together to make all those words."

"It's enough then?"

"It's enough."

And then she leans down, slowly and deliberately, and kisses me.

I let this first part go slow. I let it torture me. Because this kiss is everything right now and I want to remember every single second of it. Her lips are soft and tender. And when she opens her mouth and slips her tongue right up against mine, I am crushed by all the seconds I've wasted in life without her by my side.

I see everything that I've missed in this one moment. All condensed, and squished up, and packed into a single fleck of time.

And then that moment passes and I can't take it any longer. I reach up and grab her face and kiss her good. When we've had our fill of that we pull away, breathless. Then she's scootin' backwards. Getting away from me. I grab her hand, but she put her finger to her lips and says, "Shhhhh."

So I let go.

And she stands up, smiling at me, something coy about it too. And then she hikes her Revival costume dress up her thighs and then the next thing I know, her panties are dropping to the floor. Then she puts her bare foot right up between my legs and starts rolling down her stocking.

I about die. "Woman, what the fuck are you trying to do to me?"

She just smiles—more coyness comes with it—and she does this same move with the other leg too. Then she grabs my tie and pulls on it until I get the hint and stand up.

I have to admit, I'm smiling as well. Not coyly. Not at all. Maybe a bit loftily. And then she's sliding my suspenders down my arms. And before I even get a chance to catch up, she's got her dainty little fingertips on the top button of my trousers. All five of the buttons down my fly come open.

I might die again.

And she knows this, because she laughs as she pushes me, making me fall back into the couch cushions. Then she steps up to me, looking down at me, smiling at me—and she sits herself back in my lap. Arranging her dress to flare over her thighs. Placing her hands on my shoulders.

"Do you want me to keep going, Collin Creed? So you can watch with your mouth open a little longer?"

I almost guffaw. Almost. Instead, I grab her hips, flip her sideways onto the couch—which makes her squeal like she's a teenager again—and then I push that dress right out of my way with one hand, getting my hard-on out of my pants with the other, and even though she deserves more than just a little bit of foreplay time, that can come later.

Right now, I just want to be inside her.

And a moment later, there's where I am.

I brace myself on my elbows, take her face in my hands, and I look her in the eyes as I love the fuck out of her for the second time ever. And this time, maybe the setting could be a little nicer, a bit more romantic, but either way, it's everything I ever wanted from lovemaking.

Lowyn closes her eyes, opens her mouth to moan a little, and then her back is bucking up as I slip in and out of her and then before I even have a chance to calm her down, she's coming. Writhing under me as Fleetwood Mac softly sings about lightning striking—maybe once, maybe twice.

And it is twice. In our case, at least.

Because this is everything a man could ever want in a second chance.

When I come, I do not pull out. And I'm not gonna regret that tomorrow. This is the woman I will marry. I don't care that she doesn't want a husband. So when she's calmer, and I've got my face buried in her neck—kissing it, nibbling on her ear—I let her know this.

I say, in a soft, soft whisper, "When the trying times come, we will hold hands. And when the heavy times come, we will walk them together. And when the depressing times come, and you feel the burden of life to be so vast and wide that you feel forsaken, I will be there to carry you. No matter how long it takes or how far we must travel, no matter how many miles it be, I will carry you, Lowyn McBride. I will carry you."

She is holding her breath that whole time I'm whispering. And when I'm done, she lets it out real slow. "That's a Revival wedding vow you just recited, Collin Creed."

And I just smile into her neck as I squish us together on the couch. "Indeed it is, Miss McBride. Indeed it is."

She turns her whole body into me. Burying her face in my chest. Pressing herself up so close to me, I can feel her heart thumping in her chest.

And this, I think, is probably the best night of my life. And for the first time in more than a decade, I slip into sleep without a single thought of how much blood I have on my hands.

I STARTLE AWAKE, rubbing my eyes and groggily trying to open them. "What the fuck is that noise?"

Lowyn groans beside me, pulling my arm over her head to try to cover her ears, not the least bit interested in waking up.

But I can't help myself. I would love to stay on this used couch from the Seventies inside her store, but that noise... "Oh, shit." I sit up, taking Lowyn with me.

"Mmmmmmmm," she protests.

"Lowyn, get up. We slept through Saturday."

"What?"

I'm already on my feet, buttoning my trousers back up.

"What are you talking about?" Her question is sexy as all hell because her voice is so... low, and deep, and filled with satisfaction.

"Listen." I point to the ceiling.

She squints her eyes. Like this might help her hear better. And then I say the words with the loudspeaker outside. "'When you look upon the hills, the sun shining on the peaks, and you hear the rumble in the distance, don't you ever forget that behind it comes the glory. And as that rumble resonates into the echo on the water, let it be a sign! A sign that the righteous will find comfort in the brave. And the danger will exist only in the damaged. Because when you give yourself to something higher, you will feel the relief that comes with the emptiness of anger and you will know, in your heart, that the blessing of grace is now upon you!'"

And then I look at Lowyn, who is standing now, her hair all askew and a little bit of dribble at the corner of her mouth. She manages to say a few words. "Is that what I think... but... it's not Sunday. We could not have slept two nights, Collin! It's not possible!"

"Those are my daddy's words." For some reason, I'm upset about this. Like... borderline angry about this. "Why the fuck is my daddy's voice booming through the town loudspeakers when it's Saturday morning of opening weekend and there is no fuckin' Revival scheduled?"

Lowyn pats at her hair, still trying to wake up. "I don't know. What's goin' on?"

"Put your panties back on, Lowyn. We've got to go."

"*It's Saturday.*" I'm looking at Collin when I say this. He's brushing his teeth in my little McBooms bathroom using one of the new toothbrushes I keep stashed here. "There is no Revival on opening Saturday. There has never, in the history of this town, been a Revival on opening Saturday."

Collin shrugs, spits, rinses his mouth, and turns the water off. I hand him a towel to wipe his face. He does that grin at me. "How should I know, Lowyn? I just got here."

"I know. I'm just thinking out loud. It's just weird."

"You know what else is weird? My daddy's voice coming out of those speakers. Why the hell are they using my daddy's sermon when he's not even the preacher no more?"

"Well, they never stopped using that one. Even after he was fired. It's the call to Revival now. That little snippet of his Easter Day Revelation sermon has been playing non-stop, in some fashion or another, for thirty-five years. I guess it was just too much tradition to part with."

I can't tell how he feels about this. He looks a little bit annoyed. But then again, he looks a little bit composed. Is he pissed, but trying not to show it? I can't tell.

"Is that what you're wearing on your feet?" He's pointing to my shoes.

Which are Fifties saddle shoes that came from Sears. I just pulled them off the McBooms sale rack. It's not authorized apparel and I think it's cute that Collin noticed. "I'm not putting those pumps back on. My feet were sore yesterday. So this will have to do."

"You little rebel." Then he slips his hand around my waist, pulls me close, and kisses me with his minty-fresh breath.

But just as our lips touch, the bells start ringing.

Collin pulls back. "What in God's name is that?"

"The bells."

"I can hear the ringing, Lowyn. Why the hell are they doing it now? There are no churches in Disciple."

"True. There aren't. But when Simon came on board to replace your daddy, he took offense to the Easter Day Revelation sermon being the call to Revival, so he insisted on adding in bells as last call. So this is last call. It's about to start. Should we get going?"

Collin's in a pretty good mood. He did get laid last night. And it was me he was getting laid by. Maybe I'm not anything special in the wider world, but I am to Collin Creed. Even I know this. So his mood has been good. Up until this point.

He sighs. "Maybe we should just skip it."

"I can't. You can, if you want. But I have the booth. The teenagers will run it during Revival—I am playing Fainting Woman with Fan for week one, so I gotta be at the service to collapse at the proper time—but after that, Bonnie and Lydia are wrangling the children's choir between performances and Mark and Matthew are running the rides. So it's just me in the booth today. Bryn can't take off two days in a row at the inn. Guests would shit a vintage brick if they had to eat pre-made sandwiches and chips two days in a row."

His smile starts small but it grows pretty quick. "Do you even realize how weird this place is? Or have you just grown immune to the insanity?"

I bob my head a little, thinking. "Little bit of both, I guess. I do know we're special. And I do know I like it." I grin back at him.

"OK." He offers me his hand, resigned to the fact that he's part of this again. "Let's go then."

As soon as **we turn** the corner and start heading up Main Street, the cry of newsie boys catches our attention. There are a lot of people on Main, all of them heading up the hill to the tent. The kids hawking the *Revival News*, boys and girls, are dressed up in their proper costumes, including the trademark cap.

"Prodigal son returns! One dollar! Get it now, people! Don't miss this edition! Get it now!"

That's what they're all crying.

Which makes Collin grumble. "Prodigal son. It doesn't even make sense."

"It's a show, Collin. It doesn't need to make sense. You're just playing a part like everyone else." I steer us over to the nearest newsie—a little girl called Amy. She's got her long, brown hair tied back, and her sweet face looks very, very cute under that newsboy hat. "I'll take one, Amy."

She makes a face at me. One of those wide-eyed, all-teeth-smile faces.

"What? What's wrong with you?"

"Ummm. Miss McBride, I hope you don't hold it against me. I'm just a delivery girl." And she holds up the paper. It features Collin, of course. Someone snapped a picture of him yesterday because he's in his costume and he's looking angry about something. That was expected.

What we didn't expect is a picture of me—Fainting Woman with Fan.

Only I'm not Fainting Woman with Fan. I've been recast as Widow Cries as Murderer Returns Home. They're using a picture of me from Season Four, when my character was called Distraught Woman in Stockings and I was crying because my fictional sister was rounded up and put in the paddy wagon with a dozen other young ladies for prostitution in Revenant.

Collins grabs the paper. I open my little purse and give Amy a dollar so she can scuttle out of the way and avoid the meltdown that's about to happen. Collin shakes the paper at me. "What the actual fuck?"

And just as he says that, someone yells, "There he is! That's him!" And when I say 'someone' I mean Rosie Harlow. "That's him! The murderer! Collin Creed, the murderer!"

I make a face of *what the hell are you doing, Rosie?*

She makes a face back. Hers says, *Sorry, but Jim Bob told me to.*

Suddenly, the crowd of people who just a moment ago were peacefully heading up the hill to the call for Revival all turn and look at us.

"What are you doing with him?" Lettie Gainer accuses, pointing her finger at me. "He killed your husband!"

"Oh, my God." Collin sighs. "This is crazy."

I pull his arm. "Don't say anything. Let's just keep walking."

We don't really have a choice, so Collin leads me up the hill and the crowd of people—who are mostly not townspeople, and therefore almost as confused as we are—simply part for us. Like we're Moses stepping through the Red Sea.

The bells stop ringing when we're about a hundred yards from the tent. And then the children's choir starts up with 'Amazing Grace.' I sigh a little as I listen.

Collin nudges me. "Taking ya back?"

I chuckle. "We sang this song when I was in the choir."

"I know. I used to watch you sing this song. You were right across the stage from me."

"I used to look at you with awe."

"And now look at us. I've murdered your husband and corrupted your honor."

"Who says you corrupted my honor?"

"No one. But that's where this is going. I can see it coming. But it's interesting."

"What is?"

"You didn't object to the part where I killed your husband."

He's right I didn't. Because, in a way, he did kill my husband. My future husband, which was supposed to be him. I lost him that night. But now he's back, so I'm never gonna think about that night again.

I can't tell him this, though. We talked it out last night. It's over. And I'm just about to turn and say this when the choir stops and Simon starts preaching.

"There is nothing more wicked than the wayward son!" Simon is really putting on the theatrics this morning because his voice is booming, and his arms are stretched out wide, and his face is already beet red and the sermon just started. "The son who disrespects! The son who courts evil! The son who lies, and cheats, and steals for nothing more than instantaneous pleasure. Gratification *is a sin!*"

Less than a minute into his sermon and I'm starting to panic. Because this is the sermon that got Mr. Creed fired from the Revival.

And it's all about Collin.

"Oh, God." Collin looks down at me. "What the actual fuck is this shit?"

"Your… daddy's final sermon?"

"Are you fuckin' kidding me?" He just stares at me for a moment. Like he always knew his daddy was an asshole, especially after Collin joined the Marines, but this has taken things to a whole new level.

But actually, Collin has no idea just how much of a son of a bitch his daddy really was. There was a lot of anger in that man. This sermon was just the tip of the iceberg.

185

"Sons who disobey the will of their fathers will live a life of hell on earth!" Simon is practically screaming now. It's not like him. Not like him at all. He's a very soft-spoken man. I didn't even know he had it in him to sound like Billy Sunday threatening us all with an eternal sentence in Hell.

We stop just short of the tent, standing at the beginning of the sawdust aisle that leads right up to the stage where our normally low-key preacher stands behind the pulpit, roaring about Satan.

Collin and I both sigh. Him because it's a completely unfair accusation, and me because I thought we had put these dark sermons to rest nearly a decade back. If this whole season is nothing but a replay of Preacher Creed's unhinged sermons about his son, I might have to step away until after Fourth of July.

I already lived through it once, I don't want to do it again.

Suddenly Jameson Grimm steps into the aisle in front of us and there is a moment here. A moment when time kinda stops and scenarios start running through my head.

What is he gonna say?

What fresh hell is about to start now?

I tilt my head at Grimm and I see his eyes narrow a little. But I can't tell if he's narrowing them because of malice or because he's cringing at what comes next.

And just as I have that thought, Grimm points at Collin. "There he is!" He yells this. *Roars* this. "That's him! Collin Creed! The murderer!"

The audience gasps, the actors—my fellow townspeople— gasping the loudest, of course. I wonder, vaguely, if this was a cue for me to faint. Because several women in the audience actually do that now.

Then my fellow townspeople take it one step further. One step too far, actually. And they all point to Collin. And they all start chanting.

"Murderer! Murderer! Murderer!"

Then there is bedlam.

Collin has my hand, and he is tugging me away. But the chant follows us. Rosie appears screaming, "He's hypnotized her! He's hypnotized her!" Pointing at me.

Hypnotism was a kind of a big scare back in the Twenties. It pops up a lot in the Revival story as a red herring for the Devil. And now I'm the poor woman who had her soul captured by a murderer using hypnotism.

It's so ridiculous. I've always thought that the hypnotism thing was an unnecessary exaggeration, but the people eat it up. We draw big crowds for that side story.

Collin is still pulling me. He's about to head out of the tent grounds, but I pull back. "I can't leave, Collin. I can't. I have the booth!"

"Fuck." He pauses to run his hand through his hair, and all the while, Simon is still preaching in a loud and shriek-y way that is so not like him, I get chills. It's even coming through the loudspeakers set up around town. I can hear his over-excited words echoing through the hills and off the far river bank.

"It's just a story. You know this, Collin. It's just a fiction. You grew up in it. Don't let any of this get to you."

"How do I not? I murdered a man. Right here in this town. Right here in your house. And now the story's about me being a murderer? What the fuck, ya know? What did I ever do to these people?"

I grab both his shoulders and shake him a little. "It's *not real*."

"I know that. But... what the hell? Why do they have to do this? Why can't they just leave me alone?"

"Why?" I mean, is he really asking me that question?

"Yeah, why?"

"OK." I pause here. But then I hear people coming and a lot of whispers behind us, so I drag him through the aisles of tents until I find mine, sitting high on the special platform that allows me to see the whole tent grounds, and tug him up the stairs. Once we get there, I take one last look over my shoulder —most of the crowd is still in the tent listening to Simon—and then pull Collin inside, startling the teenagers.

"Miss McBride!" Bonnie says this like I've walked in on something.

"Sorry to startle you, girls."

But just as I say that, Mark says, "Mr. Creed! So nice to meet you." He walks towards us and extends his hand towards Collin.

Collin looks a little confused, so I quickly explain. "Collin, meet teenagers. Teenagers, meet Collin."

Collins allows Mark to shake his hand, which Mark does enthusiastically as he speaks. "I was talking to Mr. Parrish last night at the bowling alley, and he says you're looking for a few new men." He nudges Matthew. "We're gonna join up with Edge Security." Both boys smile at Collin, like they are awestruck.

Collin blows out a breath and withdraws his hand from the shake. "OK." But that's all he's got.

So I take over. "You all are dismissed. Go on. I've got it now."

Lydia and Bonnie both give me a little curtsey, a customary response when talking to adults on a show day, then dart out of the tent. And Mark and Matthew give Collin a little salute.

I pull the flap closed and turn to Collin. "Listen, you're taking this way too personal. It's a production. And you... well, I hate to say this, but you asked. Why are they fucking with you? Why are they giving you a leading role? It's because you walked out, Collin. And for nearly four years, things fell apart around here. Your daddy went nuts. Started preaching shit like that." I nod my head in the direction of the Revival tent. "It almost ruined everything. And now things are good. Real good. You saw the contracts. We're making millions here. Tens upon tens of millions each year."

"So why the hell are they bringing it back? Why would they do that? Why fuck with a good thing?"

"Because they want to punish you." I shrug. "It's as simple as that. And you can either freak out like this every weekend until Fourth of July when the story turns, or you can play along and let it go."

Just as I say that, the tent flaps open and Amon comes in, grinnin' like a fool. "Wow. That was amazing."

Collin is still pissed. "What the hell was so amazing, Amon? They're calling me a murderer. How is this not fucked up on an epic level?"

Amon is still laughing. "Oh, it's so fucked up. But it's gold, man. They printed up these new story programs, twenty-five bucks a pop. They are selling like fuckin' hotcakes out there right now. They can't get enough of you two."

I take a step forward. "What are you talking about?"

Amon pulls a rolled-up program out of his back pocket and hands it to me. "Prodigal son comes back to town, has to face the widow—you"—he points to me—"after killing her husband twelve years ago. He's looking for redemption and has to prove himself to the town."

I look at Collin, who is already looking at me, and I give him a smug I-told-you-so smile. "What did I tell you?"

"This is fucked up."

"Collin." Amon puts a hand on his friend's shoulder. "It's fake, dude. No matter how much you feel this is personal, it's not. This town loves you."

"Then why would they do this to me?"

"I told you why, Collin." I'm still giving him that smug I-told-you-so smile when he glances over at me.

"Just play along, Col." Amon is sure taking this in stride. "It's actually a cool role. I'll round up a script for you so you know what to expect tomorrow. That one you got yesterday? Throw it out. The whole thing's been rewritten." And with that, Amon Parrish blows out of my tent, just as quick as he blew in.

COLLIN

I *leave Lowyn's tent* and head straight into town to confront Jim Bob. That's what he was yellin' about when I was in there the other day. 'The programs,' he said. The printer must've been in Revenant because Jim Bob was threating to cut off a percentage of profits if they didn't have them delivered by six a.m. this morning.

I wasn't paying much attention at the time—didn't know that whole program change was about me in that moment, did I? And I was maybe a little preoccupied. Not a good thing to be when you're supposed to be running an elite security team.

God, coming back here has affected me more than I figured. Seeing Lowyn again has put me all out of sorts.

But I'm laser-focused now and I'm gonna have it out with Jim Bob before this day is over. He knew he was gonna do this when he slid that contract across his desk at me. And he deliberately left this part out.

In my world, willfully withholding information counts as a lie. And I only give liars one chance. One. That's it. And little lies, like the one Lowyn told about my bedroom to spare my feelings about how my daddy hates me and thinks of me as trash, that's nowhere near enough to make Lowyn my proper definition of a liar.

That was different.

What Jim Bob did—while not completely unforgivable, this

was my first business dealing with him as an adult after all—is setting a very bad precedent. And unless he does something really spectacular to gain my trust back, I will never make a deal with that man again.

He burned a bridge with me.

When I get to the tiny stone building where Jim Bob Baptist does his government business I barge right in, making the door slam as I enter. But it pops back open again because I slammed it too hard.

Then I stand there in the doorway to check things out before I make a scene.

Ester is type-type-typing away on her keyboard. Doesn't even look up at the commotion. Just keeps goin'. "He's expectin' ya. Go right in."

Expecting me. What a dick.

"And don't you dare leave that door open, Collin Creed. You were not born in a barn."

I kick the door closed and stride across the reception area, entering Jim Bob's office without knockin'.

His considerable body is sitting in his substantial chair with his feet up on the desk like he hasn't got a care in the world. "Have a seat, Collin." He points to one of two chairs in front of his desk with an unlit cigar.

I don't sit. I walk right up to his desk and slap the paper and the program down on the wooden top. "You didn't think to mention this when I signed that fuckin' contract?"

Jim Bob straightens up, puts his feet back on the floor. "See, Collin, I kinda know you a little bit better than you seem to think I do."

"I guess. Since you've been spying on me all these years."

He gets a real serious look on his face. "Son, I am not spying on you. Who do you think got you and Amon those jobs?"

"What?"

"You never asked yourself, 'Why me?' Never once did you wonder how the hell you got so lucky?"

"Lucky?" I almost snort. "*Lucky?* Jim Bob, I spent the last decade killing assholes all over the fuckin' planet. That's not my version of luck. Lucky is winning the lottery. Lucky is gettin' in a motorcycle accident and living to tell about it. Lucky is—"

"I get the point. But you're missing it entirely."

"Please." I laugh. "Enlighten me."

"Boy, do you have any idea what life in the regular Marines would've been like for you? And ask Amon if he feels lucky to have learned how to train military dogs."

"Well, I'm not Amon. And I didn't spend the first two years playing with the world's best dogs. I spent the first two years doing counterintelligence and learning fuckin' secrets I never asked to know about. Secrets so deep and disgusting, I went back to my room that first day and puked up my fuckin' lunch."

"But now you know. And that can't be undone."

"You need to get to the point, Jim Bob. Because you are seriously starting to piss me off. And if you know me even half as well as you seem to think you do, then you should be shaking in your fuckin' boots right now."

"Calm down, Collin. And take a fuckin' seat." He points at the chair again. Still using his unlit cigar.

I sit. But I protest loudly with a sigh as I do this.

Jim Bob leans back in his chair, smiling. "I know you think I didn't tell you everything the other night."

"Think? I don't *think*, Jim Bob. You *didn't* tell me everything. And now you've got some stupid show running about my past that is way too close to my real past, and I don't like it. I don't wanna be a part of it. And I think you should let me out of that contract. If Amon wants to play your game, that's his business. But I'm out." I sit back and fold my arms across my chest to punctuate my point.

"It's just a show, Collin."

"It's a show about *me*! Why me?"

"It's not really about *you*, son." He sighs. "It's about where you've been. And what you did that fateful New Year's Eve night. It's about who you come from, Collin. And how I need that reputation of yours right now."

"Jim Bob. What the *hell* are you talkin' about?" He opens his mouth, but I already know he's about to lie. So I point at him and my words come out low and mean. "Listen. And you listen good. I'm not waitin' no year for my answers. I want to know what the fuck is going on. And before you get all high and mighty and start thinkin' you know me because you know where I've *been*, you had better think hard, Jim Bob Baptist. Because you have no idea at all about what I've been *doing*."

I pause and take a breath. I hate gettin' angry.

"Now," I say, my anger toned down a bit. "Let's hear it. And let's hear it from the beginning."

Jim Bob sighs mightily. "I can't tell you everything." I start to protest, but he puts up a hand. "Calm down. I can't tell you everything, but I can tell you some. Because this part is common knowledge."

"If it's so common, then why don't I know about it?"

"You do know. Some. You know a stranger came into your house on New Year's Eve when you were just a teenager. You know that man was tryin' to kidnap your sister."

"Go on."

"Collin, do you know the difference between a gang and a cartel?"

"What's this got to do with my sister?"

"Do you, or don't you?"

I huff a little bit of air. "A gang is... a group of likeminded people doing likeminded things."

"And a cartel?"

I look him in the eye. Because the pieces are startin' to fall into place. "A cartel is a group of likeminded organizations, not people."

"That's right, Collin. That's exactly right. A group of likeminded organizations. A group such as... a trinity of towns."

"Disciple, Revenant, and Bishop."

"You're a smart boy."

"I'm not a boy, Jim Bob. I haven't been a boy for twelve years now. And now I'm gonna ask you again, and this time I want an answer. What's this got to do with my sister?"

Jim Bob blows out his own breath now. "I'm getting precariously close to the edge here, Collin. I'm at the boundary. But I will tell you this—her kidnapping was a redress."

"A redress?"

"Vengeance? Retribution? All good words, but not technically accurate. Redress really is the proper term. If you're not familiar with the dictionary meaning I suggest you go look it up. Now. What I'm really trying to say here is that there are contracts in place, Collin. Big, important contracts in place. And you only know about some of it."

"What's that mean?"

"The trinity. It means three. Father, Son, Holy Spirit, right? Well, a cross has four points, ya know. Not three."

"What? How did we go from the dictionary meaning of redress to the points on a fuckin' cross?"

"That's all I'm gonna say. There's more. A lot more. But you're not gonna get a single bit of it from me until your year is up." I make to protest, but he keeps going. "I don't care how much you threaten me, I won't give that information up early. You can kill me if you want, this is a thing I will take to the grave."

He stands, looming over me like the considerable man he is. I haven't seen any pictures of him as a young man in a long, long time, but I can pick them out of my memory. He might be big, but Jim Bob Baptist is not soft. And if my memory serves, he was military police when he was in his twenties.

"Why Grimm?" I ask him.

"What?"

"Why Grimm? Last night you said the only people who

know what the contracts are really about are Ester, Joseph, Ruth, Tommy, Able, and Grimm. So why Grimm?"

"Because his granddaddy and I came up together. Just like your granddaddy and I came up together."

"And Ester?"

"Ester knows everything, son. There ain't no way for anything to be happening around here without Ester knowing about it." He shrugs. "But she's my number one. She and I have no secrets."

Huh. I make a connection here. Because Rosie Harlow is Ester's niece or something. There's a generation missing there, maybe even two, but it doesn't matter. "Does Rosie know?"

"She might. But don't bother asking Ester about it, Collin. She will never tell you who she's told."

This answer surprises me. Especially after all his grand-standing a few minutes ago about taking shit to the grave. "What's that mean? I thought you said it was fuckin' secret. Why's she tellin' anyone at all? I mean, shouldn't the answer to my question be 'no'?"

"Son, what good is having a fuckin' secret if you cannot use it? And in order to use it, other people need to know about it. Everyone who knows has told someone else. A secret like this is always more powerful when others know about it."

He's got a point. A big secret *is* dangerous. It can get you killed right quick if you don't know how to preserve it. You have to pass it on. You have to tell someone, it's like insurance. And if I were a bettin' man, I'd put all my chips on Rosie Harlow being Ester's vault.

Rosie comes off as a blabbermouth, but she's got a cunning side to her. I mean, she is the only single mother in the entire fuckin' town. And it's got nothin' to do with people accepting her past mistakes. I haven't been here long, but the only possible reason Rosie's still living inside city limits and taking her profit share is because she refused to leave. She would not be run out like all the others who came before her.

"So who did Grimm tell?"

Jim Bob smiles at me. Like it ain't none of my business. And then he changes the subject. "Who would you tell, Collin? If you had that secret right now?"

My first inclination would be to tell Lowyn. But I would never tell Lowyn. It would put her in too much danger. "Amon."

Jim Bob nods. "Good choice."

"So if we both get this truth at the end of the year, we should each tell someone else?"

"Makes sense."

I kinda scoff here. Some secret this is. "So everybody knows, Jim Bob?"

Jim Bob makes a big ol' shrug with both hands. "Perhaps. But the only people on record knowin' is what counts. You hear me? And there are only seven names on that record, including mine. But just the fact that you're here would be enough for them to guess."

"What the fuck does that mean?"

"We're gonna say 'good day' now, Collin. I'm sorry the Revival story brings back bad memories for you. But they're really not that bad, son. They're really not. Olive is alive and living with your parents. That alone means you won."

He holds out his hand. Which is my signal to get to my feet. So I do that. I don't have to shake his hand. I know this. It's his decision to offer it, but it's my decision whether or not I want to complete the transaction.

Which seems to be fair, I guess. If I put in my time, he will give me the truth.

I accept the truce, gripping his hand hard as I lock eyes with him. "I want you to know that you've burned a bridge with me, Jim Bob." He sighs, but it's a small one. I have not yet let go of his hand. "You tricked me." He shakes his head no. But he's wrong. "If you cared about me, you would not have brought me into this. So I'm gonna have to go ahead and assume you do not care about me, Jim Bob."

Then I end the handshake. Turn around. And walk out.

WHEN I LEAVE **Jim Bob's** little government building my brain is going so fast, I feel like one of those crazy conspiracy theorists like you see on TV shows. The kind with a wall covered with newspaper clippings, and photographs, and red strings goin' this way and that, connecting all the dots together.

Except I'm not that guy. Not yet, anyway. I'm standing in a basement room with windows near the ceiling. A single light hanging from the rafters. Swaying, maybe, throwing shadows. But the walls are empty. Maybe one or two things on there, but that's it. Because I am not at the end of a journey, connecting dots with pieces of red string. I am that crazy man on day one of his quest. Back when he was sane.

Redress. According to the internet there are ten definitions of redress. But the one I home in on is this: Act of correcting an error or a fault or an evil.

I don't know what that evil could be or how it's connected to that night I killed that man for trying to take my little sister. And really, how important could it be? It's been twelve years. If there was some big, important secret out there that needed to be known, wouldn't I know it? Or be suffering some kind of consequence for not knowing it?

It all feels dumb.

I walk back up the hill to the Revival and slip into the security tent where I left Mercy. She's lying down in a corner, not even tied up, paying no attention to anything.

When you tell a dog like that to 'go to bed' that's exactly what they do. That command is no different than 'sit,' or 'stay,' or 'bite.'

No one else is in there, everyone's on duty. And I'm neglecting my post on the north side, but I'm sure Amon has someone over there. Even if it is just a bunch of construction workers.

"Let's go, Mercy."

She gets up, walks over to me, and I snap her lead on. Then we head back on out for patrol.

I FIND **Amon at his post** near the east gate. The children's choir is singing not too far away, so 'Pie Jesu' floats through the air like flowers on the wind as I make my way over there.

He's watching me as I come towards him. Like he knows something just happened. "What's up?"

I let out a breath. "I need to talk to you in private. But not here."

"Whyyyyy?" He draws this word out. And not in a mean or irritated way.

"Because I just learned something that I think you should know about."

Amon lets out a breath. "Why can't we do it right now?"

I consider his request, then settle on this. "We need to SCIF this one."

His eyebrow goes up. "Really."

"Truly."

"Shit, Collin. What'd you get caught up in now?"

"It wasn't me. It's just... we'll talk later at the compound."

"Is Lowyn coming?"

"For sure." Then I walk away with my dog and head for my post. But as I'm walkin' I'm calling Ryan.

He picks up first ring. "What's up?"

"Where are you?"

He's eating something because I hear chewing. "South gate. Right where I'm supposed to be. Why? Where are you?"

"Heading to north gate. I need you to set me up a SCIF for tonight."

"Why?" He's still fuckin' chewing.

"What the hell are you eating? You sound like a cow."

"Funnel cake. Dude, do you know MacyLynn? Is that a real name? She's running the funnel cake tent."

"What? Who cares? I need a SCIF."

"The SCIF is already set up in the bunker. Do you know MacyLynn or not?"

"Uhhh…" I think back. "Kinda. I did, at least. In high school."

"She's fuckin' adorable. I'm gonna hook up with her. She mentioned she's a widow, which makes her sound old, but she doesn't look old to me. Late twenties, I figure."

"Why are you tellin' me this? I don't give a fuck about your love life, Ryan."

"Asshole." Then he ends the call.

Mercy makes a little noise here, like she heard that whole call and she's laughing at me. I look down at my dog and give her a look. "Mind your business, girl."

She answers me with a sneeze.

This is when I notice that people are lookin' at me. And whisperin'. I catch a few words here and there, but don't stop. Just keep walking.

But then, there she is—Rosie fuckin' Harlow off to my left, about ten feet away. She must be a full-time character because apparently she is not needed elsewhere and can just lollygag around, followin' me, most likely, trying to stir up trouble.

She points at me and I brace for it. And then, just before she opens her mouth, she winks. "That's him! That's him! The murderer!"

Another group—all from Disciple and dressed up in dresses much like the ones Lowyn wears—turn and gasp. Spitting out their lines.

"Someone should run him out on a rail."

"I heard he killed a lot more than just one man."

"And he steals too!"

Fuck's sake. "Yes." I direct this word at the nearest group. "I'm the bad guy. So what?" I pan my hands wide and turn a slow circle. "Get a good look, ladies." Then I'm facing the strangers. The guests from out of town. "You like what you see?" A couple of teenage girls giggle. A couple of boyfriends or husbands laugh. "Get a good fuckin' look."

I'm not supposed to swear at the guests—this has always been a rule—but I don't care.

I finish my circle, let out a breath, and Mercy and I go on our way.

But every step I take there is someone whisperin' about me.

Fourth of July. Fourth of July. I repeat this in my head over and over as I make my way to the north gate. When I get there, I find a man fillin' in. He's blond, blue-eyed, and probably early twenties.

He must know who I am because he smiles when I approach, greeting me by name. "Come to take your spot, Collin?"

He's definitely local. I can hear the accent. But he's not a townie, I don't think. He doesn't look familiar. Granted, I've been gone for twelve years, but still, I just don't think he is. "Thank you." I say it plainly. "I appreciate you fillin' in. I had some matters to attend to."

He stretches out his hand. "Siah. Nice to meet you."

I shake his hand. "Siah, as in Josiah?"

"Yeah." He nods. "That's right."

"Are you from Disciple?" He's got a disciple name, that's why I ask.

"Nah. My granddaddy was, though. I'm workin' for you guys now. Amon gave me a job."

"Nice. I'm... glad to have you."

"OK." He's not nervous, exactly, but he's definitely a little jittery. "I'll... uh, I'll see ya around."

Then he takes off, walking straight out of the Revival grounds like he's got somewhere to be.

I make a mental note to ask Amon if we're doin' drug tests on these guys. But as soon as I have that thought I feel like an asshole. Still, you can't ever be too careful.

West Virginia isn't any worse in this respect than most places. Every town has got a drug problem these days. But I find that I am judging the men around here and it's not fair. It's not their fault there's no work. It's just... when a man can't work a job and make a decent living, it's typically the beginning of the end.

We've hired at least hundred people from the area and even though it's not my department, I find I am suddenly interested in what they were all up to before Edge showed up.

I make another mental note. Background checks for everyone.

Just as I have that thought a rumble roars up and a few seconds later, there are bikers everywhere. Revving their engines, yellin' and hollerin'. Doing donuts in the grassy park on the other side of the narrow street, tearin' shit up.

"What the fuck?" Mercy barks once and I look down at her. "Right? Now what the hell is going on?"

She looks up at me, and if she were a human, I swear she'd be shruggin' her shoulders.

I let out a long sigh. I know who they are. They're all wearing cuts—cut-off vests in denim or leather—and they're all wearing colors for Deceivers too.

The MC club in Revenant. Archenemies of Disciple.

Not really. The feud's fake. Just like everything else around here.

Didn't take long to get this party started, I guess.

They keep circling, hootin' up a storm. But then one breaks away and comes towards the gate like he's gonna ride right through it.

I'm currently standing right smack in the middle of the entrance, but I do not move. I shoot him a look like I'm bored.

He's a big guy. Blond beard that covers his neck. Long hair, little bit lighter than the beard, all tied back. All decked out in leather and too many patches on that shit to count.

Now, we might all be in costume—and in Disciple this costume is supposed to be kinda upscale Great Depression, if that was ever a thing. But Revenant and Bishop all have their own costumes. So he's all Keanu Reeves—if he were a Viking— and I'm all Pretty Boy Floyd.

In my opinion, this is a clash of sorts. Two different worlds meetin' in the middle. And it should not be happening.

But this guy is coming towards me like he's on a mission, so I figure… it's gotta be part of the script.

He stops an inch away. His front tire is practically between my legs.

Neither Mercy nor I make any attempt to avoid him.

He grins, wearin' shades. But he lifts them up and I find his eyes to be… I mean… mesmerizing really is the right word.

They are hazel, kinda like mine, actually. With a whole lot of teal blue and golden brown mixed with green. And this is when it hits me—

"Hey, cuz." He bellows out a laugh. "Long time no see, Collin Creed."

I squint my eyes at him. "Lucas? Is that you?"

He guffaws again, nodding.

"Last time I saw you, you were ten."

He points at me. And then squints those eyes and sets his jaw. Puttin' on a show, I realize. Everybody's watching. He growls, real low so no one but me and Mercy can hear him, "No time to catch up though, friend. I'm on the clock. Come by the bar when you get a chance. We got a good band goin'. Drinks are on the house."

The he revs his bike, whoops out a battle cry, backs up and spins around—spittin' gravel out from under his tires—tears up the grass one more time, then leaves with his club the same way he came.

I just stand there, not sure what to do.

I've been to dozens of different countries over the past decade, but I swear on my life, there is no place like the Trinity anywhere else on this earth.

And I gotta admit… I've kinda missed it.

he day goes by spectacularly quick, in my opinion. Probably because every female inside the Disciple city limits—and even a few who live on the other side of that line—feels the need to come by my tent and ask me questions about Collin Creed.

Interesting questions, to say the least.

Taylor Hill comes by first. "Well. Are the two of you gettin' cozy again?" She asks this without preamble or explanation, but of course, she's talking about Collin and I.

"We are, Taylor. We're gettin' along just fine." She's about five years younger than me, so we never did run together or anything. But she was a helper in our souvenir tent once when she was in high school. Pretty much everyone in town has been a helper here over the years.

Well, her question was one of the more discreet ones. Rosie comes by and, unlike Taylor, she has no boundaries. "Did ya sleep with him yet, Low? Please tell me you did. Don't make that man pine for you." She holds up her hands like she's praying to God about my sex life. When I just smile in response, she loses her cool. "Oh, my God. What's he like? It was good, right?"

I don't tell her anything. Luckily some people wander into the tent and save me. One day, though, I probably will. Since Clover moved away to her super-fancy-fancy hotel job I don't really have a best friend. It's been years now. And I like Rosie above and beyond as an employee.

Then there are the almost-strangers who live outside city limits. "Does he have a brother?"

"A best friend?"

"A cousin?"

Anyone in town would know these answers already—no, yes, and yes—even if he has been gone twelve years. There is no brother. Amon is most definitely the best friend. And his cousin is Lucas, one of the more colorful MC members from Revenant.

I heard the rumble of bikes roaring into town earlier. And I knew they were at the north gate because it was in the script, but I bet Collin never read the script so he was probably surprised when Lucas showed up making a scene.

I wonder if Collin even recognized him.

Anyway. That was my day. Females for hours on end, asking about Collin Creed.

He has that effect on people. Amon is certainly the charmer of the two, but Collin has this mystery around him. He's quieter than Amon, does not wear *anything* on his sleeve, and those eyes of his are penetrating when you're his target.

I bite my lip and sigh just thinking about that gaze of his.

And last night was pretty nice.

Tonight, though… I let out a long breath.

Then the bells start tolling and snap me out of it.

"Six o'clock already?" I check my little time-period-appropriate gold watch, and sure enough, it's quittin' time.

There are a few people lingering and it takes about twenty more minutes to wrap things up in the tent, but once I'm done I go outside and close the door behind me, standing on my little porch —which is six steps high and gives me a nice view of the Revival grounds. I look north, but can't quite see the gate from here.

Collin will have to stay at his post until the grounds have

been cleared, so I start heading that way with the lollygagging crowd. I catch little fragments of conversation as we all head towards the exit. Mostly people are talking about the bikers. But a few of them are talking about Collin.

Most of the time people come for the weekend. There are shows on Saturday and Sunday most weekends. But Revenant has the nightlife and Bishop usually has the early mornings and late afternoons. They do all kinds of chore things in the mornings and afternoons over in Bishop, which some people are into, I guess. They draw the crowds for... horse pullin' or something.

Typically, the Revival happens from eleven to noon.

But nothing was all that normal about today.

Of course, once I read the script it all made sense. But they must've had teenagers and twentysomethings out last night spreading the word about the extra Revival meeting this a.m. because there was quite a crowd and opening day is always on Sunday. Not Saturday.

Until this year.

Not until Collin Creed came home. Who is shooing people out the gate as I approach. He winks at me, waving people through. And I watch him do this like he's catching a football or something.

He's got his dog with him. But she just sits right at his left knee. Tongue falling out, eyes bright, happy, I guess. Content to watch.

I lean against a post near the gate. It takes ten more minutes for the all-clear to sound, but I don't mind. Collin is smiling at people. Talking to them. Like he forgot he's the bad guy and everyone's supposed to hate him.

It's after six, though. So the show's over.

Finally, he closes the gate, gives instructions to two men who must be on the night shift, and turns in my direction, tippin' his hat to me. "Sorry. People. They just take their sweet time like we've got nothing better to do in this world but say goodbye."

I walk over to him, wrap my fingers around his lapels, and lean up on my tiptoes.

He kisses me. Nice and long, too. A few people start calling out, but he doesn't stop. Eventually, though, all kisses end. And when he pulls back he says, "Did you have a nice day, Lowyn?"

I let out a breath, look around a little, find Rosie and Taylor off to the side of April Laver's bakery givin' me a thumbs-up, and shake my head.

"No? How could you have a bad day in a place like this?"

I look up at Collin. "Sorry. No. I was shaking my head at the prattle-prates over there."

He looks and finds his little fan club waving at him. Then he shakes his head too. "This place, Low. It hasn't changed a bit, but everything is different. When did the Revenant bikers start harassing people and tearing up grass?"

"Oh, about five years ago, I guess. People love the fuckin' bikers. They can't get enough of them, so it's good for everyone if they come by and tear up the grass every now and then. Keeps the sod farm in business, at any rate."

Collin plays with my hair, smiling down at me. "You wanna come over for dinner?"

"At my house?" I ask, chuckling.

"Oh. No. The compound. I gotta have a little meeting with Amon. I figured you could pick the church while I did that and then we'd have dinner."

"Dinner at the compound?"

"Nash has the nice house. He's throwin' a little party tonight for all the new hires. Which, I have to be honest, is no small thing. But he's into that kind of shit. How about it? Sound fun or…?"

He lets that question hang there for a moment. And I like it. I have to be honest. I like that he's not taking my answer for granted.

"Sure. Sounds like a really good time."

It also sounds like a date.

Collin does feel like my best friend, and it would be very easy to just slip into the past. But that would be a habit and I would prefer that we start something new instead. So I'm glad he's asking me instead of assuming. Even though we're already kinda living together.

At least temporarily.

"Great. Let's go. I can't wait to get out of these fuckin' pants."

I just shake my head. But he takes my hand and that's how we walk home.

Holding hands.

THERE ARE QUITE *a few people* still lingering in town and the highway is backed up at both ends with cars trying to leave— one end leading to Bishop, where people choose to stay the night, the other Revenant, where people choose to party. So this walk home with my high-school boyfriend isn't anything particularly special as far as the scenery goes.

But I feel like I'm floating and I have a weird awareness of... safety. Which makes sense, I guess. Collin does run a security company.

Oh, Lowyn. That's not why you feel safe with him.

No. It's not. Two seconds. That's why I feel safe with Collin Creed.

Soon enough we're at the house. Collin has his key ready and I really have to pause here, at least internally, because this man who has been missing in my life—has been a gaping hole in my life for a dozen years—is now living with me.

Last week we didn't even know if the other was alive.

I want to slow it down. Kind of. Not just to enjoy it, though I do want to enjoy it. I wanna slow it down because it's just going so fast. Not *too* fast, mind you. Just... I don't know. I'm not sure what this feeling is. It's anxiety, maybe. Or something less negative. Like... uneasiness.

Because it's all happening like a dream. Like a movie script or a book. Like it's not real.

And I am desperate for this to be real.

We go inside and Collin drops his keys on the counter like that's where they've been living his entire life. Then he looks at me, smiling. "Do you wanna take a shower with me."

It's not even a question. It's a statement. Not like he's expecting me to say yes, but more like this is just something we do. We shower together. And like he's asked me this question a million times already.

"Sure." And I answer him in the same no-big-deal way. Like I always say yes when he asks to get naked with me. "Come on. The really great bathroom is upstairs." I take his hand and lead him over to the stairs on the far side of the living room.

"That's three, you know."

"What?" I look at him over my shoulder. He's smirking at me. And my God, not only do I feel like I'm in high school again, but this look he's shootin' me reminds me of the boy I once knew.

"The number of times you've invited me up to see your bedroom."

We've reached the stairs and now we're climbing. "You're keeping track, are you?"

"Mmm."

I love my bedroom. I designed every corner, every windowsill, every door, every floorboard—the paint, the curtains, the rugs, the furniture. And it's not retro, either. The color scheme from downstairs has been modified.

As we come around the landing and continue to climb, I take in a breath. Wondering what he will think of it. Wondering if he will even care.

But then there we are, at the top of the stairs. "Wow, Low. This is nice." I step aside so he can walk past me and I can enjoy the way his gaze wanders around, taking it all in.

The walls have been covered in reclaimed shiplap I found in Ohio and painted just the lightest shade of sage green—real name cucumber. And the floorboards and trim are painted an antique white. The floors up here are even more spectacular than the ones downstairs. The wood planks are wide and dark, with many imperfections that just add to the character. The structural beams above us are the same color. I got those out of a barn on a trip to eastern Pennsylvania. The entire attic was removed from the house to expose those beams and they really look nice contrasted against the cucumber shiplap ceiling.

Most of the accents are the same antique white—the sheer curtains over the brand-new floor-to-ceiling windows, the giant rag rug under the bed, and the cushions on the window seats in the dormers. But the other accents are a pewter gray, like the bed, which is king-size and the mattress is nearly four feet off the ground the way antique beds often are, not because I particularly wanted a bed that big, but because I found a hundred-and-fifty-year-old iron bed frame in Kentucky that I just had to have. I stripped every bit of paint off that thing and then brought the old iron back to life with a wire wheel on my drill, polishing it up until the entire thing looked just like those pewter mugs they serve beer in at the Pineapple Pub in historic Bishop. It took almost a year to finish that bed. But it was worth it.

"I don't know why, but I pictured a canopy bed." Collin looks over his shoulder at me, winking.

"Because I had one of those as a girl?"

"Lots of memories up in that room of yours." He grins, pausing for a moment, maybe to relive a particularly favorite memory. We never did have sex in my girlhood room or nothing like that, but we did spend time in there, just hanging out, listening to vinyl records and doing homework. "But this really is special, Low." I like the way he calls me Low. He turns to face me. "It feels like home."

Then he's coming towards me. And a moment later, his hands are on my hips and he's kissing me. His fingertips bunching up the fabric of my dress until he's got it up to my waist. I hold in a breath and look right into his mesmerizing eyes, like I'm caught in a trap, and then the dress is coming over my head and the next thing I know, I'm standing there in my stockings, and garters, and underwear.

Collin lets out a long breath. "I could stand here and look at you for years, Lowyn McBride, and still never see all the ways in which you are perfect."

My God, this man and his words. "Well," I say, "I could say the same." And then I've got my fingertips underneath his suspenders and I'm sliding them down his arms. He holds his breath, I think, his head slightly tipped down as he watches me do this. Then he looks up, smile gone. Hunger in his eyes.

I stare at him, almost unable to breathe, as I take my fingertips to his shirt buttons. And one by one, I undo them and spread the shirt wide open. He's wearing an undershirt underneath, as one does when they are in costume. But I find that this is a detail I like. One that is missed on modern men.

I slide the shirt down his arms and let it drop to the floor. "I like this look."

"The sleeveless undershirt?" Collin chuckles. "I had forgotten how many fuckin' layers of clothing the costumes have."

"But it's nice though, right? I mean, if I wasn't in costume, I would not be wearing stockings and garters, would I?"

"You've got a point there, peaches."

And this makes me grin. "God, I've missed you. I'm so glad you're home. Have I told you that yet?"

He reaches up to put a hand on my face, his thumb caressing a line along my cheek. "I think it goes without saying at this point. But I will go on record here and reciprocate that sentiment right back at you. I am so happy to be home, Lowyn. And you're the reason why."

He reaches around my back and a moment later, my bra is loose. I just stand there and let him slide the straps down my arms the same way I did his suspenders. And then that bra is dropping to the floor.

I stand there and let him look. I let him get a real long, good look. And when his eyes come back up to meet him, he's not just hungry, he's starvin'.

He presses himself up to me, both hands on my face, and kisses me like it's our first kiss ever. Only better. Because there is nothing awkward about this kiss. There is no hesitation. Not from me, not from him. Our bodies press together, my breasts sensitive to the feel of the ribbed cotton of his undershirt. And then he's taking my hair down. Pins drop to the floor with a small *ting*. And then the whole thing comes apart.

I think we both come apart with that hair. Because he's taken his kisses to my neck, and this has always been a weak spot for me, so a little moan escapes my mouth.

His hips press up against me, letting me know he's hard. And then there's a clink of his belt, and my fingers cannot get those fly buttons open fast enough. When I take him in my hand and squeeze, he moans back. Biting my shoulder.

I lean into him, breathing heavy and kinda stunned. Because I don't recall ever being as turned on with a man—not even him—as I am now.

Collin turns me around as I'm having these thoughts and then he's walking me backwards to the bed. The backs of my thighs hit the mattress and I begin to fall back, but I should know better. Collin won't let me fall. He *doesn't* let me fall. His large hands—both of them—are around my waist, fingertips right at the small of my back, thumbs gripping my hipbones, and I am lowered down by his strong grip.

A moment later he's kneeling in front of me. His teeth grazing up my thigh. And I've got my fingers threaded through his hair.

"Holy Mother, Low. I just wanna fuck you." I open my eyes and look at him, a little bit surprised, because he's never talked to me that way before. "Sorry." He shrugs. "Slipped out."

"Well, don't stop on my account. Let it slip all it wants."

He grins at me, those eyes of his a little bit wild now. And I realize something in this moment. What we did last night was kind of a remnant of the past. Us, as teenagers.

But what we're doing right now is something else entirely. Us, as adults.

Is he thinking the same thing?

Undoubtedly. Because what I just said was something along the lines of permission.

He drops his head between my legs and then he's licking me through my panties, his tongue skimming along the thin, silky fabric. My back comes up right off the bed, arching from the sensation. Gripping his hair tight now, because I'm about to come undone the same way my hair did. And it's not gonna take much to push me through to the other side.

I don't want it to stop yet. So I suck in a breath and grip his head with both hands, stilling him. "I'm gonna ruin this good time if you keep going like that."

"Ruin it?" He chuckles, blowing a breath right up against my sweet spot.

I hiss and squirm. But he's got his hands on my hips, holding me steady. His tongue still working between my legs. I'm biting my lip, and clawing at his shoulders, and moaning, and protesting, and writhing.

But he keeps going.

And then things are coming out of my mouth that I've

never said before. "Yes. Oh, my God. Lick me, Collin. Yes, yes, yes... right there. Lick me right there."

I'm coming—my body shaking, legs trembling, head thrown back, mouth open and moaning—just as he slips my panties aside and pushes a finger inside me. Then I'm absolutely losing my shit. It's like... I don't even know what it's like. I've never experienced a climax like this before in my life. It's wave after wave and I can't even contain the groans and whimpers slipping past my lips.

Collin pulls back and I open my eyes just in time to see him lick his lips. Then he pushes my legs closed and rips my panties down my legs. He grins as he pushes my legs open and I'm still feeling the waves of pleasure from the climax. Yet I am ready for him again.

He stands up, his dick long and hard falling out of his pants. I'm instantly drawn to the motion of his hand as he jerks himself off. All the while his eyes are locked on mine.

Taking a step forward, he reaches for me, grabbing me behind the knees and pulling me towards him until my knees are gripping his hips.

Collin smiles a wicked smile—one that is also very alluring and sexy at the same time—and then he leans forward and slides his hands up my stomach until they are gripping my breasts. A moment later his mouth is over a nipple, teasing it with his teeth. Nipping it, then soothing it with his tongue.

At the same time, he's right up against my entrance and even though I just came seconds ago, when he pushes inside me, I'm nearly ready to explode again.

He's hard, and thick, and I have a moment to think about how he's stretching me, and how good it feels, and then... I just do it again.

Bucking, and arching, and moaning, and begging. Oh, my God, I'm begging. "More, Collin. *More*. Go deeper."

"You don't need to tell me twice." Collin growls this out, his voice all husky and filled with desire. And then he's thrusting up inside me. Once. Twice. And then we're just fucking. His hips going faster as I lift mine up and back, keeping up with the new rhythm. He's biting my neck, and squeezing my breasts, and I'm coming again.

It's all a blur after that. Wave after wave of explosion. Like I've never had sex before in my life. Like I'm starving, and thirsty, and he's a sweet piece of fruit and a cool drink of water at the same time.

It ends, eventually. And then next thing I know, he's got his arms wrapped around me, his face pressed into my neck, and we're lying together on top of the covers, breathing hard and heavy.

But he's not still. His hands are wandering. Caressing my thigh and hip.

I could go again.

I could go all night with this man. And I'm just about to ask him what he thinks about that when his phone buzzes.

"Shit." He sits up in bed, fishing around in his pocket because he's still got his fuckin' pants on. "Yeah." He answers the phone. "Yeah, yeah. We're on our way. Be there in like thirty." He ends the call and lies back down, reaching for me. "Amon. He and I have a meeting tonight. I wanna say no. I wanna stay here with you, but it's business I need to talk out with him. So…"

I sigh. "Well, I was just about to ask you if you'd like to fuck me all night. But it's fine. Let's get you to your meeting."

I make to get up, but he grabs me, pulling me back down and laughing. "Lowyn, I'm gonna give you a three-hour reprieve. But if you think I won't be fucking you all night when we get back here later, you're out of your damn mind."

He squeezes me, ticklin' me a little. And I giggle like a fuckin' girl. But it's good. And… yeah. I could fall right into this. Right back into him.

And I think I will.

COLLIN

I think about the shower Lowyn and I took the whole drive back to the compound. I told Amon thirty minutes, so we didn't have time to do much more than soap each other up and wash each other's hair, but it was enough.

More than enough.

The thing that stands out, though, is how comfortable it feels. We never did this kind of shit as kids. Kissing, a little fooling around with my hand up her shirt. Her hand in my pants. That one time up in the hills in the tent. It was truly teenager stuff. There was no showering together. No getting naked in front of each other. No oral, either.

But everything about us being together right now feels like that. Like no time has passed. Like high school is just right behind us. Like everything is the way it should be.

And it's just weird how two people who didn't even part on good terms can fall back into a life together so easily, even though the life we're fallin' into didn't even exist until now.

There are a lot of romantic notions wrapped up in these thoughts. Something about soulmates, maybe.

When I glance over at Lowyn, shadows dancing across her face from passing under the occasional street light, I find her looking at me. "What? What's on your mind, Low?"

"You. There's nothing on my mind but you right now, Collin Creed."

I smirk at this. "You're thinking about tonight, aren't you? You're thinkin'..." She's already giggling. "You're thinking... 'How in the world am I gonna last three hours without his mouth between my legs?'"

She huffs out a breath. "I swear to God, I had no idea you were a dirty talker in bed, Collin."

I grin, then wink at her. "This is OK with you? Or shall I be poetic or somethin' instead?"

"Nothing wrong with both."

Now *I'm* practically giggling. "Is that the only note you have for me? Your request list is dirty poetry. Is there anything else I can improve upon?"

She hums a little. Which, I'm not gonna lie, comes out pretty fucking sexy. Enough to have me wishing I didn't ask for this stupid SCIF meeting with Amon. "Well, I have to be honest here, Collin. I wasn't aware you wanted notes when we got started earlier, so I wasn't in a takin'-them frame of mind. But I tell you what. Next time I will pay closer attention and then we can discuss it when it's over, how's that?"

"Peaches." I say this with a dead serious face and voice. "If you give me notes on what I can do better, I swear to the fuckin' Mother, I will go above and beyond."

She's biting her lip when I look over, but she's grinning too.

"Am I scaring you?"

Lowyn slowly shakes her head. "You wish, Collin Creed. You wish."

"That feels like a challenge."

Her eyes are all squinty, she's smilin' so big. "You can take it any way you want."

And so I do. So I do.

WHEN WE PULL **in to the compound** it's already almost eight o'clock. Earlier I was thinking we'd get here right after shutdown, I'd have my little meeting, we'd grab some barbecue, and we'd be home pretty early. Long before the party Ryan, Nash, and Amon are throwing for the new hires really got started.

But the sex kinda threw that timeframe to the wayside and now we're arriving in the thick of it.

"What the hell is going on here?" Lowyn is turning around in her seat trying to take it all in.

"The new hires. They're gettin' the welcome treatment."

"Did you hire every unemployed man in the state of West Virginia or what? There are hundreds of people here."

She's right. Every time I come to this place we seem to have more and more people on the fuckin' payroll. "All of West Virginia and parts of Ohio too, by the looks of it."

It's a slow crawl to get past everyone and up to Nash's house, which is the first one you come to when you pull in, so getting to my house—not that there's any reason to go there— would be nearly impossible. But I manage it and pull my Jeep right up to Nash's front porch.

Lowyn laughs at this. "You never did care much for driveways and parking lots."

I turn the engine off and shake my head. "Don't see much point when there's empty spaces everywhere. But I will not park on your lawn, Low." I take her hand and kiss it. "Don't worry."

We get out and make our way up the porch stairs and into Nash's house. I see Amon first. He's got a beer in his hand and he's talking to a group of men, a couple of whom I saw today working the Revival. Not Lowyn's teenagers, other guys. A little bit older.

I catch Amon's eye and nod at him. So he excuses himself and comes over.

"Hey, Low." He pokes Lowyn in the ribs, making her squirm. "Lookin' good, peaches." Then he winks at her.

Lowyn grins at Amon nearly the same way she grins at me. "Why, hello there, Amon. This is a nice place you got here."

"Isn't it?" Amon looks at me. "It's home now, huh? Even though you're not even living here."

"It's hard to live in a house with no windows, Amon."

"For sure. That's why the windows are missin' in the first place, Collin." Then he looks at Lowyn. "You can thank me later, peaches."

Lowyn laughs. Shakes her head a little.

"All right." I blow out a breath. "Where's Nash and Ryan? I need someone to keep Lowyn company while we talk."

"The SCIF is in the bunker," Amon says. "And you made me save all that junk for Lowyn to pick through, so she can just come with us and do that while we're downstairs. No one will bother her in the church. It's all been reinforced. We just finished it up this afternoon."

"How about it?" I ask Low. "You wanna pick through junk while we have our meeting?"

"Pick through your junk, Collin?" She raises an eyebrow, then laughs. "Yes. That sounds perfect."

We walk back outside and Amon is amused. "You two seem to have picked up right where you left off."

I take Lowyn's hand as we head for the church and silently agree. We sure did.

We stop at the front door—which, just a few days ago, was made of wood and there were two of them. A nice, churchy double door. But now there is just one and it's made of solid steel, making the front side look more like a bank vault than a house of God.

"I'll give you the code to the door downstairs, Col." Amon is punching in his code as he says this.

"This is some door you've got. Are those shutters over the windows?" Lowyn is craning her neck to see around the porch.

"Stained glass on the inside, solid steel on the out." And with this statement, Amon opens the door. "After you."

He waves us through, so we enter. Then he closes and locks the door behind us.

We get about ten paces in—past the leftover, broken-up statues in the inside vestibule—and enter the nave.

"Wow." Lowyn is looking around. "This is really nice, you guys. Are all these pews original?" Then she's looking down at her feet. "Slate floors, my God. They're incredible."

"She's gonna be just fine in here, I think," Amon says.

"You gonna be fine, Low? It'll only take about fifteen minutes, I think."

She's already let go of my hand and has started walking towards the nearest pew. They are all crowded with junk for her to pick through. "Better than fine, boys." She waves us off. "Go do your thing. I'll be right here when you get back."

I follow Amon down the middle aisle of the church, then into the back, where we find the stairs that lead to the bunker. "There's a brand-new door down here too," Amon says.

And even though I can recall two small windows on the way down the last time I was here, there are no windows now. Just bricks. "Shit, you guys have been busy since I've been gone."

"Feelin' guilty for slackin' off?"

"Not a bit."

Amon laughs. "Nor should you." He stops at the new stainless-steel door and looks over his shoulder at me. "I told you when we started putting this together last year, I'm gonna handle it. You do your thing, Ryan, Nash, and I will take care of the rest. How'd you like Mercy?"

"The dog? Yeah. She's no trouble. She did her thing without comment. Well, she did shoot me a look once."

Amon is smilin' as I talk about his dog. "What kind of look? Rolling her eyes kinda look?"

"Maybe more like... 'Yes, sir.' But with a mocking tone behind it."

His whole face lights up when you talk dogs with Amon. And his eyes get all excited. "Yup," he says. "That sounds like Mercy." Then he opens a black box sitting on a table just next to the door. "Put your phone in there."

He drops his in, I drop mine in, and he closes the lid.

Then Amon opens the door, waves me though, closes it, and turns to me. "The whole room is secure. You say whatever you want in here, Collin. You know we don't have permission for this, and it's never gonna be accredited, but Ryan did it right. No one's gonna hear nothin'. I'd stake my life on that."

A SCIF is a room you use when you absolutely want to make sure no one else will ever know you said a thing. It's built special with electromagnetic shielding. What's said in the SCIF stays in the SCIF. Unless someone blabs, that's it. But neither of us will be blabbing about nothin'. And maybe what Jim Bob told me earlier doesn't exactly warrant this kind of security, but then again, maybe it does. And it's always better to be safe than sorry.

"I trust ya. And anyway, this isn't that big of a deal. I just need to tell someone something, and you're my someone."

Amon shoots a finger at me. "Got it, Sarge. Let's hear it."

"Don't call me Sarge. Not in here, not out there."

"Sorry. Habit."

"And that's Master Sergeant to you, soldier."

"Well, excuse the fuck outta me, *Master Sergeant*." He salutes me and clicks his fuckin' heels, eyes going serious as he stares off in the distance.

"Shut the fuck up."

Amon relaxes and punches me. "All right. What's up?"

So I tell him all about my little meeting with Jim Bob this morning. The little bits and pieces I was given, anyway.

"Well, of course I knew he was holding out, ya know," Amon says. "I knew there was something about your sister in the whole you'll-learn-the-truth-at-the-end-of-your-contract bullshit. But what it all means?" He scoffs. "I don't know. And that shit about the cross having four points? What the hell? Is it code? Is he talkin' in some code?"

"I don't know, Amon. But it's weird, right?"

"Agreed. It's weird. But..." He pauses to think a little. "In the grand scheme of things, is it any weirder than everything else around here?"

I blow out a breath and huff. "Well, someone tried to kidnap my sister and I blew his head off over it, so I would not exactly call that *normal* weird."

Amon looks past me for a moment, like he's thinking about something. Then his blue eyes lock with mine. "I've thought about that, ya know. How that guy came into your house and grabbed your sister like that. And I've got four little sisters myself. So back then I would think... what would I have done? And ya know what, Collin? It would've ended the exact same way. Even if he did put his hands up. Fuck. *No.* No one gets to come into my house and touch my sisters. I don't know if you did the right thing, but it doesn't even matter. People wanna fuck around and find out? Good. Let them. This is what happens when they step over the line. And now everyone around here knows exactly where they stand with you."

Amon and I have never talked about this before. We weren't really friends when he and I ended up in the Marine recruiting office in Charleston together. We were just neighbors trying to get the fuck out of this place as quickly and efficiently as we could. Of course, he knew what I'd done, but he never asked me about it and I never offered it up.

Murdering a man in cold blood felt like a really important thing about myself back then. Like a defining thing. But now? It's just one among many things that have defined me over the years. So there's been no real reason to rehash that shit.

Until now, I guess.

"Redress," I say. "That's what Jim Bob called it. Something

about redress, and he told me to look it up in the dictionary. So I looked it up. Figured he wouldn't have said that unless he wanted me to understand the details. And it came up as the correcting of an error, or a fault, or an evil. Which I don't much like the sound of, ya know?"

"Yeah. Anything with 'evil' in it has got to be... evil."

"Not just that, but what I wanna know is, am I the one correctin' an evil? Or the one being corrected?"

Amon doesn't answer right away. Just blows out a breath. But when he does answer, he's switched the subject, avoiding that last question completely. "The fourth point on the cross. It's gotta mean there's, obviously, another entity involved. Who could it be?"

I shrug. "I got that feeling too. But it came off like a feud, or something. There's definitely someone else involved in all this business. And whatever agreement Jim Bob has hammered out with them, whoever 'they' are, it's tenuous. That was my major takeaway. Everything they've got set up around here looks really solid but at the same time, it feels kinda fragile."

Amon huffs a little air. "Agreed. But we both lived here for eighteen damn years and never once did I ever hear anything about a feud. Do you think it's got something to do with Revenant?"

"Why do you say that?"

"It's... you know, Revenant."

"Yeah, but... it's fake. Just like the Revival. We're not really feudin' with Revenant, Amon."

"Maybe we are and we just don't know it?"

"I don't think so. Jim Bob was swearin' up a storm at some printer over there because the new program you were so fuckin' happy about this morning might not have been printed on time. I heard him yelling about this yesterday. So he's not afraid of no one in Revenant. Plus, I got family over there. I saw Lucas today."

"Fuck. Little Lucas. I haven't seen that boy in... well"—Amon laughs—"twelve years."

"He's not little anymore. I think he's actually running the MC."

"No shit?" Amon pauses to consider this. "That's quite a role. How old is he?"

"Twenty-two, twenty-three? Somewhere around there. 'Bout the same age as Olive, I think. Maybe a year older, I guess."

"Hmm."

"He invited me to come by the bar. Said the drinks are free."

"Well, it's a good place to start, don't you think? We should take him up on that. Let's make a date. How about Monday?"

I nod at Amon. "Sounds good. Not like I've got anything else to do during the week. We've got jobs lined up. Just waiting for the construction to be done and the people to show up on my end now."

Amon's nodding back. "But you want me to go with you, though, right?"

"For sure."

"OK." He blows out a breath. "It's a date. We done?"

"One more thing, since we're here. How did you screen the guys we've hired?"

Amon narrows his eyes at me. "Whyyyyy?" He drawls that word out. His accent has gotten a lot thicker since we came home.

But so has mine. "I dunno. I just got a feeling about that guy you sent to watch the north gate for me."

"What guy?"

Now it's my turn to narrow my eyes at him. "What do you mean 'what guy?' The one who was standin' at the gate when I got there after my meeting with Jim Bob."

"When was this?"

"Fuck's sake, Amon. You saw me in Lowyn's tent during the

Revival. And then I came up to you after my meeting and that's when I told you I needed to talk to you in a SCIF."

"Yeah. But I didn't assign anyone to take your place at the north gate."

I blow out a breath. "He said his name was Siah. Josiah."

"Disciple boy?"

"No. He said not. But his granddaddy was or something."

"What'd he look like?"

I shrug. "Kinda like Lucas, actually. Same age, same build—no tattoos that I could see. Blond hair, blue eyes. He knew who I was. Said..." I pause here to think back. "Something like... 'You come to take your place, Collin?' Something like that when I walked up. Then he just... left. Came off as nervous."

Amon stares off in the distance for a moment. "Yeah. OK. I think I know who he is, and I did hire him, but I didn't put him at your gate. He should've been back at the compound. Maybe Ryan or Nash sent him up? I'll ask. And yes, I did background checks on everyone. Penny Rider did them for me."

"Penny from DC?" My eyebrows go up.

"Yeah. Why?"

"Do you think it's a good idea to use DC people for this?"

"It's Penny. She's like... seventy years old. And besides, she likes me. She did them all for free. I sent her a spreadsheet, she ran it through her big fancy computer program, and two hours later I had my answers."

"Did you drug-test them?"

"What is *up*, Collin?"

"I'm just asking. This Siah guy, I just got a feeling about him. He came off as jittery."

"You think he's on... what? Meth, or something?"

"I don't know if he's on meth, I'm asking you if he's on meth."

Amon lets out a long breath. "I didn't do drug tests. Everybody's testing positive these days, Collin. You know that. They all got a medical marijuana card."

I'm shaking my head as soon as he starts talking. "Amon—"

But he puts up a hand. "I know. I feel the same way. But I needed a hundred and fifty men. I want this shit done fast and there's no good reason to drag it out in phases like we first planned. We've got the money, Collin. We don't have to concern ourselves with a budget. Get it done, get it over with. And if I had drug-tested every single man I hired, we'd have twenty guys, if that."

"I don't want these guys around. I don't like this. There are way too many locals here, Amon. This is an operation, for fuck's sake. Not a fuckin' employment office for every goddamned jobless man in West Virginia."

"Calm down. That's why I did it this way. They're gonna be gone in like three weeks."

"Three weeks? You told me two."

"Two weeks is a meme, Collin." He winks at me, but then goes serious. "Shit is getting done. I'm telling you, moving up the timeline makes this worth the risk. I'll keep my eyes on this Siah guy. And I'll talk to him. OK? He's not gonna bother nothing. And in three weeks most of them will be moving on. In five weeks the other men will be here and it'll all be cool."

"I hate fuckin' construction."

Amon chuckles. "Why the hell do you think I put you over there with Lowyn?" He slaps me on the back. "You're welcome, by the way." He gets up. "We done now for real?"

"We're done. Just… keep your eyes and ears open. See if we can start to figure this shit out without Jim Bob's help. Because I don't feel like waitin' no year for the truth."

"Will do, Sarge." Then he salutes, but grins like a fool at the same time, cooling me down before I can yell at him.

WHEN WE COME BACK UP into the church Lowyn is dragging a huge mirror across the floor, using an old wool blanket to scoot it along the slate floor. She blows out a breath when she sees us, then smiles and points to her treasure. "Look at this. Will you look at this? I love it. Do you think it'll fit in the Jeep, Collin? I want to take it tonight. I know I won't be able to start strippin' it until Monday, but we're here and we might as well, ya know?"

That's when I spy a whole pile of junk propped up near the door. "Woman, we've been gone ten minutes. How'd you get a pile of shit that big in ten minutes?"

"Shit? Collin Creed! I'll have you know I found a Hitchcock chair. They are fancy-fancy. I think there might be another one around here somewhere. People usually got them in pairs." She looks around the church, like this chair is hiding behind a pew or something. "And this mirror? Not famous or nothing. Which is why I'm gonna strip it and paint it. But just look at this thing." She sighs, lookin' up at it. "Isn't it glorious?"

It is a big-ass mirror, that's for sure. Probably seven feet tall and three feet wide. "There is no way that's gonna fit in the Jeep."

Lowyn lets out a disappointed breath and I feel sorry about that. I brought my bad mood up from the bunker with me and now it's ruining hers. "We'll pick it up tomorrow, Low. We'll get your truck and trailer and load it as soon as we can get away from the Revival. OK?"

This makes her smile. Which makes me smile.

"Look at the two of you," Amon says. "Long-lost lovers, finally reunited."

I roll my eyes at Amon as I walk over to Lowyn and start tugging the mirror across the floor. We take it over to her pile and prop it up against the wall and I offer her my hand. "Let's eat. I'm fuckin' starving."

. . .

*OVER AT NASH'S **house*** the party is in full swing. I just want to go home, but if we leave now, we'll have to pick up food from somewhere. And that's a waste. The barbecue is good, there's lots of beer, and as soon as I get a few of those in me, my mood improves.

But three hours later, I'm also a little too drunk to drive home.

"Give me your keys." Lowyn is holding out her hand. She didn't drink. Not even a single beer.

"Are you the DD?" I wink at her. "Gonna take care of me tonight?"

She nods, trying to hide a smile. "I don't know what you and Amon talked about down there in your secret room, but when you came up you looked like you needed a drink, Collin Creed. And that's all good. But you're not driving home."

I hand her the keys and get in the passenger side. "I'm not that drunk. I'm just in a happy place."

She starts the Jeep, pats my leg, then backs up and we're heading home.

Home.

It's literally home. And all the way there I think about that. How Lowyn McBride is the reason I still have a home in Disciple. And my room is still there.

I look over at Lowyn. She's focusing on the curvy bit of road that leads into the Disciple river valley. Her face is lit up by the dashboard lights, a fingernail tapping the leather steering wheel. "Why are you staring at me, Collin?"

"You're pretty."

She smiles. "I think you might be drunker than you realize."

"I don't get drunk."

"OK." She laughs.

"I've missed you. I mean... I didn't really know I missed you until I came home and saw you in that bar in Bishop."

"Of course you had to go there. Right to the night when I was drunk and you had to drive me home." She chances a look at me, but it's just a quick one. Her eyes go back to the road because she's responsible like that.

"I'm gonna marry you, Lowyn McBride."

She huffs. "Is that so?"

"Yup. I'm gonna ask you to marry me in some spectacular way. And you're gonna say yes. And we're gonna do that in front of everyone. The whole fuckin' town. And then I'm gonna take you somewhere. Somewhere nice. Like... like... I dunno. I'll think of a place. Somewhere you've never been. Never heard of, even. And we'll get a nice room with pretty things in it, and I'll fuck the living shit out of you on that bed."

She starts laughing.

"What's so funny?"

"You. That's all. First you're all dirty-talking me during sex and now you're all dirty-talking me on the drive home."

"Shit." I let out a sigh and look out my window. "This ain't nothing."

"Hmm."

"What's that 'hmm' for?"

"Your promises are intriguing."

I smile. Grin, actually. Like a drunk-ass fool. But she's intrigued.

I leave it there, staying silent for the rest of the ride home.

WHEN WE GET THERE, and get inside, I realize I do kinda feel buzzed. Not proper drunk, but definitely buzzed. And I'm still running Lowyn's words through my head as she and I go upstairs like we're some kind of couple and this is normal. Like we do this every night. We go out with friends, and come home, and go upstairs, and get in bed, and I get to touch her all over before we fall asleep together. And then wake up and do it all again.

She flicks the light on and her beautiful bedroom appears. The covers on her bed are all a mess, but it doesn't matter because we're gonna be under them any minute now. She stops in the middle of the room and turns to me, reaching for my leather jacket, sliding it down my arms. It's heavy and the zippers jingle a little as she takes it over to a chair that sits in front of a vanity and drapes it over the back.

She's wearing jeans, a tight-fitting t-shirt, and an oversized flannel as a jacket. She takes the flannel off, drapes it over my jacket, and then sits down on a bench at the end of her bed. Smiling up at me as she takes off her boots.

I don't even move. I just stand there and watch.

When she's done she gets up, comes over to me, and starts taking my shirt off.

I hold my breath until it comes up over my head and she's tossing it on the floor.

Then she looks at me. Like *really* fuckin' looks at me, her eyes taking in my chest. When they slide up my body and meet my eyes, I take a step forward—because that's all the distance there is between us—and then I'm pulling her shirt up too. But I don't take it off. I just hike it up to her neck and start fondling her breasts through her bra, never breaking eye contact.

"Intriguing, huh?"

"What?" She's a little bit breathless.

"You said… 'Your promises are intriguing.'"

She presses her lips together and nods. "To say the least."

I let go of one breast so I can reach up and touch her face. "Which part intrigues you?"

"Hmm." She hums this out in a sexy way. "All of it, I guess. I don't know you as a man, Collin. I knew you as a boy. So..." She shrugs her shoulders up. "I'm intrigued, is all."

I reach down and pop the button on her jeans. She closes her eyes for a second, sucking in a breath of air, but opens them quickly.

"You don't have to look me in the eyes if you don't want to, Lowyn."

I watch as she processes this statement, not quite sure what she thinks of it. But her answer is good enough for me. "I want to. I love those eyes of yours."

I push one side of her jeans down over a hip and stop. Staring at her.

She huffs a little. "Do you want me to help you?"

I shake my head. "No. I just want you to stand here while I figure out the most intriguing way to take off your clothes."

"Couldn't we just... you know, do it real quick?"

"What's the point of that?"

She smiles big now. "OK." She licks her lips. "I think I might be getting an idea of where this is going."

Now it's my turn to smile. "I really don't think you do." Then I kneel down and start kissing her stomach. My hands on her hips now. Gripping her tight and holding her close.

Immediately her hands are on my head, fingertips threaded into my hair, her breathing quickening and starting to get ragged. I grip the waistband of her jeans with both hands and tug them down to her knees. But that's where I stop.

She huffs again. "You're trying to make this painful?"

I laugh a little, still kissing her stomach. But she's on the right track now. Not painful. Not at all painful. Not in the literal way. I pull back a little and look up. She's got her teeth together but her lips are parted, like I caught her sucking in a breath of air. She lets that breath out, just staring down at me.

"Anticipation, Lowyn. It's not painful, it's just anticipation."

"Hmm. That's... also very intriguing."

"Do you want me to touch you?"

"Oh, man. You're gonna tease me, aren't you?"

"Only if you want me to. Should I tease you, Lowyn?"

She thinks about this because she understands that I'm asking her a real question and her answer is gonna dictate what happens next.

If she says no, I won't. I'll start right in and in a few seconds, I'll have a finger inside her and a few minutes later she'll be coming all over it. After that she can do me, or we can fuck, and then we'll go to bed all snuggled up and cozy.

It's a nice option A. I won't mind in the least if she chooses option A.

But if she says yes... well, that's option B.

And that's when she learns my definition of 'intriguing.'

LOWYN

OK. *He's got me*. I knew there was more to Collin Creed than the man he was showing me this past week. I could sense it. I mean, how does a teenage boy kill someone, disappear for twelve years, and then show back up as the same person he was when he left?

That's not how it works. And I knew this.

Should I be afraid of his truth? Of what he's been up to all these years?

Probably. Not in the strictest sense of the word, but I'm almost a hundred percent sure that I don't want to know what he's been up to.

And if he was simply… I dunno, shopping for a gun, or talking about his business, or reliving old times with Amon about the military—or whatever it was they were in—I'd gladly walk away from that and just let him do his thing.

But this isn't about him, it's about us.

And not in the old us kind of way, either. This is about the new us. Grown-up us. It's about how we're going to be intimate with each other, and that? Yes. That I want to know.

He wants to tease me. I'm not even sure what that means. But I do understand what it doesn't mean. We will not be getting naked and jumping into bed. This is not a direct route to an orgasm.

It's a long and winding road to something that I can only describe as worth the wait.

He's on his knees with his mouth practically on my stomach, lookin' up at me with those eyes of his. Waiting, patiently, for my answer. My jeans are stuck around my hips, his hands are holding my thighs, and I'm already tingling inside and we haven't even gotten started.

So I say, "Yes. I would like you to tease me, Collin."

And this makes him smile all the way up to his eyes. He tugs my jeans down to my knees and places his mouth on my stomach—still looking at me. Then he begins to drag his tongue down between my legs.

I still have my hands in his hair. And I'm caught in whatever spell this is because I cannot stop watching him. I cannot help but imagine what it's gonna feel like when his tongue runs out of stomach, which it does pretty quick. He angles his head up so his chin is right between my legs. Touching me right where I want to be touched.

But then he stops and goes still.

I close my eyes and let out a breath. Willing him to keep going.

He doesn't. He's not going to. This is his game and he's gonna make me play it.

Or… say 'No, thank you,' I guess.

"You know what to do next, Lowyn. So do it."

Again, I don't know him. I think I do because he feels so familiar. But it's an illusion. Something held on to from long-ago days.

It could take weeks, or months, or, hell, even years to tease out the real Collin. He's got his guard down tonight, though. He had a stressful day and then had a couple too many to drink. And that's probably why he's giving me something real like this.

And I don't want to wait weeks, or months, or years. I don't even want to wait hours. I want a crash course in him right now. So I angle my hips forward until I can feel the pressure of his chin. I bite my lip, wondering if I'm really gonna do this. Am I really gonna grind against his face and get myself off? Because that's what he's set up here. That's what he wants me to do.

"Come on, Low." He's encouraging me now. Maybe thinking I might lose my nerve.

And maybe I might. So I like his encouragement. Because I do want to keep going.

So I move my hips again.

"Yeah. Like that, Low. You got it." And this time, when he talks, he adds a little bit of pressure to my motion—pushing forward and driving me wild.

I'm breathing fast now. Biting my lip and closing my eyes, getting excited just thinking about what's happening in my bedroom. There's a really big part of me that wants to stop this. But that's because it's kind of embarrassing. Not because I don't want to follow through.

And I don't like making decisions just based on emotion. Though I'm not sure my argument holds, seeing as my payout here is nothing but emotion.

Still, I grip his hair tighter and continue to move my hips. The tender skin of my inner thighs sensitive to the scratchiness of his unshaven jaw.

Collin reaches up with his hands and begins to fondle my breasts and when I open my eyes and look down at him he's staring back at me with the most intense look I've ever seen. Not just on him, but any man.

I'm so close. It won't take much. And it's like he's reading my mind because one hand slips down my stomach and thumb is right between my legs. Putting just a little bit more pressure where I've already got plenty.

I last about five more seconds and then I thrust forward and my whole body goes stiff as the climax flutters through my body in waves.

Collin stands up, his fingers still between my legs, pushing me back onto the bed. But he doesn't ease me back onto the mattress this time, he turns me around, places his hand between my shoulder blades, and presses me forward.

"Stretch out your arms, Lowyn. Stretch them out on the bed in front of you."

Collin's voice is dripping with lust and when I do as he asks, I'm suddenly ready again. He grabs the cuffs of my jeans and drags them the rest of the way down my legs. Then he taps his boot against the inside of my ankle, signaling me to open my legs. I suck in a breath—so fuckin' turned on I can barely stand it—and scoot my feet along the rag rope rug until he leans forward, pressing himself against my ass. He grinds against me a few times, then he eases back and the next time he comes forward, he's inside me.

He starts slow, but his pace quickens when I push back, allowing him to enter me deeper.

Then he's grabbing my hair. A whole fistful of hair. Wrapping it around his hand. Pulling it as he leans forward and fucks me like I am the only woman he's ever gonna have for the rest of his life.

Just a few moments later, he pulls out and comes all over my ass.

There's a moment now when we're just spent and I know he wants to flop over onto the bed. Maybe he's not drunk, but he's definitely buzzing. So I kind of expect him to do that.

But he doesn't.

That's not something Collin Creed would do. He picks up his shirt, or my shirt, or whatever, and cleans me off like the gentleman he usually is. Then he's kicking off his boot, dragging his jeans down his legs, and pushing me over so I'm on my back.

I'm smiling at him when he finds my face with those eyes of him. And I know what he's thinking.

Did I go too far?

But he doesn't say it out loud. He sighs instead. Then kisses me on the lips.

A nice, long I'm-sorry-I-got-weird-there kiss that makes me laugh right into his mouth.

He pulls back a little, also chuckling. "You liked it, didn't you?"

And I just nod.

Because I did.

My doorbell wakes me from a very nice slumber. Not to mention a sexy dream involving the man who's got his arms around me right this very moment.

"What. The fuck. Is that?" The aforementioned man growls this into my neck.

"That, dear Collin, is a costume change."

"What?"

I crack one eye open, find the vintage clock face on my nightstand—squint a little to force it to make sense—and nod. "That's right. When someone rings my doorbell at seven a.m. on a Sunday morning during Revival season, it means a costume change."

"I hate this fuckin' town."

"No, you don't."

"I'm not wearin' a costume today. I've had about enough of the fuckin' Revival."

"Well, you do you, Collin. But..." I push him away and start to get out of bed.

He grabs me back and leans his face into my neck so when he whispers, "Don't leave me," it's right up against my ear.

"I'm not going far, you baby." Which makes him chuckle. "But I need to see what my costume is. I hope it's a pretty dress. It's Easter, after all."

This kinda shakes him out of his hungover stupor. "Shit. I forgot about Easter."

I scoot out of his grip and get out of bed, naked.

I think he kinda forgot I was naked. Not in the logical sense —we were all cuddled up together skin to skin, after all—but in the general sense, because his eyes go big and his smile goes wide.

I let him look all he wants as kind of a consolation prize for leaving him. Then I smirk, pull on a robe, and go downstairs.

Outside my door is an Easter basket, of all things. A giant— like two-feet-wide—Easter basket. And it's filled with packages.

I gaze up, studying the sky, and take note that there's a storm coming. Then I look around, checkin' other porches on the street. There are no houses directly across the street from me because it's just woods that lead down to the river valley proper. But I can see five or six porches in both directions to make my comparison and none of them are showing any signs of an Easter basket. Three of them, however, do have brown paper bags.

Hmm.

I pick up the basket and take it inside. Collin is coming down the stairs wearing his jeans and nothing else. They're not buttoned or zipped so I get a good, long look at that happy trail of his before I shut the door and meet his eyes.

"What the fuck is that?"

"Do you need a coffee, Collin?"

"I feel like I need a cigarette."

This makes me laugh. "Do you smoke?"

"Not really. But I've been known to."

"Would you like one?"

"Do you smoke?" He's squintin' his eyes at me.

"Not really. But I've been known to as well."

He lets out a breath. And I can tell he's moody about the early hour and probably wondering what fresh hell is waitin' for him today. Because it truly does seem like Disciple is trying to piss him off every chance it gets. "What do we do for Easter?"

I blink my eyes at him, mostly due to the change in subject, but also because I'm really not following. "Pardon me?"

He points to the basket I'm holding. "Do I buy you flowers? Candy? Is there a big dinner waitin' at the end of this day?"

I can't help my laugh. It comes out a little bit barky, too. Because he's just too much. "Well, I would not turn down flowers and candy, but it's not necessary. And you know as well as I do that Easter is just a pretend thing around here. So I don't think anyone's gonna have us over for dinner." He looks disappointed, so I hold up a finger. "But, if you would like me to rustle up a spiral ham and a couple of side dishes, I would be more than happy to do that for you."

"I forgot Easter isn't a thing here."

"Have you been celebratin' Easter all these years, Collin?"

"Not specifically celebrating it. I don't go to church, if that's what you're asking. But the mess hall always had a nice spread. And even when we were overseas, someone brought us a fuckin' ham."

"Well, hmmm. It appears that thinking about missing Easter dinner is making you cranky, so I will rectify this. Don't you worry, Collin. You will eat good tonight. Does that make you feel a little better? Can you face the day now?"

He's noncommittal. Just gives me a shrug. "I guess." Then he points at my basket. "What's in there, anyway?"

"I don't know." I heft the large basket up onto the kitchen counter and walk around the other side of it so when Collin comes over, we're facing each other. He looks tired. "Are you hungover?"

"What?" He was studying the basket, but he looks up at me.

"No. I mean… I do have a headache. And…" He pauses. "About last night…"

I raise an eyebrow. "What about last night?"

He lets out a breath. Like he's unsure where to go from here. It takes him another five whole seconds to even get the first word out. "When I…" He cranes his head back, massaging his neck with his hand.

"Are you worried what I think about you after the dirty sex, Collin?"

Finally, this man smiles. And it's weird seeing him so uncomfortable, especially about sex. "Maybe a little." He winces. "I might've been a little bit buzzed?"

"Is that your excuse?"

"Do I need an excuse?"

I slowly shake my head. "I'm a grownup, Collin. If I didn't want your face between my legs last night, your face would not have been there."

He nods, looking me straight in the eye. "OK."

"Should we unpack this basket?"

"No. We should probably burn that thing."

"Come on now. It's not gonna be that bad. And it's all so pretty, isn't it?" I reach for the top package. It's a hat box, I already know that. But it's not just any hat box. It's pale yellow with lavender flowers all over it. And the handle is a braided satin cord the color of green apples.

There are at least a dozen packages in this basket and they are all held in place with yellow and white baker's twine, so I get the scissors and cut them all free. Collin takes them out of the basket and places them on the counter.

He's moody about the Revival, and the costumes, and countless other things that come with being a part of this town. But he's caught up in the spell this morning. Not because he wants to be, but because he can't help it.

None of us can.

I know the people over in Bishop probably think their town

is pretty special. I mean, really, how charming are those big horses lugging things around town? It's like a twenty-four-seven Heritage Day parade. And I know that the people of Revenant probably think their town is remarkable as well. It's exciting over there. It feels like... life. I don't know how to describe it. Not a constant party. That's too vague. But... more like a Fourth of July picnic that never ends.

But here in Disciple it's all about... the look. And the mood. And a sense that you're part of something bigger. It's just an old-timey feeling. Like you're living in the long-ago 'better days.' But not in the same way as Bishop, because no one in Disciple has to wake up at five a.m. to milk cows. And not in the same way as Revenant, either, with their marina festival, and their bikers whooping, and hollering, and drinking.

Because we're not crass here. We're kinda classy here. The women are mostly... well, women. Monday through Friday they are raising kids, and doing book club, and cooking dinners. But then every single weekend for nine months out of the year they wear tea dresses and white gloves. Cloche hats with satin ribbons and felt flowers on them. They play cards, and gossip, and prop up the script doing fun things like fainting and fanning themselves.

And the men are mostly just men. Hard workers during the week, doing jobs like everyone else, some more important than others. But on the weekends, they are doing something extraordinary that's not only fun, most of the time, but earns them enough to dream bigger and make plans for a better future at the end of every year. They wear their fancy suits and bowler hats. And their kids dress up like papergirls and boys, and sing in the choir, and practice good manners as they learn their place in our community.

If Revenant is a Fourth of July picnic and Bishop is a Heritage Day parade—then Disciple is a garden party. A lovely, pastel-perfect garden party.

And never is there a time, all through the year, when this feeling is more tangible than on Easter Sunday.

The package underneath the hat box is wrapped in thick brown paper and held together with more baker's twine. Collin's name is written across the front in neat calligraphy. "Yours, good sir." I smile, starting a pile for him.

There are ten more packages, all wrapped up in either pretty pastel paper for me or brown paper for Collin.

When that's done, and I look up, I find him smiling. "Is your mood improved?"

He lets out a sigh. "I was thinking back. When I was like... eight, or something. Olive wasn't born yet. And we got a basket like this for opening day. I don't know what it was about, but I got a new suit." He squints his eyes at me. "You know what's funny?"

"Tell me."

"I remember you that day."

"Hmm. That was my second year in the children's choir and I had been given a solo on Easter Sunday. I sang—"

"'Rise and Shine.' You sang 'Rise and Shine.'"

"I did." I giggle a little. "I was lookin' right at you on the stage that day. Your suit was gray. With a cream shirt and tan waistcoat."

"Yeah." He kinda laughs this word out.

"And usually you just wore navy blue."

Collin nods. "I hated those fuckin' suits." But he's not upset. He's actually smiling pretty big. Then he lets out a breath. "All right. I get it. It's special. Let's just... play along, I guess."

I bring my hands up like I'm praying and clap them together. Then we open our packages.

They are all clothes. A dress for me and a suit for him. I've been given a gorgeous, drop-waist silk flapper dress in the prettiest peach color. Glass beads everywhere giving it the kind of heft I just die for because of how it will fall just so over my curves. It's sleeveless and it's got an art deco motif, a deep v-neck, and a handkerchief hem.

There's a capelet too. All fussed up in tiny sun-colored glass beads and silver pearls. It's very short, just barely enough to cover my shoulders. But with the dress, it's just perfect. The lariat necklace is a double string of gold pearls that are so heavy, I swear, they might be real. I slip it over my head immediately. The two strings come together at my waist where a bronze clasp holds them together, then a single loop descends from there, dropping nearly to my thighs.

I even got a matching bag. More beads, more art deco motifs—stars and a starburst. Not to mention a dainty chain to balance it on my shoulder.

My breath comes out in a rush as I stare down at everything, wondering what part I'm playing today that they have given me such an outfit.

"Wow." Even Collin seems impressed. "You're gonna look good in that, Low."

I smile at him, shrugging my shoulders up a little with excitement. "I am. What'd they give you?"

He pulls out the various pieces of a three-piece suit in a light brown color. Not wool, this time, but linen. There's a peach tie that matches my dress, plus cufflinks and a pocket watch on a long gold chain.

"That's nice, Col. And it looks a little more fitted than the last one."

"Yeah. It does." He looks at me and squints his eyes. "They're letting me look nice? Why, do you think? What do they have planned?"

"Let's see." I dig through the basket. "Is there a script in here?" There's an envelope with both our names on it. I pull it out and hand it to Collin.

He takes the envelope, opens it, but it's just a card. Like a postcard.

"What's it say, Collin?"

"It just says, 'Welcome to Revival, Season Nine: The Prodigal Son Returns. Have a nice day.'" He puts the card down and looks at me. Unsure what to think.

"Maybe they just want us to have a nice day?"

"That's funny."

"Well, here's the bright side. There's no new script."

"I didn't even read the old one."

"Well, I did. They didn't give us any lines."

"OK. So what are we supposed to do? I mean, I know what I'm doing. I'm standing at the north gate with the dog."

"And I'm sitting in the pew fanning myself, waiting for my cue to faint."

We both laugh. Then Collin says, "This is stupid."

"I don't know. If we don't have any lines, maybe we really are just supposed to have a nice day."

"I think it's more likely that they didn't give us any lines because I am not about to follow the script. So what they did is give Rosie Harlow lines. Or fuckin' Grimm lines. Or whoever. So they can nudge and prod the story along without our participation."

I take a step towards him, closing the little bit of space between us, and drape my arms over his shoulders, clasping my hands behind his neck. Then I lean up and kiss him. He kisses me back and while we're doing that I whisper, "I had fun last night."

This makes him smile. "So did I."

"I would like to put it on record that we can do that again any time you want."

He laughs a little. "Noted."

COLLIN

*A **phone rings upstairs*** just as I'm about to give Lowyn another kiss.

Lowyn pushes back, turning toward the sound. "Well, who could that be?"

"No one good, I'm sure."

She pats my chest. "I'll be right back." Then she darts up the stairs, her robe flaring out behind her.

I look back down at the costume I was given. It doesn't look much like a gangster costume. What it looks like is a church outfit. And that doesn't make much sense, because I'm gonna be at the gate today, not inside the fuckin' tent.

Lowyn comes back down holding her phone. "OK. Yep. I understand. I'll be ready. Thank you!" She ends the call. "Well, that was Rosie. She and the girls—Taylor, April, MaisieLee, MacyLynn, and Bryn—are all coming to pick me up at eight-thirty."

"Whyyyy?" I try my best to say this nicely, but it comes out dripping in cynicism.

"I'm not sure. She wouldn't say."

"Script change."

"Probably. But listen, Collin, don't fight it. It's opening day."

"No. Yesterday was opening day."

"I don't really know what yesterday was, but opening day it was not. You know this as well as I do. Today is opening day, that tent is gonna be packed tight, and it's gonna be fun." I must be wearing a look that says 'I do not believe you' because she comes right up to me, slipping her hands around my waist—which, not gonna lie, feels pretty great—and pushes herself into me. "Opening day is always nice. Think back a little. You know this is true. And they gave us spectacular costumes. Just go with it."

Then she kisses me. I'm just about to throw her down on the couch and fuck the ever-loving shit out of her when she pulls back and pats my chest. "Let's get the wrinkles out of that suit."

AT EIGHT-THIRTY ON THE DOT, a horn honks outside. We're both ready, but this is Lowyn's ride, not mine. I'm not showing up to that tent a half hour early. So I take one last look at her—she looks so damn pretty, it's a shame to waste this day on the fuckin' Revival—and then kiss her. Because I know she's excited about this day and it's about to start right now.

"I'll see you in a bit." She blows me a kiss, straightens her cloche hat—which is a pretty light green color and has little felt daisies on the satin band—and then she's gone. I walk over to the window and pull the sheer curtain aside so I can watch her get in a minivan filled with women.

But just before she gets in, she turns, looking at me, then waves and smiles, and I like the idea that she knew I'd be watching. So I wave and smile back.

Then she's inside and a moment later, she's gone.

I let out a sigh, missing her already. I wish we could just spend the day together and not have to deal with this fuckin'

Revival bullshit. I would like to take her out. Such a waste to be wearing that dress and have to spend it working a souvenir booth and sitting inside a tent.

A crack of silent lightning races across the sky in the distance and this is when I look up and realize it's gonna storm today. It's not raining now, but there are more cracks of lightning shootin' off in the distance against a backdrop of purple-gray clouds.

Wonderful. We're all dressed up and it's gonna rain.

But... maybe there's a bright side?

Maybe the whole fuckin' day will be cancelled.

Just as I think that, thunder booms through the town. Then the lights flicker and go out.

"Fuck." I go find the basement door—same place as it was when I was a kid, right off the back mud room—and open it. God, it smells the same. Like old bricks and dirt.

Our house was built over an older foundation sometime back in the nineteen fifties. And this basement was part of that original house. It's all made of stone, but near the back side of the house, some parts of the basement floor are still dirt. It used to flood a little when I was a kid, but it's dry right now. So I go down, grabbing a flashlight hanging on a hook that has been there for thirty years.

Not really. It's a flashlight and it's in the same place, but it's not the one we had when I was a kid. So when I flick it on, there's light.

The breaker box is just at the bottom of the stairs. High enough that flood waters never bothered it. And close enough that you can open it up and flip the breakers without leaving the steps, just in case it was flooded.

A bad place to put a breaker box, if you ask me. But no one ever asked me.

When I get to the bottom, I open the little compartment, but the moment I do that, something falls out and makes a clinking noise on the concrete.

I shine light on the floor and spy a key. An old, rusted skeleton key. I pick it up and look at it, then shove it in my pocket and turn to the breakers.

The box is empty. I should've figured Lowyn would get new electrics when she redid the place. So I close it and go back upstairs, then hit up the garage and, sure enough, there's a nearly brand-new box just next to the door.

I flip the breakers that were tripped, go back inside, and the lights are on again.

As soon as I close the door to the garage, a horn honks outside.

I let out a long breath, already tired of this day. But when I peek out, I have to laugh. Because Amon is leaning against a very fancy car right out front. Fancy-fancy, as Lowyn would say. And when I take a closer look, I realize it's Old Man Hunt's 1933 Rolls Royce Phantom II. "What the hell?"

Amon spies me in the window and starts yellin' for me to hurry up. He's wearing a costume that's very similar to mine. And then I see Ryan and Nash are in the little backseat, dressed up with new clothes too.

Something is up, that's for sure. I dunno what Jim Bob has planned for me today, but it's definitely something. What can I do but play along? I go outside to my smiling partners and get in the fuckin' car.

"Like my new threads?" Ryan says.

I look over my shoulder at him and Nash. "The two of you are gonna regret this, ya know. You have no idea how much you're gonna wish that you never put those clothes on by Christmas Eve."

"Oh, stop, Collin." That's Amon chastising me from the driver's side, which is on the right in this car. "You act like Disciple is some kind of evil cult or something. It's a fuckin' tent revival."

"It's a scam is what it is."

"Correct me if I'm wrong," Nash says, "but isn't 'scam' the dictionary definition of 'tent revival?'"

I turn in my seat to point at him. "Correct. Scam from day one."

"Why the hell did you want us to come back here if you hate this place so much?" Nash asks.

"Two words," Amon says. "Lowyn"—he looks at me, winkin'—"McBride."

"That's not even true. Y'all know that we needed to meet some very specific requirements as far as the compound goes. Our place was the only place for sale that met all the conditions."

"It's kinda weird, don't ya think?"

I look back at Ryan. "Weird how?"

"That it came up for sale right when we were looking. And it's literally next door to yours and Amon's home town. And practically came complete with a high-school girlfriend and a fuckin' side show paying out a million dollars every New Year's Day."

"How'd you know about that?" But there's only one way. So I direct my gaze back to Amon again. "You told them?"

"We're partners," Nash says. "It's his job to tell us."

"I hope you boys don't expect no money on the first of the year. Because I don't care what Amon told you, Jim Bob Baptist is not gonna pay no fuckin' outsider part of his profit share."

"We'll see," Ryan says.

"What's there to see?"

Ryan looks at me. "If we're valuable team members of the Revival, then who's to say that Jim Bob Baptist won't change his closed-up mind?"

I turn around and face forward, then huff out an incredulous sigh. "Keep dreaming, Ryan. You'll see at the end of the year. And I'll be tellin' ya, 'I told ya so.'"

Just as I say this, we turn, heading up the hill towards the

Revival grounds. And for a moment I kinda get lost, unable to process what I'm seeing. "What the hell is that?"

"What the hell does it look like, Collin? It's a fuckin' tent."

A *tent*? I mean… it's kinda pitched like one. And it's all made out of canvas or something that looks similar enough. But this is… an engineering miracle.

Those words in my head come out in Jim Bob's voice, making me recall that first meeting when he was talking about how my daddy spent the entire year after I left working on plans to take the Revival to the next level. "Four-season festivities," Jim Bob's voice says again.

So that's what I'm looking at—a four-season, five-acre-square tent city covering the entire Revival grounds—when we pull up to the east gate where security headquarters are. Only now, instead of just a gate leading into the park, there's a… tunnel. That's the only way to describe it. Made out of tent canvas and all ready to protect people from the rain once it starts.

I can only presume the security tent is still here, but now it's inside the mother tent.

"How the hell did they get this done overnight?" I'm not really talking to anyone in particular, and my words are barely more than a whispered mumble, but Nash answers me.

"There's some kind of mechanical framework attached to the boardwalk buildings on either side of the Revival tent. I was talking to some old fart yesterday named Joseph. We were just shootin' the shit about the weather and he started telling me about how they could put a roof over the whole park with a push of a button."

The town clerk. A quarryman. A jewelry maker. A diesel mechanic. The chief of police. And a real estate agent. Joseph is the quarryman. Probably the only guy in town who owns a crane, so I guess it makes sense to give him a nice profit share when you're lookin' to build a five-acre roof made out of canvas.

There's even a little makeshift garage for Old Man Hunt's Rolls Royce. And that's right where Amon parks it.

"It's pretty cool," Ryan says. "It reminds me of a circus, but an old-timey one. Something you'd see in the movies. I can't believe we live here now. I fuckin' love this place. It's all hilly, and green, and that river sounds like it wants to kill you every moment of the day. Just roaring by, non-stop, twenty-four seven. I love it."

"At least we're not gonna get our new fancy clothes wet," Nash calls, already out of the car and walking towards the tunnel gate. Ryan follows.

And I do have to admit, he's not wrong. The tent is kinda blowing my mind in this moment.

Amon turns the engine off and looks at me. "It is openin' fuckin' day, Collin. Are you ready for this shit?"

"Shut up."

He pretends to punch me in the arm. "Enjoy it, Sarge. You're only ever gonna get this day once."

"What are you talking about?"

"I'm supposed to let you know that yesterday was your practice run. Jim Bob wanted to see how you'd react. It was predictable."

"What?"

"Yeah. They just wanted to light you up. You did not disappoint."

"Why would they do that?"

"Because they want you to play along, Collin. And they needed you to get it out of your system yesterday so you would not fuck up today."

"I'm not acting in this stupid show. I was hired to run security and that's all I'm doing. They can fuck right off about this whole prodigal son thing."

"Well, see… they knew this about you, Col. So today, and for weeks to come, actually, the whole story is just you and

Lowyn falling in love. Today is the day you meet her for the first time."

"No, it isn't."

"You're gonna bump into her, and have a little moment with locked eyes or something. And you're gonna have some coffee, and sit next to each other during the Revival, and then have a little lunch, and dance. Hold hands and shit."

"You're one of them, aren't ya?"

He laughs.

"They got to you. They took my friend, Amon, sucked out his brain and all his common sense, and put some alien thing back inside his head. I'm gonna go to my gate and stand there until this day is over. Then I'm gonna go home and enjoy a spiral ham with a couple of sides because Lowyn has promised to rustle that up for me. That's what I'm gonna do."

He pats me on the shoulder. "We'll see, friend. We'll see. Because everyone in this town has been instructed to go out of their way to make it special for the two of you. So. I would not have high expectations for the highlight of your Easter Sunday being a spiral ham and a couple of sides."

Then he gets out of the car and walks into the tent.

I sit there for another moment, but in that same moment there's a flash of lightning and, a moment later, the crack of thunder.

The rumble and the glory.

That's what my daddy used to call thunderstorms when I was a kid. They used to scare me and he would come into my room at night and recite that passage from his book of sermons. 'When you look upon the hills, the sun shining on the peaks, and you hear the rumble in the distance, don't you ever forget that behind it comes the glory.'

We used to say it together. Every time it stormed.

I don't know when I grew out of that. Maybe seven or eight. But even so, every time there was a crack of thunder, we'd stop what we were doing and say that little passage.

Shit, I've caught myself reciting that passage all over the world when I hear the thunder.

I let out a long sigh. Because I kinda miss that man. I miss the father he used to be. I miss how he used to look at me before I killed that fuckin' kidnapper. Like he was proud of me. Like he loved me.

And all of that disappeared in two seconds.

I get out of the car and go inside the tent. Immediately, Mercy gets up from her little dog cushion and starts barking at me.

"She's mad at you," Amon says. Then he points to her. "Settle, Mercy." And Mercy settles, going quiet and sittin' nicely.

"She's got no reason to be mad at me."

"You leave her behind when you go home. She's the only one who gets left behind."

"What are you talking about? She's a… co-worker. She doesn't live with me, Amon."

"She's your partner, Collin. And from now on, you need to take her home. She's been sleeping in the security tent all weekend."

"What? Now I feel bad. How come you didn't tell me this?"

"Why would I need to tell you that? She's your partner."

I look over at Mercy—who actually appears to be followin' this conversation—and sigh. "Fine. You can come home with me. But you better be good or Lowyn will kick you out."

She barks once.

"Come on, let's go." She comes over and heels like she's stuck to my left knee. "I'll be at the gate," I tell Amon. Then we walk out.

But I catch him chuckling. Like there's gonna be a surprise at my gate.

And sure enough, when I get over there, it's already being manned by three men who don't act jittery or look like they need a background check.

"Hey, Sarge," one of the guys says.

"What did you just call me?"

"Uh…" He looks a little panicked. "Sarge? That's what Amon told me to call you. But I can call you something else. What should I call you?"

"How 'bout my name?" I snap. "Which is Collin."

"Cool." He nods. "Yeah. Great. Nice to meet you. I'm Chuck, this is Darrel"—he points to the guy right behind him—"and that's Matty." He points to the third guy.

"All right. What are you doing here?"

"We're… manning the north gate."

"I man the north gate."

"Right. But… I'm supposed to tell you that Lowyn… she's waiting for you."

"Who told you to say that? Amon?"

"No, sir. Jim Bob told me. She's waiting for you at the east coffee tent."

"Right now she is?"

"Right now, sir."

And I guess Amon was right. Because if Lowyn is waiting for me somewhere, I'm gonna show up there. "OK," I sigh. "You call me if you boys need anything."

He salutes me.

I almost yell at him to stop doing that, but I already know that Amon told him to. He's trying to piss me off from afar. It would be stupid to take it out on this guy because he doesn't know any better, so I let it go and walk away.

But it's hard to stay irritated right now. Because the Revival grounds have been transformed into something altogether different than I've ever seen before. So my attention is on the details in front of me and not on all the ways that Amon is taking Jim Bob's side.

It kinda feels like a fairy forest underneath the massive tent roof. Since these whole five acres are truly outdoors, and this pitched-tent roof is just a temporary thing, there is grass along some of the side walkways that aren't planked with wood like a boardwalk. There are trees in here, and birds in here, and flowers. The spring tulips aren't as bright as they might be out in the sunshine, but there are little patches of orange, and yellow, and purple spoutin' out of everywhere. And I am certain they are as new as the canvas roof above my head.

I look up and find long strings of garden lights. There're people up there too, hanging off the extensive steel scaffolding, still stringing them along.

But that's really the only sign that this is all fresh and wasn't like this yesterday.

I don't know how they did it, but it's nice. And kinda romantic.

At the next little intersection I turn onto the main boardwalk, my new fancy shoes quieter than my boots usually are. The grounds aren't open yet, so it's just Disciple people doing last-minute things before everything gets going. And every single one of them shoots me a smile and a wave.

I shoot a smile and a wave back because it's kinda rude not to.

And just this simple act of being smiled at and smiling back is enough to lift my mood. But even if it wasn't, catching sight of Lowyn in the gazebo near the coffeeshop—sittin' all alone like she's waiting for me and wearing that gorgeous dress— well, that would be enough to lift anyone's spirits.

I come up the steps to the gazebo and she turns to look at me, smiling. "Can you believe this? I mean, I've seen it like this a hundred times at least, but not in the spring. Not on opening day. The flowers, Collin. The trees have leaves! I don't know." She looks around like she's trying to take it all in the same way I was. "It's just kinda magical."

I come up to her, lean down, and kiss her hello on the cheek even though I just saw her half an hour ago. She looks up at me, still smiling, her eyes bright and happy. "I've missed you too, Collin."

I chuckle a little and take my seat across from her, telling

Mercy to lie down at my feet, which she does without complaint.

"What is all this?" I pan my hand to mean the gazebo and the fact that we're sitting in it when we should be working. But honestly, I mean all of it. Our costumes. The girls picking her up. Amon driving Old Man Hunt's Rolls Royce.

"Script change." Lowyn shakes her head a little, like she can't believe it either. "Bryn is taking over the booth today."

"Really. Well that's interesting. Because the north gate has people manning it who are not me as well."

"I've been told that we are the stars of the show today."

"I've heard the same rumor. But I'm not followin' a script. I don't care how much trouble they've gone to to put this place together, I'm not gonna play along."

"So here's the interesting thing, Collin. There is no script. Not for us, anyway."

"What do you mean?"

"We just get to... be on a date all day. As long as we don't stray out of the Revival grounds, and we hang around until six, we've done our part."

"How's that figure into the prodigal son? I mean, yesterday we were front-page news. They were calling me a murderer."

"Yesterday doesn't count. Did they tell you? It was some dress rehearsal and all the guests were from Bishop and Revenant. So you can just relax, Collin. We're playing the part of a couple on a first date. You can manage that, right?"

"What about next weekend?"

"I don't know. But there is no reason to worry about next weekend when we're still in this one."

As soon as she's done saying that a waitress appears, a teenager who I don't know, but Lowyn obviously does because she says, "Good morning, Lucy. How are you today?"

Lucy blushes and she sets down a fancy tea service set in the middle of the table. Then she curtseys and addresses Lowyn in a small voice. "I'm fine, thank you. This is your coffee, it's not tea, Miss McBride. I'll be back with your pastries in a moment." Then she curtsies again, leaving as quick as she came.

Lowyn's face is the picture of delight when she looks at me and points to the tea set at the same time. "Fancy-fancy."

Which makes me laugh. And with that laugh, I settle and lean back in my chair. "It's like a vacation day."

"Exactly. Think of it just like that."

"What are we gonna do all day? I mean, I'm not really interested in shopping. That's pretty much all there is to do here."

"We're gonna walk around. And hold hands. And talk. And go to the Revival." I'm about to protest, but she puts up a hand to stop me. "There's not gonna be no trouble, Collin. I got that straight from Rosie."

"How does Rosie know?"

"Ester told her. So we're just gonna go to the Revival like everyone else and watch the show."

"Well, if we're the stars, and we don't have lines, how will there even be a show?"

"I think it's about the boys today."

"What boys?"

"Your boys."

"You mean Amon?"

"And the others from the compound."

"How many of them are here?"

"Twenty or so, I think."

"What are they gonna do? Get in a fight or something?"

"I don't think so. I was told that this was just gonna be a nice day. So the two of us will find out together when the Revival starts. But here's something interesting." This is when I notice there is a program for today's Revival sitting on the table in front of her. And when she picks it up, I realize it's really two. She holds the top one out for me and I take it.

I look down at it, read the main article on the front page, then look back up at Lowyn. "What's this?"

"Apparently, this is the real program for this weekend." She holds up the second program. "The one with us on the front page was only for yesterday."

"What? So... we're not the stars of this show?"

"I think we are. But we're on page five in that one." She points to the program I'm holding.

I turn to page five and sure enough, there's a picture of us from Friday. And the headline is different. It says, 'Local Man Returns to Run Father's Business.' I look back up at Lowyn and shake my head. "So what is this? I get a choice? Be the man who murdered your husband or be the preacher of the fuckin' Revival?"

"They're gonna pigeonhole you into something or other, Collin. You might as well just accept it."

I set the program back down on the table. "I'm going with option C. None of the above."

"Well, I do think it's kinda crazy how obsessed Jim Bob is with you."

"What do you mean?"

"He's certainly not obsessed with me that way. When I said I wanted out—mostly out, not all the way out—but when I said, 'I've got a business to run, Jim Bob, and that's my number one priority,' he didn't even blink. He just said, 'OK, Lowyn. That's fine with me. Good luck.' Or something of that nature. He didn't care. He didn't care when Clover left. Hell, her whole family left. So why is he so stuck on you?"

"You tell me."

"The only thing that sets you apart is what you did twelve years ago and how you reacted to it afterward. But how does any of that relate back to being the preacher? Because I can't see the connection."

"That makes two of us." But it's a lie on my part. And I suddenly have an urge to tell Lowyn about the secrets Jim Bob is hiding. To tell her all about the fourth point on the cross and how there's more to the story about my sister almost being kidnapped.

But then Lucy is back with a platter of pastries, so the quiet between Lowyn and I continues while she pours our coffee, does another curtsey, and disappears.

And by this time, the subject of the conversation has shifted to food. Lowyn picks up a small, round pastry covered in large sugar sprinkles and layered with cream cheese and berries. "Want a bite?"

She holds it out to me and I take one. "Fuck, that's good."

"April is one hell of a baker." Then she takes a bite too, moaning a little when all those flavors hit her taste buds.

I add some cream to my coffee and sit back, sipping it. Just watching her polish that little pastry off. She nods and sighs once it's gone.

"There are more. Have another." I point to the tray, which is holding way too many pastries for just two people, and they are all as exquisite-looking as the little berry pie.

She picks up something in the shape of a pinwheel and eats that too. Then she dabs her mouth with a real cloth napkin, and sets it back in her lap.

"Now what, Lowyn?"

"We're just gonna sit here and have a nice time, Collin. Tell me about what you've been doing. Tell another story about where you've been."

Most of what I've been doing is not appropriate conversation for a fake first date. But I do have one or two stories that fit the bill.

So I start talking.

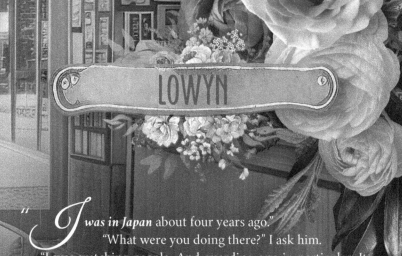

"*I was in Japan* about four years ago."

"What were you doing there?" I ask him.

"I was watching people. And guarding one in particular. It was Chinese New Year, and they have this incredible lantern festival in Nagasaki. For me, just a guy from West Virginia, it was chaos. And loud. And bright." He pauses to smile here. "Maybe you don't know this, but lantern festivals tend to have a lot of light."

"Is that where they send balloons up with candles in them, or something?"

"Yeah, kinda like that. But they're not balloons. The ones that float up are lanterns. The hot air inside them is what makes them do that. But they've got more than just lanterns at these festivals. Not just that shape, I mean. Some were in the shape of giant animals, and people, and some floated on the water. It was just really cool."

"I wish I could've been there."

He sighs. "It would've been way different if you were."

"How so?"

"Well, I would've enjoyed it more, of course. The whole thing was kind of annoying from a security standpoint."

"Were you guarding someone special?"

"A minister of state's six-year-old daughter."

I picture this and smile. "Was she a handful?"

"I am embarrassed to admit that she got away from me twice that night."

"Oh, no!"

"She was that kind of kid. Always up to something. I actually lost her for about twenty-five minutes the second time. I found her curled up with a kitten in a pachinko arcade." I laugh, but he lets out a long sigh. "She got me fired. I had been working that job, protectin' that damn kid for six months. And what she did that night got me fired."

I tsk my tongue.

"But the funny part of this story is that two years ago she wrote me a letter apologizing for being bad and she invited me to her birthday party in Paris."

"Did you go?"

"I couldn't. The congressional hearings were just getting started."

"Did you ever talk to her again?"

He nods, but stays silent for a moment. "Her father was assassinated about a year later and by that time the hearings were over, we had been cleared, and so I saw her at the funeral in Tokyo."

"Why was he killed?"

"You know. Same old thing. Too many good ideas."

"Hmm. That's a very cynical answer, Collin."

"The world deserves my cynicism."

"I'll take your word on that. I don't get out much."

"You travel all the time."

"But I meet people just like me. I don't meet ministers or daughters thereof."

"You meet people like Sassy Lorraine."

And this makes me smile, even though his story was sad. "I have a feeling she's gonna hang around in my life for years to come."

"Should I tell you a happier story now?"

"I'd like that. But first, I want to know why you told me the sad one to begin with."

"Because I spent that whole night thinking about you, Lowyn. And how you would've loved that lantern festival. That's why the little girl got away from me."

I reach over and take his hand. It's a little bit cold, so I hold it in both of mine, trying to warm him up. "What's the happy story?"

"I saw you on TV once."

"Oh." I'm surprised. He hasn't brought up Jet Shadows yet. So I guess I figured he didn't know about him. But I guess I was wrong.

"Don't worry, Low. I'm not gonna pry into whatever was going on with that Jet guy. But I was back in America—in Georgia, actually—taking a meeting with Charlie, one of my DC contacts. And we were in a bar and there you were on the TV. Your name all printed up on the screen."

"When was this?" I'm only asking because the actual filming of that was a long time ago now. But they play reruns all the time.

"About six years ago."

"Well, six years ago Jet and I had already gone our separate ways."

"Did you date him?"

"Briefly. For a few months. He helped me a lot. He's really the reason I'm so fortunate now. And as successful as I am."

"I doubt that, Lowyn. You seem like a real hard worker to me."

"Well, this is your happy story? Because this doesn't feel like your happy story."

"Well, it is a happy story because I was in pretty bad place that day. I learned something about the people I was working for that kinda changed my life in… not a great way."

"What did you learn?"

He stares at me for a moment. And while I might not be a mind reader, this pause does not warrant that level of skill. It's pretty clear he's trying to figure out if he should tell me the truth or not. For a moment, I'm sure he's not going to. But then he says, "One of my men died," and I absolutely know this is the truth.

"How did that happen?"

"He had some kind of reaction to a... treatment they were giving him."

"Was he sick?"

"No. Not quite."

"Then what was he being treated for?"

"He was still in the Marines. So... yeah. If they tell you to take a treatment, you take the treatment."

"And this killed him?"

He nods at me. "It did."

"Did you ever take that treatment?"

"No. We were out. Contractors, remember? Anyway. Charlie made me come see him to talk about that. And I was in the worst mood. And then there you were. And even though I could tell that you were maybe a little bit enamored with that Jet guy, it didn't matter. You made me smile."

I picture his life all these years, something I've tried not to do since he came home. But he's told me three stories now and two of them involve death. So I'm starting to get the feeling that Collin Creed has seen more than his share in the past twelve years and this makes me sad.

It makes me want to change things for him. Because, for whatever reason, he and I were given a reprieve from this year's Revival story. It's a temporary one, for sure. More like a day off, really. But it's more than we had when we woke up this morning and I think we should make the most of it. I believe he deserves a very nice day.

So I stand up and offer him my hand.

He looks up at me with those eyes of his. And this time,

when I look at them, I don't just see the colors. I see the man. The honesty. The sincerity. "What are we doing now, Low?"

"Going for a walk. Would you like to take a stroll through the magical world of Revival Town with me?"

He grins and stands up, accepting my hand, and then we leave the gazebo and stroll down the boardwalk, looking at all the same familiar things that look so different now just because we've thrown a tent over them.

People appear. Then crowds of them. And soon it's time for the Revival. I know Collin doesn't want to go, so I don't bother asking him. But he surprises me and starts leading me that way once his daddy's voice comes across the loudspeakers talking about the rumble and the glory.

His dog, Mercy, follows. He doesn't even have her on a lead today, but she stays right by his side like they've been partners forever.

The Revival is beautiful, as always. Particularly because of the children's choir, which has always been my favorite part, but also because Simon isn't loud and charismatic like he was yesterday. He's never been as good a preacher as Mr. Creed was. He will never fill those shoes. Mr. Creed could really wring the emotions out of a person.

But Simon's sermon is nice. It's all about new beginnings— fitting, for Easter Sunday and the springtime in general.

And right during the middle of it, the rain starts. Coming down hard on the overarching tent above the one we're in.

People stir a little, but there are no leaks. And after just a few minutes, the pounding rain and cracking thunder becomes just another part of the show. A backdrop soundtrack or something.

Rosie and Bryn both take turns fainting when Simon raises his hands up for some reason or another. I notice Amon off to the left shoutin' particularly loud 'amens.'

Old Man Hunt is led up to the front for healing, and of

course, there's a miracle and subsequent rejoicing. Then more music, and more singing, and fainting.

It's a good show. Kinda like it was back when I was a kid.

When it's over, people linger and chat, but Collin and I just wander out with the guests like we're not playing any parts at all. I do notice that Jacob Wonder is taking a lot of pictures of us, which means we're probably gonna be back on the front page of the program next weekend, but I don't mention this to Collin. There's no need to worry about things that haven't happened yet.

We go over to the river on the far side of the tent grounds. There's no tent roof here, but there is a little tunnel of canvas that leads right to the same dock where we spent time on Friday.

When we get there, I have a little worry that we won't be able to fill this day and it will be nothing but a whole lot of awkward silences and such. But then Collin starts talking, telling me more about his time away. Not sad stories this time. Just regular stuff. Starting off with how he and Amon spent the first two years in the Marines before they were discharged.

"What does a counterintelligence specialist do?" I ask him.

"It's a spy thing."

"You were a spy?"

"No. I was just learning how it all works. I didn't go out into the field at all those first two years. I just sat in that room filled with computers looking at other people's computer screens and listening in on their conversations with their assets. Which means people. Which actually means snitches and shit. I was just there to observe."

"Sounds boring."

"It was so fuckin' boring."

"You didn't have a choice in this?"

"Nope. They just told me what to do, and then I did it."

"After the two years, though? Did you have a choice in that?"

"Sure. I did. And I could've said no, I guess. But what else was I gonna do? I wasn't in the Marines anymore. If I did it the way they wanted me to—set up a private security team—then they would pay for all that start-up shit. And it would all be in my name."

"All of it? What about Amon?"

"No. It was all in my name. Which isn't a great thing, actually. It's just someone to blame when the shit goes sideways."

"Did they blame you?"

"They tried." Collin takes a moment to laugh here. "They did try. But I didn't do anything wrong. I was offered military contracts signed by a five-star general, not to mention a whole horde of his underlings. I didn't do a damn thing wrong."

"Why do you think they set it up that way?"

"What do ya mean?"

"That you would get off scot-free, and those men would take the fall."

He blows out a breath. "Well, the only real explanation is that they still need me. And those guys who took the fall were no longer necessary."

"Yeah." I look out over the water, just watching the rain as it pelts the surface, making it all jagged with splashes. "That's how it looks to me too. But you're not workin' for them?"

"I already told you I wasn't. But..." He pauses. "I mean, the government is my main client, Lowyn. So it's all very same-same, ya know?"

I nod at him. And I do understand this, I'm just kinda worried about what it might mean.

Mercy barks and both Collin and I look over to find her staring down at the river, which is flowing really fast right now since it's spring and raining.

Collin walks over to her, peering down into the river, then looks at me and shrugs. "No idea what this dog is barking about. Probably saw a rabbit or something. Maybe I should take her back to the tent. It's probably time for her to eat, anyway."

"You go ahead, I'll wait here." The security tent is not that far away. If I get up on my tiptoes, I can even see it. So Collin nods, tells Mercy to follow, and they go off in that direction.

I continue to look out at the river, just watching it go by. But then I spy a large pile of debris coming my way. Like a tangle of twigs and leaves. But something else too, because it's a big clump. Suddenly it breaks free and starts coming at me fast. That's when I realize it's not just trees, but... I squint as it goes rushing by, then pull my head back, confused. Because I swear I just saw *bones* in that clump.

"You should be careful, ya know."

I let out a forced breath. Then I turn and face him. "What can I do for you, Grimm?"

Grimm is standing there at the end of the dock wearing one of the special new outfits, like the ones made for Collin and his friends. He's pretty much the definition of handsome with that dark hair and matching dark stubble on his jaw. He doesn't shave, he grooms. And even when he's not dressed for Revival, he always looks nice. Like he could've been a male model if he had walked out of Disciple and went somewhere like New York or LA.

"I'm just telling you. You need to be careful around him."

"You don't need to tell me anything, Grimm. Go away." Then I turn back to the river. It's not that I hate Grimm, it's just... we dated. Briefly. A long time ago. I was in a weird place, my mama had only just died like a year before and there was trouble. He was kind of part of that trouble, but only in an auxiliary way. Still, he was there in the periphery and that's how I think of him these days. He just makes me edgy.

"He's not what you think. I know. Whatever he told you about where he's been and what he's been doing, it's not what you think."

Against my better judgment, I turn back around. "How would you know, Grimm?"

"I've got access to privileged information. You know that as well as I do. Collin Creed is here for a reason and I am just warning you to be careful."

"What reason?"

"Ask him yourself." Then he turns and walks away.

I grumble under my breath. Fuckin' Grimm. He's always known exactly how to push my buttons. "Just ignore him, Lowyn." I say this out loud. Over and over again, like a mantra. "Just ignore him, just ignore him."

But it's always been easier said than done and this time is no different.

"All right."

I whirl around, surprised. Collin is coming towards me again. "Are you OK?"

"What?" I wipe my hands on my dress. They are sweaty for some reason.

"You look... startled. Did I come up on you too quiet?" He's already next to me now, his hands slipping easily around my waist as he grins down at me with mischievous eyes.

And this makes me happy for some reason. He's different now. Calmer, for sure. And he's enjoying this day at the Revival grounds. Something he probably didn't think was possible. "You didn't scare me, Collin. Not in the least."

He offers me his hand and I take it. Then he leads me away from the river and back into the tent where the people are.

But there's a little voice in my head now though. Grimm's voice. *You need to be careful around him.* I want to push it aside and just ignore it, but deep down, I know there's some truth in what he said. Collin *is* here for a reason. And it doesn't have anything to do with me. He's already told me his reason and I don't doubt him—I certainly don't think he's a liar—but lots of people find omission to be their pathway to the truth. Myself included. Hell, everyone in this town included. So I can't just throw Grimm's comments away.

That doesn't mean his comments matter, either. Because they don't. Not to me. I don't care why Collin Creed came home. I don't care what he'll be doin' out there on that old compound.

I'm just glad he's back.

"What happened to your dog?"

Collin looks over his shoulder, then back at me. "She's in the security tent. I'm not patrolling, so I figure she could take a rest. But..." He winces here.

"But what?"

"She's coming home with me tonight."

"She is?"

"Every night, actually."

I smile, then laugh. "We've got ourselves a dog now, do we?"

"We do. I don't think she'll be any trouble. She speaks four languages."

"I think bringing that dog home is a fine idea."

Just as I say this, a child begins to sing. So I look in that direction and find little Bethylynn Baptist—Jim Bob's great-granddaughter—stepping forward from a crowd wearing the prettiest dress a little girl has ever seen, and I'm willing to bet my whole reputation that her dress was wrapped up in paper on her doorstep this morning, probably sitting inside a two-foot-wide straw basket. She starts belting out 'Sing Me an Old-Fashioned Song' as a boy with a guitar comes forward. A pair of girls start fiddlin' and then the unmistakable sound of a standup bass thumps from inside the crowd—which is getting thicker as the moments pass—and just a second later, there are dozens of kids from the Children's Choir surrounding Collin and me, like they are serenading us.

Guests crowd in too, clapping along, and then someone yells, "Dance, everyone, dance!"

Which is a cue, because suddenly half of the crowd—who

are all Disciple people—scatter around, forming up, and start twirling, and stepping, and hopping. Their shoes and boots stomping loud on the wooden boardwalk to a feisty beat.

"Holy shit," Collin mumbles. Then he looks at me. "What are they doing?"

He's not asking because he doesn't know what they're doing. He's asking because he does.

Because they're doing the final dance that has ended the season every single year without fail, since it started almost a hundred years ago.

It's a purely Revival way of dancing that combines the polka, the square dance, and the quadrille while adding in a little bit of local flavor to sweeten it up. It starts out with four pairs to a square, and you do different parts of the dance with each other's partners for a good little while. But then everyone forms up in a line in a fast-paced modified quadrille as the watching crowd claps out a beat.

It's chaos. Beautifully coordinated chaos. And this one dance, done by all the Disciple kids, is the whole reason people pay a pretty penny to attend the Christmas Eve show when the season ends. It's been that way since before Collin and I were born.

So his question is not what dance are they doing, but why are they doing it now, on opening day?

And I don't know.

That song ends and another child—a boy this time—starts singing 'There's Better Times A-Coming.' A banjo joins in, then all the kids are dancing again.

"Come on, everyone!" Rosie yells. She's standing on the elevated wooden porch that leads to the bakery, her arms waving in the air and her face lit up gold from the strings of lights hanging down from the tent ceiling. "Dance with us!"

And of course, when you invite people to do something, some will most certainly go ahead and do that. So people start dancing. It's a very complicated dance, so they're all Disciple people too. But when you look at the guests you can see it in their faces. How much they want to be a part of this. How much they want to feel this joy. And some of them don't care that they have no clue what they're doing. When they are invited in by an extended hand, they take it and do their best.

Collin comes out in front of me and offers me his hand as well.

I think I blush like a fucking teenager, because my whole face goes hot.

"Come on, Lowyn. If I remember how to do this dance, I know damn well you do too."

He's right. I've been doing this dance since I was four.

I give him my hand and suddenly I'm swept up in a wave of delight as he moves me around, and through, the dancing crowd. The next thing I know Rosie and Amon are in our group. And the pair of us join up with Jacob Wonder and April Laver. Then Bryn is there, dancing with Ethan Sardis, who runs the mechanic shop on Third and Maple, and we've got ourselves a square.

The dance is never-ending, that's what makes it so fun. When the song ends, some other child in the choir starts singing 'Can't You Hear Me Callin', and we just keep going. I don't know even know how long it lasts. Half an hour? Two hours? A lifetime? All I know is that I haven't danced this much, or smiled this much, or felt this good since before that one dark night when everything went wrong.

But eventually, it all slows down, and little Bethylynn Baptist is back crooning out 'Down to the River to Pray' in her angelic six-year-old voice, and we all slow too. Collin and I face each other and I rest my head on his shoulder as he holds me, just listening to the words echo inside him as he sings along. We all sing along. Even if most of us are just whispering or catching our breath.

When that's over, it's all over. People start clapping, all of us. It's a familiar moment because it comes every year on

Christmas Eve when the season ends. And even though we all complain about the work, and the stress, and the baking, and the fainting, and the crafting, and everything that comes along with being a part of this Broadway play of a town, we're *always* sad when it ends.

Even Collin looks sad. And there's not even a reason to be sad because this is opening day.

It's just conditioning that we're feeling.

Because that dancing we just did means somethin's over.

COLLIN

*W*e *spend the afternoon* with Amon, Ryan, Nash, and Bryn—who I guess is OK with me now, or at the very least is being polite, because she doesn't even shoot me a dirty look. But right around three o'clock they all disappear, leaving Lowyn and I alone again.

We can't leave until six, so she takes me to the souvenir tent and we let the teenagers leave and enjoy what's left of opening day.

There are a lot of people inside the tent with us, all buying things, and I help out when I can, but it's mostly non-stop busy for the next couple hours, only thinning out after five o'clock passes.

Lowyn leans against the counter, lettin' out a breath. Her eyes sparkle bright as she looks at me. "I think this might be the best opening day ever."

"Because you sold so many crafty things?" I wink at her.

This is an invitation for her to come over and slip her hands right around my waist. She leans up and kisses me on the cheek. "Can we still go get my mirror tonight?"

"Peaches, I had that mirror delivered to McBooms at lunchtime."

"You did?"

"I did. When I went to drop Mercy off in the tent, I told Amon to take care of it. Rosie gave him a key and that whole pile of shit you had stacked up near the door to the church is sitting in the back of your store."

She gazes up at me like I'm a fuckin' prince. "That was pretty nice of you, Collin."

"We don't have time to be deliverin' shit tonight. We gotta hit the grocery store for a spiral ham and a couple of sides."

"Oh, now it's my turn to surprise you. Because we don't need to do that."

"No?"

She's smiling big now, like she really is about to surprise me. "Nope. We've got ourselves a reservation at the Bishop Inn tonight. They *looooove* Easter over in Bishop."

"I can't imagine they had an open table when you called Jessica and asked for one this morning."

"I'm sure they didn't. But I didn't call and ask Jessica. I asked Bryn."

"Well, well, well." I grin just picturing it. "I guess we're gonna have ourselves a proper dinner then."

She pats my chest. "Just you wait. The only kicker is, we gotta show up in costume. Give the Bishop folks a little encore, so to speak. Because Bryn tells me that Jessica and Michael are gonna go all-out for this."

"Well, I am certainly intrigued and that's all fine with me. I think this might be the nicest suit I've ever worn and it would be criminal to make you take that dress off before we're ready for bed."

Her eyes do a little wild dance. Like she's picturing us going to bed tonight.

"Just one thing." I hold up a finger. "We gotta take Mercy. Because she and I are partners now."

"Of course we can. She's a lovely dog anyway. Why don't you go grab her while I close up and I'll meet you over by the east gate and we can walk home and get your Jeep."

"Sounds like a plan." Then I lean down and kiss her. But it's not a cheek kiss. Not at all. It's a good, long one with lots of tongue. And when she pulls back, she's breathless and her cheeks are all pink.

R YAN IS **the only one** in the tent when I get there. He's busy packing things away in the safe, but when I enter, he looks over his shoulder and nods at me. "I like this place, Collin. I like your people too."

I walk over to Mercy and bend down to pet her. She yawns sleepily, like she's been having the best time of her life just lazing around in this tent all afternoon. "Well, I'm glad to hear that Ryan. They are not bad people, that's for sure. But don't get too cozy with them." I look him in the eye for this next part. "It's nice. It's… a little bit magical at times, I guess. But this is an inside job, if you get my meaning. And even if you married into it, the best you'd get back is a smile to your face and overly polite words. They will never see you as one of them."

He lets out a breath, opens his mouth like he wants to say something, but then decides against it, nodding at Mercy instead. "She's been good."

"Of course she has." Then I stand up, snap my fingers, and the next thing I know, Mercy is sittin' at my left knee. "Where is everyone else?"

"Amon's making the rounds for night shift. It finally stopped raining."

"Shit. I kinda forgot it was raining. This tent is something else."

"A goddamned engineering marvel is what it is," Ryan agrees. He hesitates again. But this time when he opens his mouth the words actually come out. "So... this MacyLynn girl? You were saying earlier?"

"Was I sayin' something earlier?" He rolls his eyes and I grin at him. "She was a freshman when I was a senior and she's got a twin sister called Maizie Lee. I really don't know her. Know *of* her, yes. But that's it. You got a thing for MacyLynn, Ryan?"

"I could maybe have one, if it was a worthwhile investment."

"Define that."

"You know. If she's into me, I'd be into her."

"Do you want me to pass this message along?"

He smiles. "If you don't mind, I actually would."

"These Disciple women scaring ya a little bit, Ryan? Because I don't recall you ever needed a proper introduction to get yourself a woman."

He huffs a little bit of air. "This place is..."

"Weird?"

"Kinda. But these people are..."

"Culty?"

He laughs. "I was gonna say old-fashioned? But maybe culty works too. I bought one of her funnel cakes."

"OK."

"And she was nice to me."

"I'm following."

"But, as you mentioned, it was a very polite nice to me."

"Like maybe you're cute, and worldly, and interesting, but that's just not enough for her?"

He points at me. "That. This girl is running a funnel cake tent at a carnival—no offense."

"None taken. This place is exactly like a carnival."

"And I'm a former asshole rich kid who's been all over the world doing shit I'm not even allowed to talk about, it's so damn important and interesting, and she looked at me like I was trying to sell her insurance when I smiled and said, 'Hello.'"

My chuckle comes out quick. "Sounds about right."

"So what's the deal? These Disciple women don't date

outside men? The place is not that big. How could you not all be related by now?"

"Don't be a dick, Ryan."

"Sorry. It's just a fact."

"Well, the truth is, they most certainly do date outside men. Almost everyone has a parent who wasn't from here. At the very least, they've got a grandparent who wasn't. So it's not a rule or nothin'. But the profit share is something we guard. She's not gonna waste her time on just any old fucker, Ryan. She's not gonna mess up the good thing she's got by birthright. And she's not gonna share it with just anyone. So if you like this woman, you'd better brush up on your manners. Regardless of how Amon goes through life here in Disciple, you're not Amon. He put a spell on this town and he did that back when he was five or six. They love him. They do not love you. So do not follow his lead."

"So... it's OK for me to ask her out? Or not?"

"Ask her out. But if you put your hand up her shirt on that first date, she'd better have her hand down your pants before you do that. I'm not saying the women here are prudes, but don't disrespect her. You need to give her a reason to like you. And before you ask her out, you had better find out if she's got a man already. And if she does, stay away from her."

Ryan thinks about all this for a few moments. Then looks me in the eye and nods. "OK. Thanks for the tip."

"It's been a pleasure. Now, I'm gonna get the fuck out of here. Lowyn has planned me an Easter dinner."

I catch Ryan grinning as I turn, but I don't say anything else. Just walk out of the tent with my dog.

Lowyn is waiting for me at the east gate. She's talking to a few guests, smiling at them as they ask her questions, or whatever. But then, when I get closer, I hear that they are talking about McBooms.

"We're generally open during the week if you want to stop by," Lowyn is saying. "But your best bet is to look on the website because everything I have for sale is online and can be shipped." She notices me and excuses herself from the two older ladies. "Ready?"

I nod and offer her my arm, which Lowyn takes gladly and easily. Like this is something men still do. Because here in Disciple, it is.

We walk down the hill slowly, just looking out at the river and the thick forest on the other side of it. I'd forgotten how nice of a view it is when walking home from Revival. This is the same view from my front porch—Lowyn's front porch now —so it's all very familiar, but surprising at the same time.

Then we cut over to the right when we get to my street, which is a nice street for being in town. There are no busi- nesses on the side I live on. And my backyard bumps up to a hillside covered in trees just like the one across the river. I spent a lot of time up in those hills when I was a kid. Grimm and me both, since we were pretty close when we were young.

Mercy stays right at my side like the well-trained security dog she is.

"It was really nice today, don't you think?"

I look over at Lowyn and nod. "It was. But it was weird too. I mean, why the sudden change? It was a completely different vibe from yesterday."

"I've been thinking about that all day myself. And I think Jim Bob's intention was to remind you of all the good things about Revival."

"You mean that warm, fuzzy feeling we all get when it's Christmas Eve and the whole fuckin' thing is over?"

Lowyn chuckles. "Yeah. Probably. But it did remind you, didn't it?"

"I cannot deny that his plan was clever. It was fun. Really fun. Why don't they just do that every weekend, ya know? Why bother with all this story stuff in the first place?"

"I imagine they bother because things aren't special if they happen all the time. And closing day is filled with things we don't normally do."

"So it's just a plan. Jim Bob knows what he's doing. He's kind of a master manipulator, if you ask me. He thinks the cozy atmosphere under the big tent, and the hazy, soft glow of garden lights strung up everywhere—plus the dancing—will be enough to entice me to participate. But I'm telling you right now, it's not gonna work. I don't want to be a part of the show. And if he would just let me be, I'd gladly show up and dance with you on the boardwalk every now and then to make it all special."

"He's not gonna give up on you. He wants you here, Collin. You might as well make your peace with that."

I would like to object here. Say more. But we're home. I take my keys out of my pocket, click the key fob, unlocking the Jeep, then open the passenger door for Lowyn.

But in this same moment, Mercy starts to bark. At me, no less. She starts nosing my hand, whining. "Stop, Mercy." I open the back door and point to it. "Get in." Which she does without hesitation, but I think I catch a bit of dejection when her gaze catches mine.

Fucking Amon. He treats these dogs like people and it's starting to rub off on me.

BISHOP IS A FUCKIN' **madhouse** of cars circling for parking spaces. You can't go into downtown using a car. You have to park and walk in, or take one of the horse-drawn carriages. They do have a nice big parking lot, but it's a half a mile away, at least. They run big old streetcars with teams of Belgians pulling them to shuffle people in and out of the central historic district. And I see dozens of these streetcars as I circle the block, looking for a space to park.

"Damn," I say, under my breath. "Bishop is going off."

"We get the crowds from nine to six, Bishop gets the family folk after that, and all the partiers go to Revenant. That much has not changed. But the crowds are definitely bigger with each passing year. At least here in Bishop. I don't know what Revenant looks like these days, but I assume it is pretty much the same."

"We're going down there tomorrow. Lucas came by yesterday and invited me, so I'm gonna check it out, see what he's been up to, and take Amon along with me."

"I'll be busy at McBooms tomorrow. Those ladies I was talking to at the gate recognized me from TV. We're always super busy on the Monday after opening. But hopefully it'll be mostly online." She points. "There's a spot. Quick, get it."

Sure enough, a truck is pulling out just as we come up on it, so I slip the Jeep in as it leaves. "We're like seven blocks away. I hope your feet don't hurt." But just as I say that, I notice movement to my left. And when I look over, there's a horse right next to us. And behind that horse is a carriage.

Lowyn opens her door. "Looks like we won't have to worry about our feet, will we? Come on, Collin. Your Easter carriage is waiting." When I look over at her, I catch a wink.

Then I chuckle. Well. I will not say no to a carriage ride with Lowyn. I get out and Mercy is at my side, having jumped out with Lowyn.

The carriage driver points to my dog. "She can ride up here with me if she wants, Collin Creed."

I look over at Lowyn. "Did you set this up?"

Her response is a one-shoulder shrug. But it comes with a blush, so I know she did.

I direct Mercy to join the driver, then open the carriage door for Lowyn, giving her my hand as she climbs the bouncing steps and gets inside. I join her, leaning back in the cushions and slipping my arm around her shoulder just as the carriage begins to move. "You arranged a date for me."

"I did. You were so grumpy this morning, and so insistent on making a thing about Easter, I figured it was the least I could do."

I lean down and kiss her on the cheek. "Thank you. It's the perfect way to end a very nice day."

"Oh, it's not over yet." She turns her face to mine, looking up at me with a smile. "This night is just getting started."

When we get to the Bishop Inn I realize what she meant. We come in on the back side, the driver pulling the carriage up along the outside of the hedge maze. And since the hedge maze is only four feet tall, I can see that in the middle of it is a tent, strung up with garden lights, with at least a dozen people here already.

"What is this?" I ask her.

"Your Easter dinner, Mr. Creed. Complete with a spiral ham, a couple of sides, and family. Maybe they are not blood family, but they are found family, which is even better because it's fate."

There is someone standing guard at the hedge maze entrance and a little velvet rope with a sign on it that says 'Private Party.' But as we approach, the attendant removes the rope and lets us pass.

Amon is calling at me from the middle. "Hurry up, Collin. The fuckin' ham is getting' cold." And I'm sure everyone is Bishop is cringing when the f-word comes rolling out of his mouth like it's nothing.

Amon doesn't care, though. And no one likes him less when he acts like a heathen, so why should he?

We join the party and everyone from our dancing square is here. Rosie, Jacob Wonder, and April Laver, and Ethan Sardis. Even Bryn is here. She's wearing her chef's jacket, like she's working, but she's drinking a white wine too.

Ryan and Nash are here too. Sitting down, all stretched out, still wearing their Revival clothes like they are one of us. And maybe now they are. It's not every day that Disciple, West Virginia, invites outsiders in. And I think it's probable that Jim Bob did this on purpose too.

It's a way for him to tell me that my friends are welcome here, without actually telling me.

Even though the hedge maze is not tall, it is quite long. So it takes us almost ten minutes to make our way to the center where everyone is waiting, sitting under the tent around a long wooden table that was probably handcrafted locally by a talented woodworker. The table is set with pewter plate chargers, and fine china, and wine glasses that reflect the garden lights, making the whole place sparkle.

There is ale in the pewter tankards and much more on the table than just a ham and two sides. It's a feast.

Every bad thing that has ever happened to me suddenly ceases to matter. Every strange place I've ever been where I've felt like an outsider fades like a distant memory.

And this is when I realize how much I gave up when I walked out twelve years ago.

It's a nice evening. The perfect evening, actually. Right at the end of a perfect day. And all the little things that have happened in the last week are starting to add up to something bigger. It's me, living in my childhood home, with the woman I loved but walked out on, and gettin' a second chance pretty much without consequence. We even have a fuckin' dog.

It's a lot. Even when it all feels comfortable and right, it's still a lot.

Not to mention I spent the entire day at the Revival and I actually had fun.

I want to see it as... I dunno. A gift. From who though? It's certainly not from Jim Bob. He's not a bad guy—at least, I don't think he is and I'm a pretty good judge of character. But he's... I mean, it's kinda cliché because of the circus he's been running for the past forty years, but the term 'carnival barker' fits. He's a fast talker and he's spent his entire life in this little town taking care of this little show. He's much more than a mere salesman and does more than just entice people to take a peek past the tent flap. He enchants them. He charms them. And if that doesn't work, he'll just bring the show to them.

Which is exactly what he did to me.

I like the thought of money, but I cannot be bought. If it were that easy to buy me, I'd be working for Charlie Beaufort. Because he has offered me fuck-you money to take that position.

But I don't wanna work for anyone. I wanna work for me, and Amon, and Nash, and Ryan.

Jim Bob has figured this out, obviously. Because he didn't offer me more money today, he offered me the one thing he had that no one else did—family.

Because I lost mine. Maybe I walked away, maybe it was always gonna end up like this, doesn't matter, because the truth is, until I came back to Disciple, the only person I had left from home was Amon.

And now—well, I'm being offered everything. Not my

daddy, not my mama, not my sister. But everything else I lost was given back to me today.

I'm not dumb, though. I know it all comes with conditions. And it sucks that people play that way. It would be nice, just once in my life, to be given something freely without an expectation in return.

WHEN WE GET HOME, I empty my pockets onto the kitchen counter and remember I put that key in there this morning. I hold it up as Lowyn sits on the couch and takes her shoes off. "What's this key to?"

She looks at it, squinting a little, slipping her shoes off and massaging her feet. Mercy barks and I turn to her and point. "Quiet now. Work's over." She gives me a look, but drops down near Lowyn.

"I don't know. I've never seen that key before. Where did you get it?" I can tell that Lowyn is exhausted because she sighs in the same way I recall from high school after a long day of homework, and football games, and cheering.

"The power went out this morning, so I went down to the basement to check the breakers. And this key fell out of the box when I opened it up."

"Oh, that's not the breaker box anymore."

"I found it. It's in the garage."

"Your daddy did that for me. He said, 'Lowyn, the electrics in this house are a mess, so I put in a new breaker box in the garage.' So I have never actually looked in the old breaker box. I don't go down to that basement. I had men fix the leaks as best they could, but that place is creepy and way too old to bother with."

"Hmm. Weird though." I set the key down on the counter.

Mercy barks again, and I finally understand. "Shit. I bet she's gotta go outside. You go up, I'll be up in a minute."

Lowyn comes over to me, places her hands on my shoulders, then leans up and kisses me on the mouth. "Don't take too long, because I'm about to pass out." Then she flashes me a smile and goes up the stairs.

I look at Mercy. She looks at me and barks. I point at her. "Don't you dare be mouthy all night long or I'll take you back to the kennel." She understands what I said, but she pretends not to, kinda lookin' up at the ceiling. "All right, let's go." I point to the back door and she trots down the hallway and sits down facing the basement. "That's the wrong door, doggie. We're goin' this way." I pull the back door open and let her out, stepping out onto the back porch as she takes off into the yard.

Other than getting the key so I could let myself in the other day, I haven't been out here. But two things have changed considerably. The porch has been rebuilt, just like the front one. Nice, too. It's screened in, but obviously Lowyn has not gotten around to putting the screens back up after winter, because they're not there and neither is the door.

Also, the back fence has been removed. Our yard—before it was Lowyn's—had a tall, wooden privacy fence around it because it backs up to the hill and the woods and my mama was always yelling at me to stay the hell out of those woods. But Lowyn has removed the fence and there's actually a little sitting area elevated up on the side of the hill. Just a couple of chairs and a little fire pit.

Of course, a fence comes in handy when you've got a new dog. But this dog is smarter than most humans, so when I say, "Stay here, Mercy," when she gets close to those woods, she pretends like the thought of going up there never even occurred to her.

After a couple minutes, we go back inside. I'm gonna have to find her a place to sleep, but not tonight. Tonight she will sleep at the bottom of the stairs. And that's the direction I'm heading when she suddenly veers off, goes over to the kitchen counter, points her nose at my keys, and gives off a single bark.

"Shhh. Quiet now."

But she barks again, then sits down, looking up at the counter. And this is when it occurs to me that she's pointing to something, the way a dog who has been trained to search for drugs might indicate it's time for a search. So I go over there and pick my car keys, offering them to her.

She doesn't move. Just barks one more time, and stares up at the counter.

The only thing up there is that skeleton key. And the moment I realize that's what she's pointing to, I get a weird feeling in my stomach. I pick it up and offer to her. She gets up, sniffs, barks once, then sits back down, just as she was trained.

I look at the clock. It's past midnight. But I don't really have a job right now, so I guess I don't mind staying up a little longer to figure this out. I offer her the key again. "Seek, Mercy. Find it."

She takes off down the hallway and when I turn the corner to see where she is, she's right where she was ten minutes ago, staring straight at the basement door.

"What the fuck." I walk over to the door, open it up, and she goes down the steps without being told. I grab the flashlight, flick it on, and follow.

For a moment I think she's following my scent from this morning because she pauses at the bottom of the stairs where I was standing when I opened the breaker box.

But then she turns, first sniffing the ground, then sniffing the air, and finally walks over to the far side of the basement where the dirt floor is. She sits down, her nose pointing at the stone wall.

I shine the light on the wall. I have to admit, I've never

thought twice about that stone wall in the basement. But looking at it now, after all the shit I've done all over the world for the past dozen years, I see exactly what it is.

Something put up quickly. Something probably not made by a mason.

Amon's words from the other day come back to me. *'I got her on special. She flunked out of cadaver school.'*

And that sinking feeling in my stomach is back.

There's no turning back now, though. So I walk over to her, bend down, and take a closer look at the wall. Sure enough, there's a break in the mortar. "Move back," I tell Mercy. She obeys, getting up and sitting down a few paces away.

Then I start prying the stone loose. It takes a good ten minutes of wiggling and in the end, I have to go hunt down a flat-head screwdriver to get it out, but get it out I do.

Setting the rock down, I shine my light into the hole and find an old metal box with a padlock on it. I take it out and Mercy stands up, barks once, and then sits back down. Telling me I'm on the right track.

It would surprise me more if the key I found in the electrical box this morning didn't open the damn lock than if it did —and of course it does.

I flip the top open, point the flashlight inside, and take out an aged plastic bag. Inside there is a single folded piece of paper. I take it out of the plastic and open it up.

"Well, this was anticlimactic." I wouldn't say I was expecting a treasure, but I was expecting something more than a scrap of paper with some chicken-scratch on it.

I set the paper back inside the box and point the flashlight at the stairs. "Mercy, let's go."

Mercy pops up and heads for the stairs. When I get to the top, she's looking straight at the back door. "Girl, you just went out. This hunt is over. Come on, let's go." I point down the hall-way, but she hesitates. "Mercy, go to bed." After one last look at the back door, she huffs some air, turns back to the hallway, and trots off.

When I join her in the living room, she's on the couch. I consider making her get down, but fuck it. I'm too tired. I go up the stairs, find Lowyn already asleep, take off my clothes, and slip in next to her.

She sighs a little when I pull her close to me, but falls back asleep almost immediately.

I don't though. I lie there with her in my arms, just runnin' the day back in my head.

I could do this. The Revival, I mean. Maybe not every weekend, but if Lowyn's got to be there, I don't mind being there too.

It's just... nice, I guess. To be here. All the ways in which 'here' is defined. Here in Disciple, here in this house, here in this bed, here with Lowyn.

It's all very, very nice.

I sigh, and close my eyes, smiling.

The next thing I know, it's morning.

*C*ollin *comes down* the stairs just as I'm pouring my coffee into a travel mug. "Mornin', peaches."

He's wearing flannel pants and no shirt, his hair all messy and tousled, and he's got a sexy shadow on his jaw. It still feels like a dream to me. Him being here. Living here. Us being back together. Acting so natural, like we were never apart and this is just how our life together shook out. "Would you like a cup of coffee, Collin?"

"Sure. Not gonna turn that down. You're off to work?"

"I have a meeting this morning with Sassy Lorraine."

"About the dognapping?"

"No." I laugh as I pour him a cup of coffee. "She's trying to revive her career and we're discussing a deal about how McBooms can help her do that, seeing as she's kinda vintage." I hand him his cup, trying my best not to get lost in those eyes of his. "What are you gonna do today?"

He looks around, frowning. "Where's Mercy?"

"Oh, I let her outside. I told her to stay in the yard, and I watched for a few minutes to see if she would do that, and she did. So then I told her to sleep on the porch."

He turns into the hallway to check on her, then comes back a moment later. "She's still there."

"Do you wanna come to work with me? It's gonna be real

boring. But if you don't have anything to do, you're welcome to hang out."

"Amon and I are going into Revenant today. I think I'll stop by the compound too. Check on my house and see how it's coming."

I smile at him, but inside I'm a little bit panicky. I like him here. And if his house is done, he won't have a reason to stay.

"I'll come by in the afternoon, though. On my way back from Revenant." He walks over to me, slipping his hands around my waist, then leans in and kisses me on the neck. "Yesterday was fun."

"It was."

"But Jim Bob is up to something and I'm gonna need to figure out what it is."

"Sounds like a plan."

"All right." He pulls back a little. "I'll let you get to work. See ya later."

I grab my purse, kiss him on the cheek, and reluctantly leave.

I don't usually drive to work, I walk. It's only a couple blocks over. So five minutes later I'm there, greeting Rosie in all her classic Valerie Bertinelli circa 1976 glory. High-waisted bell bottoms, a tight cropped sweater in orange and yellow, and wooden clogs that make my feet hurt just looking at them.

"Wasn't yesterday the best?" Rosie says, beaming a smile at me.

"I have to admit, it was a pretty fun time. But..." I frown here.

"But what? What do you possibly have to complain about?"

"What Jim Bob is up to, for one. He just had a change of heart?"

"You know how he is," Rosie says. "When he thinks things are not going his way, he resorts to manipulation."

"Obviously, but what is he doing with Collin? Why even bother winding him up like that on Saturday if he knew damn well that it wouldn't even matter on Sunday?"

Rosie cocks her head at me. "Didn't it matter?"

I let out a frustrated breath. "Rosie. If you know something—"

But that's as far as I get. Because the bell over the front door rings and both she and I turn our heads to look in that direction.

"Ladies." Jameson Grimm pretends to tip an imaginary hat.

I sigh again. He is the last person I want to see right now.

"Hi, Grimm." Rosie chirps out her greeting to Grimm in the same bubbly tone she uses on everyone. "You should've danced with us yesterday. You should've scooted in and been partners with Bryn. That would've been fun."

The funny thing is, Rosie really means this. She likes Grimm. Hell, I'm pretty sure everyone likes Grimm. Everyone but me. I don't hate him, it's just... he and I... we share secrets. And these secrets bond us in a way that might've been OK when it all started nine years ago—almost to the day, funnily enough—but is no longer OK now.

Grimm looks at me, probably picturing himself dancing in our group yesterday. Putting himself in Ethan's place as Bryn's partner. But then he kinda blinks his eyes and shakes his head a little, pulling himself back to reality. It's his turn to sigh. "Rosie, do you mind giving me a moment with Lowyn?"

I put up a hand. "That's OK, Rosie. We don't need a moment. I'm real busy, Grimm. So whatever it is, it can wait."

Grimm glances at Rosie with that look he gives, one eyebrow raised, but eyes kinda narrowed at the same time. It's not a threatening look. He's really not that kind of man. But it is a look that says, *Don't make me ask you twice.* And it works, most of the time.

It works this time for sure. Because Rosie says, "I'm gonna go organize shit over there," and then clops off in those clogs of hers.

As soon as she's across the store, pretending to be busy flipping through cassette tapes over by the jukebox, I look Grimm in the eyes. "What do you want?"

"Why do you always talk to me that way?"

"What way, Grimm?" I ask this just to be difficult. And this is exactly what he's referring to, so it comes out passive-aggressively bitchy.

"Look, I'm not tryin' to be a dick. I've left you alone. I don't interfere in your life—"

"Can you get to the point, please?"

He stares at me for a moment, like he's runnin' scenarios through his head. He blows out a breath. "OK. I'll get to the point, I guess. But there are two of them so I would ask that you let me make both of them before you throw one of your Lowyn McBride tantrums and walk out."

I scoff. "You're not gettin' off to a real good start here, Grimm."

"First of all"—he holds up a finger to indicate 'one'—"I know things about Collin. I know where he's been and some of what he's been doing, and this is just a friendly warning."

"Since when are we friends?"

He pauses and I can practically hear the insults running through his mind. But he's far more in control than I am right now, because he holds them all in, pretending I didn't even speak. "He's not the guy you think he is."

"You know that how?"

"I'm on the board, Lowyn. I've been to all the meetings about Collin Creed over the past seven years. And I've been filled in on the ones that came before that."

I don't know what this means. I didn't have any idea that the town board had been keeping tabs on Collin through the years.

When Grimm and I were closer a while back—we dated a little, nothin' serious—but when we were closer, he told me a secret. He said he had to tell somebody, so it might as well be me. I was the most trustworthy person he had ever met, that's what he said. So I do know a little bit about how the towns are all connected. But he never once—*not once*—told me anything about Collin.

This burns me a little. Because at that particular time in my life I was dyin' for information about Collin. I would've wanted to hear all of it. Any of the bits and pieces would've gone a long way to settle my soul. So learning that Grimm had details like that does not paint him in a good light. In fact, it makes me dislike him more.

"OK. So what?" This is the best I can come up with because other than the stories Collin's been telling me about his time away, I really have no idea what he's been doing.

"So he's… well, the easiest way to put it is that he's a really dangerous man, Lowyn."

Is this a surprise? Not really. I saw Collin Creed, with my own eyes, kill a man when he was eighteen years old. "Are you trying to say he's gonna hurt me, Grimm? Because that's just stupid."

"Considering the secrets you and I share, and taking into account the kind of man Collin is, and has turned into over the years, don't you feel like all this leads up to someone gettin' hurt? Because I sure do."

I force myself to stay calm and think this through.

Grimm and I do share secrets. I have one of his and he's got one of mine. His secret is about how the towns work and how they're all tangled up with the government. He learned his secret from being on the town board.

My secret is about Blackberry Hill and I learned about it from first-hand experience.

But I only told Grimm about that place because he brought the name up first.

It was a moment of weakness, in my opinion. And then I resented him for knowing that secret. It all goes back to how I don't want people to know me. How people don't have the right to know me.

Not without my permission.

And this is the real problem. I actually gave him this permission and I should not have.

If Grimm truly wants to know why I'm confrontational with him, this is why. He's got my secret I would like to take it back.

But I can't.

"What's number two, Grimm? I really am busy."

"He's gonna find out, Lowyn. Because your secret isn't really a secret. Lots of people know about it. And if it's not a secret, he's gonna find out."

"OK." I'm starting to shake a little. I mean, I knew this. I've been living with this lie—secret, whatever you wanna call it—for nine years. And of course, Jim Bob knows my secret because he's part of it. And if there's one thing I know about secrets around here, it's that they don't exist. Not really. When you get a secret in Disciple you tell someone real fast. So I know that Jim Bob told someone. I never had confirmation, not until now, but I always knew he told someone. He would've had to. It's too big not to. "Is that it, Grimm?"

"If you don't tell him, I will."

"Is that a threat? Are you threatening me?"

"I would call it an opportunity, Lowyn. Not a threat."

"You need to—"

But I am cut off by the jingling bell over the door. Grimm and I both glance in that direction.

"Hi, there, Lowyn!" Former one-time country music star

Sassy Lorraine waves enthusiastically. But she must really know how to read a room, because her smile drops almost immediately. "Did I interrupt something?"

Grimm says, "Yes."

But I say, "No. We were just finishing up." Then I look at Grimm. "Please see yourself out, and thanks for stoppin' by."

He lets out a long breath, looking me in the eye one last time. "I mean it, Low. You tell him, or I will."

Then he tips that same imaginary hat at me and turns away, tippin' it again as he passes Sassy and opens the door, leaving all the tension he created behind him.

"Well," Sassy says, "I don't know what that was about, but it was a thing, wasn't it?"

I exhale, gather myself, force everything Grimm just said out of my mind, and smile at Sassy. "It was nothing. I'm so glad you're here. We've got a million things to discuss. Let me introduce you to my assistant."

Then I walk over to her, offer her my arm, and escort her over to Rosie. Who immediately takes over, chattin' a mile a minute, so I can pull myself together.

I have always known that this loose end would come back to haunt me. I've always known it.

But it has been so long now that I guess I just... believed, maybe, that there would be no consequences for what I did on the one-year anniversary of my mama's birthday after her death.

The original get-drunk day. The very first one-night-stand day. The day I made the biggest mistake of my life.

COLLIN

After Lowyn leaves, I go to the front window and watch her walk off. I wish she didn't have work. I would like nothing more than for her to take the day off and to fuck her silly all morning.

That's one thing I hate about the Revival. It takes up your whole weekend. And yeah, it was fun. But I get tired of crowds. Sometimes you just want to be alone with your pretty girlfriend and not have to put on a show for strangers.

I will have to talk to Jim Bob. But not now. I just want to forget about all that crap.

I take my coffee out to the back porch where Mercy is, checkin' on her. She's just sleeping like she hasn't got a care in the world. Then I remember our little midnight treasure hunt. I left that piece of paper in the metal box down in the basement. And since I'm right here, just a few feet away, I go back inside, open the door, go down the stairs, grab the paper, and come back up. Then I take it and my coffee back into the kitchen so I can look a little closer.

Last night it looked like a bunch of scribbles, but this morning, with more light and a clearer head, I can tell that it's something like a crude map. In fact, at least one of those chicken scratches looks kinda like a skull.

After a couple more seconds, I come to the conclusion that this map starts at my house.

Well, Lowyn's house.

And then I'm thinking that whatever this piece of paper is, it belonged to my daddy. He drew this map.

I look up and around, then down at the map, trying to orient it. It begins at the back door.

"Hmm." Do I want to fuck with this? Or should I just leave this alone?

If Jim Bob had not told me that there was some big-deal secret waiting for me at the end of my one-year contract that has something to do with my baby sister's would-be kidnapper —i.e. the man I fuckin' killed—well, I might leave it alone.

But I already know that the secret is most certainly related to that and so there is no way in hell I am not gonna follow this map to see where it takes me.

I go upstairs, pull on some jeans and a t-shirt, slip my feet into my work boots, grab my jacket, and then go out the back door to Mercy.

She hops up, wagging and smiling at me.

I show her the map, then tell her, "Seek," just to see if this map was the reason she wanted to go outside last night after we found it.

She sticks her nose up into the wind, sniffin'. If Mercy was trained for cadavers, and Amon said she was even if she did flunk out, then she tracks scents through the air as well as the ground. This map has been in the basement for God knows how long, so I'm not expecting much, but she did bark last night. And I really do think that she smelled something relating to this map, or maybe the key that opened the metal box.

Mercy looks at me, then at the woods in the back of the house, and takes off in that direction.

"Well, fuckin' A." I shake my head, but I follow.

The hillside behind the house is muddy from yesterday's downpour, so I grab a stick to help pull myself up the trail— which really isn't much of a trail, since I haven't come up this way for nearly two decades, but it's easy enough to see it once I start looking. Plus, wherever Mercy is heading, it seems to be along the path.

The hills in West Virginia are some of the prettiest around because they are covered edge to edge in thick trees. And while this certainly looks nice when you're gazing out a window, it's actually not that easy to walk through. Especially when you're going uphill.

When Mercy gets to the top of the first hill right behind my house, she stops and sniffs the air again. There's a lot of forest up here, but typically I didn't go much higher up as a kid because all the interesting things, in my childhood opinion, were to the left.

The river winds around Disciple in a horseshoe, but it curves back and forth like that in hundreds of places up in the hills. That's how you can have a view of it from the front porch of Lowyn's house, another view of it from the back end of the Revival grounds, but still have to cross it when you venture up this way. Goin' left was the best part when we were teenagers. Because there's a waterfall up here. That's where all the high school kids gathered back then, and I'm pretty sure they probably still do.

But Mercy doesn't go left. She goes across a meadow and into the next bit of forest. I lose sight of her quickly and I find myself wishing she had a bell on, but once I get back under the canopy of leaves, I see her ahead. Waiting for me in a clearing.

As soon as she sees me coming, she takes off again, going straight up a hill, and there's no path at all this time. She makes it to the top in thirty seconds. But it takes me ten whole minutes to pull myself up the steep incline and come out into another mountaintop meadow.

Mercy barks. She's all the way across it, waiting to go into the next set of woods and trek up the next fuckin' hill.

I look out across a cliffside and figure I'm about done with this. But when I look over at Mercy to call her back, she's gone.

"Mercy!" I call her, then wait. I expect her to come back

because she's not a pet, she's a protection dog. And she has spent every minute of her short life learning how to follow commands.

But she does not come back.

I call again, "Mercy!" Louder. But still, no dog appears. "Fuck." I let out a long breath and follow her. I certainly can't leave her up here, Amon would throw a fit.

When I get into the next level of forest the hill is not as steep and there actually appears to be a slight deer trail weaving through the underbrush. Then I hear barking. It sounds far though. "Mercy!" I call, loud as I can. Then wait, straining to hear anything up ahead.

I take a step forward, trip over a root or something, and almost fall, only just barely catching myself on a nearby tree trunk. I look down to see what it was and have to shake my head and blink.

What the fuck? I bend down, pick it up, and hold it in my hands, feeling like I just stumbled into my own personal *Blair Witch Project*.

Because it's not a root. It's a fuckin' bone. Like a leg bone. Like a human-sized leg bone.

That's when I look up and see skulls. One, two—at least ten. They are hanging from the tree limbs, more than ten, dozens of them, strung up on vines. Hanging down like a curtain of horror.

When I look around some more, there are more bones hidden in the dirt and leaves.

Mercy, the cadaver dog, brought me to a boneyard and I'm guessing that if I were to look at the map and trace my steps, this is exactly where that map leads.

Yep, I've seen enough. "Mercy!" I yell it as loud as I can. "Mercy, come here!"

I grew up here in these hills so of course, I've heard the stories about the mountain men and the granny witches and such. But they were ghost stories. Never in my life did I ever see any evidence of them.

"Mercy!"

The sound of an animal coming through the brush fills the air. I know it's probably Mercy, but it could be a boar, or a bear, or a bobcat, and I reach for my sidearm.

Except it's not there. Because I haven't carried a gun since I got here.

The sharp cry of a dog fills the forest and my gut sinks. "Mercy!" I run forward, my boots crunching over bones with every step, and come out into another cleared circle inside the forest. This time there is a definite pattern to the hanging bones. They make a circular curtain around a cleared patch of dirt. And inside that circle is Mercy, strung up in a net.

I stand there trying to make sense of everything. Trying to understand how the hell I went from Lowyn's house to this nightmare in the span of thirty minutes.

Then someone behind me pumps a shotgun.

I put my hands up and don't move.

"Collin Creed. You're trespassing on hallowed ground."

"Who—"

"Shut up." The barrel of the shotgun jabs me in the back. "I don't know how you got up here, or why you brought that dog, but I don't care either. This is your only warning and you're only gettin' it because the contract says I can't kill you without a tribunal."

"What—"

"Shut up." He jabs me with the gun again. "I'm not finished. And just in case you start to get any ideas about bringing your men up here to start some trouble, I want you to take a good look around."

He whistles sharply and from out of the brush, people stand up. Dozens of them. All wearing ghillie suits. Not homemade ones, either—not some sticks and leaves glued to a tarp, but real fucking military-grade ghillie suits. Their faces are all painted up in black and green with one eye squintin' down a sight that is aimed squarely at me. Another quick check and I realize they are all sportin' GhostMachines, which is a mighty fine semi-automatic bullpup rifle that goes for just under three grand apiece and is worth every fuckin' penny. We've got two dozen of them down in our bunker, so I should know.

With less than ten seconds to make a first impression, these boys have let me know that they are not fuckin' around.

And I believe them.

I don't know who they are, why they know my name, or what they're doing up here in these hills, but I believe them.

"Do you understand me, Collin Creed? You've got five minutes to cut your dog out of that trap and leave. Because if you don't, fuck the contract, I'll shoot you both."

Then they all seem to disappear. Almost silently. One by one, when my eyes sweep the area, they are gone. And when I turn, there is no one behind me.

"*So you think*," Sassy says, "that my best bet is just puttin' out a record on my own dime? That's how the kids do it these days?"

"Well, some of them do vinyl. Most go the digital route. You know, SongTunes and such."

"Shouldn't I be doin' SongTunes?"

"Sassy, I'm not like… a record person. You said you'd give me the toys dirt cheap if I helped you plan a comeback. Of course you should do SongTunes. But I'm a vintage girl. Not only that, *you're* a vintage girl."

I think she might blush here because I called her a girl. But as a girl myself, I hope people never stop calling me a girl. Because inside, I'm still eight years old and I think that remindin' a girl that she's a ma'am now is just plain impolite.

"And the people who know you, Sassy," I continue, "they're vintage girls too."

"Hmm." She thinks about this thoughtfully for a moment.

Which gives me a moment to think about Grimm. And how I can't get a hold of Collin to check and make sure that Grimm didn't already find him and tell him something he really doesn't need to know.

"So you're thinking somethin' old-fashioned."

"Old-fashioned?" I pan my arms out wide to indicate my

store. "In case you haven't noticed, Sassy, old-fashioned is in. I'm worth seventeen million dollars."

She puts a hand over her heart. "Shut. Up."

People are always surprised when they learn just how rich I am. And for sure, there are many out there who are worth a lot more than I am. But for a woman under thirty who did it all on hard work, fierce determination, and a few lucky breaks, it's quite a big deal.

"A lot of it comes from appraisals," I tell a stunned Sassy. "I do live online consults while people are at auctions or flea markets. They can make an appointment or can call me up spur of the moment and I'll tell them if it's a good deal or not."

"Well, who knew?" Sassy declares.

"Certainly not me. My friend, Jet Shadows, from the TV show? He's the one who told me about that. Said I'd make a killing. I don't know if I'd call it a killing, but I do have appointments Thursday through Sunday almost every weekend of the year. Not last weekend, of course. Revival opening and all. I also bought up the contents of a barn about eight years back and in that barn, buried under layers and layers of dirt and junk, were trunks, and trunks, and trunks filled with old-time concert posters. Framed in glass, even. Pristine condition. I'm talkin' Johnny Cash. The Beatles. The Rolling Stones."

"Wow." Sassy's eyes go big. "That was some find."

"It's the real reason I'm where I'm at. I still have a few. I keep them for a rainy day. Or a dry day, more likely. So anyway, my point is, you should target your old fans first. Then, after you get a little traction, you should release something new, and shiny, and digital."

"Do you think they'd let me play at the Revival?"

Now, I knew she was gonna ask me this. When a person is looking to make a deal, such as she is looking to make a deal, they want to leverage everything. I have a face that's on TV in reruns, I have one famous friend, I have a very popular antique store, and I have the Revival.

Normally, my answer to her question would be an immediate no. But she played me some of her music when I was at her house and it's kinda our thing. It's not country. Not in the modern sense. It's not even vintage like Loretta or Patsy. She is Carter family all the way. Folksy and bluegrassy—if that's a word. Not only does she play the banjo, but she can fiddle, for fuck's sake.

She's old-timey, for sure.

And we are nothing if not old-timey around here. So I'm gonna put a good word in for her.

"Now listen," I say. Sassy leans in, eager. "I can't promise anything and you should not get your hopes up, but I will speak to Jim Bob—he runs this town. And I will play him a song. And I will remind him that you could bring in new people. It would be a win-win. But we've never—and I do need you to understand this, Sassy—we've *never* had an outsider play music for us. The kids do all the music. It's always been that way."

She deflates a little.

"But I would not waste my time or potentially get your hopes up if I didn't think that Jim Bob would at least listen to it."

She lets out a breath. "That sounds fair." Then she sticks out her hand. "This is good enough for me."

We shake on it. And I make her a promise. "I'm a woman of my word. Thank you very much, Sassy. Those toys are… well, let's be honest here, they're a gold mine. But I will fulfill my end of this deal. I will pitch you to Jim Bob with my utmost sincerity and I don't know how it's going with the whole dognapping thing, but I'm pretty sure Collin and Amon are considering it."

Her whole face lights up. "Oh, thank you so much, Lowyn. I

think meeting you has been the best thing that has ever happened to me." Which is a pretty big thing to say, considering who she is and what she's done in her life. "Do you want to come pick up the toys yourself? Or should I ship them?"

"I would be more than delighted to drive back down and spend the day with you and pack them up myself, if that's OK."

"Oh, I'd love that Lowyn. Thank you." She grabs my hand and shakes it again. "Now I'll get out of your hair. You let me know when you wanna come down and I'll clear my schedule."

"I will talk to Jim Bob this week and let you know by Friday."

She leaves, happy as can be.

But as soon as she's out the door, I've got my phone out and I'm calling Collin.

It goes straight to voicemail.

Shit. What could that mean? Did Grimm find him and start blabbin'? Is Collin already not talkin' to me?

I call Collin again, but this time I use the store phone so he can't recognize the number.

Straight to voicemail.

I call Amon. He picks up first ring. "Lowyn McBride. What can I do for you?"

"How'd you know it was me?"

"I know everything, Lowyn."

Thankfully, that's not true. Because if he did, he'd know why I am starting to feel a panic inside my chest. "Have you talked to Collin this morning? I've been trying to get a hold of him, but it goes straight to voicemail."

"Well, I haven't had a reason to get a hold of him. Hold on, let me try. Be right back."

He puts me on hold and I let out a breath.

A few seconds later, he's back. "Nope. Same thing here. Straight to voicemail. Weird. But we're going into Revenant later. I'm sure he'll pop up soon. And when he does, I'll tell him you were lookin' for him."

I let out a breath. "OK, thank you, Amon. Oh, and by the way, Sassy Lorraine was just here. I like her. A lot. Do you think you're gonna do that dognapping thing for her?"

"I was just fuckin' with the drones I ordered to plan that very escapade."

"You got more than one drone?"

"Oh, I bought a small army of those things." He laughs, then goes serious. "But don't tell Collin."

"Where are you boys getting all this money to hire those people, fix up all those houses, have a whole kennel of genius dogs, and buy a small army of drones, Amon Parrish?"

"Sorry, Low. That's all top-secret shit. I'll see ya later."

The call ends before I can say anything else. And now I'm not only wondering what kind of damage Grimm is gonna do to my new relationship, where the hell Collin is, and why Amon needs a small army of drones, but also where they are getting their funding from.

I know drones *can* be cheap. But I'm worldly enough to understand that those are not the kind of drones Amon is talking about. He certainly didn't buy a toy to airlift a chihuahua out of the Bahamas.

I let out a long sigh. Yesterday was so nice. Today is stressful.

And it's all stupid Grimm's fault.

Why can't he just leave me alone?

Just as I think that my phone buzzes in my hand and when I look down, the screen is lit up with a text message from Jim Bob, which reads: *Come to my office right now. We need to talk.*

Great. Just great.

I want to ignore this text. Pretend I didn't even see it.

But when you are a Disciple girl and Jim Bob Baptist summons you to his office, you had better get your ass over to his office.

"I'll be back in thirty," I call out to Rosie. "If Collin comes by, tell him to wait for me, please!"

"Sure thing," Rosie calls back.

And then, like it or not, I get my ass over to Jim Bob's office.

COLLIN

I turn back to the clearing and focus on the net with my dog inside. She's whining a little because the net is still swinging, but she's not thrashing, so that's good. "Hold on, Mercy. I'm coming." While I might not be carrying a gun—something that I will never do again—I always keep a pocket knife on me.

What's interesting, though, is that they left me a knife. It's stuck in the tree where the trap is set up. It's a really nice skinner knife with an engraved blade.

But I don't study it. I go over to the ropes and start sawing, holding the main rope so when the tension breaks, I can do what I can to slow the long fall down for Mercy.

She still hits pretty hard and cries out, but it's better than it could've been.

I go over to her and start untangling her from the net. It takes a good few minutes to do that, but finally she is free and back on her feet.

I'm bent down, lookin' her in the eyes. "You all right?"

She pouts a little, probably embarrassed that she got caught in a trap.

I pat her head. "It's OK. We all get caught every once in a while. Come on. Let's go."

I take the knife with me and look around, without seeming

to look around, as we make our way back through the woods, over the bones, and down the first hill.

They're still watching me. I know that for sure. So I just keep going across the pasture, hit the next hill, and go down that one too before I let out a breath.

I'm sure they have cameras everywhere. That's how they knew I was up there. Because that boneyard, whatever it was, it wasn't where they stay. They saw me coming and they got their team together.

I've been trying to figure out how they disappeared like that. Like magic.

It's not magic. It's probably tunnels. And if I had rooted around a little, I'd have found them.

This leads me to the next question—who the fuck are they? Who has time to make a network of tunnels up in the hills? They wanted me to think they were mountain men and granny witches with those hanging bones. And maybe that boneyard is sacred ground. But then again, maybe it's not. Maybe it's just cover for somethin' else?

Regardless, there's an operation up in the hills above Disciple and these people have access to money, time, equipment, tunnels, and very nice weapons.

And I have a really strong suspicion that these men, whoever they are, are connected to the secrets that Jim Bob is holding dear.

I think a visit to Jim Bob's little stone building is in order.

But as I'm heading down the last hill, my phone buzzes. I answer. "Yeah."

"Where are you?" Amon says. "People been lookin' for you all morning."

"Who?"

He laughs. "Just Lowyn. She says she was tryin' to call you and it went straight to voicemail."

"I was up in the hills above the house. Mercy took off."

"What? That's impossible. Mercy don't take off."

"Well…"

"Before you start this story, are you home yet? Because we're going in to Revenant, remember? And I'm pulling up to your house right now."

"My house? Or Lowyn's house?"

"Same difference."

"We're coming down the hill. I can see you. Be right there."

When I come out of the woods I throw the knife, stickin' it in a stump. Because I'm not gonna tell Amon about what just happened. Not right away. I'm gonna talk to Jim Bob first. So when we get down to Amon's truck, I just direct Mercy into the back cab and get in the passenger seat.

"Damn." Amon is lookin' at my muddy boots. "She took you on a chase, huh? What was she after? Because my dogs do not take off. They track or they hunt. So she was doin' one of the two."

"She saw a rabbit."

"Ahhh," Amon groans, then turns and looks at Mercy. "We've had this discussion ten times already, Mercy girl. You went clean and now you gave in to the temptation. You're gonna be in a world of hurt tryin' to kick this habit again."

I just shake my head. And when I look back at Mercy, she's practically rolling her eyes because she knows damn well she's covering for me.

"In all seriousness," Amon says, "she probably needs a few more weeks of training at the kennel. I'll take her back with me tonight."

"Nah, that's OK. She's fine, Amon. She's good just the way she is."

"Ah-ha!" He points at me. "You love her, don't you? I knew it. I knew you'd keep a dog if I just gave you a little push."

I smile and look out the window. "Whatever." But he's right. I do like Mercy. She's not a pet, she's more like a partner. She's so well trained too. I can practically ignore her and she just knows what to do.

*AMON TALKS **about*** Sassy Lorraine's dognapping caper as we drive down the winding road into Revenant. The three towns are all located on a loop that cuts off the main highway right at Revenant, then takes you up into the hills to Disciple, curves around over the river, and goes back down to Bishop where the loop ends at the same highway where it began, but about twenty miles down the road.

So Revenant is actually pretty busy because of this fact. If the town wasn't owned—like one hundred percent owned—by the Revenant Corporation, there would be apartments and townhouses all over the damn place. But that corp owns about a thousand acres to the west and Bishop owns all the acres to the east. So try as they might, the developers will never take over Revenant because this land is in a perpetual contract with the Trinity that has no termination.

Disciple and Bishop are the same way. There will be no 'progress' as far as the Trinity is concerned.

And it's nice, I think. Because even though I have not been in Revenant for over a decade—we came in on the Bishop side of things when we were buying the compound outside Disciple —it still looks the same. Other than new paint on the buildings and a newly blacktopped road through downtown, it's exactly how I remember it.

Of course, if you're gone twelve years then the people change. Lucas is my example A. Since the last time I saw him, he was ten and now he's some big-ass blond biker.

If Disciple is old-timey, and Bishop is historical, then I would describe Revenant as quaint. Which is not a word one typically uses to describe a biker town. But it's right on the river. Not only that, it's a wide part of the river so there's actually a little cove with a tiny fishin' marina. So the whole thing brings out a bit of character that one mostly finds in New England, and not West Virginia.

It's charming, I think. With the brightly painted Cape Cod buildings. Some are big, some are very small, and some are even stately. And when you mix all that in with the line of bikes parked diagonal and crowding every street in downtown, it's an appealing contradiction.

Every other bike parked down here doesn't even run. They are just props so the aesthetic of downtown maintains its biker roots at all times. Only every other bike, though. So bikers can come in from the city and get a nice space in front of a bar, or a hotel, or a restaurant.

Which means we have to park blocks away. But it's fine. Amon does that and then we head into the downtown area on foot, Mercy heelin' right at my left knee.

*E*ster is *type-type-typin' away* when I enter the little stone building where Jim Bob does his town business. "Go on in." She doesn't even look up. "He's expectin' ya."

"Thanks," I say, passing her desk and approaching Jim Bob's massive door. It's always been intimidating, this door. I was a little girl of only nine the very first time I was called down here. Ester, who was a lot younger back then but, in my memory, looked exactly the same as she does now, was waitin' for me when I got off the bus from school. She said, "Come with me, little Lowyn. Jim Bob needs to speak to you."

This was not unusual. Everyone has been called into Jim Bob's office at one time or another. But lookin' back, nine was a little young. There was a good reason, though. I was going to sing a solo at the Christmas Eve Revival and Jim Bob wanted to give me some direction. I don't remember much about the meeting, but I do remember that I sang my little heart out for that show.

I open his door and peek my head in. "Ya busy? I'm here."

"Come in, Lowyn." He's sittin' at his desk, kinda leaning back in his chair. And he's wearin' a scowl.

I walk up to his desk and decide not to sit. I am not nine years old anymore.

Jim Bob notices this. "Please, have a seat, Lowyn. I think you might need it."

My heart thumps and I sit. "What do you mean?"

"Guess who I just got off the phone with?"

"Uh…" I shrug. "Jim Bob, it could be anyone. Just tell me what the fuck is going on."

"Ike. I just got off the phone with *Ike*."

My stomach drops. It shouldn't come as a surprise. Not after the way Grimm's been behaving these past couple days. I take a breath and calm myself. "Does Collin know?"

"Does he know what?"

"You know… me… and Ike."

"I can only presume he knows something, Lowyn McBride, because that call from Ike was about Collin."

"What?" I squint at him. "Why would Ike be calling about Collin?"

"Because apparently, your man was up at the boneyard this morning snoopin' around."

"What?" I am truly stunned. "Why would he do that?"

"He had that dog with him. Ike thinks he sent him on a track."

"It's a girl."

Jim Bob scowls at me as he sits forward in his chair. "*What?*"

"The dog. Mercy. She's a girl, not a boy."

"Who gives a flyin' fuck, Lowyn! Did you not hear what I said? Your man went up to the Blackberry Hill boneyard with a trackin' dog! To say that Ike is pissed off would be an understatement."

I let out a breath. "Sorry. I heard you."

"You promised me"—he's pointin' his finger at me—"that if I let you come home this would not come back to bite me in the ass. Do you recall that conversation?"

I nod. "I do." Then I swallow.

"Well, somethin' just bit my fuckin' ass, Lowyn McBride! And that somethin' is named Ike Monroe! Now I'm gonna need you to go up there and set this right."

"No." I stand up. "No. Nope. No fuckin' way, Jim Bob. I am *not* going up there."

"Oh, you are, Lowyn. You are. Because he was talkin' crazy on the phone. He knows as well as I do who Collin Creed really is. And he's proper freaked out about what just happened. You're the only one who can get up there without gettin' shot. So you're going. And you're gonna tell him that Collin made a mistake, he will never be back again, and nothin' will ever come of this."

"You don't understand—"

"No!" He's loud now. And this 'no' shuts me right up and makes me sit back down. "*You* don't understand, Lowyn. We have a contract with Blackberry Hill and Collin just violated it. Do you have any idea what could happen if we don't fix this?"

"I mean… I can take a guess. But no, Jim Bob—"

"Stop it!" he bellows. "Just stop it. I know damn well that Grimm told you what he was told to tell no one."

I'm shakin' my head. Because, of course, Grimm did tell me. This is the very secret he shared with me all those years ago when I shared mine.

But he also said that should anyone ask if I know this secret, my answer is no. Even if he asks me himself. "He didn't. He never told me anything. I don't even talk to Grimm."

"That's funny. I heard you were talkin' to him this morning."

"He came into—"

"Enough! I don't care that Grimm told you, Lowyn. We all tell someone and I always knew he told you. None of that matters. What matters is that you understand the contract." He stops and stares at me for a moment. "Right, Lowyn? You understand the contract."

I gulp and nod. "I do." It comes out as a whisper.

"And not only that, but you are a debt owed to Blackberry Hill. You understand that as well, correct?"

I sigh and nod again. "I do." Which is a funny thing to say, twice in a row, because it was these exact words that got me into all this trouble in the first place.

"Go on up there and make Ike happy, Lowyn. Smooth this out."

I stand up, resigned to what I must do. "But... Collin? He's OK?"

"Last I heard Ike trapped his dog in a net, but yes. He's alive. He was told to cut the dog down and leave and never come back. And as far as Ike could tell, that's what he did."

My breath comes out in a rush, but my heart is beatin' like crazy.

"Go. And don't you dare call Collin and tell him anything. Do you understand? This is your mess, Lowyn. You're gonna fix it."

"OK." I nod my head, swallow hard, and walk out.

I don't say anything to Ester as I leave, just go outside and try not to cry.

I was not expecting that. Like... having to go up and talk to Ike Monroe was not even in the top million things I was worried about today and now it's number one.

I walk home in a daze, hoping that Collin is there so that maybe he can see that I'm upset and make me tell him what's wrong so I don't have to take responsibility for blabbing my mouth off and I can just let Collin handle all the things.

His Jeep is there, but when I check inside, he's not home.

I might be the damsel in distress right in this moment, but unfortunately for me, there isn't a prince in sight. So I just get in my truck and start making my way up the hill. Because today—nine years after I walked out of Blackberry Hill under the protection of the entire town of Disciple—I'm going back in under explicit orders of Jim Bob Baptist and no one has my back.

What will Ike do?

Will he yell at me?

Will he hit me?

I really don't think so. He wasn't that kind of man the last time I saw him.

But that was nine years ago and he's a *much* different person now.

COLLIN

he streets are mostly sleepy even though it's a little after eleven by the time we enter downtown.

Amon must notice too, because he says, "Everything's closed on Mondays, right? Is that how it works?"

"I don't know. You'd know better than I do. I never came here much when we were kids."

"I can't really remember it being a thing, but it makes sense. Weekends are big here. Lots of partyin', ya know. Sure looks deserted though, don't it?"

"Yeah," I agree. "Maybe this is a big waste of time."

"Well, we're here, so we might as well check it out." He points to a building about halfway down the street. "Let's try McGills. Back in the day, that's where I used to go."

McGills is a tavern and it's got a sign on the door that says 'open,' so what the hell. We head that way and when we get there, Amon just pulls the door open and walks in.

There are a handful of customers inside. Two sittin' on opposite ends of the bar, one fucking with the jukebox, and two more playing pool.

There's also a bartender. Girl, maybe twenty-one. Blonde hair pulled back, black t-shirt that says 'McGills' on it in white letters, and very big blue eyes. Amon walks up to her and says, "We're lookin' for Lucas. Can ya help us?"

She eyeballs him. Then me. Then back to him. "Depends on

who's askin'."

"Amon Parrish and Collin Creed. We're from Disciple."

"Lucas is my cousin," I add. "He told me to come by and visit. I just got back into town."

"Hmmmph." That's all she says. But she turns, walks away, and disappears behind a swinging door.

"Why do I feel like we walked into something here, Amon?"

"Keep cool. It's typical paranoia." He turns to smile at me. "You just forgot how it was."

"Maybe." I sigh. But of course, I did get threatened by mountain men just an hour ago, so maybe I just never understood how complicated the fuckin' Trinity is and today is my day to be schooled.

A moment later the girl is back. "He's down on A Street. Go out here, take a left, then your first right. That's A. He's the second house on the right. It's big and white, ya can't miss it."

"Thank ya very much," Amon says, tipping an imaginary hat at her.

But she's already turned her back to us. So I just do the same and head out the door.

"We should just go," I say, once Amon has caught up outside.

"Why? We're here to fuckin' visit. It's not a big deal. We just come off as outsiders, that's all. Once we set them all straight, it'll go better."

"Well, I don't really have anything to say to Lucas. I was just coming by to be polite."

"So be polite."

We find the house easy enough. It's massive. One of the stately ones, not simply big. We climb the stairs to the significant front porch and Amon knocks on the door.

Both of us lean in, trying to hear something. A few seconds later, we hear footsteps thudding across a wooden floor. The door opens and—

"What the fuck?" Amon laughs. "What the hell are you doin' here, Grimm?"

Grimm doesn't answer Amon. He looks straight at me. "I was coming here to talk to Lasher about you and Lowyn."

I fuckin' knew it. I fuckin' *knew* it. Something is going on here.

Amon is confused. "What the hell are you talkin' about, Grimm?"

The door opens wider and then another man appears. Very tall, maybe six-two—six-three. Muscular, a little bit older than me, long blond hair and a beard to match. He looks even more like a Viking than Lucas. I vaguely remember him, but only because Grimm just used his name a few seconds ago. "Lasher," I say. He's my... step-uncle? Lucas's step-father? My mother's one-time brother-in-law? Kinda?

It's... complicated. As relations tend to be when towns are this small and people change their minds about marriage.

"Long time, Collin," Lasher says. "I think you might want to come inside and take a seat. Because Grimm here has something very important to tell you about the woman you seem to be fallin' in love with."

Amon looks at me and I just look back at him. I don't really wanna go inside, but whatever this is, it's been chasing me all morning and I'd rather just get it over with.

I go first, Mercy at my knee, and Amon follows. Lasher leads us through a very fancy foyer with the biggest crystal chandelier I've ever seen, down a hallway, and into a... maybe a library, maybe an office. At any rate, he points to a group of four wingback leather chairs. "Have a seat. I'll get us a drink."

I put up a hand. "I don't need a drink."

Lasher shoots me a look from over his shoulder, already reaching for a whiskey decanter on the bar. "You're gonna want this drink, Collin. Take my word on that."

"OK, what the fuck?" Amon hates riddles and this day is turning into a beauty of a mystery right before our eyes. "You guys need to explain what the hell is going on. I can't take this fuckin' tension!"

"Sit down, Amon." Lasher hands him a drink. "You're here for moral support."

Amon, not typically one to take orders from anyone but me, decides he will take the drink and the seat. He sits and I take the chair next to him.

Grimm settles in the one across from me, but he doesn't sit back. He leans forward with his elbows on his knees.

Lasher offers me the drink and I take it. Just to have something to hold.

Lasher sits across from Amon and he doesn't sit back either. I notice he didn't pour himself a drink. Or Grimm, for that matter. Even though Grimm is the only one in the room who really does look like he needs one.

Grimm starts. "Collin, you and I were friends. You remember that? And it wasn't just some casual relationship, either. We did everything together as kids."

"Sure," I say. "Eagle Scouts. Football."

"Well... just... keep that in mind—"

"Spit it out, Grimm. Just... fuckin' spit it out."

He shrugs and sighs. "Lowyn, Collin. She's... *married*."

I just blink at him. Like these words do not make sense.

"Not just married," Lasher says. I look over at him. "She's married to Ike Monroe."

"Who the fuck is Ike Monroe?" Amon asks. Because I don't seem to be able to talk.

Lasher looks Amon right in the eyes. "My twin brother. He runs Blackberry Hill." Amon and I both must have blank looks on our faces because Lasher kinda laughs. "Oh. Shit. I forgot. I guess I didn't realize that the two of you left town before you could be told."

"Told what?" Amon asks.

"About how there's a fourth town in the Trinity contract. And Lowyn McBride married the man who runs that town nine years ago when she was just twenty years old."

LOWYN

There is a turn-off from the highway that leads up to Blackberry Hill. I've tried my best to forget about it over the last nine years, but you don't just forget about a man like Ike Monroe.

I don't care who you are, male or female, once he walks into your life, he's an obsession.

Everything that happened to me that weekend—my mama's very first birthday after she died—was because my little car hydroplaned on the wet road during a thunderstorm and I slid into that little scrap of a road and right into the woods and hit a tree smack-on.

Just a few seconds of time changed my whole life. Because I was stuck there, and I had hit my head, and I didn't actually know where I was because I was just drivin' blind. Crying. Everything was blurry. Not just from the rain pelting down on the windshield, but from my tears.

That first anniversary hit me hard. It was tough. The whole season of Revival without Mama. I had to do everything. I had to quit school, and come home, and look out for Bryn, and make sure she didn't ruin her life in some way. I was exhausted by the time Christmas Eve came. And then it felt like I slept away the whole rest of the winter in a depression.

When I woke up it was spring and the Revival was startin'

again. And I couldn't take it, I guess. I just kinda lost my mind. I got in my car during the storm and I just drove around the hills. I didn't have anywhere to go.

These days, if that happened, I would go to Clover. Spend a weekend with her in the spa. But she was still in school. And I didn't feel like driving all the way over to West Virginia University just to be reminded of all the other things I lost when my mama died.

So I drove, and I wrecked, and I spent the whole night out there in those woods. It was cold, and my car wouldn't start to keep the heater goin', and I was too scared to walk up to the road in the middle of the night and wait for someone to come by and save me.

Someone did, anyway. Ike Monroe came. I don't recall why he was up so early, but I do recall the time. It was six-thirty in the morning and the rain had stopped a couple hours before, so everything outside was all wet, and crisp, and pretty, and clean when the sun first started peeking up from the horizon.

And then there he was. Something out of a Viking movie. Tall, and blond, and muscular.

He knocked on my window, but of course, the battery was dead so I couldn't just buzz my window down. I had to open the door.

And once I opened that door, it was over. The life I had before was over and the new life that took its place was one where a man like Ike Monroe existed.

We talked a little. He started asking questions. And as soon as I said who I was and where I came from, he changed. Like... he saw me different in that instant.

And I would wonder, for years afterward, if it would've turned out different if I had said I was from somewhere else. Not Disciple, or Bishop, or Revenant. Then he might've called me a tow truck or something—a cab, an Uber—or just taken me straight home, but then of course, he would've taken me to Disciple, so he would've known anyway.

If I was an outsider, he most certainly would not have taken me up to Blackberry Hill. And I wouldn't have stayed the weekend. And I would've never seen their little festival, or met any of his family or friends, or nothing.

I would've known nothing.

That's what I think about that now. That I would've forgotten about him if he had just called me a tow truck.

But it's a lie. From the moment I laid eyes on him, I was obsessed.

Of course, less than forty-eight hours later I had snapped out of it. But the point is, it was done. One look at him, gettin' one look at me—that was it. Life as I knew it was over.

These days I don't think about him at all. Like ever.

There was that one moment when Collin took me to dinner down the Watauga River and he asked me, 'Where is your husband?' and I about choked. But Collin, of course, wasn't talking about Ike, and Ike's face only flashed through my head for a split second as that whole thing played out over a series of moments, and then... I promptly forgot about him again.

We're not *really* married. Not in a legal way.

But in a Blackberry Hill way? Well, I guess there's an argument for that.

Whatever spark there was between Ike and me that wet morning nine years ago, it was a faint one. It needed to play out. However that happened didn't really matter. But Ike Monroe isn't the kind of guy you can just forget about until you have a good reason.

I needed that good reason. So that's why I'm thankful that it happened as quick as it did. Otherwise my obsession could've lasted for months, or years, or still be in full swing right now.

The dirt road ends and I park my truck next to a couple of others. By now, they probably know I'm coming. So I debate here. Should I wait in the truck for an escort? Or should I just start hoofin' it up the hill?

I get out and start walking, passing the barn on my right.

There could be a horse in there, but I am not stupid enough to take one of their horses without permission. It's a two-mile trail up the hill and they use horses from here on in because the trail is most certainly not a road. Now there *is* a road that goes up there—I know that for sure because when I was up here last, I saw a whole bunch of cars and trucks—but *how* they got up there, I don't know. Some secret back road, I guess.

I only get about two hundred yards before I hear the clip-clop of hooves.

And then there he is. Looking like a fuckin'... whatever.

His hair is long and blond, almost exactly the same as his brother Lasher's out in Revenant. They've got the same build too. They are twins, after all. They used to have the same temperament, but not anymore. That's why Lasher left this place back in his early twenties.

There can be only one boss of Blackberry Hill and that boss is Ike, not Lasher.

He doesn't get off his horse, just kinda stands there. It's a big horse with lots of energy, so it's prancing and making me nervous.

He doesn't offer me a greeting, so I guess it's up to me. "Hi," I say. "I... um... Jim Bob told me that there was a misunderstanding this morning and..."

He turns his horse around, like he's about to go back the way he came. But then the horse starts backing up and I let out a breath.

"Listen, Ike—"

"Get on, Lowyn. We're gonna have this talk up the hill." His voice is the same. Deep, and rumbly, and... well, different too. Because it comes out kinda mean.

But there is no way out of this. I have to have this conversation and I already knew when I got in my truck that it was gonna happen up on the hill. So I walk over to the horse, and he offers me his hand. I raise my arm up and he grabs it—tight

—right at the elbow, and then he says, "Jump up," and the next thing I know, I'm sitting on that horse right behind him.

There's no saddle or nothing. Just me and Ike on the back of a horse. And a moment later we're galloping up the hill at a breakneck speed and I'm holding on to him like my life depends on it.

COLLIN

"Are you OK?"

I don't look at Amon when he asks this. Just stare out the window as we make our way back into Disciple.

Lowyn is married. Not proper married. Lasher—who, I guess, was not only my mama's brother-in-law because he was hooked up with her sister at one time, but is also Lowyn's brother-in-law because she was hooked up with his brother at one time?—anyway, he said it was a festival wedding. The Blackberry Festival, to be precise. Never heard of it. Regardless, festival weddings—while legitimate in the eyes of the people in attendance—are not legal as far as city and state requirements go.

Which doesn't really make me feel any better, because up here people don't care much about city and state requirements. What folks up here *do* care about are local customs and traditions. So if those Blackberry people think Lowyn and this Ike Monroe guy are married, then they damn well are.

"Collin?"

"Yeah, I'm fine."

"You don't look fine."

I turn my head so I can see him. "Well, I just found out the girl I love—the only girl I've ever loved—has been hillbilly-promised to a mountain man who lives in the woods doing

God knows what and might be better armed than a Mexican cartel. So… yeah. I could be a little pale or somethin'."

Amon is chuckling before I even finish. "Collin Creed. You and those words of yours."

I just turn away and look back out the window. Grimm was so apologetic. I really do think he sincerely felt bad about having to be the one to tell me.

He said, "I don't know what you think of me, Collin. But you were my best friend all growing up. When you left, I'm sure you never thought about me again, not with all the things that were going on with you. But I thought about you a lot. Lowyn and I became friends. Dated a little here and there, but nothin' serious. I was just a shoulder to cry on, really. And I didn't care much that she got herself caught up in the Blackberry stuff. She snapped out of it pretty quick and Jim Bob stepped in to get her back, but the ceremony had been done. As far as anyone around up there was concerned, she was really and truly married."

I pressed him, and Lasher, for more information about this Blackberry Hill place. I have thousands of questions. But they shut up real quick. And then Lasher said the conversation was over and I needed to go see Jim Bob to get any more information.

So that's where we're going.

"Do you wanna stop by Lowyn's first, Collin?"

"I dunno. What do you think?"

"I think you should. Just ask her what's goin' on. She's not gonna lie to you."

This makes me think back to our date out there at that place on the Watauga River where she ate spaghetti and meatballs and I asked her where her husband was.

I was asking because it was too good to be true that she was still single. But she had a little reaction that I didn't notice at the time, or maybe just interpreted the wrong way. She was just about to take a sip of her wine when I asked her that, but she stopped, and if she had taken that drink, she might've choked. The answer she gave was something else too. It was her opinion on the merits of marriage. Or... no. Her opinion on the merits of a *husband*. 'I don't want a husband,' that's what she said.

When we get back into town Amon doesn't stop at Jim Bob's government building. He goes around the block to McBooms and parks right in front.

I look over at him and he shrugs. "Just... go ask her. Then we can sort this out with Jim Bob."

"What good is asking her, Amon? We already know the truth. What good is making her say it to my face? It's not gonna change anything."

"Well, what else are ya gonna do? Just walk away?" When I don't say anything, one of his eyebrows shoots straight up. "You're not walking away from Lowyn McBride, Collin. Don't be fuckin' stupid. It was one weekend when she was twenty years old. It was one year after her mama died. Two years after you walked out on her. Don't judge her for this."

"That's not what I had in mind, trust me."

"Then what is the problem?"

"The problem is... she wasn't gonna tell me."

Amon sighs and looks out his window. "I get that. But it's only been a week. She needs more than a week."

He's not wrong. So I get out of the truck and go inside to McBooms.

Rosie Harlow is fucking with some cassette tapes over by the jukebox and greets me with her trademark good-natured smile. "Hey, Collin. What's up?"

"Is Lowyn around?"

"Not right now. She was called over to Jim Bob's."

"How long ago was that?"

Rosie glances up at a clock and makes a face of surprise. "Well, look at that. It was a while ago, I guess. I was so busy I didn't notice. But I'd say about two hours, maybe?"

"A two-hour meeting with Jim Bob?"

"Maybe she went to home to eat lunch?" Rosie shrugs. "She did tell me that if you came by, I should tell you to wait for her. But"—her face screws up a little—"she's been gone way too long for that. You should call her."

"Thanks. I'll do that."

I pull my phone out and leave. Then press her contact and stop next to Amon's truck and wait for it to ring.

It goes straight to voicemail.

"Figures." I get in the truck. "Take a ride over to my house. I wanna see if she's home."

Amon chuckles. "Your house, her house. Same thing, I guess, huh?"

I don't say anything to that.

A minute later we're there, but there is no truck in the driveway. And it was there earlier, right next to my Jeep, when I came down out of the hills and Amon picked me up.

"Now where?" Amon asks.

"The only place left to go, I guess. Jim Bob's."

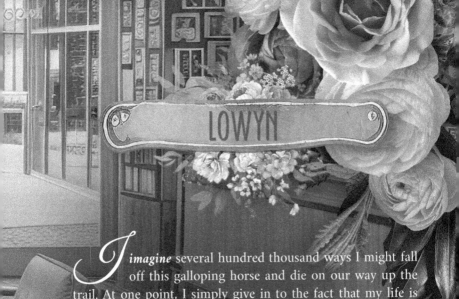

I imagine several hundred thousand ways I might fall off this galloping horse and die on our way up the trail. At one point, I simply give in to the fact that my life is over. But then I just hold on tighter. Which, I believe, is probably the whole reason Ike is doing this to me. To scare me and make me hold on tighter.

We finally stop just shy of the mountaintop clearing that contains the village of Blackberry Hill and as soon as this happens, I let go, get my leg between him and me, and slide right off that horse's back. When I turn and glare up at him, he's smilin' down at me like an asshole.

I try to stay calm and project an outward sense of control, but internally I'm seething. "You could've killed me, you jerk."

Ike scoffs. "You're still here, aren'tcha?"

"No thanks to you."

He tilts his head at me, those blue eyes of his dancing with… I would like to say mischief. People often mistake him for mischievous, but he's not. Because mischievous kinda implies that he's being playful in a teasing way and that's never been my impression.

Well, perhaps at first—the early hours of that first day nine years ago—I might've fallen for the charm. But it was a very short-lived mistake once I saw what was really happening in Blackberry Hill.

Then I just saw him as menacing. I got the impression that he *likes* to scare people. He enjoys it. He cultivates fear to keep his people in control.

Right now, he's looking at me like he's a cat and I'm a half-dead mouse he'd like to torture for a few hours before leaving me to die.

I haven't had any kind of interaction with him for all these years, but I did see him around a couple times. Once, when I was waiting at the stoplight in Revenant, right there at the highway. He was turning right, going up the hill. And I was in the left turn lane, about to go down into the valley. We locked eyes as he passed, but that was about it.

Another time I saw him in the Bishop Inn pickin' up food. I was lookin' out the back windows at the hedge maze, waiting for Bryn to take her lunch break—she was a maid back then—and Jessica came and hurriedly ushered me into the kitchen so I didn't have to talk to him.

There have been a few more incidents like that over the years, but no conversations. Not a single word between us since Jim Bob came up this very hill and walked me back out the way I came in.

Ike's last words to me were, "I do not ever want to see you again." And I just meekly agreed because I was young and afraid I'd get stuck up here forever if I didn't just shut my mouth and let him have his say. And... whatever. Like I cared.

Obviously, I didn't want to stay. I didn't care if I ever saw him again.

But, as the years went by, I would think about that day and roll that last conversation over in my head. Trying to remember every word. And of course, years and years later, I would have a proper comeback for that. Something along the lines of, *If you were the last man on earth...*

But it wouldn't have been true at the time. Even though I did not want to stay, I was still quite caught in his spell when he let me go. If I hadn't accidentally seen something I shouldn't have in that short time I was with him, I might've stayed up there forever and just let him take care of me.

That's just not how it happened, though. And I'm glad I saw what I saw. It would be far worse to be caught up in his lies and live as a fool than it was to admit he was just a liar right from the start and excuse myself from the situation.

What I saw scared me. I didn't really understand it, but I knew there was something bad going on and I knew it was a secret. After that, nothing about him—not those eyes, not that body, not that face—nothing about him was enough to make me stay.

He didn't know I saw what I did. If he had... well, I don't know what would've happened to me. I just know I wouldn't be living this life. There would be no McBooms. There would be no buying Collin's childhood home. There would be no Collin.

I need to get this conversation over with quick and then start back down the hill and be gone.

"Well," Ike says, still sittin' on that horse so he's even more imposing than he would naturally be. "Why are you here, Lowyn? Should I take a guess?"

I let out a sigh. Jim Bob already told me Ike called about Collin. So he knows why I'm here and there's no reason to beat around the bush. "Jim Bob sent me."

Ike laughs. "I bet he did."

"Do you mind gettin' down off that horse?"

"Am I too big for you, Lowyn?"

I turn my back on him and just stare down the hill. I want to walk away so bad, but I can't. Not until I set things right. So I turn back and my wish has been granted. He's on the ground now, only slightly less imposing.

He spreads his arms wide. "Well, I'm listening."

I take a breath and begin. "I'm not sure what happened this morning—"

"You're not *sure?*" He cuts me off with the most incredulous look. "You're. Not. *Sure?*"

"I don't know why Collin came up here. The dog ran off, maybe. He doesn't have a reason to come up here."

Ike lifts one eyebrow. "Is that so? So he doesn't know we're married?"

"We're *not* married. That was *not* legal. I was distraught, and... and sad... and..." I let out a long breath. "It wasn't legal. We're not married."

"Well, now that's funny. Because all this time I've been saving myself for the day you came back because I thought you were my wife."

I just squint at him, confused. He was... saving himself?

A laugh bursts out of him. It's so loud, it startles me and I take a step back. He points. Right at me. "Your face." He laughs again. "Oh, my God, your face, Lowyn. You really thought I'd been saving myself for *you!*" Another guffaw bursts out. "That's amazing. You always were gullible."

"Anyway." I huff this word out. "I just came up to tell you that it's not gonna be a problem. He doesn't know anything. And when I say anything, I mean *nothing.* He doesn't even know you guys are here."

Ike's laughter is dead now, his face angry. "Well, obviously he does. Because I saw him in my boneyard this morning. Him and his trackin' dog. And I know that's a trackin' dog, Lowyn McBride, so don't try to deny it. I've had men on the inside of his compound since the moment Amon started hiring them. He's got a whole kennel of special dogs and a bunker underneath the church with a SCIF in it. So what hell is he doin'? Why the hell does he need all that shit?"

"Ike, I don't even know what a SCIF is."

"It's a private room. Everything's encrypted, all phone lines are secured. No recording devices. It's a custom-made private room that prevents high-level spying, that's what it is. So why the hell does he need one of those? That's government shit,

Low. And if he's doin' something for the government, I need to know about it. So what's goin' on?"

"You're asking the wrong person. But they do own a security company. It kinda makes sense to have protection dogs and private phone lines, or whatever. My point is, it was a mistake and it won't happen again, so… we're good, right? I can go home and tell Jim Bob we're good?"

"Go home?" He laughs yet again. "Why would you wanna go *home*, Lowyn?"

"Oh, I dunno." I sneer at him. "Maybe because I have a *life*."

"You're not goin' nowhere, Low. Not yet. Not until Collin and I have a little chat. So you're gonna come with me—"

I take off runnin' down the hill. I don't waste any breath arguing with him, I just book it. I don't even look back. It's a long way and I'm not really a runner and he's got a horse, so I know this is dumb. But there's no way in hell I'm just gonna give up without even tryin'.

He passes me on the horse, making the giant animal turn and then rear up just a few feet in front of me. I put my hands up, stumblin' back, and then I fall on my ass.

The next thing I know he's on the ground and got me by the arm. Then he starts tyin' my hands together with a piece of nylon rope!

I pull away, getting free before he can finish. But he's reaching for me again. "Stop it!" I'm yellin', trying to kick him.

But he just grabs my foot and stares at me. "We can do this the easy way, or I can throw you over my fuckin' shoulder and cart you back up this hill myself." He bends down and leans forward, so close to me. "Choose. Because I'm not fuckin' around here. He's working for the government, Low. And I know what you saw when you left me."

"What?" It comes out as a tiny whisper.

"I've always known. It never occurred to you that I had cameras all over that house?"

I don't know what to say. I just blink at him.

"You know what we're doin' up here. And you know it's illegal. If he's here to spy on us and report back—"

"He's *not!*"

"How would you know?" He yells this. Right at my face. His eyes blazing. And it's certainly not mischief I see in there. Certainly not.

Then he must realize that he's losin' his temper, because he lets out a breath, releases my foot, and stands back up, offering me his hand.

I don't take it, but I do get up, dustin' off my ass as my mind whirls around with this new information, tryin' to force it to make sense.

He's wrong about one thing. I *did* see something, but I didn't know what it *meant*. And even though Grimm did tell me they're working for the government—the military specifically—that's all he knew. I don't know what they're doin' up here. I just know I don't want any part of it.

"He's here to suss us out, don't you understand?"

I shake my head. "I asked him that, Ike. Straight up, I did. It was one of the first things I asked him—'Do you work for the government?'—and he said, 'No.'"

Ike scoffs. "Do you really think he's gonna tell you if he's working on some secret operation for the government? You don't know what a SCIF is, so let me explain what it means that he has one. He's either getting secret information or givin' it. So which is he? The guy gettin' the secrets? Or the guy givin' them?"

I don't say anything. I can't really know what Collin is up to, but he's definitely up to something, Ike's not wrong about that. It's just... I can't picture it. And even if I could, I don't want it to be true. I want him to be here for me, not Ike Monroe.

I deflate a little and this must satisfy Ike, because he takes a step back and runs his fingers through his hair, looking off into the woods. Then he must remember he's got a horse—who is standing quietly close by like none of this is happening—because he gets it and walks it over to me. Then he offers me his open palm. Not so I can hold his hand, but so he can give me a leg up.

I look him in the eyes and shake my head. "I don't wanna go up there, Ike. I don't wanna know what it looks like these days, I don't wanna know who's up there... just let me go back and I'll send Collin to the bottom of the hill and the two of you—"

"*No.*" He says this very firmly. "Now get on the horse, Lowyn. Because if you don't, I'll just put you on the fuckin' horse myself."

I'm not gettin' away. Not right now, anyway. So there's really nothin' left to do. I put my knee in his hand and I swing my leg over the horse's back as he lifts me up.

I expect him to get on too, but he doesn't. He slips the reins over the horse's head and begins to lead me forward towards the mountaintop village of Blackberry Hill.

A little while later we come out from a thick copse of tall shrubs and then there it is. I don't remember a lot of details about getting up here or my first look—which is this same view here—but my first impression is that it looks the same. Two buildings appear first, both low and long and made of logs. The trail leads right between them and I know from memory that the one on my right is a stable and the one on my left is a blacksmith.

Sure enough, when we come out between the two buildings, that's what they still are. No one is working in the blacksmith's. It's all shuttered up and doesn't look like anyone's worked there in a while, maybe because it's still a little bit winter up here. There's still snow on the ground, though not a lot of it.

But the stable is open and that's where Ike stops. I feel stupid for being up on this horse. There's no reason for it this time, unlike last time when I was injured. Though I didn't have to ride alone. Ike was riding with me.

So I don't really see the point, other than he wanted to order me around. I wouldn't be the least bit surprised if that was the only reason. That's the kind of man he is. Some might call that bossy the same way some might call his eyes mischievous. But the eyes are menacing and this alpha thing he does, it's authoritarian, not bossy.

"Get down, Lowyn." He offers a hand to help.

I don't take it. I just swing my leg over and slide down on my own. I don't ride horses a lot anymore, but Clover and I had our horse-crazy years as pre-teens, so I'm not afraid of a dismount.

A man appears from inside the stable. Not much more than a teenager. And Ike hands him the horse without comment and then he takes the horse inside.

Now I turn and look at the village. Like my first impression, it all comes off as familiar. But upon closer inspection, I can see that it's been fixed up a lot in the last nine years.

Even though I've lived in these parts since the day I was born, before Ike found me in my wreck of a car and brought me up to these hills, I never even knew people lived up here. The cabins were all here nine years ago, of course. And they were fine. They had windows and front doors. And, of course, log cabins always do come with a certain amount of charm. They were fine back then and that's really all you could say about the various buildings in this village.

But today they are more than merely livable. Curtains hang in the windows. Shutters hang on the outside. Some of them have window boxes with spring flowers coming up. Red and yellow tulips and purple hyacinths. The front porches have rocking chairs on them. There's new metal roofing, and gutters, and there's even a street—kinda of. It's made of dirt, but it's actually a really nice fine gravel the color of sand, not gray like most of the rocks around these parts. Some of the cabins have a second floor now. And balconies.

It's... nice. They've spent a lot of money up here. And this makes me angry.

But I can't afford to be angry right now. I need to keep a clear head. So I dial it down and just let myself see it.

"Looks different, huh?" Ike says.

I nod, but don't look at him.

"I'm over here now. Let's go."

I don't go. I turn and face him. And he must've known I was gonna object, because he hasn't walked off yet. In fact, he looks like he's expecting this confrontation. "Why do you want me here?"

"Because, Lowyn, Collin Creed and I are gonna come to an agreement today and I'm gonna use you to get what I want."

This is not a surprise. So I don't really react. It's just the kind of man he is. "What is it you want, Ike?"

"I want the truth." He's holding up a finger, making a list. "I want a promise." He holds up finger number two. "And I want to know who he's working for." That final finger comes up.

"Why can't I just call him up and ask him these things?"

"Because I need him to know that I will take you any time I want, just like I take the others. And I need to look him in the eyes when he comes to that realization."

These words rattle around in my head for a moment as I try to put them together. "What... *others*?"

Ike smiles at me. One could mistake this smile for charm, but it's not charming. It's... ugly. And when his words come out, they're ugly too. "He owes me, Lowyn," Ike says, his voice deep and threatening now. "He owes me Olive and the man he killed that night when we came to take her back."

And this is when I realize I don't know him. Not a little bit, not at all.

But at least now I do know what he did.

Ike Monroe, and all the other people up here on Blackberry

Hill, are the ones responsible for changing our lives that one horrible New Year's Eve twelve years ago.

He's the reason Collin killed someone.

He's the reason Collin left and joined the Marines.

He's the reason why, in just two seconds' time, all my dreams were crushed.

COLLIN

When we come through the door to Jim Bob's office Ester is typing her little heart out. She doesn't look up. "Go on in," she says, nose pushed up against her computer screen. "He's expectin' ya."

Amon and I share a look. But who cares how and why he knows we were coming?

I walk forward—Mercy still at my knee—then open the door and go in.

Jim Bob is on the phone. "Yep." He nods to us, pointing to the chairs. "I hear ya," he tells the person on the phone. "Not to worry. And I gotta go now, I have a meeting. Goodbye." He sets the phone back down in the cradle and lets out a long breath. "Do you know who that was?"

I take a guess. "Lasher?"

"That was Lasher. He wanted to remind me of our contracts. Which I am well aware of."

Amon and I look at each other, not sure what this is about. "OK," I say. "You wanna explain that? Or should I just assume it's related to why I'm here and just get to the point?"

He clears his throat. "Collin, you are a thorn in my fuckin' ass today, do you know that?"

"Jim Bob, this is not a friendly visit and I'm not an eight-year-old kid who was just called to the damn principal's office.

367

I'm the pissed-off owner of a small army, that's who I am. And I've got questions."

"Save your breath, Collin. I don't care about your questions or your little army." Amon huffs here, taking exception to the minimization of our organization. "I told you when you'd get your answers and you're not gonna get them a minute early. I'm here to ask you what the hell you were doing up on that mountain this morning."

"What mountain?" Amon looks at me. "Does he mean when the dog ran away?"

Jim Bob ignores him. He's staring right at me. "Well?"

I let out a breath. I'm pissed off and being angry is never the right way forward in a negotiation. I will get my answers today, but I need to play this right. "I'm not gonna waste time here because I have shit to do that doesn't involve you. So I'll tell ya, even though it's none of your fuckin' business."

Jim Bob is unfazed by my f-bomb. "Let's hear it."

"Amon here specializes in military dogs." I point down at Mercy. "She's one of them. And the other day the power went out, so I went down in Lowyn's basement to check the breakers and a key fell out of the breaker box. I didn't think much of it, but later I noticed that Mercy was acting a little weird. Like she caught a scent. And later that night she took me back into the basement like she was on a track. And she pointed me in the direction of a loose brick, behind which was a box with a lock. Key fit the lock, I opened it up, and there was... a map. Kinda. I didn't know it was a map, it just looked like a scribble. But the next morning I gave her the map and told her to seek. And she caught something on the wind. Turns out"—I look at Amon for this part—"it was bones."

Amon laughs. "She flunked out of cadaver school."

"She most certainly did not." Now I look back at Jim Bob. "It wasn't just one bone, but I'm guessin' you already know that, Jim Bob. It was an entire boneyard and it was surrounded by weird granny-witch shit."

"Where was this?" Amon asks.

"Don't tell him, Collin." Jim Bob shoots me a stern look. "Do not. Tell him."

I look Jim Bob in the eyes. "Straight up the hill just back of my house. About a thousand feet up."

"That was a mistake," Jim Bob says. "A mistake you'll regret, Collin. Mark my words."

I keep goin'. "There were people up there."

"What kind of people?" Amon asks.

"Hill people. At least"—I pause here to watch Jim Bob's face—"they wanted me to *think* they were hill people. But they're not, are they, Jim Bob? They're military, aren't they?"

"What the fuck?" Amon says. "What the hell is the military doin' up there?"

Jim Bob sighs. "This is a mistake. A very big mistake. I sent Lowyn up there to smooth things over—"

"You *what?*" It comes out mean. Loud, too.

"I sent her up there to have a talk with them. They're pissed. You have no idea how badly you have pissed them off, Collin Creed."

"I pissed some military people off and you decide that the best course of action is to send my fuckin' *girlfriend* up there? What kind of asshole does that?" I wave a hand in the air. "This is why I'm actually here. Lowyn. Lasher just told me that she's married to some guy called Ike Monroe? A festival wedding nine years ago? And this guy runs a place called Blackberry Hill. Let me guess… I stumbled into Blackberry Hill this morning, didn't I?" I narrow my eyes at him, because I might want to be calm, and I might know that calm is the best way forward here, but I am not calm. "Is this your secret then? Blackberry Hill, whatever that place is, is part of the Trinity?"

Jim Bob huffs. It's kind of a laugh, but not quite. "The Trinity." He huffs again. "You know how those Catholics are always making that sign of the cross?"

My anger is building, so he better get to the point.

"They cross themselves and say Father, Son, Holy Spirit and all that shit? Well, don't you think it's kinda weird that they call it a trinity when it's a cross?"

"I'm losing my patience here, Jim Bob. What the hell are you talking about?"

"I told you this already. You just didn't catch on. There's four points to a cross, Collin. That's what I'm talking about. It has never been a trinity. There are four points to a cross and Blackberry Hill completes the quad. But here's the funny thing..." He stops. I wait. But he doesn't continue.

"Well? What's the fuckin' funny thing?"

"Never mind. I'm gonna keep that one to myself. But here's what I'm gonna tell you now, Collin. And then you're gonna get the fuck out of my office, go home, and let me handle this shit."

"Yeah, right," Amon says.

Jim Bob ignores him. "When you signed that contract, I promised you answers about that night you killed that man. And that's what I'm gonna give you. I'll pay you early, but understand that you owe me now."

I'm clenching my jaw, so fucking angry. "Let's hear it."

"That man who was trying to kidnap your sister? He wasn't kidnapping her. He was trying to take her home. Your sister isn't your sister. Your mama found a runaway girl when you were about nine years old. This girl was pregnant and she came from Blackberry Hill."

"Holy shit," Amon says. He looks at me. "What the fuck is this?"

But I don't know, so I can't answer.

"She hid this girl in your basement."

"No fuckin' way." I can't believe it. I shake my head.

"You were away for a week or so. A Boy Scout camping trip. Does that ring any bells? At any rate, during that time, the baby was born, the girl ran, leaving the baby behind, and your mama and daddy come to me with an infant, told me the story, and asked to keep her. I said yes. I didn't know Blackberry Hill was a thing because Blackberry Hill *wasn't* a thing. At least, not like it is now. And that's all I'm gonna say about that. The point is, Olive wasn't your sister, that man that night was her rightful father, and you killed him because he tried to take her home."

I take a seat and lean over, putting my head in my hands. Running these words back through my head. It's not true. It can't be true. I remember... well. I'm not sure what I remember about Olive's birth. I was nine. I didn't know anything about babies. Where they come from or how things happen. Did I ever see my mama pregnant?

I can't say either way. I just know one day I had a baby sister.

But it kinda makes sense. It's a reason, at least, for why a man would break into my house and try and kidnap her.

I look up at Jim Bob and let out a long breath. Anger not in check. "Why the fuck didn't you tell me this earlier?"

Amon is pissed too. "Yeah, what the fuck, Jim Bob! What the actual fuck!"

"Collin," Jim Bob says. "You guessed right. These people are military. This operation they're running is beyond top secret."

"There's no such thing as beyond top secret," Amon says. "Trust us, we know."

"Then you know damn well that there are special considerations for that, then, don't you? This operation they're running up there is called Blackberry Top Secret. That's what I was told. That's all I know. I don't know what they do up there."

The military is all compartmentalized. It's all need to know. There is a chain of command and if you're not on the chain, you don't get to know. So I do believe that Jim Bob is telling the truth about this. But it's really bad sign. I know better than most that there's a lot of corruption in the military. Congressional hearings, Exhibit A. So whatever is going on up there, that's how it's gonna end. Eventually. One year, or five years, or fifteen years from now someone will blow the whistle and that's how Blackberry Hill will end.

Or... maybe not. Maybe it's so much more than illegal private armies and experimental biological treatment and it was made to last forever. Either way, doesn't matter. I might not know any details but I got a secret this morning. And people, like this Ike Monroe guy, are pretty upset about that.

"OK," I say, pulling myself together. "How the hell does Lowyn fit into all this?"

"She's the only one knows how to get up there besides me. She's the only one of us who's ever been *inside*. I'm too damn old to walk two miles up a fuckin' mountain these days. So I sent her up to smooth things over with Ike because you found his fuckin' boneyard, Collin. I had to send her up there because of you."

"How long ago was this?" Amon asks.

Jim Bob looks at his watch. "About... two hours ago."

"Two hours?" I stand up. "What the fuck has she been doing up there for two hours?"

"Smoothin' things over, I assume."

"This is why you couldn't get through," Amon says. "There's no signal up there."

"Well, there must be some kind of signal," I say. "A landline, or somethin'. Because Jim Bob already admitted he got a call from Ike. So you call him, Jim Bob. You call Ike Monroe right the fuck now and tell him to put Lowyn on the phone."

"It doesn't work that way, Collin."

"Then how's it work, Jim Bob? Because I'm holding my shit together right now, but just barely. And you're the one I want to be angry at."

He takes offense to this because his chin juts back in surprise. "Are you threatenin' me, Collin?"

"You're damn right I am."

"Even if I could"—Jim Bob glares at me—"after your threat, I wouldn't. But as it is, I can't. *They* call *me*. It's a satellite phone.

I have no way to contact them at all. And if I tried to go up there, or you try to go up there, or any one of your small army tries to go up there, they will shoot you, Collin. If you learned nothing else at all this morning, I hope you learned that. They will *shoot you*."

"*Surprised?*" Ike is smirkin' at me.

"That you're the one who ruined my life?" I scoff. "Not in the least."

Ike scowls at me. "How the hell do you figure that I'm the one who ruined your life?"

"You sent that man to kidnap Olive?"

"That man?" He laughs. "That man, Lowyn, was Olive's real father."

"Bullshit." This word comes out quick and it comes out mean too. "That's bullshit. You're just making things up!"

"Oh, am I?" He leans down into my face. "You have no idea what is really going on around here. You saw something nine years ago. You got into my security room."

"You left the door open. I didn't force my way in."

"You went snoopin' around." He straightens up to his full height, which is considerable. Way over six foot. "So you saw a secret on those screens. Good for you. But that's just the literal tip of the iceberg, if, of course, the iceberg is a mountain. And it is."

"What?" I don't even know what he's talking about. I did see screens in his security room. There were like twenty or thirty of them in there. But I didn't really have enough time to make sense of what it all meant. I saw… lots of… places? Rooms? Hallways? I don't know. The only thing I did know was that they were not the part of Blackberry Hill that I had already seen. These places, they were in secret buildings or something. It looked military and it looked secret. That was my takeaway.

Ike grabs me by the arm and starts pulling me. I resist, but he yanks harder. And there's no way to resist if he's yanking me. I stumble along with him.

But as we're walking people emerge. Like maybe they were hiding, waiting to see what was gonna happen. They look… well, just like local people, I guess. Not as poor as they looked the last time I was here. There were a lot of people back then who were still wearing raggedy things. Dirty things.

They are neater now. Cleaner. Richer, I decide. Because of course they are. But still, I know in my heart that they are local. Descendants, maybe. From some hill clan.

We pass one of the larger buildings. It's made of logs. Everything is made of logs. And pressed against the nearly dozen windows lining the front of this building are the faces of children. They are watching Ike take me through the village.

It's weird, the way they watch me. Like they've never seen a stranger in their lives.

Maybe they haven't? Maybe they never leave this little place?

Last time I was up here I saw cars and trucks. Signs all over that there were ways leading up here that went beyond that horse trail.

But this time, there is none of that. No signs of any kind of transportation except for horses and, oddly enough, something that might be a helicopter pad. A wide-open space with a smooth blacktop square on the other side of the village—right in front of us actually, because we're walkin' that way. And I guess it makes sense. Not only is it not safe to live so isolated— there has to be some kind of emergency way in or out—but if they are military, helicopters would be the easiest way to come and go.

So maybe it's true? Maybe they are so isolated up here that I *am* a novelty to these children?

There are some old folks too. Mostly sitting on porches in small groups, but some are looking out the windows as well. They don't look at me with curiosity though. They look at me with... I dunno. Contempt, maybe.

Finally, after what seems like an eternal walk of shame, we arrive at a porch. Ike practically drags me up the steps, opens the door, and pushes me inside ahead of him.

I want to object to his manhandling, but the interior of this space has redirected my attention. It's... nice. And... homey. And... normal. And so far, this trip has been anything but normal, so I'm not sure what to do with this change of perspective.

It's all very new. And country. Kind of like the way I designed my bedroom, only more masculine. All done up in black and gray. There's a nice wide-plank wood floor, and cotton-rope rugs, and a fireplace with a huge raw-edge tree trunk as a mantel and a river-stone chimney climbing up the wall, all the way to the ceiling.

I turn and face Ike. "What is this place?"

He huffs. "My home? Where else would I bring you?"

I don't have an answer for that. Just more questions.

"You can snoop all you want in this one." He smirks at me again. "Not gonna find any secrets here, Low."

I'm just about to ask him what the hell that means when he turns and leaves. Closing the door behind him.

Then I hear the click of a lock.

He locked me in!

I could rush over to the door and make a scene. Pound on it for a while. Scream. Kick it. Break a window.

But I have a feeling that Ike Monroe would not respond well to a temper tantrum. And there's no point, anyway. I'm here until he has his words with Collin. So I sigh, walk over to the couch, and sit down. Just running this day back through my head so I can make some sense of it.

I just don't understand why Collin would decide, right out of the blue, to send Mercy on a trackin' job up the hill out back of the house.

It makes no sense to me.

I skip ahead to the next mystery, which might actually be solved. If Ike is telling the truth and Olive wasn't Collin's real sister—I'm not sure how that could be, but just for the sake of argument, let's say it's true—well, that kind of explains a lot. Why that man was there in the first place. Why he put his hands up so readily. Why everyone wanted to make it go away after Collin killed him.

Why Mr. and Mrs. Creed wanted to move away, and... why Ike Monroe thinks Collin Creed owes him something.

I sit there on the couch for a while, not really sure how much time passes. But eventually I get hungry and there is a very nice modern kitchen on the other side of the room. Since Ike practically gave me permission to snoop—*Not gonna find any secrets here, Low*—I figure I'm allowed to help myself to some food.

So I get up and walk in there, but just as I'm reaching for the refrigerator door, I spy a photo album on the kitchen table.

For some reason I look over my shoulder. Who am I kidding? I know the reason. He's probably got cameras in here, too.

But curiosity gets the better of me. A photo album is a treasure trove of information. I've picked my share of vintage photo albums so I know that images, even without a running commentary—though lots of them do have that—are a very good way to understand people.

This album looks a lot like those others that I have picked. Very thick and made of leather that is cracked and worn, like it's been collecting photos for generations.

I pull it towards me, then take a seat in a chair and open it up.

The inside title page says 'Monroe Family' and there's an image of a family tree with lots of names and dates starting down at the roots and going all the way up to the highest leaves at the top.

Ike is near the top. But not the very top. On his same level are a couple of women too. And, of course, Lasher, his twin. They share the same bough. I do the math and figure out he's thirty-four. I didn't actually know that. It always felt like he was so much older than me because nine years ago, I was practically a child and I can't imagine Ike ever being small.

But he's only three years older than Collin. Which is kinda weird, since Lasher is the same age and he was, at one time at least, Collin's uncle.

I have to shake my head here. Of course, this wasn't by marriage or blood. Lasher was dating Collin's aunt—his mother's little sister—and that's how the relations got that way. That's also how Lucas got to be Lasher's stepson.

Who Lucas's real daddy is, I have no clue. Maybe one of these Blackberry people and that's why Lasher took over like that?

For the first time I begin to wonder why so many parents in these Trinity towns run off and leave whole families behind.

Then I scoff. I mean... these parts are weird. These towns are weird. And it's a small, small world out this way. It makes a lot of sense to run off if you're the kind of person who likes a bigger world better than a small one.

But to leave your kids behind? And Lucas, God, he was a gorgeous kid. Not that it matters—anyone who runs off on a kid, regardless of how they look, might be an asshole. I say 'might' because I don't know what the situation was and it's really not my place to judge.

Lucas, though. Gorgeous child. I remember him. And... well, I have to laugh here. Because he was so much like Collin.

Because that's almost exactly what Collin looked like as a boy too.

I turn the page and find two very fine old photographs of a young man and his bride. The names below these pictures say 'Ginny McMann' and 'Theodore Monroe.' They are pretty people too. Even if they are rather skinny and gaunt. I bet they had a hard life up here in these hills. They might even be the original people from this village. The ones who built those cabins.

I turn the page and find more people. Smaller, less fine pictures. And in groups. All with names under them. More Monroes, of course. Then I have to squint my eyes and blink a little, because I see the name McBride under one of these women. It's dated nineteen twenty-two and her name is Lindyn.

I just look at her for a while, seeing a little bit of myself in her light hair and eyes. I can't tell what color they are, since the picture is in black and white, but she does look like me.

She's got two brothers. Oren and Acacius. And when I page forward, I see that Acacius married a woman called... Elowyn.

"Oh, wow." I whisper this out loud as my fingertip glides across the woman's face. Elowyn. Lowyn. She is related to me. Or, at the very least, I think I was named after her.

I keep paging forward, but there are no more McBrides. Lots of other names appear. McGill, and McMann, and dozens of others along that line.

Sometimes they look hardened and tired. Like they work way too much. I might not know first-hand what it was like to grow up in the Appalachian hills, but I know more than most. No running water, no electricity, just a wood stove in the winter to keep you warm. No washing machines, no dishwashers, no TV. So these people probably didn't even know how hard they had it.

It's the life of a pioneer, is what it is.

Now, in this house, Ike has everything. All the modern

comforts. When I look around, I don't see a TV, but everything else seems to be here. There are speakers, so there's some kind of sound system. Plus, I saw that room with all the computer screens last time, so I know he has those. Maybe not here, but he's got them somewhere.

Ike changed the direction of this town. He was born here—this album proves it. But he's part of something bigger too.

That's why I asked Collin if he was with the government. I didn't specifically think he was connected to Blackberry Hill, but it did cross my mind that he might be. So I asked him and he said no.

But I know as much about Collin's business as I do Ike's at this point.

I blow out a breath and turn the page again. Now it's the current generation. Baby pictures of Lasher and Ike. And their sisters and mama. A few more page turns and they are teenagers, then practically men.

The next time I turn the page there's a picture of me. I nearly gasp out loud. I even pick up the album and put it right up to my face, trying to see every detail.

It was... my wedding day. I'm wearing a borrowed white dress and my hair is piled on top of my head and sprinkled with flowers.

Ike's sisters did that. I don't know how old they were back then—fourteen? Fifteen? They were so excited. They danced around me that day like little fairies, trying to make me pretty and happy.

I was pretty, but I wasn't happy. I don't know what I was thinking, actually. This man appears and rescues me. He takes up into the hills on a horse and feeds me, and makes a fire, and we talk. Well, he talked mostly. It was some kind of shock, or something. I did hit my head, and Ike wouldn't let me sleep. He said I had to stay up for twenty-four hours to make sure there was no concussion. So we talked all night. Twenty-four hours of... spilling guts, I guess. I didn't talk at first, but he was so chatty and nice. He rescued me, made me feel safe, took away all the worries I had been carrying around for the past year after Mama died, and I think that's why I said I wanted to stay.

I was done. I wanted a husband to just take over. The accident was the last straw for me. Leaving Blackberry Hill and going home meant that all my problems would be there waiting for me.

Or maybe I'm just making excuses.

Regardless, I am the one who brought it up. I am the one who put the idea of marriage in his head. It was me. It was *all* me, really.

And I just don't know what I was thinking.

What I do know is that after I saw that secret room, I came to my senses. And that's when the phone calls started, and deals had to be made, and Jim Bob came up the hill and walked me back out. Furious as a raging fire.

I turn the page again and then there's a picture of all of us. Me and Ike—he's even smiling. His sisters, his mama, his granny. I don't know what happened to his daddy or grandad. I only knew the man for one weekend total, so it never came up. But there are no other men in that picture, just him. Lasher was already gone by then, I guess.

This is when it occurs to me, while I'm looking at these pictures, that while the wedding might've felt fake to me—maybe I was concussed, maybe I was just depressed—it doesn't matter because the point is, it wasn't fake to *them*.

My wedding to Ike was real. It was their festival day. There was food, and dancing, and laughing, and photographs being taken. It was a big party. And in the middle of that, there was a wedding.

Looking back, it feels really strange to me. I mean, that's just not how weddings happen in Disciple. They are a big deal and they are planned far in advance. They happen during a Revival with tons of singing, and dancing, and fanfare. It's part of the show. They are also legal. There is a license and a preacher.

But people living up here—maybe not so much these days, but back in the old days—they wouldn't care if there was a preacher, or a church, or a license. If they wanted to get married, I imagine it happened for them the same way it happened for me. On a festival day with friends and family as their witness. They said words, made promises, and then they kissed and they were married.

For the first time in nine years I begin to see my wedding through a different set of eyes. I see it though Ike's eyes, and his sister's eyes, and his mama's eyes.

And then I imagine what they thought of me when I walked away.

The front door opens and I stand up quickly, almost knocking the chair over as I do this.

Ike comes in, his boots thudding across the floors. He looks for me and his squinting eyes find me in the kitchen. "What are you doing?"

I point to the table where the photo album is still open. "I... I was looking."

His eyes dart down to the table, then immediately back up at me. I get the feeling that maybe he was lookin' at that photo album earlier and he forgot he left it out. He sighs, but doesn't say anything.

That's OK though. I know just what to say. "Ike, I need to see your mother. I have something to say to her."

COLLIN

We leave Jim Bob's quietly.

We get back in Amon's truck quietly.

He drives. At first, I'm not sure where we're goin', but when he glides right past Maple Street—which is the right turn towards my street—I realize we're just goin' back to the compound. "Maybe I should stay in town."

"What for?" Amon doesn't look at me. Just keeps his eyes on the road.

"To wait for Lowyn."

Amon scoffs. "You think she's comin' home?"

It had occurred to me that she might not. But I wasn't gonna say it out loud. "She could settle things up and come back."

"She could," Amon says. Then he finally looks at me. "But we both know she didn't." He takes his eyes back to the road. "That fucker's waitin' for you, Collin. So I think we should probably just… get you on up there."

"Well, the way to the boneyard is back at my place. That's the only way I know how to get up there."

"Fuck the boneyard."

We both stop talking after that. He's cooking up something and I'm cooking up something too. So we just stay quiet and make our plans. But when we get to the compound—which is busy as hell, hundreds of workers—he goes right to the church and parks in front of it.

He still doesn't say anything. Just gets out and goes inside.

I stay in the truck for a moment. I don't really have anywhere to go because my fuckin' house isn't done, but I wanna make a phone call anyway.

Charlie Beaufort answers on the first ring. "Collin Creed! Most dangerous mind in the world. The mental prowess of a... a"—he gets lost here, but recovers quickly—"an AI, counterintelligence genius extraordinaire, and the man I'd pay half my salary to if he'd just let me order him around a little. How are you doin', son? How are you doin'?" He's his usual smoke-blowin' self.

I let out a breath. "Yeah, well, here's the thing..."

I tell him my problem. Every single bit of it. Because it doesn't matter what kind of secret you tell Charlie, it's not a secret. He already knows about it. No one ever elected this man. Hell, most people have never even heard of this man. But no one, and I do mean no one, in DC does anything with the military or intelligence without the explicit permission of Charlie Beaufort.

"Ike Monroe," he says, once I finish.

"You know him?" It's not really a question, but it feels polite to try to maintain some semblance of chain of command here, even though we both know he's running the show.

"I know him. And his operation. Which I unfortunately cannot share with you, Collin." He's more serious now, all jokin' aside.

"It's all right. I don't need to know. But here's what I do need, Charlie. Because if I don't get this, I'm gonna take a team up there. And your shit is gonna go sideways before this day is over."

I just threatened him. He knows it, I know it. But it's just the first half of the conversation, so he also knows it's his move.

"So we're gonna do each other a little favor here, Collin? Is that what's happenin'?"

"Yes, sir. That's what's happenin'."

I can hear him smile on the other end of this conversation. "How much time can I have?"

This is why I respect Charlie Beaufort. I would not say I like him, but I do respect him. Because he respects me. We're making a deal and he knows that whatever I want today, it's a small thing in comparison to what I could do for him. I will not work for him, but I will do a job for him in exchange for what I need. And my time, as a person for hire, is billed hourly.

"Ten hours."

He lets out a breath. It's a nice offer and he knows this. I could do a whole operation in ten hours. "Does that include travel time?"

"Nope. Travel time is on me."

"Does it include a team? Or just you?"

I know he wants the team, but this is personal, so I can't promise him that. What I can say is this: "It's just me. But if they want to help me out, I will let them."

"Deal." He can't say it fast enough. "How can I help you today, Collin?"

So I tell him. And thirty seconds later he says, "I'll be in touch within the hour."

WHEN I GO **inside the church** to find Amon, he's lining up dozens of little black cases in the middle of the chancel. When he notices me walking up the nave he straightens up and nods. "We've got forty-eight. I think it'll be enough."

"Forty-eight what?"

"Drones. They came in just yesterday."

Even though this day sucks, I laugh. "I never even gave you permission to buy *one*, Amon. And you bought forty-eight?"

"Fifty-two, actually. But the last four, they're too big for this job. These little fuckers though"—he looks down at his drones like they are his children, or dogs, actually, that's how proud he is of them—"these little fuckers are sneaky."

"And what, exactly, are you plannin' to do with said little fuckers?"

"Mostly just send a not-so-polite message." He smiles at me. "Because I know damn well you've already got a plan. But I'm gonna get my jabs in too. And these little fuckers are gonna do that for me. We need to teach these people a lesson, Col. They don't get to do this shit. Maybe what Jim Bob said about Olive is true, but that don't matter. You do not break into a man's house and steal his child. If they knew Olive was there, and she was one of theirs, the polite thing to do—the smart thing to do —is have a fuckin' conversation. And now they what? They've taken Lowyn hostage or something? To get back at you for stumblin' into their stupid fuckin' boneyard?"

"Sounds about right."

"Well, that shit is over now. We're here and we're not playin' that game."

"What's all this got to do with drones?"

He smiles at me. It's one of those wicked 'I'm Amon Parrish' smiles that I only ever see when we're workin' a job and his mind is abuzz with ideas. "You'll see. I'll set them up and then you'll see. In the meantime, do me a favor, will ya?"

"What's that?"

"Go tell Nash to pay all these motherfuckers off and send them home. We're gonna finish this place ourselves."

Finally, he's talkin' sense.

I turn to do this, but he calls me back. "Hey."

I look over my shoulder at him. "What?"

"You missed your dose. We all took ours at breakfast. I was gonna bring you yours last night, but I forgot because we had that dinner in Bishop. So… make sure you drink that, OK?"

I give him a little salute and walk out of the church.

WHEN I GET to Nash's house, he's in his office fuckin' with paperwork. His place looks pretty nice. I did see it the other night at the party, but there were too many people to really get details. It's clean now. And he's got new furniture.

He looks up when I walk in. "What's up, Col?"

"Where do I start?" I kinda laugh these words out. Nash just looks a little confused, so I elaborate. "Amon says to send all these boys home. We've got security issues with them. They can't be trusted. Pay them off and tell them thank you."

"OK. I'll do that." Nash salutes me.

Which I hate. But I don't say nothing. I just walk out of his office and go into the kitchen—which, in the span of one week, has all been redone. Shiny new appliances and stone countertops even.

I find a single stainless-steel canister waiting for me in the fridge. They are delivered weekly on Sunday nights. I take it out and set it on the counter, running a conversation I had with Lowyn yesterday though my head. *Did you ever take that treatment?*

I told her no. It wasn't a lie. Not exactly. When I was telling her about that time I saw her on TV and I was having a real bad day because one of my men died from a treatment, I wasn't a Marine at that time, so I wasn't getting those particular treatments.

But we all got treatments while we were official military.

And we still take them because we don't have a choice anymore.

I twist the cap off the canister, smell it—kinda fruity, like always—and then drink it.

Because I don't have a choice.

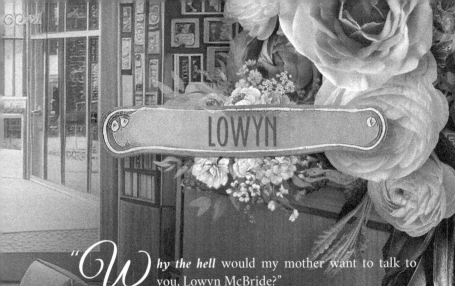

LOWYN

"*Why the hell* would my mother want to talk to you, Lowyn McBride?"

Ike's response kinda shocks me. Probably because I was looking through that photo album, so my temper has simmered down a little. But he's been outside doin' whatever, so his must still be boilin' over.

"She probably doesn't." I force myself to stay calm. "But I have something to say to her."

"Well, let's hear it. And I'll pass it along."

I sigh. I could insist, I guess. But this direction feels like a brand-new fight and I'm trying to defuse things. "I would just like to apologize to her. And your sisters. And…" I force myself to say this last part. "And you, too."

His brows are all furrowed up. "For what, exactly?"

"For… running away, I guess."

"You *guess*?"

I'm mad now, I can't help it. "Ya know what? Fuck you, Ike. I was hurt that day. Probably did have a concussion. But above and beyond that, I was sad. It was my mama's first birthday after her death. I was missing her that night. And I was tired. I did the whole fuckin' Revival myself that first year like I was a grown-up, and I wasn't. I was a kid." I point at him. "You knew that."

He points back. "You wanted to stay. You're the one who brought it up."

"I wasn't thinking clearly."

"And you weren't a kid, Lowyn. You were twenty years old, for fuck's sake. People around here, they've got three kids of their own by the time they're twenty."

"Well, I'm not from here! I was a newly dropped-out college student in the middle of a new adult crisis and fighting off depression and fear. I'm allowed to make mistakes. And I get it." I point to the photo album. "It was real to you people—"

"To *you people*?"

"It was real to you, but it wasn't real to me. And it wasn't legal." So much for that olive branch I had been plannin' to offer.

"You think we're just a bunch of stupid hillbillies, don't you?"

"I was gonna apologize and you just went and ruined it. Forget it. I'm not sorry. I'm mad. You took advantage of me—"

"Fuuuuuuck. You!" he says all dramatically. "I pulled you out of a wreck. Probably saved your life, since you had a concussion and all. Where was Collin Creed that night, huh?"

"He's got nothing to do with this and you know it."

"He killed Olive's daddy!"

"That man broke into Collin's house and tried to kidnap her!"

"She was his child! That's not kidnapping!"

"It most certainly is." I growl these words out. The fucking audacity. I just can't. "If he really was Olive's father—and I really don't believe you. I mean, you people can just say and think whatever you want, fuck proving it true, right? But even if she was, he broke in. We were all scared. Collin did what anyone would do. Even you. Are you really trying to tell me that if Pastor Creed had broken into one of these houses and tried to steal a child, none of you would've blown his head off?"

I scoff. "Jim Bob made me come up here today to sort this out because he said I was the only one who could get up the hill without being shot. That's the reputation this place has. Not to mention all your fuckin' secrets." I put up my hands to stop him, because he's opening his mouth to talk back. "I don't want your stupid secrets. I don't care what you're doing up here. I'm fuckin' sorry that I broke your heart, or whatever—"

He guffaws. "You wish."

"Then what the hell is wrong with you, Ike Monroe? Why are you such a flaming asshole?"

His eyes blaze up and he comes at me. I step backwards—again and again—until my back is pressed up against a wall and Ike Monroe is looming over me, his face red with anger.

He's embarrassed, I think. I've embarrassed him. "I think you liked me," I whisper. His face is so close, we could be kissing. But he's so hot with anger, I know with a hundred percent certainty that he's not thinking about kissing me.

He wants to *hit* me.

But I don't care. I'm gonna say what I've always thought and he can do whatever the hell he wants with it. "I think you liked me a lot. And when I walked out, you took it personal. Like a fuckin' teenage boy. Because that marriage ceremony we had, it wasn't about love, was it, Ike? No." He's grittin' his teeth and clenching his jaw as he leans into my face. "It wasn't about love, it was about power. Your power over me. And maybe over Collin, even though he'd already been gone two years at that point. You are a small, small man with an ego the size of this mountain."

He slaps me. *Hard*. Right across the cheek. My head jerks to the side and I let out a breath, very surprised that he lost control like this.

But I haven't lost control. Not at all. No one has ever slapped me. Ever. So I haven't been conditioned to be afraid of it yet.

I turn my head back and look him straight in the eyes. "You're a monster. I'm glad I left you. It was the best decision I ever made. No one will ever love you. And fuck you, and fuck your mother"—he slaps me again, but I just laugh this time and look him in the eyes again—"and fuck this whole place."

He takes a step back, and for a moment I think it's over. But then I realize he's making a fist and the next blow is probably gonna knock me out.

I look him in the eyes and dare him to do it. In fact, I take it one step further. Because if I'm gonna get hit by this piece of shit, then I'm gonna make it worth it. "No wonder Olive's mama wanted to leave."

"You bitch," he snarls. "Don't you—"

But I cut him off. "No wonder Lasher walked out too."

His fist is still in play. And he's seething. But there's a moment here when he maybe wavers. Then his anger is too much and I know he's gonna do it.

But in that same moment, something outside draws his attention. There's a commotion. People yelling, but also… something else. Something that sounds like a loudspeaker.

I let out a laugh.

Ike walks over to the closest window, looking out. "What the fuck is that?"

My breath comes out in a rush. "That, you asshole, is the Call to Revival."

He leaves the kitchen and opens the front door.

I follow, because this is over now and he knows it as well as I do.

Two seconds.

That's how long you have to push Collin Creed into action.

Two seconds and then he takes care of business.

Outside people are panicking. Running all over the place. And from within the trees comes the sermon, in Pastor Creed's own voice, just like it does every day during Revival.

"When you look upon the hills, the sun shining on the

peaks"—this is coming from off to the left—"and you hear the rumble in the distance"—this is coming from my right—"don't you ever forget that behind it comes the glory!" That comes from above and everyone looks up. There is—I squint, because for a moment I think it's a bird, but it's not. It's a drone. And it's belting out Revival words.

I laugh out loud as the sermon continues. "And as that rumble resonates into the echo on the water"—these words come from the forest—"let it be a sign! A sign that the righteous will find comfort in the brave"—there are too many drones to count, and now they all call out in unison—"and the danger will exist only in the damaged. Because when you give yourself to something higher, you will feel the relief that comes with the emptiness of anger and you will know, in your heart, that the blessing of grace is now upon you!"

It ends the way it always ends. With Pastor Creed doin' his best impression of Billy Sunday back in the righteous revival tents of the Great Depression.

Ike has a gun out now, and he's shootin' at them.

I scream, and start running. Because he's crazy! He slapped me just because I said some words he didn't like. He was gonna hit me with a closed fist next. He's angry and out of control. And that gun could just as easily point in my direction.

The shootin' stops, but I don't have time to be relieved because I can hear him coming after me. He reaches for my jacket, gets a hold of my hood, and the only reason I get away is because I unzip it and fling my arms backwards, letting it slip off me.

I run harder towards the trail that starts between the blacksmith and the stable that will take me the hell outta here. But it's far, and I know Ike is already back on his feet.

Then there's a noise—a thumping in the air—and when I look up there is a giant military helicopter with two propellers, one on each end, coming down right at us.

The wind from this massive piece of machinery blows everything around and almost knocks me down.

And even though there is a helipad on the other side of the village, it does not waste time landing on the helipad. It lands right in the gravel street.

I'm on the ground now, and there are men everywhere with guns. Village men, not military.

Stairs fold down from the helicopter and out comes... well, some military man. An older gentleman with lots of colorful things on his very important-looking uniform. He's got a bull-horn to his mouth and he yells, "You motherfucking mountain men had better stand down, because if I get shot today, every one of you assholes will be goin' to Hell with me."

I look back at Ike, who is still on his feet, and he must know this man, because he lowers his gun and salutes him.

When I look back at the helicopter four soldiers in all-black armor—helmets and everything, so you can't see their faces— jump out from behind the man, who must be a general or something. They fan out in a pattern, but they are all coming straight at Ike and me with their weapons up and ready to shoot.

Three of them walk up to Ike and push their rifles right up against his face. Hard enough to press into his skin.

The fourth comes over to me, flips the faceplate up on his helmet, and offers me a hand.

Collin stares down at me. "Come on, Low." He's not smiling. He looks pissed. "Let's go."

I take his hand and he helps me up. But before we leave, he lets go of my hand, turns to Ike and aims his rifle right between his eyes. "If you ever come down off this mountain, consider yourself a target. I will take you out, Ike Monroe. And you won't ever see me coming. And then, when I'm done with you, I will firebomb this whole fuckin' place. And if you think I can't get permission to do any of these things, take a look at your commanding officer right there." He juts his chin towards the general in front of the helicopter. "Because he's the guy who gave me a ride in today."

Then he lowers his faceplate, grabs my hand again, and leads me over to the helicopter.

His team follows us, and the next thing I know, we're in the air, heading off the mountain.

COLLIN

owyn's cheek is red. Hell, it's practically got the shape of a handprint on it. But I don't ask her any questions because if she tells me he hit her, I will go back up that mountain tonight and take care of things, with or without official permission from Charlie Beaufort.

I know Amon, Nash, and Ryan see it too, but they don't even raise their faceplates in the helicopter. They sit and behave like we're on duty. And I guess we are. Because this was a sanctioned operation, not some half-ass rescue scheme.

We land at a base about an hour away from Disciple by car, but only ten minutes by 'copter.

When we get out, the men and I salute General Forbe, then he offers me his hand and I shake it. "Nice seeing you again, Collin. Don't be a stranger."

"Yes sir, General. Thank you for your help today."

"It was my pleasure." Then he walks off with his underlings and finally, Amon, Nash, and Ryan put their faceplates up. We look at each other, then I nod in the direction of our armored truck, which is parked along the side of a small building.

Lowyn doesn't say anything, just keeps hold of my hand.

We open up the back and start stripping out of our armor. Ryan hops inside and takes our weapons, then each piece of armor as we strip it off, hanging it all up in its proper place. Then, when we are done and only dressed in base-layer fatigues, Amon and Nash take the front and start up the truck. I get in the back with Ryan, lending a hand to Lowyn, pulling her in with me. We sit across from each other.

Then Ryan closes the doors and we're on our way home.

Lowyn is the first one to speak. "I didn't marry him. I mean—"

"Peaches," I say, looking her in the eyes as I cut her off, "I don't need an explanation. So I hope you don't feel like you need to give one." I do my best not to look at that cheek of hers. But it's kinda hard and I have a feeling I'll be dreaming about murdering that asshole Ike Monroe until the day I die.

I decide to change the direction of these thoughts by pulling out my phone and pressing Jim Bob's contact.

Ester answers, of course. "City Hall, how can I help you?"

"This is Collin. Put Jim Bob on."

She hesitates. Like maybe she's thinkin' about denying my request. But she must think better of it. "One moment, Collin." And she puts me on hold.

Ryan's lookin' at me like he wants to ask questions, but he knows better to ask questions when I'm in a mood like this. So he shrugs and shuts up, looking at the little window between us and Amon and Nash in the front seat.

It takes Jim Bob three minutes to get on the phone. "Collin. I… I just heard."

"Good. Good for you, Jim Bob. This is a courtesy call. I'm just letting you know that me and my men have done our part as far as our security contract goes. We look forward to that million dollars apiece on New Year's Day. Oh, and I know you don't have their last names, so take this down. It's Ryan Desoto and Nash Skinner. Don't fuck it up on the checks."

"Uh…" Jim Bob kinda stammers here. Because, of course, Ryan and Nash are not on that contract that promised us a million dollars each. At least they weren't. But they sure as fuck are now. "Well…" I can hear Jim Bob swallow.

"I told you"—I look Lowyn straight in the eyes for this.

There is no point in hiding it anymore. We will have no secrets from this day forward—"that you burned a bridge with me."

"Son—"

"I'm not your son, Jim Bob. And you need to shut up and listen. We're out, but we *will* get paid. Whatever beef you had with the men up that mountain is over now, thanks to us. Lowyn's out too. She will give you nothing." I'm still watching Lowyn as I say this, my eyebrows raised. Like… if she wants to object, now is the time.

She holds up a finger.

"Hold for a moment, please." I put Jim Bob on hold. "What is it, Low?"

"Well, I made a promise to Sassy Lorraine that I would ask Jim Bob if she could sing in the Revival. Can you make him do that for me? I really like her."

I smile and take Jim Bob off hold. "One more thing. Low's friend is a singer. And she would like to sing in the Revival. You're gonna make that happen."

"Now look, Collin—"

"No, you look, Jim Bob. Lowyn's out, we're out. And Sassy Lorraine *will* be singing at the Revival. It's not a request, it's a stipulation. You better give her good parts, too. And stay the fuck away from us. Because if you don't, I will ruin Disciple the same fuckin' way I just ruined Blackberry Hill."

Then I end the call.

Ryan starts laughing. "Thanks, man. I don't really need the money, but fuck it. I'll take it."

I let out a breath and look at Lowyn. "I'm not gonna be stayin' in town anymore and I think you should move in with me."

She stares at me for a moment. Then she nods. "I would love to. But I have one more request."

"What is it?"

"Can I be in charge of decoratin'?"

All of us laugh. And let out a long breath too.

Then I scoot across the aisle, sit next to her on the bench, and slip my arm around her. She leans her head on my shoulder, still shaking a little, but trying to put it behind her. "Of course you can. If you fill that whole place up with junk, I promise to love every bit of it."

CLOVER BRADLEY LOOKS like the very same girl I last saw twelve years ago. Long golden-red hair, bright green eyes, and tiny body. Which makes me laugh because she's one of those powerhouse short girls. Athletic, but very cute. She did gymnastics, cheer, track, horse showin', and rifle club. The girl can do a flip off a pony while shootin' a target from twenty yards out and never drop her pom-poms.

Well, that's probably stretchin' it, but if challenged to do that, Clover Bradley would find a way and she would nail it. She's that kind of girl.

Unlike Bryn, who is just Lowyn's sister, Clover was the best-best friend. So if I wanted to date Low back in high school, I had to get approval from Clover.

I mean, technically, this probably isn't true for Lowyn. She loved me no matter what. I know that in my heart. But Clover could've made life difficult for me if we hadn't gotten along.

Plus side to all this—I like Clover. Have always liked Clover. And she gets extra points for getting us a spur-of-the-moment, long-term cottage rental at her super-fancy-fancy hotel in Virginia, the Dixie Yonder.

Would Lowyn be safe in Disciple while our compound house is being remodeled? I have no doubt. But do I want her there? Hell. No.

I'm very much done with all those Trinity towns. Even the ones I might not even know about yet. Because I've been thinking about that cross analogy that Jim Bob was going on about and it has occurred to me that there are not four points on a cross, but five. Because everything meets in the middle, doesn't it?

Now, though, it's no longer my problem. Nor is it even my business.

It's a relief, actually. To have that part of my life permanently put to rest. The moment I came into town I could feel the manipulation. Jim Bob is kinda slick, but he's really not that smart. Still, he was pulling me back in and given enough time, he probably would've gotten me behind that pulpit.

"Oh. Mah. Gosh," Clover says as she looks me up and down. "Collin Creed, as I live and breathe." She looks over at Lowyn, who I guess did not tell her I was back when she called and asked for a cottage. "Where the hell have you been hidin' him?"

"Believe it or not, he's only been back in town a week." Lowyn looks at me and we both laugh. What a helluva week it was.

Clover studies us both with a critical eye, takes a long, long look at Lowyn's cheek, which is still red, then her eyes go to me. "Hmmm. OK, then. Welcome to the Dixie Yonder." She pans a hand towards a path lined with flowerbeds and elm trees. "Follow me."

That's another thing I have always liked about Clover. She is confrontational, like Bryn, but she's also quiet about it, like Lowyn. She's not gonna bring up that handprint on Lowyn's cheek. But she took note and she's gonna tuck that fact away for a time in the future when she might need it.

I know she doesn't think I did it.

I'm also fairly certain she has an idea who did. Because I've been thinking about that wedding up in the mountains and how Jim Bob managed to pacify those Blackberry Hill people so Lowyn could get out of it. And I have a pretty good hunch about how he pulled that off.

Clover pulls Lowyn away from me as we walk, hooking arms with her and leaning in to her shoulder. I dutifully pull our suitcases and let them get a few paces ahead so they can have their little whisper talk. And it all must check out, because when we arrive at the cottage, Clover shoots me a smile and says, "Make yourselves at home. I've already had dinner, but how about we meet up for breakfast tomorrow?"

Lowyn squeezes Clover's hands. "That would be amazing. Thank you so much. I owe you."

Clover laughs that off. "You owe me nothing." Then she twiddles her fingers goodbye while shootin' me a smirk, and leaves back the way we came.

When the door closes and we're alone, Lowyn lets out a sigh as she looks around. And I watch her as she takes it all in. It's vintage in her sense of the word, but it's old stuff. Antique shit. She walks over to the desk, pulls the chair out, and looks at it. There is a painting on the front of the chair back. Sleighs and horses or something. A kind of folk art painting from long-ago times.

"Somethin' interesting about that chair, Low?"

She looks over at me while pointin' to the chair. "What are the chances that we'd go a hundred miles away from the last Hitchcock chair I saw and find a match to the set in our long-term cottage rental at the Dixie Yonder? This is the very chair I was lookin' for in your church." She beams a smile at it, then looks back at me. "If I were an outlaw, I would steal this chair."

The only possible reaction from me is a shake of my head and a laugh. Because, while she didn't mean to, that sentence right there perfectly sums her up. If she were the kind of person who steals things, she would take a chair. Not someone's money. Not anything to get power. Just an old chair that makes up a matching set.

She is good.

And I'm really not sure I deserve her.

This discrepancy in our morals bothers me. So I walk over to her, take her face in my hands—careful not to press hard against her red cheek—and look her in the eyes. "Lowyn McBride. When the trying times come, we will hold hands. And when the heavy times come, we will walk them together. And when the depressing times come, and you feel the burden of life to be so vast and wide that you feel forsaken, I will be there to carry you. No matter how long it takes or how far we must travel, I will carry you, Lowyn McBride. I will carry you."

Her smile grows even wider and her eyes dance with happiness. "I know you will, Collin Creed. I know you will."

Which is exactly how the Revival wedding vow goes.

I promise to carry her, and she promises to trust me.

*M*y heart nearly stops when he makes his vow to me. And I almost can't remember what my promise back is, even though it's so short compared to his. But I manage it. I believe in him. That's my part in all this wedding vow stuff. I will believe in him.

The people of Disciple have been making this wedding vow for over a hundred years now and every once in a while, someone will wander into my little tent and ask me about it. There is nothing about loving, or honoring, or respecting in there. There is no promise to be loyal.

Not those words, anyway.

And sometimes strangers have a hard time with that.

But the people where I come from understand that marriage isn't really about love, or honor, or respect, or loyalty.

It's about trust.

Collin Creed could promise me anything. To come home every night for dinner. To wash my hair on the weekends. To clean the dishes after I cook. It doesn't matter what the promise is. The only thing that matters is that I believe him.

Marriage is about having one person in this world whose promise to you is law and your belief in them is absolute.

That's the definition of love around here.

"I broke my promise to you, Low."

"You hadn't made one back then, Collin."

"It's not true and you know it. I might not have said those words, but I did make that promise. And then I forgot. I forgot what it meant to be me and I left." He stares at me for a moment. "Jim Bob was making you pay those hill people, wasn't he? He was taking your profit share and giving it to Blackberry Hill, wasn't he?"

I nod. Because it's true. "It was the only way Ike would let me go."

Collin looks sad. Then he looks angry. And I know he's thinking about today and not the past. About my red cheek, and the fact that he had to reveal himself to me. How he had to show me the best and worst of him in a single moment. And now he's thinking about how they made me pay for a stupid mistake that I made when I was young, and sad, and feelin' overwhelmed.

It's not fair. None of it's fair. It's just life.

"I'm gonna get that money back, Low. Every fuckin' penny of it."

"No." I shake my head. "I don't need that money, Collin. There are people in this world who will do anything for money, but I'm not one of them. And, if I'm being perfectly honest here, I don't think I'd be the person I am today if life hadn't shit on me that weekend. Jim Bob taking my profit share and giving it to Blackberry Hill was the motivation I needed to work harder. To make my own way without the safety net of Disciple propping me up. Those two men made a deal using me as their collateral. They took almost everything I had left that day I walked down that hill."

"It was a mistake. Being angry and demanding... *redress*"— he hisses this word out—"for a mistake is just plain fuckin' evil. And I hate evil."

"Evil doesn't care if you hate it, Collin. So why bother? And anyway, I was wrong. You didn't ruin me that night you killed that man. You revealed me as well as yourself. You set us on a path to be ourselves. And then, for whatever reason—under the guiding hand of some higher power, maybe—you came back. And now we're ready to make our promise and live up to it. We will be one of the few couples who makes our vow without regrets. That's a pretty special thing."

He takes his hands off my face and then leads me into the bathroom. Then he runs a tub and squirts some bubbles in it. I undress him and he undresses me, and then we get in the tub, facing each other. All squished together.

And then we talk. He tells me everything he's done. Every moment that he remembers. And I learn some really terrible things about him, and the US government, and people who love power and money.

Then I tell him all my moments too. I confess, for the first time ever, just how sad I was in those early years. But each misfortune made me work harder and as the years passed, I got stronger.

Collin and I get clean in that tub.

We wash away every sin.

And when we get out, we dry each other off, crawl into bed, and hold each other tight all night long.

*PACKING **my bags*** and leaving my house turned out to be way less traumatic than I thought it would. That little house in Disciple was where we started. Collin and I had so much history there. But of course, it was also the root of the problem.

It's where everything changed.

And even though it didn't feel like the same place to me—even before I did all those renovations, I just didn't see it as the house where Collin killed someone—it was still that same place to him.

I offered it up to Rosie Harlow as a gift. Not to keep forever, but just to live in for as long as she wanted to. Of course, she jumped on it, her eyes bright with gratitude. And since I was leaving all the furniture and décor, she and Cross have already moved in—after Collin had a little chat with her landlord and got her out of a lease.

He's pretty persuasive.

Neither Collin nor I have any history with the house on his compound. It won't be ready for the move-in for a few more weeks, but it's been stripped to the bones and will be put back together while we're living in the cottage at the Dixie Yonder.

As far as what happened up in the hills... well, I don't know exactly how he got a military helicopter and a five-star general to take him up that mountain to save me, but I do know he made a deal with someone to make it happen.

When that debt comes due, I have no idea.

But I'm not gonna worry about it for now.

And anyway, Collin Creed is the most capable man I've ever met in my life.

ABOUT TWO WEEKS LATER, once things have started to settle down a bit, I call up Sassy Lorraine—brand-new headlining star every Sunday at the Disciple Revival startin' with the turn-of-story on Fourth of July. *Thank you, Jim Bob Baptist. But we don't owe you one, you still owe us.* I didn't even bother asking how they were gonna salvage the seasons since both Collin and I were out, but I'm sure they'll pull it off.

Jim Bob is mad, but it's not hate-your-guts kind of mad. It's more like you're-ruinin'-my-business-opportunities mad. Which can be worse in most cases. But it turns out that Jim Bob was tickled pink when I brought him Sassy Lorraine. He remembered her. She sang for his brother's wedding years back. Jim Bob's brother didn't stay in Disciple. He started his life down in Knoxville. And that's Sassy's stompin' ground.

So. Maybe Jim isn't happy, but he's nearly satisfied and that's the best I can do.

Sassy answers on the first ring. "Lowyn, my girl. How are you doin' today?"

"I'm just fine, thank you. I'm calling to let you know that Collin and Amon have a plan for your doggie."

She squeals. "That's great! How soon can we do it?"

"They tell me there's a jet scheduled for this Wednesday. We're all goin' to the Bahamas on vacay. Would you like to come along?"

She gasps. "That would be the highlight of my life, Lowyn McBride! I would love it."

"Pack your things, Sassy. And be here at six a.m. on Wednesday."

She squeals again. Then we say our goodbyes and hang up.

Her toys are what I'm cataloguing today. It's a gold mine. A 1978 Luke Skywalker Action Figure. A Monopoly game, but not just any Monopoly game. This is the very first one ever made—hand-drawn on oil cloth—and owned by the game's inventor. This is just the start. Sassy gave me four trunks of comics that together are worth more than three million dollars.

A gold mine in exchange for the safe return of one teeny-tiny chihuahua called Prissy.

Sassy thinks this is an even trade because part of the deal is that I have to put it all online so she can send the links to her ex-husband and picture him crying his eyes out as I sell it all off.

"He'll probably buy it all back, Lowyn!" she told me with bright eyes. "Wouldn't that just be the most ironic thing ever?"

It might not be the most traditional version of happily ever after, but it certainly is satisfying.

COLLIN

Prissy the chihuahua was delivered via basket. This was Sassy's idea. "She has been sleepin' in this basket since the day she was born. Trust me," Sassy told us. "If we lower it down, she will hop right in."

Amon wanted to use some kind of claw attachment for the drone that didn't come with it, and therefore set us back another five thousand dollars. So I was a little bit hot that we bought that thing and didn't even use it. But Amon said, "Relax, Collin. It's a writeoff. And a claw really comes in handy." Then he slapped me on the back and went back to whatever the fuck he was doing.

Sassy was right about the basket. We took a jet down to the Bahamas, rented a yacht for a day from a guy Amon and I knew once upon a time, and flew that drone right down to Mr. Former Sassy Lorraine's boat dock where the dog was sleepin'. We put a little speaker on the basket, just in case, with Sassy's voice callin' Prissy to go to bed.

"That's all ya got to say," Sassy said. "'Go to bed' and she'll jump right in."

She was right. The whole thing took about thirty minutes. Then we had a nice lunch on the deck and were back at our hotels by dinnertime.

Sassy and Amon went home, but Low and I stayed for a couple days to relax a little. We'd never been on a trip together and it was nice. And when we got home, our house was ready for us to move in. We don't barely have any furniture yet, but we don't mind.

Mercy stays inside at night, but during the day she guards our porch. Amon says I'm wastin' her. "She's only two, Collin! She wants to work!"

Maybe. But personally, I think she prefers the porch. So that's where I let her spend her days. Amon should've kept her for himself if he wanted to boss her around.

McBooms is still open and Lowyn still goes into town for that, but when she gave Rosie a free house to live in, it came with a full-time job. Rosie minds McBooms now, and Lowyn spends her time doing consultations and picking people's junk and puttin' it online.

I took Amon's advice on that pickin' trip and now we do that together. One week a month we get to take a little vacation. It might not be fancy-fancy, but it's more than enough for us.

But today isn't about any of that.

Today is about our men.

Two buses pull into the compound at three forty-five in the afternoon. They stop right in the middle of the road, about halfway between Nash's house and our house.

There are sixty men inside those buses and Amon, Nash, Ryan, and I are waiting when they all pile out. Big men. Dangerous men. Unstable men. They don't fit in anymore. Every single one of them was found either in a homeless shelter or in jail.

This is their second chance. A fresh start using the skills they built so carefully over the years. They were giants in the military. The best of the best. They came home from things no one ever wants to talk about.

And that's the problem, really. You gotta have someone you can talk about that shit with. That's the whole point of a war story. That's why old men tell those stories. They can't just file them away and forget.

Once you get used to that team, it's there forever. You can't just walk away from a team.

So we brought them here, to the edge of Disciple, West Virginia, and they are now on our team.

They stand there, lookin' around, most of them smiling. The ones who aren't are just a little more cautious than the rest. They'll come around.

There are ten houses. Six men to a house. It's all part of the paycheck.

We will have a boot camp for the next six weeks, then two weeks' R&R, and on August one Charlie Beaufort will be here to tell us what to do next.

I don't know what kind of job Charlie will have me do, but he's not gonna waste that debt on something small, I do know that much. So it probably won't come up for a while and that means I don't have to worry about that debt until it comes due.

Amon starts in with his speech, welcoming them, pointing out the houses, which have been turned into barracks. They nod and listen. And when he brings out the dogs and starts handing them out, assigning each one to a pair of handlers, not a single man is frowning.

Some of them are just puppies and they will be trained by these men. Some of them are breeders, and they will be cared for by these men. And some of them are pretty much ready to go. And these dogs will be their best friends.

Every man in Edge will get his own dog eventually. But for now, it's enough.

I let Amon, Nash, and Ryan do the talking and take myself down the road where Lowyn and Mercy are waiting for me on the porch.

Lowyn's smiling big at me. Probably because I'm smiling big at her.

We have a lot of dark days in our past. There was a lot of thunder in those storms.

But I guess that all those preachers who came before me were right.

Because behind that rumble comes the glory.

END OF BOOK SHIT

*W*elcome to the End of Book Shit. This is the part of the book where I get to say anything I want about the story you just read or listened to. It's not professionally edited and really has nothing to do with the reader, it's just my thoughts and feelings about the story and writing process.

The Rumble and the Glory spent a lot of time up in my head. Since I finished this book in 2023 and it's now mid-2024 (and it has been waiting to be released for nearly a year now,) it feels like a really long time ago when I first started plotting this series. I'm fairly sure that this idea came to me some time in 2022 because I was writing a whole bunch of other things when I got this idea and so it had time to morph a bit before I actually sat down to flesh it out.

I knew a few things going in. One. It was going to be a small-town romance and it was gonna take place in West Virginia. Two. It had an enemies-to-lovers main trope. And three, it was the start of a new world and a long series. Most of that stayed the same, though I would say that the end result is more second-chance romance than enemies-to-lovers. Though it does start out enemies-to-lovers.

What I did not have, and would not have until I was actually a few chapters in to writing it, was the set-up of the three towns. Since it was many books ago now, I can't even recall

423

where this whole Revival thing came from. I'm completely drawing a blank at how I came up with that idea in the first place. lol I think it started when I did the research on West Virginia and the Appalachian Mountains. In fact, now that I mention that, I recall finding an article about a man called Billy Sunday. He was a real tent-revival preacher and was pretty famous back in his day.

I kind of remember coming up with the idea of three towns, but I'm pretty sure I had already decided that the town was putting on this tent revival show as sort of a scam to make money before I came up with the trinity of Revenant, Disciple, and Bishop. Now, that old movie, Leap of Faith with Steve Martin, has always been a favorite of mine, so for sure, I would say it was inspiration once the ball got rolling.

But I didn't want the story to really focus on the actual show. I just wanted it to be a backdrop. Once that idea took hold, the rest of it all fell into place as I got further and further along in the writing. But I knew absolutely nothing about the towns, or the shows, or what Collin Creed did to make him run away and join the Marines when I started chapter one.

In fact, I didn't even know Lowyn was an antiques dealer until I started describing her house. And now that I think about it, I didn't even know that was Collin's house until it came out on the page. I think that was really the defining moment in so far as where I took the series. But it was a nice meet-cute, even if it wasn't a real meet-cute since they knew each other.

From there, it was mostly a matter of Collin coming to terms with being home again. A place that he thought was hostile due to the bitter way he became estranged from his family.

Of course, the town felt otherwise. And Lowyn was no different. I made her put up a little fight, but these two were always destiny.

I had imagined Rumble as a JA Huss take on a small-town

cozy. Which makes me laugh out loud as I type this because this so NOT a cozy. But if you've been reading my books for any length of time, you can kinda see it. It's got the makings of a cozy, but the twists and turns that I am sorta famous for pretty much cancel that cozy stuff out.

Still, I wanted readers and listeners to be invested in the towns and the people who lived in them. I wanted Trinity County to feel comfortable and real. Like, maybe, if you took a right turn on some random highway in West Virginia, you might actually find yourself passing through biker-covered Revenant. And if you went a little further up the hill, you'd stop for the Revival and maybe take a peek inside Lowyn's antique store. And then, you'd get hungry and head on over to the Pineapple Pub in Bishop for a burger and fries at the bar, and walk the downtown area at sunset, enjoying the clip-cloppy sound of hooves on the brick roads, and spend the night at the Inn, waking to the smell of Bryn's five-star waffles.

In other words, I want readers and listeners to get comfortable. Because this is the start of a very long journey. I knew this would be a multi-book series from the very start because I had just finished up the Creeping Beautiful series, which is the tail-end of what began as the Rook & Ronin Series, then turned into the Company World, and then the Bossy Brothers got involved (not to mention the Misters) and between all the spin-offs and one-offs, the books in that twisted hydra mess totaled in the high twenties and spanned a good ten years of my writing career.

You can't end something like that without a new beginning. And I know, I know, I *know* that I'm gonna get all kinds of messages asking if this is a Company book. Because it *feels* like a Company book, doesn't it? It's got all the makings of the Company. And if you're new to me, and haven't read all those twisted books mentioned above, then good for you. You don't see the connections so you don't have to think about it.

But for those of you who have, I'm gonna go on record here

and say that this will not interconnect with anyone in the Company world and there will not be a revised graphic for the reading order of Rook & Ronin/Company/Bossy/Misters/Creeping series. (I have said I was done with it, and I meant it, though I reserve the right to go back and write inside it any time I want).

But just to be clear, Rumble is something all brand new.

The Rumble and the Glory will release June 27, 2024. Book two will release July 25, 2024. And the third book in the Disciple Trilogy will release August 22, 2024. I knew from the first day I started Rumble that the trilogy would have a summer rapid release and so that's what's happening.

There will be more books to come and this series will grow over time. Some might release in trilogy sets like this one while others will release as standalones. All books in this world will connect and I plan on writing approximately three per year.

In other words, this small-town stuff I'm doing is all VERY big. And I hope it will have all the intrigue, suspense, and spice everyone loved so much in the world we just left behind and will keep you entertained for another decade to come.

I hope you enjoyed your introduction to the Sacred Trinity Series. Thank you for reading, thank you for reviewing, and I'll see you in the next book.

Julie
JA Huss
March 28, 2024

ABOUT THE AUTHOR

J A Huss is a scientist, New York Times Bestseller, USA Today Bestseller, and a cowgirl who rides English. Five of her books were optioned for TV/film, several of her audiobooks have been nominated for the Audie and SOVA Awards, and she was a RITA Finalist in 2019. She has been an indie author in both fiction and non-fiction for seventeen years and lives on a ranch in Colorado with her family, horses, dogs, goats, donkeys, and chickens.